"You're going to say no."

Rosie felt a surge of disappointment. Not least because it meant she'd be losing all contact with him.

Chase shook his head. "I can't bury my disquiet," he said. "I'm of two minds about whether or not to allow an expedition like this on Three Moons. Still, it was great to see Mick show such enthusiasm. He's always been on about the Egyptian connection. A lot of people up here still are."

She stared up at him. "And you?" she asked.

He threw her a sidelong smile. "I'll admit this is all fascinating stuff. I do have an imagination—but I also have a cattle station to run."

"Yet you're afraid to let us go off by ourselves?"

He answered with some force. "I'm afraid to let *you* go off, Miss Summers. I appreciate that you've had terrifying times covering your war stories, but you can equally well get lost or killed in the jungle."

"I'm game," she said with a shrug. "But let me point out that you, Mr. Banfield, are the ideal man to head this expedition."

"What would I get out of it?" he demanded.

A nearly audible chord of excitement vibrated in the air between them as attraction assumed real shape and substance.

Rosie had never felt so vulnerable in her life, literally quaking. "You can hardly be suggesting we become lovers." Even saying it aroused her....

Dear Reader,

For years now, I've wanted to write a book about an ancient Egyptian presence in Australia. This is it!

My interest was captured as a young woman when I read in the paper about a find of hand-forged Egyptian bronze, copper and iron tools, pottery and coins dating back more than two thousand years. This discovery took place on an excavation site less than thirty miles from where we lived. The following year, five hundred miles away in tropical North Queensland, an Egyptian calendar stone, gold scarabs and gold coins were found.

There's a well-known story of a North Queensland cattleman who used to serve his dinner guests off gold plates fashioned from melted down gold coins found on the station!

Objects that appear to be from ancient Egypt have also appeared in Western Australia and New South Wales.

These finds excited me. I had been an avid student of ancient history in high school, perhaps because of a vivid and romantic imagination, so I knew quite a lot about ancient civilizations. Egypt has always had a strange fascination for me, akin to my love of ghost stories and the supernatural. Perhaps you feel the same way.

So *was* there an ancient Egyptian presence in Australia? My heroine, Rosie Summers, thinks so, although cattle baron Chase Banfield is skeptical. See what *you* think!

Margaret Way

The Cattle Baron
Margaret Way

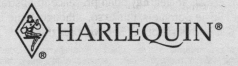

HARLEQUIN®

TORONTO • NEW YORK • LONDON
AMSTERDAM • PARIS • SYDNEY • HAMBURG
STOCKHOLM • ATHENS • TOKYO • MILAN • MADRID
PRAGUE • WARSAW • BUDAPEST • AUCKLAND

ISBN 0-373-70966-8

THE CATTLE BARON

Copyright © 2001 by Margaret Way, Pty., Ltd.

This edition published by arrangement with Harlequin Books S.A.

® and TM are trademarks of the publisher. Trademarks indicated with
® are registered in the United States Patent and Trademark Office, the
Canadian Trade Marks Office and in other countries.

Visit us at www.eHarlequin.com

Printed in U.S.A.

The Cattle Baron

PROLOGUE

3500 B.C.
The Great South Land

BURU BURU CROSSED the beautiful crystal river without incident, though a gigantic crocodile cruised downstream, its massive head turned Buru Buru's way. The crocodile's yellow eyes were open, unmoving, narrowed against the molten brilliance of the sun. Another crocodile almost as monstrous had taken up a position on the white sandy bank of the crossing, steadily watching its territory. Buru Buru was not afraid. He chanted a magic song beneath his breath. These were Dreaming Crocodiles, sacred to his people, keepers of the tribe's secrets, its ancient rituals.

Inside the enormous reptiles lived mythical beings, spirits from the Eternal Dreamtime, which held every black man in its stream. The black man's culture had existed since time began; now it was pressed to desperation by the arrival of the copper skins, who worshiped strange gods and turned everything to fear and anguish. These frightening newcomers had come from the sea. Not on rafts or in the small long-nosed bark canoes the men of Buru Buru's tribe used to hunt fish and turtles, but in large painted vessels that moved swiftly like the clouds.

In the early days of the terrible invasion, many of his people had been captured and killed, too bewildered by

what was happening to run and hide. The people of Buru
Buru's tribe were gentle, peace-loving, unused to violence.
The dreadful debbil-debbils came from a different world.
A world where men killed fiercely for no reason Buru Buru
could understand. They even killed one another, laying
their victims on a great ceremonial stone slab as though
proud of the blood that dripped from the sorcerer's dagger.
These tall invaders with their cruel sharp features and beaks
of noses, not wide at the base like Buru Buru's own but
thin and straight. The lips were cold slashes over strong
white teeth. More frightening, they were strong. Bigger,
heavier, than the men of Buru Buru's clan, their tall lean
bodies wrapped from waist to knee in something softer and
more supple than the finest woven grasses. The women,
unlike his own women, covered their breasts, their heavy
long hair swinging to their shoulders, bound around the
forehead with shining ornaments unfamiliar to Buru Buru's
eyes. The women of Buru Buru's tribe wore flowers or the
colorful feathers that fell from the wings of legions of birds.
Like Buru Buru's people, the newcomers were constantly
in search of food, and they had better weapons for the hunt.
They protected their bodies, too, with heavy glinting shields
fashioned from something Buru Buru could not divine. But
even the best of them lacked his own people's skills, especially with the spear, which was shorter than the newcomers'. Worse, they had dared to take and keep many of
the tribe's boomerangs, which only the black man had the
right to carry. This and other punishable sins, such as the
desecration of a sacred site for their place of worship, had
called down the wrath of the Great Ancestors, whose power
was far beyond that of the debbil-debbil's gods.

The Great Ancestors governed the land and everything
on it: man, animals, vegetation. The Great Ancestors owned
the bright yellow gibber stones the newcomers hunted so

avidly along the mighty river's banks, even risking the
spirit crocodiles who crushed many for their transgression
between powerful jaws. Still, the invaders courted such
death. And for what? To make their pretty ornaments?
Their little figures? These yellow stones washed down by
the yearly floodwaters had been known to Buru Buru's people since the beginning of time. They saw little value in
them, except perhaps for the children, who liked to make
them skip across the stream, watching the bright pebbles
skim the waters before sinking beneath them. The black
people knew the great source of these riverine fragments.
The mother lode was buried in sacred rock walls, veins of
it like jagged lightning on the dark stone. Much as the
newcomers sought this sacred place, they would never find
it. Let them continue to wash the stones of river sand in
their vessels. They could never obtain the bright ribbons
embedded in the sacred rocks.

But the worst offense of all, and for which the invaders
had been condemned to die, was the bringing of sickness
to Buru Buru's people. Before the invaders arrived, dis-
eases had been few among the tribes; now there were many,
many deaths. The Great Ancestors had shown their wrath
in the night skies. This was the time. As an important ritual
leader, Buru Buru had sat in council. Punishment by death
except in extreme cases, like violations of sacred law, was
itself a terrible offense. But because of the great grief and
chaos the debbil-debbils had caused, the council had spoken.

He, Buru Buru, who could move like a shadow, had been
instructed to scout out the camp, to choose the exact moment. Deliberate killing would come hard to his men. Physical violence was not an accepted code of behavior. But the
black man would be merciful. The end would come quickly
and without warning. Under the cloak of night, the potent

drink the copper skins used in their ceremonies would be
laced with the juice of certain magic berries collected by
the women of Buru Buru's tribe. The juice did not kill but
induced a strange state where a man could see visions or
enter a trance during which he would be rendered incapable
of retaliation. Then the fighting men would move into the
enemy camp. Great in number, the whole of Buru Buru's
clan had been called in from the mountain rain forests, the
coastal streams, the offshore islands, all along the blue sea
with its wondrous beauty. Great hunters, all of them, with
intimate knowledge of the land and its creatures. His chest
heaving, Buru Buru climbed up onto the bank at the very
moment the great crocodile on the flood plane drove its
massive claws into the sand, propelling itself down a
smooth slide into the river, where it sank below the sparkling surface amidst a silver spray of water. Buru Buru
understood its significance. The Great Spirit inside the crocodile would join forces with the clans to drive the invader
out.

CHAPTER ONE

BY THE TIME Rosie reached Finnigans, the bar where she'd arranged to meet Dr. Graeme Marley, distinguished archaeologist from the Sydney Museum, she was already twenty minutes late. He wouldn't like that, the doctor, although she knew from experience that he was the sort of man who liked to make other people wait. But her lateness couldn't be helped. Getting through the late-Friday-afternoon traffic had almost wrecked her, held up as she'd been by her interview with a visiting film star who had a well-deserved reputation for minor rages if the questions didn't go right. Rosie knew how to get the questions right. The meeting had been so successful it had lasted right through a late lunch and well into the afternoon, with Rosie, at least, sticking to mineral water.

Eliciting hitherto undivulged but real information from the famous was her forte. Something that had won her a swag of awards and her own byline with the *Herald*. She had also done her stint in several war zones, using her skills to inform people at home of the terrible suffering that went on in infinitely less-fortunate parts of the world. The rape and murder of the innocents. Stints like that tore off every layer of skin and caused sweat-soaked nightmares, but she still kept going back. A warrior. Or so she liked to think.

A few journalists she knew were ranged around the bar, exchanging gossip and news, nursing their cold beers while they held vigorous postmortems on yesterday's headlines and the quality of reportage. They waved her over. Rosie

flashed her high-wattage smile, indicating with a little pan-
tomime of her fingers that she was meeting someone else.
All of them to a man, and every other male in range, regardless of whether he was with a female companion or
not, paused to take her in.

The verdict was unanimous. Rosie Summers was all
Woman. She was also a great "bloke," a respected member
of a tough profession. At five-nine she was a bit tall for a
woman but had a beautiful willow-slim body. A cloud of
naturally curly marmalade hair burst like fireworks around
her face; a scattering of marmalade freckles dotted her
bone-china skin. In days gone by, Rosie Summers might
have been considered plain, all cheekbones, planes and an-
gles, but the sum total fit right into the modern idiom. She
had a lovely mouth to balance the high-bridged aristocratic
nose and the wide uncompromising jaw, good arching
brows, but it was the eyes that got you. Moss-green, they
were mesmerizing enough to dive into, full of sparkling
intelligence, understanding and humor. She wore her un-
conventional clothes haphazardly, a bit of this and a bit of
that, combinations of unexpected colors and fabrics—like
now, with her orange silk shirt, brilliantly patterned scarf,
ultra-skinny purple jeans guaranteeing attention to her long,
long legs and big burgundy leather bag slung over her
shoulder. Yet the whole effect was one of great dash. All
in all, Rosie Summers added up to dazzle if you liked her,
a little too much of a challenge if you didn't.

While others speculated about her, Rosie sailed on. It
took her a moment to locate Marley, which was odd. He
was a man who lived to be seen. Maybe he was hiding
from the plebs, she thought, tucked as he was into a banquette at the far end of the room. His heavy handsome head
was bent and he was staring into his glass, apparently transfixed by what was in it. He hadn't aged a minute since
she'd last seen him. In what, two years? A brilliant aca-

demic, just as brilliant in the field, he had at first refused to be interviewed by her after his important discovery and dating of the Winjarra cave paintings in Arnhem Land in the Northern Territory. From what Rosie could gather, Dr. Marley considered women the very worst interviewers. According to him, they never stuck to the facts. She learned also that he'd read one of her pieces, an interview with a leading politician, and thought it quite dangerous. In his view, politicians had to maintain a facade, not let journalists take the scissors to them. Only when they actually met did Marlcy turn into "an old sweetheart," as Rosie later phrased it satirically to her boss. The article, a good one, with Marley saying far more about himself than he'd ever intended, appeared in a national publication and was so well received it spawned a number of television appearances for the doctor, plus a few big donations from the seriously wealthy.

Rosie had met Marley's wife, surprised that Mrs. Marley had so few obvious attractions when her husband was so striking. Helen was a quiet, almost weary youngish woman who let her husband do all the talking. Rosie figured Helen found it a lot easier that way. The odd time Mrs. Marley had opened her mouth, offering something that Rosie recalled always had a point to it, Marley had turned on her with a tight smile that quickly squashed further intelligent comment. Strangely enough, he had appeared very taken with Rosie, who was nothing if not forthright and highly articulate to boot.

"Dr. Marley?" Rosie approached the banquette. Marley didn't look up. "Rosie Summers," she said, wondering not for the first time if Marley did everything for effect. Either that or he'd developed a hearing problem.

But his surprise, as it turned out, was quite genuine. "Roslyn!" He tried to stand up, found the banquette too cramped for his height, sat down again after quickly paralyzing her outstretched hand. "How marvelous to see you. Thanks for coming. I know I was terribly secretive." For some reason he gave a hearty laugh.

"So you were!" Rosie responded brightly on cue, slipped into the banquette opposite, leaned forward, smiled. "Just enough to fan my interest, at any rate. How are you? You look well. It must be all of two years." That made him around forty-five, she evaluated.

He nodded, clearly pleased with himself, too. "Hard to believe. I'm glad you were able to come. You're often in my thoughts. You look terrific, by the way. The very picture of sparkling good health."

"I make sure I get my full quota of vitamins," Rosie answered dismissively. "What about you?" She let her eyes rove over him, waiting. There was a story here for sure.

"Things haven't been all that good for me, Roslyn," he told her, his nose pinched. "Helen and I have split up."

Rosie glanced around the room. Anything to avoid eye contact. Good for Helen! Rosie's spontaneous reaction was based on what she'd seen with her own eyes, but she could scarcely not show sympathy. "I'm so sorry. What happened?"

He took a deep breath, making no attempt to disguise his outrage, a big handsome man important in his field, charming when he had to be. He had a crest of thick dark hair with distinguished silver wings, penetrating light-blue eyes, cared-for supple skin despite all the hours digging up the great Outback, a really fit toned body from regular visits to the gym. On the face of it, his wife should have been mad for him. Obviously she had been, until rebellion kicked in.

"It's all terribly sad and I suppose predictable." He shrugged. "Helen was always a retiring sort of girl. An only child of older parents. Quite eminent academics. Helen could have had a career herself, but she chose to marry me.''

"Couldn't she have had both?'' Rosie's voice was a shade dry. ''You have no children?''

He shook his head, brushing the difficulties of parenting aside. ''Children need time and commitment. Helen and I decided early in our marriage that we needed to devote all our energies to my career. I suppose you could say she sacrificed herself for me. Of course I asked nothing of the kind. She could have found part-time work at the museum. Cataloging for our extensive library. She was an excellent student.'' He shrugged again. ''But things didn't work out. The simple truth was, she came to bitterly resent my success, though I have to admit she tried very hard to keep it to herself. She wasn't much good with people, either. Poor social skills. You'll understand I have to attend so many functions, fund-raisers, that sort of thing. I get invited everywhere.''

And revel in it. ''Those television appearances certainly helped put you in the public eye.'' All of a sudden Rosie realized she had never liked Marley, for all his suave charm.

"Haven't I always given you credit?''

"So you have,'' Rosie agreed. ''For a while. So, where's Helen now?''

He frowned so ferociously that Rosie wondered if quiet little Helen had lost all sense of good conduct and moved in with another man. ''Would you believe she's gone back to university?'' He spit the word out as though it was an accusation. ''Good God, she's nearly forty.''

Rosie swept flying wisps of hair from her face. Ah, yes, the superior male. What arrogance! Hadn't that been her first impression? ''I'm sure you regard yourself as a man in his prime, Dr. Marley. Helen hasn't hit hers yet. I'm sorry you've broken up,'' she lied. ''Perhaps it's not final?

Helen may want to establish herself. She can't *always* do what you want.''

Another tight smile. ''There'll be no reconciliation, if that's what you mean. Helen chose to leave me when I've done everything for her. End of story. I'm forced to face the fact that our marriage was a mistake in the first place.''

''I guess Helen thought so, too,'' Rosie offered wryly, completely on the unworthy Helen's side. She was surprised Helen had it in her.

Marley glared at her. ''You know, you might be a bit more sympathetic, but then, women always stick together. It's been a very unpleasant few months. Toward the end, Helen was almost a basket case. Yet her parents had the nerve to tell me it was *my* fault. I'd been neglecting their little darling. Didn't I know she'd desperately wanted children?''

''I thought that was one of the things the two of you had discussed,'' Rosie reminded him, looking amazed. ''Anyway, I'm sorry. I can see it's really hit you.'' High time to change the subject. ''So, any more fabulous finds up your sleeve? World scoops for me?''

He brightened instantly, penetrating eyes entirely focused, taking her back to the first time she'd met him, full of pride in his latest achievement, lionized by the academic world. ''That's why I wanted us to meet, Roslyn.'' He reached across the table, took her hands, mercifully not using his bone-crusher grip. ''I have in my possession a thrilling object. I've used the latest testing to date it at some five thousand years old. It was dug up on a far North Queensland cattle station.''

Rosie was less than riveted. ''Well. Okay.'' She gestured with one hand. ''It can't be Aboriginal, then? You yourself have dated beautifully finished objects many, many thousands of years older than that. Not to mention the Winjarra paintings.''

"They're not Aboriginal," Marley snapped. "Give me some credit, my dear. You'll easily identify the object just by looking at it."

"Do you have it with you?" Rosie asked more respectfully, deciding to play along.

Marley raised a dark mocking brow. "You surprise me, Roslyn. I need to be very quiet, very careful about this. Oh, I trust you. I trust your integrity. I couldn't stand to share my secret with any other person. Certainly not a journalist. I am offering you a great scoop, but what I really need from you is your persuasive power. You seem able to influence people. All sorts of people. I've made it my business to study your essays, your articles, your reviews. You have the ability to get highly sophisticated people to tell you what you want. More importantly, to get them to *do* what you want. That's not easy. It's a real gift."

"More or less," Rosie agreed modestly. "So, who is this you want me to work on? It might help if you put all your cards on the table, Dr. Marley."

"Please, call me Graeme."

He gave her a sort of we-understand-one-another smile Rosie wasn't altogether comfortable with. Although Graeme Marley was undoubtedly an impressive-looking man, she had never felt an attraction. Perhaps it related to his utter self-centeredness. Besides, he hadn't mentioned divorce, so he was still legally married to the rebellious Helen, who was at this moment throwing off her years of brainwashing. Still, calling him Graeme was hardly a sin.

He sat back, presenting her with an unexpectedly boyish grin. "Lord, I haven't asked you if you'd like something to drink."

She went to say, *Not for me,* settled for, "A Coke will be fine."

His snort was almost contemptuous. "Really?" He sounded as if she was having him on.

Rosie shrugged. "I don't drink when I drive." Though she was starting to feel pretty desperate for a scotch. "I've got the trip home, then I have a dinner lined up. I promise you I won't be driving myself home, however."

"Anything changed in that department?" he asked smoothly, signaling a passing waiter, giving his order. A Coke with ice for her. Another scotch for him.

"Meaning?" Rosie quickly said. He made it sound as though they were closer than they were.

"One doesn't think of a woman like you without a man." He tried a seductive smile, leaving Rosie to believe he'd drunk too much.

"I'm quite happy on my own," she said simply.

"No disastrous encounters?" The raised eyebrows suggested there was a story.

Rosie lifted her arm to glance at her watch. "I don't usually discuss my private life. And listen, I don't have a lot of time. If you could just let me see what you're talking about?"

He leaned forward, his rich well-oiled voice just above a whisper as though he was about to impart illicit information. "It's ancient Egyptian," he said, blue fire in his eyes. "A magnificent stone scarab."

"I love it!" Rosie wondered if Helen's defection had affected his sanity. Speculation about whether there'd ever been an ancient Egyptian presence in Australia had been going the rounds for at least a century. Still, it would pay to listen. For now. "So it was found on this cattle station?" she asked.

The light-blue eyes were those of a religious fanatic. "I'm told there's a pyramid hidden in the rain forest," Marley said urgently. "Some parts of this station are jungle. There's a river running through it with its fair share of crocodiles. The nasty beggars have been protected for too long. Some wannabe Crocodile Dundee ought to start up safaris. Let our adventure-loving tourists shoot a few. Anyway, I'm very serious about this. Egyptology may not be my particular area of expertise, but I'm extremely well-informed. I have other objects, as well. Coins, artifacts, jewelry. A cache, no less. I've seen with my own eyes rock paintings showing Egyptian hieroglyphics and pictograms, and I've spoken to a trusted colleague in the Museum of Antiquities in Cairo regarding translations. Others have blundered around in the past. Rank amateurs, mere enthusiasts who didn't know how to get a body of evidence together. Academic interest here has always been in Aboriginal rock paintings. Not non-Aboriginal."

Rosie shrugged, surprised by the intensity of expression on Marley's face. "Well, I'm no Egyptologist, either!" she said. "Although I was fascinated enough to study ancient history in high school. I know there was a set of gold boomerangs discovered by Professor Carter in the tomb of Tutankhamen."

"Indeed there was!" Marley smiled at her encouragingly. "There's also significant evidence that the ancients were well aware of the Great South Land. It's also certain that the ancient maritime civilizations were quite capable of undertaking extensive ocean voyages. Who's to say an entire fleet didn't land in our far North?"

"Certainly not me." Rosie smiled, momentarily shaking off her skepticism. "May I ask how you acquired your…cache?"

Marley glanced around to check on the waiter's whereabouts. Obviously a touch paranoid in his current state. "My dear." He leaned forward, raising his hand to the side of his cheek. "If that got out, I'd have tourists tramping around a sacred site."

Rosie looked at him thoughtfully. "The cattle station—which one is it?"

The archaeologist knit his fine brows, gaze intent. "My dear, can I swear you to secrecy?"

Rosie sat back, put a hand on her heart. "I swear I won't tell anyone. But don't expect me not to check it out."

"Good for you!" Marley beamed at her admiringly. The waiter set down their drinks and turned to Rosie, giving her an exaggerated wink. Once he'd left, Marley continued. "You've probably heard of the place. Three Moons?"

That changed everything. "Now, why didn't I think of it!" she exclaimed, rubbing her tall frosted glass. "Legendary station and all that. Cattle barons of the Far North. Give me a minute and it'll come back to me. Something to do with a tragedy." She picked up her Coke. "I was one of those who covered Senator Lamont's trip to that part of the world some years back. Banfield. I remember. I met the owner at a fund-raiser."

Marley looked absolutely delighted. "God, you know him?"

"*Met* him, Dr. Marley. As in shook hands, exchanged a few words. A largely aloof man, as I recall. Projected a great sense of distance, of incredible detachment. Very refined, wealthy, classy in an iceberg way. Older than you. Early fifties. At that time."

"But, my dear, he's not the owner at all," Marley lamented, all but grinding his teeth. "That's Porter Banfield. The uncle. He was Chase Banfield's guardian after his parents were killed."

Rosie had to think no more. It all came back. "That's it! A fire." She shuddered at the very word, plagued by her own coverage of fires over the years. The ferocity of the orange flames, the smoke, the soot, the terrible odors, the human fallout. A fire at Three Moons. How shocking it must have been. The agony, especially for the boy. That could have easily accounted for the coldness of Porter Banfield's manner. She recalled that, for the brief time they'd spoken, she'd had the sensation they weren't really speaking at all. But he'd had no hesitation in throwing his money around. The Banfields were royalty in the North. The senator hadn't qualified for an invitation to Three Moon's homestead, but it was said to be quite a place, a tropical mansion no less. "That's okay, then, if Porter Banfield isn't the person you want me to talk to," she said with relief. "To tell you the truth, I don't think he's very interested in women. Not gay—I think I'd have sensed it. More that he's one hell of a misogynist."

"Actually," said Marley, sounding as if he quite liked the man, "I've met Porter Banfield on a number of occasions connected with my work. He's very well educated, with an encyclopedic knowledge of ancient Egyptian civilization. He's also a great collector of antiquities."

Now it was Rosie's turn to cock a brow. "I thought governments didn't like their antiquities disappearing out of the country. Like the Elgin marbles," she added. "I really do think the British Museum should give them back. I'm on Greece's side."

"Hardly surprising, with Australia having the biggest Greek population outside Greece," Marley said facetiously. "Now, if we could concentrate on the matter at hand?"

Rosie frowned at his condescension. "You don't think I'm capable?"

There was a pause while Marley took another look at her glittering cloud of hair, gold, amber, topaz. "Roslyn, Roslyn, I didn't say that," he told her. "I'm just eager to enlist your aid."

"I hope you don't want me to be a snoop?"

"I want you to somehow get to Chase Banfield." Marley gazed earnestly into her face. "He's not willing to entertain me or even listen to my theories. The station isn't exactly accessible. The man even less so. He likes his privacy. I have it from his uncle that he strenuously disapproves of any kind of search on his property.''

''I guess he regards the idea of an ancient Egyptian presence in Oz a romantic notion?'' Rosie said a little flippantly.

Marley's handsome face took on a brooding expression. ''Probably he has no sense of history. No adventure in his soul.''

''Well, what do they say on the grapevine? For me, I'm just hoping he's a handsome dashing guy.'' Rosie smiled. ''Why don't we just write him a letter? Tell him what you've discovered so far. Request his cooperation. I've never met anybody—and I've met a lot of very rich people—who can't do with a bit more money. Mention a big reward. The admiration and respect of your peers all around the world. A great scoop for me. A great adventure for him. He's a frontiersman, after all. But before we really get under way, maybe I'd better look at your findings.'' *As opposed to your etchings.* Rosie's direct sparkling gaze made that point clear.

''How about dinner tonight?'' Marley asked.

Rosie waved away the winking waiter, wondering if he was trying to deliver some message. ''Can't make it. I told you I have a function.''

''Sorry, I'd forgotten. Tomorrow, then,'' Marley persisted. ''You'll have to come to my home.''

Rosie was surprised by her wariness of him. A kind of careful take-care instinct—one that didn't fool her often. ''I can't believe you'll do the cooking?''

''Come after dinner,'' he said. ''I think you'll be particularly interested in a certain piece of jewelry,'' he said, as if intoxicated by his mental picture. ''It would look marvelous around your throat. Some women can't wear important jewelry, but you...you just exude presence.''

Rosie gave him a deadpan look. ''I got it from my dad.

He's a Supreme Court judge.'' No harm in going back to the good doctor's abode, she supposed. She didn't anticipate any sexual overtures, although from the odd flash here and there she couldn't entirely rule it out. Anyway, she had insurance; her mother, who played a wonderful game of golf and tennis, had insisted she learn karate her first year of living away from home. Like her mother, she was the kind of woman who preferred to excel. Weekly classes eventually culminated in a black belt.

Marley put out his hand, clinging to her answer like a drowning man to a raft. ''Well?''

''I'm intrigued, as you well know.'' Rosie looked at him with her clear moss-green eyes. ''But what really mystifies me, given that you know Porter Banfield, is why the man who must have reared his nephew can't use his influence on your behalf. How could I possibly be more effective than Chase Banfield's uncle? Surely *he* would be your best ally?''

''It's amazing to me that he's not.'' Marley's expression clouded over. ''But by all accounts they're not close.''

Rosie sipped from her Coke. ''Well, that tells us a lot. What kind of men are the Banfields? Both brushed with the same coldness?'' she speculated. ''Is it a family trait? Or are they victims of the past? One would have thought they'd become very close—unless they were both too terribly scarred.''

Marley waved away Rosie's musings as womanly affectation. ''I really don't know,'' he said, suggesting he didn't care, either, ''but there's been a whole legacy of strife. Apparently, as soon as he turned twenty-one, Banfield turfed his uncle out.''

''Maybe Chase Banfield had a reason,'' she said. ''I feel we ought to be fair. Either that, or he's an ungrateful so-and-so. I can easily do some research on the Banfields.

They're landed gentry. There's got to be a story, and it doesn't sound like a fairy tale.''

Marley rolled his eyes. "There's always a story. Unfortunately it doesn't help me. Chase Banfield doesn't share his uncle's interests. Not in the least. In fact, he derides them. The problem is, if I can't get to Chase Banfield, I can't get onto Three Moons.''

"Where this cache was found.'' Rosie phrased it as a statement, not a question.

"I didn't exactly say that, Roslyn.''

"I think you did. If you want my help, there shouldn't be secrets between us. Presumably Porter Banfield unearthed the scarab and the rest of the stuff on the station and approached you as an eminent archaeologist. What's in it for him?''

Marley sighed, as though he wished he didn't have to choose *her* as his partner in this enterprise. "The thrill of the find, Roslyn.'' He reverted to testiness. "I told you he's an Egyptologist.''

"And nothing would please him more than sharing the limelight with you,'' she said, a touch sarcastically. "Perhaps the two of you going on a lecture tour. As I remember, he was very conscious of his own importance.''

"He's a scholar, Roslyn,'' Marley muttered. "Don't lose sight of that. Antiquities are his passion.''

"As long as he can explain where he got them.''

"That's not our business, my dear.''

Rosie rested both elbows on the table, trying to think it out. "And he was exploring Three Moons back when his nephew was a boy? He sounds like a man obsessed.''

"Why not?'' Marley stared at her with that strange look in his eyes. "Are you trying to tell me, my dear, that you don't care?''

Rosie stroked her forehead. "I'm fascinated, Dr. Marley—if it's all genuine.''

He blinked hard. "Surely you don't think I'd be party to a hoax."

"Oh, no." Rosie emphasized the *no*. "There's your integrity, your reputation. I don't mean that the objects aren't genuine. After all, finds of ancient Egyptian origin have been turning up for many, many decades. They've been reported in newspapers and magazines from the turn of the century. The big question is, where did *these* objects come from? Can Porter Banfield be telling the truth about where he acquired his treasure trove? Obviously, if his interest is antiquities, he knows all the dealers. One or two are probably shady."

"Dear God!" Marley shook his head in disbelief. "Allow me to judge the man's qualifications. With all due respect, I think I'm a better judge than you. I wouldn't have set up this meeting if I didn't think we were really onto something big. Banfield claims he knows the site of the ancient Egyptian village. He said his brother knew. Their father before them. They knew the site of the pyramid."

"And Chase Banfield doesn't? I refuse to believe it."

"Hell, why?" Marley looked rattled. "He was only ten when his parents died. For years he was pretty traumatized."

"His father and uncle never shared the family secret? I think he *has* to know. You've got to admit, Doctor, this is fairly hard to buy."

"Does everything have to make perfect sense?" Marley quivered in outrage. "There are many things out there one can't explain."

"True," Rosie acknowledged. "Particularly if the bait you're dangling is such a marvelous scoop."

Marley nodded. "It *is* marvelous, and it's real. And you're the only person I could think of who might get through to Banfield. A combination of skill and charm. Porter swears that what he says is true. The cache he left in my keeping was unearthed on Three Moons. As to how it got there? Banfield believes with every particle of faith in him that there was an ancient Egyptian village on the station. For one thing, rock paintings on the property depict papyrus, two-stem and three-stem. Papyrus was the swamp plant of ancient Egypt, as I'm sure you know. It's not indigenous to Australia. As well, there are Egyptian-like figures and glyphs depicted. I haven't seen these caves. I can't get onto the property to see them, which is enormously frustrating to someone in my position. They're almost inaccessible, so I'm told, but until I study the paintings, I can't give a definite answer as to their date or their origin. Banfield says they're very old Aboriginal drawings.''

"And who's going to brave the crocodiles?'' Rosie asked, stirring abruptly as though one was hiding under the table.

Marley rubbed his shapely hands together. "I don't think they're going to attack us if we don't attack them.''

"Maybe not the average crocodile,'' Rosie said with a shudder, "but there are plenty of rogues.''

Marley gave a dismissive little wave of his hand. "Forget the crocodiles.''

"Hell, no!''

"Nothing bad's going to happen to you,'' Marley assured her. "I've been Outback hundreds of times. Admittedly most of my experience has been with the fresh-water variety.''

Rosie groaned. "Don't West Australians keep them as pets? We're talking the saltwater variety, Dr. Marley. The ones that take you down into a death roll and shove you under a log until they're ready to party. Whichever way you look at it, saltwater crocodiles are part of your package.''

"But you look like the adventurous type,'' Marley joked. "Anyway, maybe you can get Chase Banfield himself to play great white hunter. He must know his own property like the back of his hand.''

At those words, Rosie pounced. "Isn't *that* proof there's nothing there?"

For the first time doubt sprang into Marley's eyes, yet he plowed on. "A huge slice of it is jungle. He doesn't know where to look for the site. Three Moons is vast. Some ten thousand square kilometers. Fifty thousand or more Brahmin-based cattle roam the open savannahs and the hill country. There's a farming project, as well, forage sorghum, different varieties of hay. That kind of thing. I'm no farmer.''

"Neither, apparently, was Porter Banfield." Rosie pushed glinting wisps of hair from her temples. "Not a cattleman, either. Which might account for a lot of Chase Banfield's problems,'' she added perceptively. "From the little knowledge I gained when I was up there, Three Moons station some ten years ago was almost at the point of collapse.''

"Well, that's far from the case now,'' Marley said irritably. "I understand it's back to full production.''

"So Chase Banfield is no slouch,'' Rosie offered with admiration.

"Apparently not,'' Marley responded, unsmiling. "Porter may have been a failure in some areas, but he knows his ancient history. The pyramid exists, although it's covered with eons of vegetation, hidden away in the back country. Lonely, isolated, scary country.''

"Where you want to go trekking?'' Humor sparkled in Rosie's eyes.

"I'd go trekking in hell if I could unearth an ancient civilization,'' Marley returned bluntly. "What I want to know is whether you're prepared to help me make my discovery.''

"Porter Banfield's discovery, surely.''

Marley didn't so much as blink. "He's had his cache for a while. He might be something of an Egyptologist, but he doesn't have the expertise to excavate anything, let alone an ancient ruin. Wise man, he knows his limitations. It takes an archaeologist of my training to successfully carry out a project like that. What I'm asking of you is a pact of mutual trust. If you can get to Banfield, persuade him to sanction our plan to uncover this ancient village, it might turn out to be the greatest assignment you'll ever have. To be part of an exploration group that would prove once and for all that there was an ancient Egyptian presence in Australia! Think of it. A fact, not just an interesting possibility." Fire welled up in his eyes.

"You're really serious about all this, aren't you."

"Oh, yes." Marley nodded. "And you will be, too, once you feel that necklace touching your skin."

CHAPTER TWO

MORE THAN TWO THOUSAND MILES away in tropical North Queensland, Chase Banfield, prince among his fellows, sat in the surprisingly opulent cattlemen's club, enjoying a cold beer. It was the end of a long hard day. He'd made the trek from his cattle station, Three Moons, into the small rainforest township of Isis. Now he just wanted to sit and relax before going into the town center to the pub, where he planned to stay overnight. Like most fervent hopes, it was about to be dashed. He'd barely been at the club ten minutes when Mick Dempsey lurched onto the veranda, swirling the drink in his tumbler, making the ice cubes rattle.

Chase shook off his initial dismay and waved an acknowledging hand. Dempsey, a big man who, until the untimely death of his wife, Bridget, a few years earlier, had been one of the most popular members of the cattlemen's club, was now much diminished, his black-Irish good looks eaten away by grief and the bottle. He was bone-thin, and his bush shirt and jeans hung on him, though to his credit his clothes were always clean. But when he was sozzled, which was pretty much all the time, he could be harrowing company. Even for Banfield, who had a lot of sympathy for the man. It was just that he had precious little free time these days to unwind. Three Moons, in his family since the mid-1880s took all his energy, and God knows he'd grown as tough as old boots. Now Mick was heading straight for him, ignoring the scatter of members at the other tables, who stepped up the intensity of their conversations as Mick hove unsteadily into sight.

For a split second, Banfield considered getting up, making an excuse and going on his way, but pity and genuine affection kept him in place. Mick knew all about the savage pain of grief. Most significantly, Mick had been a close friend of his father's since boyhood. Both heirs to vast cattle stations. Both frontiersmen. Things like that counted.

A sad shadow of Mick's once-famous grin crossed his face. He thrust out his huge hand, looking at Banfield with unfeigned pleasure. "Chase, m'boy! This is great! Hardly ever see you these days."

Banfield hooked out a chair for the older man, at the same time half rising and gripping Dempsey's outstretched hand. "How's it going, Mick?"

Mick sank down gratefully, eyes filmed over. Such a big forlorn man with enough black mustache to stuff a sofa, Banfield thought, torn between sympathy and a desire to bawl Mick out. Mick was smiling wanly, nursing his neat whiskey, at least the fifth since he'd come in on that torrid afternoon. "Same as always, son. I continue in my fashion."

Chase tossed off his ice-cold beer, then set the glass down on the table. "You've dug yourself into a pit, Mick. You have to climb out of it."

"Easier said than done, my boy." Mick shook his heavy dark head, still thickly thatched though the once-gleaming blue-black curls were grizzled.

"I don't dispute that. But you can do it. There's help at hand."

"Oh, how the mighty have fallen," Mick intoned. "I was someone, wasn't I, in another life? Before I lost my girl. That shattered me. Showed me for what I really am. A hollow stick."

"Listen to me, Mick—"

"Goddammit, Chase, you know it's true." Mick slumped in his chair, looking much older than his years. Fifty-eight, the same age as Lew Banfield, Chase's father, had he lived.

"You're better than this, Mick," Banfield said quietly. "None of us likes to see what's happened to you."

"I'm not a fighter like you, mate. You're a real stayer. I know I need help. I know I've got friends like you I can count on, but life doesn't mean a monkey's without my girl. She was everything to me. My better half. No question. I tried for a while. Maybe if the kids had stuck around, but neither of them liked the life. Bridget held us all together."

"She was a fine woman, Mick, a good woman." Banfield understood how he felt. "Why she had to die so young, I don't know. Don't ask questions. There aren't any answers."

"You'd know, son." Mick continued to swirl the whiskey in his glass without drinking. "Losing your mum and dad the way you did. Having that bastard of a Porter run your life for so long. I suffered that bloody Porter for your dad's sake. Could two brothers have been less alike?" He sighed. "Bridget and I always had a big interest in you. Always knew you'd get Three Moons back to what it was."

"Hardly that yet, Mick." Banfield grimaced. "Porter might've been born into a cattle dynasty, but he didn't know the first thing about running Three Moons."

"Never woulda had to, I expect," Mick said in a lugubrious tone. "Second son and all that. Who would ever have thought your mum and dad would go so early? A tragedy if ever I heard one. You'd have been a goner, too, except for old Porter. Reckon saving you was the one bloody thing he's ever done in his life. If he did it." Mick snorted. "Always had an idea m'self it was Moses." Mick referred to Three Moons' leading stockman, a full-blooded Aboriginal and the finest tracker in the Top End.

"Moses denied it unequivocally. Does to this day," Banfield said calmly, unwilling to give Mick any encouragement. He raised a hand in greeting to a member on the veranda who, about to bound over, caught sight of Mick and abruptly veered off.

"Why the hell wouldn't he?" Mick shot back with some of his old fire. "Porter would have kicked him off the place. Off his tribal land. What the hell did it matter if Three Moons lost a loyal employee and supreme stockman? Porter had to play the hero."

"Don't work yourself up," Banfield said. He'd heard Mick rant on in this vein many times before. "The police accepted Porter's version of events. No reason not to. He *is* my uncle. I was overcome by smoke inhalation. I knew nothing until they found me staggering around in the bush. Hell, I was only ten. I couldn't do anything. I couldn't do anything," he repeated, all these years later still caught up in the old anguish. "If only I'd been older...stronger."

Mick screwed up his face, breathing heavily. "I know, my boy. I know the grief and the rage. But bloody Porter! The bastard spent a fortune. Your money, son. Your inheritance."

Banfield's face took on a somber cast, though he spoke matter-of-factly. "The west wing had to be rebuilt. Anyway, let's not talk about Porter, Mick. He's pretty much out of my life. He only comes to Three Moons now and again. It's no secret we have a poor relationship, but I can't lose sight of the fact that he saved my life."

"I dunno, Chase. He certainly took the credit, the old vulture. How come the fire was confined to the west wing? Your mum and dad's private wing. Why didn't it start down at Porter's end of the home?"

"You're talking murder, aren't you, Mick." Banfield looked directly into the older man's eyes. "Porter may be many things, but I can't see him doing away with his own brother.''

"I guess not," Mick said, hanging his head and taking a deep reflective breath. "But he had a compelling reason. Your dad inherited just about everything from your grandfather. The station, the investment portfolio, most of the money.''

"Porter got enough. Why dredge it up now? There was plenty of money for both of them. Porter always knew he wasn't going to be the heir.''

"I reckon it twisted him.'' Mick was nothing if not persistent. "Anyway, it wasn't about your bloody uncle I wanted to speak. Some doctor guy arrived in town today, askin' after you. Him and his girlfriend. 'Struth, what a looker!'' Momentarily Mick was released from the chasm of grief, kissing his fingertips. "Masses of orange hair. Eyes like a new leaf, plenty of dash to her. The sort of woman a man would fight for. He's a distinguished-looking bloke, but they don't seem to match up somehow.''

"So you still notice, Mick?'' Banfield sent him a sardonic glance.

"Hard not to. A man doesn't see exciting women all that often. Anyway, it appears they want to meet you.''

"The hell they do.'' Banfield glanced at his watch. "I don't have time for this. I'm betting we're talking about a Dr. Graeme Marley. He rang me some time back. Wanted us to meet up then. He's an archaeologist with the Sydney Museum. Very respected. Published a lot of stuff.''

"So I believe!'' Dempsey actually chortled. "He was the guy who discovered those cave paintings in the Territory. Winjarra, wasn't it?''

"How do you know all this stuff, Mick?'' Banfield asked, genuinely wanting to hear the answer. There was Mick, sozzled most of the time, yet he always knew what was going on.

"I asked Lyn at the pub, of course. Lyn knows everything. Makes it her business."

"Like you." Banfield chuckled, and the sound made Mick laugh. Not altogether happily.

"For a while there, after Bridget died, Lyn thought she'd latch on to me, poor deluded woman. I found the one woman to love and I lost her."

"But you did know love, Mick, didn't you?" Banfield murmured. "You and Bridget lived for each other. Not everyone's so lucky. You ought to let the good memories come. It might help."

Mick's veined blue eyes glistened, though he gave the younger man a cagey look. "I know I make you mad. Your dad would probably have dealt with it, but I'm not ready yet, son. Not yet. If ever. Anyway, I don't want to go upsetting you. You have a big job on your hands."

"Tell me about it!" Banfield let out a pent-up breath. "I'd sue the pants off Porter if he had anything left, but he went through his inheritance, as well as a fair bit of mine. God knows what on. A partial rebuild can't account for it. My mother had refurbished the whole place only a few years before...."

"Those bloody antiquities." Mick pulled his chair closer. "The whisper is, he's got a lot of stuff he shouldn't have all locked away from prying eyes. Remember how he was always going on about the ancient Egyptians having some sort of village on Three Moons?"

Again Banfield's face changed. Became full of humor. "He believes it, too." He rolled his eyes. "I think he'd have dug up every inch of Three Moons if he'd been allowed to."

"Well, he did find those coins and the bits of pottery." Mick smoothed down his magnificent mustache.

"Ptolemy IV." Banfield nodded. "A couple of hundred

years before Christ. Someone could easily have brought them into the country."

"Who?" In the old days Mick had been fascinated with the whole question of an ancient Egyptian presence in Australia. "Spanish or Portuguese explorers?"

"Why not? The station fronts onto the sea," Banfield pointed out. "They came in ships."

"Why not the Egyptians, then?" Mick sounded a lot more focused now. "'Struth, they've found amulets, scarabs, hieroglyphics on cave walls. They're there to be seen. The Aboriginal cave paintings show characters in Egyptian-style dress. They've found silver and bronze jewelry, even gold figures."

"I know, Mick." Banfield gave the older man a lazy smile. "It's all very fascinating, but I'm far too busy to hare off after treasure, even if you and Porter are hooked on the old stories. And maybe this Marley guy. My uncle left Three Moons in pretty bad shape. I don't know what would've happened without our old faithfuls like Moses and his crew to hold the fort. I know how many times you tried to offer Porter advice."

"Porter just hated taking advice," Mick said with considerable disgust. "If you ask me, he became drunk on power. Bloody near certifiable. He always wanted power and money, but without the responsibilities."

Both men fell silent for a while, lost in their reflections. Both never quite free from the past.

Mick was the first to rouse. "Let me shout you another beer, son," he said, turning. "I won't have another scotch, if that's what's worrying you."

Banfield answered quietly but with genuine feeling. "Nothing would make me happier than to have you back, Mick. And yes, I will have that beer. I'm not planning to drive home tonight. I thought I'd stay over at the pub."

"Bonza!" Mick clapped a big friendly hand on Banfield's arm, signaling a very unsure-looking waiter. "You can have dinner with me."

"I didn't know you ate anymore," Banfield said dryly.

"I will tonight. And no more booze. Count on it." Mick spoke earnestly. "That's if you'll honor your dad's old mate."

"Suits me fine," Banfield said with more kindness than truth. He'd heard Mick's promises before.

"Then we might get to meet this doctor guy." Mick perked up. "Take a closer gander at the girlfriend. Never seen a woman as striking in me life, unless it was your mum. You've got your father's rangy height and his strong cast of features, but you have your mother's eyes. Tiger eyes, Bridget used to call them. Never saw a tiger in her life. Pure gold." He shook his head. "The things we hand down to our children. You were the son of privilege, Chase. Heir to a great station. And wealth. But I reckon you'd give it all up to have your mum and dad back."

Banfield leaned back in his chair, memories piercing his heart. "You're right about that, Mick."

"It's the same with me." Mick suddenly stood up and pitched the rest of his whiskey into the lush tropical garden. "Are you sure you can't listen to what this professor has to say?" he asked. "I've got the funniest feeling it's something to do with that cache old Porter dug up years ago. The coins and the pottery."

"You and your treasure, Mick," Banfield scoffed. "There is no treasure. There was no village. The ancient Egyptians were never on Three Moons."

Mick plonked down again and summoned the hovering waiter. "How do you know?" he countered gleefully. "You weren't there."

MICK STUCK to his promise for the hour they stayed on at the club, drinking soda water with a dash of bitters, wincing with every mouthful as though it was poison. As the place filled up and the other members became aware that Mick was as close to sober as he'd been in years, a lot of the old camaraderie returned.

Banfield was a generation younger than most of the others, but as his father's son he'd had been granted full membership as a matter of course. Being heir to a vast station was one thing. Running it when Porter Banfield had almost brought it to the brink was another. It didn't take Chase Banfield long, three years at most, to establish that he could take his place with the best of them. From the day he returned home from university with an honors degree in economics and business administration, he had taken to calling in at the club. Not to drink, although he always had time for a quick beer, but to talk to his fellow cattlemen. Or, as he admitted openly to much friendly banter, to "pick their brains." These were top cattlemen like his father. He had much to learn. A month later he turned twenty-one, and his uncle Porter's guardianship was over. John Chase Banfield was in full control of his inheritance—his trust fund, his father's business portfolio and historic Three Moons station. It was also the day he evicted his uncle. At last he was free to take over the reins and restore Three Moons to its former position as one of the great cattle stations of the world's leading beef-producing country. He was afire to succeed. He had the brains, the strength, the determination, and he was a very fast learner.

IT WAS ONLY a short four-mile trip from the club into the town of Isis, the drive winding through towering banks of bougainvillea gone wild. A veritable jungle of the ubiquitous cerise and deep-purple flowers, with their dangerous hooked thorns. A drawback certainly but they looked magnificent, brilliant foils for the soaring palms and vivid orange-scarlet of the flame-of-the-forest that lit up the bush.

In this part of the world, an enormous range of bougain-villea cultivars, the Thai golds, the pinks, the bronzes, the burnt oranges and scarlets adorned home gardens, showy and relatively easy to handle, but they never assumed the incredible height and splendor of the original bougainvillea gone wild. His mother had planted bridal white when she first came to Three Moons, training it over walls and per-golas and the balustrades of the veranda. Now great billow-ing veils of it made an unforgettable sight.

His mother! Would he ever in his lifetime be released from the grief? The might-have-beens? But grief had to be lived with. He was a Banfield and it was up to him to carry on a proud tradition, which Porter had almost wrecked. He'd never seen his uncle grieve, but perhaps he had in private. Porter was a strange one, with his own inner life, layers and layers of secrets. He was incapable of showing affection, if indeed he actually felt emotion outside his love of precious objects, especially antiquities. Inanimate pos-sessions were the thing, not human relationships. Chase couldn't begin to understand his uncle. He had long since stopped trying.

The sun had lost the worst of its heat, the cloudless co-balt sky giving way to another glorious tropical sunset. There were Mick's Spanish galleons sailing majestically above, sweeping down the sky, their sails billowing crim-son and gold. Poor old Mick! He held out no real hope that Mick would show up for dinner. Probably someone would let him sleep it off at the club.

After he'd gone a mile, he turned off the side road and onto the highway, saluting as always his grandfather, the town's founding father who'd had the foresight to line the route with royal palms. They soared a uniform eighty feet, forming a superb entry into the little rain-forest town. Then the poincianas suddenly replaced them, forming an inter-locking canopy over the main street, turning the air rosy when they were in bloom. North of Capricorn was a fantasy world, a paradise, a celebration of nature. He had visited other parts of the world, sailed around the glorious South Pacific with two of his university friends, but there was nowhere on earth he'd rather be than the place he was born. Three Moons. His great-great-grandfather, Patrick Banfield, an Englishman in search of adventure, had named it after the three almost perfect moon-shaped lagoons on the vast selection he'd taken on from the colonial Queensland government. Their characteristic feature was magnificent water lilies, and Patrick Banfield had realized they would be easily seen from the Malaysian-style homestead he planned to build.

All kinds of water birds still thronged to the lagoons—ibis, egrets, pelicans, ducks, magpie geese, pygmy geese, the brolgas, the blue cranes that mated for life. There were no beautiful water lilies farther back, in the swamp country. There the surface was completely overgrown with aquatic plants, the thick vegetation hiding the waterfowl and the crocodiles. The common crocodile mostly, freshwater, harmless, living mainly on fish. But the big stream the Aborigines called Gongora, the place of the sacred crocodile on Three Moons coastal border, was home to a few estuarine crocs that weren't particular about what they ate. Anything and everything that might come to drink at the water's edge. Birds, reptiles, mammals, tortoises, cattle, men.

The station had suffered three crocodile-related disasters over the years, which was close to a miracle, considering no one seemed to heed the warnings. Victim one at the turn of the century—an unwary stockman. Another in the 1930s when a visiting English cousin deliberately went after the legendary Munwari, the gigantic sacred crocodile said to be thousands of years old. Ah, the thrill of the kill! Everyone had warned him not to interfere with the crocodiles, a species that had survived unchanged for more than 150 million years, but according to the cousin, this was even better than hunting rhino in Africa. He'd made it to the upper reaches of Gongora, deep into country few white men had ever traveled; he'd never returned. A large search had been mounted, but it was as though he'd vanished from the face of the earth. The Aboriginal version of events was that the earth and not the Great Spirit guardian had swallowed him up; either way, he was never seen again. His story was part of the saga of the Wilderness Coast. A zoologist, the author of many scientific papers on reptiles, including crocodiles, lost a leg right up to the thigh in the course of his study of Munwari. That was in his father's day. Porter had never allowed anyone else onto the station after that. Chase didn't intend to, either, and that included Dr. Graeme Marley.

The last time, and it had to be two years, Marley had tried calling him. No go, especially when Marley had used Porter for a reference. Now Marley had decided to show up in person with his girlfriend in tow.

Girlfriend? Surely he'd seen a photograph someplace of Marley and a wife? A little brown hen to Marley's peacock. It could even have been on TV. Marley had made quite a few appearances after he'd discovered and dated the Winjarra paintings. Ah! He remembered now. There was a journalist involved. A young woman. Banfield started to make the connections. A redhead. His mind ranged back over Mick's description. Masses of orange hair. Obviously she wasn't bothered by the fact that Marley was a married man.

Well, time hadn't changed his mind. He had no intention of allowing Dr. Marley and his girlfriend to run around Three Moons uncovering more bric-a-brac. Probably stuff buried by poor old Porter, whose imagination worked on overdrive. Porter might be obsessed with "proving" the existence of some ancient Egyptian village in the wilds of the up-country, a real no-man's-land; Chase was far more interested in what was happening on Three Moons here and now. The mustering had to be completed before the onset of the Wet between December and March. They were well into September, spring in the state capital, Brisbane, more than a thousand miles away. Life at Three Moons was dictated by the season. The Wet and the Dry. A creek that was little more than a trickle in the Dry could become a raging torrent in the Wet. If a cyclone blew in from the Coral Sea to the east, the Timor to the north, the Indian Ocean to the west, all hell broke loose. It was either one thing or the other—drought or flood—presided over by the timeless culture of the Aborigines. Banfield had great respect for the Aborigines and great sympathy for them as they coped with the problems that beset them as traditional life broke down. It wasn't easy trying to adapt to the white man's culture, almost diametrically opposed to their own. Aborigines were intimately attuned to the land. They weren't terribly receptive to material gain. But they were the backbone of the big stations, splendid stockmen, trackers, horse breakers. The bush owed them a great debt. His childhood mentor had been Moses, not his uncle Porter. Moses was Three Moon's leading stockman, the most loyal of employees and a tribal elder. Moses had been asked to look out for him in his childhood days when he'd been running wild. Moses had taken the job very seriously. Banfield didn't know what he would've done without him in those first terrible years after he'd lost his parents and Porter had withdrawn to a place inside himself that could not be reached. Moses was a remarkable man. In many ways a foster father. It was men like Moses who had helped him win the battle to reestablish Three Moons.

CHAPTER THREE

HE WAS NOSING down a sharp rise when he was snatched out of his reverie by one hell of a sight. A small white car in the distance suddenly swerved off the road and took off down the thickly vegetated slope facing the sea. He saw at once why. A wallaby was still standing foolishly on the center line. The driver of the vehicle equally foolishly had swerved to avoid the animal. Just how far should you put yourself at risk? He felt a rush of anxiety for the driver gunning the accelerator and covering the distance in record time. The main business of life was staying alive. No one would deliberately want to hit a harmless animal, but when the alternative was careering off the road, the only safe option was to hold course. If this accident had happened a mile back, the car would have hurtled down into an old volcanic crater. As it was, with the slope nowhere near so steep, the driver had a good chance of surviving. Still, it would be one hell of an experience, crashing wildly into the brush.

His four-wheel drive with its formidable bull bar slammed to a halt at the spot where he'd seen the small car go over. The tires had left skid marks on the road, and the trail led straight over the side. God! He pushed trailing branches of bougainvillea aside, taking the blood-raising lash as they snapped back, and looked down, wincing at what he might see. Instead, he felt a rush of relief and, it had to be said, admiration. The small car had come safely to rest in a dry gully with a bed of glittering stones, narrowly missing a huge boulder a few feet away. No sign of the driver, but then, he was looking at the passenger side.

Swiftly he got on his mobile and passed a message to Chipper Murray, the local police constable, then he reached into his vehicle for a good strong rope, knotting it securely to the bull bar. He touched his neck, felt a smarting, bleeding raised welt. Mercifully the gully was bone-dry. He went over the side, working his way down in a series of jumps much like the rappelling he used to enjoy. He got down easily, covering the small clearing to the car. The birds were singing. The sky was a cloudless peacock-blue. The air was sweet with the scent of the many species of wild herbs his boots had crushed.

He was almost at the driver's door when it suddenly opened and a young woman swung her long jean-clad legs to the ground and leaned out. "Hi!" she said in a husky but otherwise perfectly focused voice. "What did I do wrong?"

He laughed over a hard wave of relief. This was a remarkably composed woman. "Regardless of what you did wrong, you're obviously one hell of a driver." He approached, studying her with considerable interest. Masses of marigold hair, skin as white as a snowflake, a sprinkling of freckles standing out in high relief, extraordinary eyes, green with gold flecks in them like sunlight on a deep lagoon.

"Skills get sharpened when you're interested in staying alive," she answered wryly. "It was the wallaby. No one warned me the darling little thing was out there waiting for me."

"Next time slow right down, beep your horn and let it cross," he advised, keeping an eye on her, afraid that she might pass out from delayed reaction.

Instead, she tried ineffectively to smooth down her magnificent hair. "It happened much too fast for that."

He nodded in appreciation. "How are you feeling?" From the look of it, shock hadn't yet set in. Either that or she was downright fearless. Just about anybody would have been a mess.

"I'll be fine when the adrenaline levels out."

"Good," he replied. "Can you stand up? I want to see if you're still in one piece."

He put out his arm to assist her, but she rose unaided, tried a smile and stumbled. He caught her, hauling her along his chest.

"Okay, rest a minute." His hand somehow found the back of her head, shaping its contours as though it had found a will of its own. She smelled of sunlight, fresh air, a bowl of limes.

She wasn't about to argue, letting her marigold head fall against his shoulder. Tall for a woman. Slight, but he could feel the luscious press of her breasts. He couldn't decide if she was teetering on plain or was the most striking woman he had ever seen. Either way, his reaction to her was strong and immediate, or maybe he was swept up in the sheer romance of it all.

She stirred after a moment and he murmured, "Take your time. Look on the bright side."

"Which is?" At that she lifted her head, stared up at him with sparkling eyes.

"It could have been a lot worse. In the Wet that gully runs a torrent."

"I have to get my thrills somehow." She leaned back slowly and steadied herself by gripping his strong rugged arms. "Where did you spring from? Thanks for coming to my rescue, by the way."

"I was right behind you when it happened."

"So you saw the whole thing?"

He nodded. "I pretty much had a heart attack. I'm feeling a lot better now that I know you're safe. Look, why don't you slip back into your car? Rest quietly. The ambulance should be here soon."

She did a double take. "What ambulance?" Her voice, which had been vibrant and musical, turned sharp and dismayed.

He stared down at her, raising his eyebrows. "The one that's going to take you into town. I know you're a defensive driver at the highest level, but you've had one hairy ride. Shock will set in. Believe me."

She laughed, although her temples were beaded with sweat and her skin was whiter than white. "Get on your mobile. Tell them not to come."

"I'm not sure that's a good idea."

"I'm talking to you, aren't I? I'm quite rational."

"Hold out your hands," he ordered gently.

She did so without an instant's hesitation.

"They're trembling." They were, too. Beautiful hands, long-fingered, elegant, the nails unpainted, but a nice length.

"I'm a bit shaken up, that's all." She shrugged, more easily able to size him up now. Her first impression was of someone larger than life, a man of mythic proportions. Hercules, Apollo, a bit of both. "Listen, I don't want any fuss. You can drive me back to town, can't you?"

Frowning, he studied her face. "If that's what you want, but I have my doubts I'd be doing the right thing."

"I've been in worse situations."

"Yeah? When?" he asked skeptically.

"Try East Timor. Or dodging bullets in Afghanistan when you're trying to talk on camera."

He gave a devastating smile of approval, looking good enough to play the hero in a big adventure movie.

"Well, that doesn't leave me with much else to say. Hang on a second and I'll see if I can stop the ambulance. I'm Chase Banfield. And you're…?"

One quirky eyebrow shot up. He probably knew exactly who she was, but she identified herself, anyway.

"Roslyn Sum-m-mers." She'd briskly put her hand in his, then dragged out her name as a jolt of electricity flared through her body. *Chase Banfield.* Who else? She watched him as he half turned away, punching numbers into his mobile. He was wearing jeans and a bush shirt, and James Bond couldn't look as good in a tuxedo. Tall. A lot taller than she. About six-three. Wide-shouldered, lean-hipped. A mane of deeply waving bronze hair. A wonderful gold tone to his skin. Beautiful topaz eyes, resembling a tiger's. A strong distinctive face, sculpted, not chiseled like her own. High cheekbones, brackets around a handsomely cut mouth. Thirty, thirty-two. A man in full possession of his space. A man on his own territory. A fighter. A cattleman with the polished speaking voice of the elite. After Porter she wasn't prepared for his *maleness,* his virility and splendor.

Chase Banfield. What else was there to say? The fates had thrown them together.

"So that's okay," he said, pushing the mobile back into the pouch on his belt. "No ambulance. Chipper is going to take a run out, though, and see what you've done."

"Whoever Chipper is." She could feel her heartbeat gradually returning to normal.

"Chipper Murray is our local police constable," he explained. "A good man. He sees that nothing much goes wrong around here."

"What's he going to do? Arrest me for creating this mess?"

"Arresting people is part of the job, but no, you have nothing to fear. He'll have enough on his hands trying to retrieve the car. Hire car, isn't it?"

Rosie turned her head, kicked a tire lightly. "This is going to cost a pretty penny."

"At least it didn't kill you. So, Roslyn, what do we do now?"

Enterprising though she was, she didn't think she could handle Chase Banfield. He was dynamite. Rosie took a long look up the slope. "I saw the way you got down. Piece of cake."

He groaned. "Are you serious? A piece of cake for me. I don't know about you."

"Watch me."

He was beginning to wonder if he could ever *stop* watching her. She was dressed like him in jeans and a shirt, only, he was never so entrancingly violently colorful. Her cotton shirt was a bright saffron. She had a couple of strings of multicolored glass beads around her neck and an ornate beaten-silver belt around her narrow waist. She reminded him of a field of wild poppies waving in the sun.

"Hang on," he said, grasping her arm. "I can't let you go just like that."

"Of course you can. You wouldn't believe some of the places I've been and the things I've done."

"It's my rope, girl." He spoke softly, yet she listened.

"I'm sure I can make it up that slope." She changed tack, smiled at him appealingly.

"There's bougainvillea at the top." He spoke almost with disgust. "It could rip you to shreds."

"Then you'll just have to go up first and cut it off. I'll bet you've got something to do it with."

He nodded grimly. "That's right."

"I would've put a thousand bucks on it. Anyway, if you can get up there so can I. All I need is a hand."

He stroked his lean bronzed cheek, taking a moment to verbalize his thoughts. "The problem is, what do we do if you faint?"

"I never faint." She had once, but he didn't have to know that.

"Tough girl."

She put her hands on her slim hips. "Believe it."

In fact, her color was coming back. Bone china as opposed to snow. "I guess I can haul you up." He continued to stand over her. "You know anything about knots?"

Her face brightened. "Do I ever! I used to sail with my dad around Sydney Harbour."

"Perfect!" He could see her in a T-shirt and white shorts. A tomboy with a woman's body.

"You want me to knot the rope around my waist?"

"Uh-huh," he drawled laconically. "Don't rush. We've got time."

Actually, they had very little time. Soon the brilliant sunset would fade to a brief mauve twilight, then total darkness would set in.

Rosie watched as he made short work of hauling himself up the slope, hand over hand, obviously a man who spent his life outdoors, rain or shine. She could never hope to emulate his prowess, but she sure as hell was going to try.

Moments later, he'd reached the top, walking to a big powerful-looking four-wheel drive with a really scary bull bar just in view. She laughed out loud when she saw him return with a yellow chain saw.

"Take care," she called lightly, although she was serious. Not that she had reason to worry. She'd rarely met anyone who inspired such confidence.

In no time at all, he'd cleared an area of the spectacular purple bougainvillea with its lethal thorns. He gave her a brisk wave.

"Do you still want to do this?"

She looked up at him outlined against the flame-colored sky. "As long as you can," she shouted.

"I think I'm up to it."

"Right!" The rope firmly knotted around her waist, Rosie went forward, trying not to think about snakes. This was the Garden of Eden. There were bound to be a few lazing around. *Okay, Rosie, you can do this,* she urged herself. *Part of the job.* She had to make a huge effort all the same. She was feeling very shaky. Still, it felt good just to be alive.

Twice on the way up she lost her footing, dangling in space, swearing mildly while he held her weight and called out words of encouragement. "Come on, kid. You can do it!"

"Kid?" She was twenty-nine. Nearly an old maid, if her mother was to be believed. What she wanted, she thought suddenly, was a husband, children. Obviously, it took dangling off a precipice for that realization to hit.

At the top he grabbed her as though were she a feather pillow, while she, in an excess of joy, flung her arms around him. "Rosie," he drawled, throwing back his bronze head and laughing. "You've made me proud."

She returned his wonderfully infectious smile. "How did you know to call me Rosie?"

"Seems to suit you better than Roslyn," he said, topaz eyes lighting on her hair. "Is that for real?"

"Goes with the freckles, doesn't it?" she challenged.

"It's quite possible you've painted them on, they're so fetching. What are you doing here in Queensland, Rosie Summers?" All of a sudden he sounded like a detective with a suspect. Even the drawl had a sharp edge.

"Would you believe looking for you?" She'd been an investigative reporter too long not to know when it was time to be direct.

"So this was a setup?" His eyes glinted as he gazed down at her.

She considered that, rubbed her cheek. "Hey, I'm inventive, but this was sheer coincidence. It's glorious country up here. I wanted to have a look around."

"Then I'd advise you to have a damned good look for

wallabies, kangaroos, brolgas and wild boar while you're at it.''

''You mean they all cross the road?''

He moved abruptly, fighting a brief violent desire to kiss her. ''I can't take you to task now. You're still very pale.''

''I know,'' she answered almost apologetically. ''I've been cursed with very white skin.''

''I'd say blessed.'' His comment was as dry as ash.

''Would you?''

For the first time he got the full effect of her smile. ''Spare me the seduction, entrapment, whatever,'' he told her shortly, bending his strong fingers to untie the knot at her waist. He slipped the rope free, walked back to his vehicle, unfastened the other end from the bull bar and wound it into a neat coil, which he stashed away in the rear. ''Come along.''

She started after him obediently. ''You make me feel I should ask you what the charge is.''

''That's because you *are* guilty of something, aren't you, Rosie?'' He rounded on her, making her feel incongruously as small as a marmalade kitten.

''I paid for the hire car. I didn't steal it. Incidentally, is it all right to leave it here?''

He opened the passenger door for her and she hopped in. ''It's not going anyplace,'' he muttered.

They were back on the road before he spoke again. ''Aren't you up here seeking permission for a dig? Specifically on my land?''

She swung her head in surprise, caught his accusing glance. ''Aha, someone's been talking. The question is, how did they know, let alone inform you?''

''The answer is, I have spies everywhere. This is my town.''

''You mean you own all the buildings?'' she asked brightly.

"I own much of the land the town is built on. Is that enough of an answer?"

"Goodness, yes. The Banfields must be very rich."

"You have an interest in rich men?"

"Not in cozying up to them. I'm a working girl, after all." She paused. "Do you think you might listen to what I have to say?"

"Regarding what?" He flicked her a brief daunting glance.

"I've heard you're difficult." She made it sound like a little grumble.

"Really? I don't hear that too often. Most people up here think I'm very reasonable."

"Just being a Banfield might account for that. Listen, I'm not a crank."

"Thanks for the tip," he said dryly.

"If you know about me, you must know about Dr. Marley."

"Aren't you clever?" he mocked. "Marley's the boyfriend, isn't he? Hasn't he got a wife?"

"He's not the boyfriend!" Rosie burst out as though he'd offered her an insult. "And not that it's any of your business his wife recently left him."

"Oh, nice!" He nodded in cynical fashion. "That gives you a bit more leverage. I guess she wants to live a little, not fade away in Marley's shadow."

Exactly Rosie's reflection. "You know her?" she asked in surprise.

"I once saw a photograph of her and Marley in the paper. A few years back. She seemed a repressed little soul. Too sheltered."

Rosie had no words to deny it. "Right! But Dr. Marley is very highly regarded in his field. You know about his finding and dating of the Winjarra paintings?"

He looked at her hard. "I don't spend all my life on a horse."

"I love horses," Rosie breathed, getting an instant mental picture of Chase Banfield as Alexander the Great.

"Is that so? How are you feeling now?" he added, shocked that he'd almost forgotten what she had endured.

"Light-headed."

"When we reach town, you can get a good meal into you."

"I could go for that," she said, leaning her head back. "A nice dinner…"

"With Marley?" He couldn't resist it.

Her eyes flew open. "I told you I'm not involved with him in any way other than professionally."

"Okay." His voice soothed. "So why are you tagging along with him?"

"I should have told you. Dr. Marley thinks highly of my persuasive powers."

He gave a brief laugh that made her squirm. "Don't kid yourself."

"You're not being very complimentary. You know what my accident means, don't you? The fates have chosen to throw us together. I doubt if I'd have got back up the hill without you."

"You're dead right," he said, sounding pretty final.

"Of course, I could have screamed for help."

"Why do I have the feeling no one would have heard you? Though I suppose Marley would have noticed when you didn't show up."

She wished he'd accept that the situation with Marley was not as it obviously seemed. "Can't we forget Dr. Marley for a minute?" Rosie asked wearily.

"No." His answer was flat. "I had one conversation with the man. It could last me all my life."

"Is there a reason you're not being cooperative?" Rosie complained. "What I need from you—"

He chopped her off. "Do you honestly believe Three Moons was the site of an ancient Egyptian village?" he asked, exasperation in his tone.

Rosie had learned a long time ago to tell the truth. "I honestly don't, but it would be one heck of a discovery if it was. As I see it, Marley's not a fool. He's a brilliant scholar, a renowned archaeologist. And he has something in his possession I think you should see."

"Don't tell me, a mummy." A mocking smile touched his face.

Rosie shuddered. "I wouldn't be too happy about a mummy. No, this is a scarab."

His look clearly conveyed *I could have told you that.* "So where did he get it? One of his mates in Cairo?"

"Are you willing to be open-minded?" she implored.

"No." He shook his head. "Plain enough, Rosie?"

"Something tells me you haven't lost the spirit of inquiry, of adventure." She turned to him earnestly. "Despite your stubbornness."

"The answer is still no."

Now she clicked her tongue, folded her arms across her chest. "You're letting your dislike of the man overrule your intelligence."

At that he laughed spontaneously. "You know I'm intelligent, do you?"

She patted his arm encouragingly. "I'm not one of those who thinks brawn can't be matched by brain. Let him talk to you. No more than an hour. There's only one pub in town, unless you're staying with a friend. You have to have dinner. We'll throw in dinner."

His amusement was still evident. "That's mighty generous of you, Miss Summers. I take it this dinner will be with Dr. Marley *and* you?"

She nodded. "And what you see might surprise you," she said in warm inviting tones.

"What I'd like to see, Rosie, is you dressed up to dine. Not that you wouldn't be eye-catching at any time."

"Well, I couldn't be beautiful, so I went for offbeat."

"I think you managed a bit of both."

"You're being kind," she said lightly, not considering her appearance a big issue.

"I hate women who push for compliments," he teased.

"Not me!" Rosie shook her head. "My experiences have made me anything but frivolous. To get back to the subject, you're saying you'll have dinner with us?"

"Stop it. Too easy. You're persuasive, all right. I can well imagine your getting all your interviewees to spill the beans, but guys like Marley and I don't hang out together."

"You've got to meet him all the same. I think he's on to something with this theory of his. He's obsessed with the whole idea."

"A rich fantasy life, it's called. I have an uncle just like him," Chase scoffed.

"Actually, I've met him. Porter Banfield?" Rosie's eyes studied his profile, seeing the family resemblance, but still not able to believe it. Could any two people be less alike?

Now she had surprised him. "Where?" he asked sharply. "Porter doesn't get his kicks talking to young women, however scintillating. I don't know what happened to him, but he's one miserable bastard. A confirmed misogynist."

"I think you're right," Rosie answered, nodding. "A misogynist may be misguided, emotionally bankrupt, but that doesn't necessarily mean he's stupid. He's a Banfield, after all."

He realized he was being thoroughly entertained. "Stop trying to butter me up, Miss Summers," he warned. "Others have tried it before you."

"Evidently without success."

"You haven't figured me out, either."

"True, but I'm not defeated. Besides, I think you owe me something for saving my life."

He laughed, a rich chuckle. "That kind of reasoning is beyond me. Anyway, someone would eventually have found you. I'm even coming around to thinking you could have saved yourself."

She turned to him engagingly. "Just an hour. I swear you won't regret it."

Silence. "You're doing this for Marley?" he asked finally.

"Hell, no," Rosie crowed. "I'm doing this for myself. This is my baby. My big scoop."

"In that case," he told her. "I'll come."

BY SEVEN O'CLOCK Rosie was bathed and dressed. She hadn't had a lot of time because Chase Banfield had insisted on dropping her at the local doctor's to have her "checked out." It was easier not to argue. And it was rather nice being cared for. She hadn't had that kind of attention since she'd left home. As expected, the doctor confirmed her own evaluation of herself—she was tough, even if she didn't look it.

Tonight she'd gone to a lot of trouble with her appearance. Banfield had wanted to see her dressed up, so dressed up she'd be. Within limits. This was a little frontier town, after all. No need for the basic black and pearls. Not that she ever wore such garb. Her mother, who was a classic dresser, always said she got her outlandish taste from Great-aunt Hester, distinguished spinster in the family, now in her ninetieth year and still painting her much-sought-after nudes. Rosie's outfit for the evening was the best she could come up with on short notice. A hot-pink skirt and, wonder of wonders, it didn't clash with her hair. The top, sleeveless with a V-neck that showed just a hint of cleavage, was dark-green satin. She needed something rich to go around the middle, finally settled for a Thai-silk turquoise sash that fortuitously matched the turquoise sandals she'd brought with her. She'd long ago decided not to play down her unusual looks. For most of her early life, she'd been the clumsy duckling to her mother's elegant swan. Her height had always been a worry; her hair, a cheerful orange. Then there was the bird's beak of a nose, the wide sweep of her jaw. Again, inherited from Great-aunt Hester. There was no way she could be like her mother. Once she understood that, she had come into her own.

"There you are, Rosie," she applauded her reflection. "A woman every man would desire." It even seemed as if her hair would behave. She had arranged it in a thick upturned roll at the back, making far more of an effort than she had the previous night, when she'd pulled it into a ponytail for dinner with Graeme Marley. She sprayed her wrist again with a gardenia-based perfume. Mmm, fabulous! She was feminine enough to love perfume. *"Oh, Roslyn you're such a bohemian!"* She shook her head several times, but she could still hear her mother's voice. Rosie flashed herself another one of her saucer-size smiles. Why, oh why, did she have such a wide mouth? Well, nothing she could do about that.

She was almost out of her room, feeling extraordinarily excited, when she suddenly made the decision to wear The Necklace. It was a knockout. No one besides Marley and perhaps the hawk-eyed Mr. Banfield would know what it was. Reverently, in case some long-dead ancient Egyptian lady might take it into her head to lay a curse on her, Rosie withdrew the necklace from its soft leather pouch and draped it over her hand. Wonderful workmanship using multicolored, multitextured gold, combined with the semiprecious stone lapus lazuli—the "eyes" of the flowers, five in all, shaped like the sacred lotus, which were appended from the smooth coil that encircled the neck.

She turned back to the full-length mirror, put it on. She knew she was very privileged to wear it.

She went downstairs, smiling at the owner, Lyn Delaney, an interesting woman good for an interview, although she acted a bit cagey for all her friendliness. Rosie won a "You look marvelous" from Lyn that sounded perfectly genuine. She considered that a compliment, particularly given the exotic stylishness of this little back-of-beyond pub. But then, Banfield had said he owned most of the town.

She walked beneath the gleaming fretted timber arch into the small lounge, finding it almost full. The locals all glanced up curiously. Nobody pointed, not one expression conveyed that she looked a little freakish. They all seemed friendly and cheerful, so Rosie gave them her encompassing smile.

Banfield and Marley were already seated at a table to the rear of the room, along with a third man she didn't know. All three rose gallantly at her approach.

Marley, to her acute annoyance, bowed to kiss her cheek in much too intimate a fashion. Rosie felt like popping him one, but had to settle for discreetly moving off. Chase Banfield's tiger eyes settled on her, moving gently, very slowly, over her face and then her body. Not transfixed by the wonderful necklace but drifting past it, as if it was just the sort of thing he expected her to wear. Introductions were made. The third man, very thin, all mustache, looked burned up inside, but charming for all that. He was one Mick Dempsey, longtime friend of the Banfield family, himself the owner of a huge cattle station called Derrilan, which he told her meant "falling stars" in the Aboriginal language. Rosie pitied him and warmed to him at the same time. A tragedy there, she thought. She was sure of it.

"All pioneering families seemed to have dreamed up romantic names for their properties,'' Marley said in an indulgent voice. "Falling Stars. Three Moons!''

"Chase tells me you had quite an exciting ride this afternoon." Dempsey turned to Rosie with his still-attractive grin, as good as ignoring Marley, who looked irritated at not being in control of things.

Again Marley intervened, from long practice. "It's a miracle she didn't kill herself." He shook his head with as much vehemence as amazement. "Women and machinery simply don't mix."

Banfield threw him a contemptuous look. "I wonder how well you'd have survived the ride. Miss Summers did an extraordinary job behind the wheel.''

"Ah, but she's not the average female," Marley said with the air of someone who knew. He touched Rosie's hand, let his fingers linger.

What was this? Marley was allowing the others to assume an intimacy that didn't exist. She'd have to warn him about it in a hurry. Like before they retired to their separate rooms later that night.

Rosie removed her hand carefully. "I realize my reaction was foolish, but it's an instinctive thing to try to avoid hitting an animal."

"There isn't anything else to do, my dear," Dempsey told her kindly, pulling at the rather dashing red bandanna tucked into his white shirt. "I had a good friend run into a tree avoiding a brolga that popped down in front of him.''

"I hope your friend survived," Rosie said.

"He did, miraculously. His car was a write-off. Bull bar saved it from being ripped apart. You were very lucky Chase was driving back into town.''

"My hero!" Rosie exclaimed. "I intend to include him in my nightly prayers.''

"Include me, too, my dear," Dempsey only half joked. "I could do with the prayers of a good woman."

Marley, looking slightly bored, picked up the menu. "The food here is surprisingly good," he said, the light catching the show of silver at his temples. "A bit unusual for such a remote neck of the woods."

Patronizing idiot, Rosie thought, but Banfield said suavely, "Even our little country town can rise to a decent chef. You should try the crocodile fillet tempura, snow peas and chinois salad with a kakadu plum and wasabi dressing."

"I'm impressed!" Rosie searched in vain for it on the menu.

"Crocodile! You're joking." Marley's heavy shoulders moved beneath his summer-weight jacket.

"You'd probably think it was a delicious cut of pork," Banfield said as he helped Rosie out by pointing to the exact spot on the menu. "Or there's the tournedos of kangaroo," he added smoothly.

Rosie raised her eyebrows. "I don't fancy eating one of our national symbols. The kangaroo and the emu hold up the coat of arms."

"They're a bloody menace in the bush," Mick growled, "pardon my French, and not much we can do about it. Millions of them. I figure the best way to preserve the species, and that goes for the croc, too, is to come up with some commercially viable industry. Like cattle. The public are going to get pretty intolerant of crocs otherwise. Kangaroo, by the way, tastes good. A bit gamy to some, but very tasty. I've had it many a time and enjoyed it, but I prefer our prime beef. We produce the world's best."

"So it's tournedos of beef with potato *barigoule* béarnaise," Rosie said, sounding definite. "As you're the expert, perhaps you can enlighten me as to what a *barigoule* is. My French doesn't rise to it. I can handle the béarnaise." She turned to Banfield with a smile. He was looking incredibly handsome, not to say alluring in a sand-colored, softly constructed linen suit that sat wonderfully on his wide shoulders with a casual black cotton T-shirt beneath. The big-time cattle baron with a sophisticated edge.

He held her gaze, somewhat spellbound by her appearance, as well. This was a woman for all seasons. "A *barigoule,* and I know this only because I've had it, is a potato that's been steeped in saffron bouillon, then scooped out and filled with béarnaise sauce," he explained. "I can recommend it. It's very good. Our chef is a young Vietnamese. Lyn won't keep him long. He's too good. Some luxury hotel down the tourist coast will offer him more scope and more money, but for the time being we're dining out in style. I'd recommend the crab cream or the steamed scallops for starters, and as you're obviously a girl who doesn't have to watch her figure, the Moroccan orange tart is great."

"I'm for the ginger ice cream," Mick said gleefully. Chase could tell he was feeling better than he had in a long, long while. "You're paying, aren't you, Dr. Marley?"

Marley looked pained. "Of course."

By the time it came to coffee, they retired to the lounge, which was now almost empty. Marley stared at Mick, obviously hoping he'd go, but Mick stayed on with reckless disregard for what the doctor wanted.

"Miss Summers tells me you have something to show me." Banfield decided to get the ball rolling, giving Mick a quick, almost warning look.

"This mightn't be the moment," Marley managed, his mouth still full of a liqueur chocolate.

"You can speak in front of Mick," Banfield assured him.

"I'm not sure I can." Marley's smile was a little grim. "No offense, Dempsey, but this is fairly hush-hush."

"Would it have anything to do with Rosie's necklace, then?" Dempsey asked, affecting an Irish brogue. "Egyptian, isn't it? And isn't she just the girl to wear it? That

Nefertiti neck. I've actually seen a handmade glass amulet in a pyramid shape with Egyptian hieroglyphics on all sides that was dated by the Department of Mines at five thousand years old. How old is the necklace?''

Marley seemed angered by such an approach. ''Banfield, this is a private matter. I can't have too many people in on it.''

''In on what?'' Banfield asked in an easy voice. ''All of us here have lived with the story of an ancient Egyptian presence in the Far North. My uncle Porter has tried many times to mastermind an exploration. Unfortunately for him he needs my authority to do so. I don't have time for games. I have a big station to run.''

''That's right! Chase is a key player in the industry,'' Mick said proudly, sipping his coffee. ''Used to be myself until I lost Bridget. My wife, you know.''

''Oh, I'm sorry, Mick.'' Rosie's green eyes lit with sympathy. ''When was this?''

Mick looked down, smoothed his luxuriant mustache. ''Three years, six months and ten days. Bridget would have liked you,'' he told Rosie a little harshly. ''Bridget loved a woman with character.''

Marley leveled his penetrating blue gaze on Rosie. ''I extend my sympathies too, of course, Dempsey, but I wonder if we could keep to the agenda.''

''I thought the agenda was getting me here.'' Banfield's expression must have instantly alerted Marley that he'd said the wrong thing. ''It took Miss Summers to persuade me.''

''Call her Rosie, for God's sake, Chase,'' Mick implored, frowning at Chase in amazement.

''Miss Summers is a media power, Mick,'' Chase explained. ''One must show respect. But getting back to King Tut, talk of an ancient Egyptian presence is old news, like the forgotten race of Pygmies that hang out in the rain forest. Someone's always sighting one.''

"Someone always does if they have a mind to," Rosie said, "but there were Negritos, weren't there?" She threw herself into the argument. "I know I've read about them somewhere."

"Just a small type of Aborigine, I would suggest," Banfield said. "About five feet tall with short tight curls."

"Actually they were first officially noted in 1958," Marley intervened rather shortly, a veritable font of knowledge. "Anthropologist by the name of Birdsell. There were hundreds of these people in the rain forest at that time. There is evidence the so-called Negritos arrived about seven thousand years ago, while the Aboriginal presence in Australia goes back at least forty thousand years. This is all very interesting, but it's not what we're here to talk about." Exasperation bit into his tone.

Banfield swiveled slightly in his chair, looking to Rosie impossibly handsome and just a touch daunting. "Not if the necklace is the best you can do. I know Porter has little items like that up his sleeve. How he got hold of it I wouldn't know. He's been a collector for many years. He finds 'things' for the very rich and gets a reward. I know he has dealings with a wealthy collector based in London. My uncle is…something of an opportunist."

Marley tried unsuccessfully to cover up his resentment at the way the conversation had gone. "I realize that. Give me credit, Banfield. As deeply involved as your uncle is, he's not a professional, any more than you or Roslyn here. I, however, am highly respected in my field. My views must be taken seriously."

"C'mon," Banfield frowned. "Tell me why I should take you seriously. You'll have to come up with something more concrete than what you've got." His tone lightened. "Are you asking us to believe the necklace Miss Summers is wearing was found on Three Moons? Did my uncle lead you to understand this? Unlike me, he has the time to play games—always for his own ends. He may be using you."

"I can control people like your uncle." Marley finished his drink with a grimace. "I have other things—"

"We're going around in circles, Doctor," Banfield said, cutting him off. "Porter wants to get back on Three Moons for some reason. Maybe he has something hidden somewhere in the house. Under the big banyan tree. Anything's possible. It could even be gold. My family benefited greatly from the gold strikes in this area." He paused, shaking his head. "My parents were taken from me literally overnight. I was only a boy. There was no time to fill me in on all the family secrets. I know there have to be a few. Lost hopes. Lost dreams. This part of the world might be an opulent paradise, but terrible hardships went into our pioneering past. Isn't that so, Mick?"

"Plenty of early deaths," Mick said. "But there are so many things you mightn't know, Chase, that Porter would." He brightened. "Stuff he'd make sure you'd never find out."

Marley seized on that. "Then there's a good chance your uncle's right. All I'm asking is that you give me a couple of weeks…."

"To hare off on your own?" Banfield said with a flash of his brilliant eyes. "You could be killed if you're heading up-country." He transferred his gaze to the slender, very womanly Rosie, his attitude almost explosive. "It could be quite terrifying to get lost in the jungle."

Rosie nodded, breaking the tension. "You've sold me."

Despite himself, Banfield laughed, studying the dangerous magic of her, the warmth of her, the challenge in her almond eyes, the gorgeous clash of colors, the gleaming magnificence of the necklace around her proud throat.

"You might even run into one of those Negritos," he drawled. "I think they were cannibals."

"Really?" Rosie picked up her liqueur.

"He's joking, love," Mick assured her lightly. "He's always joking. But I've been thinking—I could help out." He looked around the table, not at all disconcerted by Chase's quick penetrating glance. "I'm as good a bushie as your dad," Mick pointed out.

Banfield nodded. Quite true, but Mick hadn't handled things well for quite a while. "What about Derrilan? How does it get on?" he asked in a measured voice.

"Hell, Chase, Arnie runs the place," Mick said sheepishly. "He's been as good as runnin' it since I lost Bridget. No, this sounds exciting, and I could do with a little excitement these days."

Banfield's eyes settled on his friend with a private message. *There aren't any pubs up-country.*

"It might help me out." Mick leaned forward to stare into Banfield's stern but caring face.

"And it could do you a lot of harm." Banfield wondered how long it would take Mick to hit the bottle.

"Once, you used to have great faith in me, Chase," Mick said gruffly.

"I learned a lot from you, Mick." In this instance, Banfield had to try not to weaken, when he normally wasn't a man who gave way easily. "So what's your proposal?" he asked Marley. "Is my uncle along on the trip?"

Marley's rich voice developed a sudden coaxing charm. "I *had* to include him."

"Oh, perfect!"

"And I've been in war zones," Rosie reminded Chase. "If that counts for anything."

He gave her a brief smile. "You're forcing my hand?"

"It's a beautiful hand." She glanced at his right hand on the table. "Strong, lean, elegant..."

"Calluses on the other side," he mocked, turning his hand over. "I'm a cattleman, Miss Summers."

"Hell, yes! None better." Mick spoke with affection and pride. "His mum and dad would've been so proud of him. Wonderful, just wonderful what he's accomplished in these last years after Porter bloody near—"

Banfield leaned toward him. "Mick, we won't waste time on Porter for the moment. I have to think about this."

"What harm could it do?" Rosie's eyes lit with green fire. "If your uncle can lead us to this pyramid—he swears it's somewhere on the station—Graeme can identify it, date it. Even if it's a wild-goose chase, which it probably is, I could turn it into a good story. Even a short documentary."

"Get Paul Hogan back and turn it into *Crocodile Dundee 3,*" Banfield suggested, sitting back, his mouth twitching. "You want to fool around with crocodiles?" he asked Rosie.

"I haven't got the nerve." She shivered. "But Mick here seems to think he has."

Mick crowed, but Marley was in no mood for frivolity. "A joke has its limits," he said, sounding very professorial. "This will be a very serious expedition. Headed by me."

Rosie picked up a liqueur chocolate, as if she was still famished. "Well, I wouldn't *want* to be leader." She shrugged. "What about you, Mick?"

Mick was enjoying this, his blue eyes brighter and more focused than Banfield had seen in a couple of years. "No way, m'dear. I'll act as your guide. It'll be grand!"

"And what will your duties be, Miss Summers?" Banfield asked suavely, knowing she would be highly capable, intelligent, resourceful, remarkably cool in a tight spot. His expression, however, suggested that at some stage they could expect hysterics.

She put a hand to the glittering necklace, aware he was being deliberately provocative. "To show the flag," she said airily. "To be of any help I can. Which probably comes down to the cooking, but I could run to a bit of first aid.''

''And where do you intend to stay during the planning stage, the initial forays?''

Mick jumped in without a thought, munching yet another pretzel, never touching his light beer.

''What's a bunch of people at Three Moons?'' he asked Banfield, as if a great idea had just come to him. ''Dammit, I know you don't want crowds marching all over the place, but this is different. And I'll be there to look after your interests.''

Between one binge and another, Banfield thought, then chided himself for not showing Mick some confidence. ''You're a real romantic at heart, aren't you, Mick.'' He smiled as he said the words.

Mick sighed. ''Bridget used to say that.'' For a moment, his expression sagged.

Banfield saw that he'd have to make a decision based not on what he wanted, but on what Mick wanted—and that scintillating, unlikely femme fatale, the amazing Miss Summers.

''I'll admit the homestead is big enough.'' His tone was brusque with an underlying hint of humor.

''So you agree?'' Rosie and Mick spoke together, picking that moment to slap a high five.

Banfield glanced at them both repressively. ''I said I have to give this a lot of thought.''

Mick nodded, laughing. ''What a character you are, Chase.''

''I am that,'' he answered dryly, catching Rosie's sparkling eyes.

''So do you reckon you'll know by mornin'?'' Mick asked with glee.

''Does it mean so much to you, Mick?'' Banfield looked at the older man with sympathy.

"Who knows what we might find, son?" Mick's blue yes glowed. "Although I don't like the idea of havin' old orter around, I can tell you that. 'Struth, the man's a fa-atic."

Marley held up his large palm. "Mr. Dempsey, you ourself are not included in our party."

"I'm in if Chase says so," Mick answered stoutly. "Am in, Chase?"

Banfield laughed. "I don't think I've agreed to anything et, Mick. But I don't see why you couldn't go if it actually omes to that. You certainly know your way around. Dr. Iarley is more familiar with central Australia and the Kim-rly than he is with this area." He turned to Marley. Wouldn't that be right, Doctor?"

Marley wasn't about to acknowledge it. "Even so, I'm experienced bushman."

"And I watched every episode of *The Bush Tucker an*," Rosie chimed in as though that settled everything. reality she was trying to keep her excitement down. very time Chase Banfield's eyes lighted on her, the most amatic things happened to her body. Adrenaline pumped. ulses raced. Even her nipples tightened. Normally she dn't react sexually to a man's mere presence.

"I'd appreciate it if I could get a decision," Marley said, early angered by the sizzling undercurrent that ran be-veen Banfield and Roslyn.

"Don't push it, Graeme," Rosie warned with a speaking ance. "I'm sure Chase will tell us when he's good and ady."

CHAPTER FOUR

THEY BROKE UP shortly after eleven, Banfield citing h
dawn return to Three Moons as an excuse.

"Couldn't drop me off on the way, Chase?" Mick ask
hopefully, following them all out into the foyer with
wealth of huge jewel-colored cushions over teak furnitur

Banfield stopped in his tracks, gazing at Mick in surpris
"How did you get here, Mick?" He'd assumed Mick h
driven in from Derrilan.

"Arnie had to come into town for some supplies." Mi
referred to his head man, now the manager. "Dropped n
off at the club."

"I see. And how'd you get here from the club?"

Mick waved a hand. "One of the blokes drove me."

One way or the other, Mick fell on his feet. Banfie
clapped a hand on the older man's shoulder. "Sure, I
drop you off. No trouble." In fact it would take him twen
miles out of his way, but what was distance up here? Mi
was bound to start again with that business about the wil
goose chase.

"Well, I'll say good-night, then." Mick smiled happil
"It's been a great pleasure meeting you, Rosie," he sai
"Some people you feel you've known all your life."

"Same here, Mick." Rosie returned the smile, givir
him her hand, which he bowed over quite gallantly.

"Take care of that necklace now," he warned. "It mig
have belonged to a very important Egyptian lady. A bea
tiful woman of high social standing. It suits you to a

Good night, Dr. Marley.'' Mick nodded in Marley's direction, his charming Irish voice flattening out.

"Good night, Dempsey.'' Marley sounded equally unimpressed. As Mick moved off to the stairs, relatively sober for once, Marley turned to Banfield with his trademark imperious expression. "There are other things you haven't seen. A magnificent scarab!''

"Probably out of Porter's safe, as well.''

"I take it I may expect your answer in the morning?'' He visibly fought down his irritation. "I've come all this way, not without good reason. I believe we have sufficient evidence to proceed. With all due respect, I might point out that I'm the expert. This expedition could mean great things for all of us. I beg you to take that into consideration.''

Banfield's eyes slid to Rosie, catching her in contemplation. "Would you care for a short stroll before bed?'' he asked. "A breath of fresh air after so much talk of an ancient civilization. Kind of a sick one, at that. Too much emphasis on death. The ancient Egyptians built their great monuments to the dead. I'm for building monuments to the living, like the ancient Greeks or the Romans did.''

"Nevertheless, we're speaking about a mighty civilization with twenty-five hundred years of great triumph and glory,'' Marley broke in before Rosie, uncharacteristically breathless, had a chance to respond.

"I appreciate the fascination, Doctor,'' Banfield said smoothly. "I'm just mentioning their strange ways. As I said earlier in the evening, I need time to think this over. You surely didn't expect a decision tonight. Let's say by the end of the week. I'm sure you can fill your time profitably. You'd probably like to visit my uncle. It may seem a harsh thing to say, but I don't want him back on Three Moons. I have my reasons.''

"And I don't want to interfere in any way.'' Marley hastened to make his position clear. "But Porter *is* the one

who claims to know where the pyramid is, or at least th
general direction.''

Banfield nodded. ''A number of people over the year
have claimed to know where pyramids are sited. I'll sa
good-night, Dr. Marley. We'll be in touch.''

It was as much as Marley could hope for. He transferre
his gaze to Rosie, who was standing quietly at Banfield'
shoulder, enjoying the sensation of having a man towe
over her. ''I'll see you, Roslyn, when you come up.'' Hi
tone implied he'd be waiting for her in bed.

It was time to put things straight. She turned around full
to face him. ''No more talking tonight, Graeme,'' she sai
firmly. ''I'll be going straight to my room—to sleep. Se
you at breakfast.''

''Is this little affair very hush-hush at the moment?'
Banfield asked as they walked out into the glorious tropica
night. A big languorous copper moon sailed above the ta
palms; the breeze was like incense.

''You're not getting to me, Chase Banfield,'' she scoffe
although the man drew her like a magnet. ''There's n
affair. I told you.''

''You'd better tell Marley,'' he suggested with more tha
a touch of irony.

''He's married.''

He laughed, taking her arm and steering her in the d
rection he wanted to go. ''I'd like a dollar for all the ex
tramarital affairs in this state alone.''

''Let me put it more plainly. I don't like him. He's a
elitist, and he's sexist and arrogant, possibly a bigot.''

''Charming.''

''He's also at the very top of his profession. His boo
on the life and culture of Australian Aborigines is a classi
His fieldwork attracts big grants. In a word, he's got to b
taken very seriously.''

Banfield considered briefly. "Speaking of grants, who's funding this?"

"Presumably Graeme's department."

"Really? Well, surely they realize that even the most brilliant scientists can have a few bats in the belfry. My concern is that Porter's using him, and Marley's making it easy because he has this burning desire to keep confounding his peers. Finding the Winjarra paintings was a huge success. But success can't stand still. Next, a tremendous discovery confirming once and for all that there was an ancient Egyptian presence in Australia."

Rosie lifted her face to the heady perfume of the night. It seemed to be coming from the cascades of gardenia-scented white trumpet vine that smothered the lattice screens. "But is it so impossible?" she asked. "How did all the relics get here? The jewelry, the artifacts, the coins—some of them were apparently buried for four thousand years. Then there's the pottery, the bronze and copper tools, the amazing hieroglyphics carved into rocks. Graeme thinks Australia was actually the Land of Punt, the mysterious southern continent referred to in Egyptian carvings. They could even have mined gold and silver and left their relics behind. Look at this gold necklace." She fingered the gleaming lotus flowers.

"I've been looking at it all evening, oddly enough."

"Where did this necklace come from?"

He glanced down at her, all his senses alive. "Again, try Porter's safe," he said wryly. "Speaking of gold, there could be gold deposits on Three Moons, for all I know. There were rich lodes up here in the old days. Tin. Collecting is an obsession with my uncle. He's run through most of his own fortune and now he has to find ways of making more. If there *is* gold on Three Moons—and one of my people, a tribal elder, believes there is—Porter as a Banfield would have a claim."

"So it's more complicated than I thought." Rosie picked a flower, then stuck it carelessly in her hair.

"It always is, especially with my uncle around."

"And you're worried about Mick, aren't you?" Her voice was quiet and sympathetic.

He stopped, took her by the shoulders, turned her around to face him. "How did you know?"

"Easy." She smiled. "I'm sensitive and highly intelligent."

And she had a strong, very womanly sexuality. It enveloped him like the perfume of the gardenias. Once again he had that hard wild urge to kiss her, taste that luscious, full-lipped mouth. He was a passionate man, but of necessity he kept it under control. There was no point at all in starting something with Miss Roslyn Summers, despite the attraction between them. Slowly he dropped his hands, walked on. "Mick has suffered badly since he lost his wife," he said levelly. "He loved her dearly and she loved him. Mick's feelings go deep. At some stage he took to the bottle to ease the pain. He's not a natural drinker. He doesn't really enjoy it. But it serves to keep his mind anesthetized."

"And you're concerned that after the initial enthusiasm wears off, he'll return to heavy drinking?"

Banfield sighed heavily. "He's not the man to mastermind an exploration of the up-country. Only a few years ago, he would have been. But I have good reason to believe he's not going to reform overnight."

"You're going to say no." She felt a surge of disappointment. Not the least of it because she'd be losing all contact with him.

"I can't bury my disquiet. I'm of two minds about everything, which doesn't suit me at all. On the one hand, it was great to see Mick show such enthusiasm. He's always been on about the Egyptian connection. A lot of people up here still are. My own grandfather claimed to have seen massive ruins of stone walls in the wilds of Cape York, which is as remote a place as one can get.''

She stared at him in amazement, struck by the male beauty of his strong features. Michelangelo would have loved him. ''You never mentioned that before.''

He threw her a sidelong mocking smile. ''There are lots of things I haven't mentioned, Miss Summers, much as you've tried to beguile them out of me. You wouldn't know, but the old Aboriginal witch doctors around here used 'knot magic,' much like the ancient Egyptians did. The knots represented blessings or curses. Where do you suppose they learned it? How did the ancient Egyptians come by their golden boomerangs, for that matter? Why did the Torres Strait natives mummify their dead using the Egyptian method? It's all fascinating stuff, I agree. I do have some imagination, but I also have a big enterprise to run.''

''And you're afraid to let us go off by ourselves with only Mick and, I presume, your uncle for guides?''

He answered with some force. ''I'm afraid to let *you* go off, Miss Summers. I appreciate that you've had terrifying times covering your war stories, but you can equally well get lost or killed in the jungle. No joke. Where you're going, the river is teeming with crocs. There are wild boar, pythons, snakes, spiders, among the deadliest in the world.''

''I'm game.'' She'd have to take good care that nothing happened to her.

''I thought you might be.'' He looked down at her moodily. ''And all you expect to get out of this is a story? A world scoop?''

''What's wrong with that?'' She didn't add she was mad keen to know him better. Instead, she stopped to stare at a bed of Indonesian torch ginger with its fantastic ten-inch red flowers. Such a clump of them! Unbelievable! ''I also get to keep this necklace,'' she added with a self-satisfied little smirk.

"Really?'' His voice was very dry. "Porter has never been known to give anything away.''

"One of the perks of the job. An inducement, obviously.'' She shrugged with apparent nonchalance. "It's a pity you're such a busy man.''

"You're so good at this,'' he groaned.

"Well, you *are* the ideal man to head this safari.''

"So what would I get out of it?'' he demanded.

A nearly audible chord of excitement vibrated in the air between them as attraction assumed real shape and substance.

Rosie couldn't laugh. She had never felt so vulnerable in her life, literally quaking. "You can hardly be suggesting we become lovers.'' Even saying it aroused her. Inside her head. All over her body.

"How could you afford to take on another one?'' he asked sardonically, surprised by his flicker of rage. Jealousy? How absurd, yet he recognized it, reined himself in. "I'm sorry. I shouldn't have said that.''

"But you obviously meant it.'' Strong feeling lapped at her, too. Primitive. Physical. A surge of sexual antagonism that went hand in hand with violent attraction. It was a problem. A big problem. Rosie drew the flower out of her hair, threw it into a dense clump of bird-of-paradise, as though renouncing temptation. "I'm going to have to insist. Please keep off the subject of Marley. There's nothing between us.''

"What on earth makes you think he feels the same way?'' Chase went on, giving her a deliberately bland look. "The man fancies you. Or he fancies that he fancies you. You're incontestably more of a challenge than the woman he married. Personally, I think it would never work out.''

"Is that all?'' she asked sweetly.

"No, it certainly isn't." He wasn't going to lie awake tonight dreaming of this. Abruptly, decisively, he folded her in his arms, holding her so there was no way she could get free.

Rosie thought plaintively of her black belt. But could she escape such dynamic energy? Did she even want to? She stood perfectly still. She was so full of sweet aches. "What are you planning to do?"

"Nothing in a hurry." He dropped his eyes to her mouth. "Is it possible, dazzling creature, that you're a little bit shy?"

So much for taking pride in her ability to mask her emotions. "Why on earth shouldn't I be?" she flashed. "I barely know you."

"I felt we recognized each other right off. Kindred souls and so forth."

"You're positive of that?"

"Absolutely!"

"I'm not ready for what you have in mind," she said simply.

"How old *are* you?"

"I hardly ever check."

He stretched out his hand to her breeze-ruffled hair. "Anyway, I have eyes. Twenty-seven, twenty-eight?"

"Sure." She made it sound like an absurd game they were playing when all the while he was getting under her skin.

"And inexplicably I see lurking beneath the delightfully confident veneer a heartbroken teenager."

His perception astounded her. "Not me," she managed to say in a casual tone. "I was greatly loved by my parents, though I have to admit my mother wished for a daughter in her own image."

"Your mother not having copper hair or resembling a sunset?"

She gazed up into his face, wondering how in hell he knew. "My mother is a beautiful woman. A completely different type than. I take after my father's side of the family."

"Well, that worked out nicely for you," he commented in a voice of easy charm.

"Come on!" She hid her continuing surprise behind scoffing.

"Come on, what? I'm beginning to believe you don't really see yourself when you look in a mirror."

"There are some things I ignore," she joked. "But all in all, I think I've found my own style."

"You certainly have!" He started to undo her hair, letting the heavy coils fall, inhaling their scent. It seemed to Rosie as erotic a gesture as starting to unfasten her satin camisole. If his fingertips grazed her breast, she thought she might burst into flame.

"So you grew up with mama taking lots of shots at you?" Now he was arranging her hair, letting it float out like clouds, studying her.

"Chase Banfield, you wouldn't be trying to turn the tables by psychoanalyzing me, would you?" she asked, trying to sidestep the question.

Instead of answering, he asked another question. "Why aren't you married?"

"Why aren't you married yourself?"

"Because the right woman hasn't come into my life."

"Same here, only make it a him."

"Maybe that's because you're so...different. The man who carries you off should be a man who relishes a challenge. Otherwise he can expect nothing but trouble."

"Thank you." For the first time she pushed herself away, and the way she did it made him laugh deep in his throat.

"Rosie, something tells me you've learned self-defense."

"Well, something's told you right," she returned smartly. "It took me ages, but I managed a black belt in karate."

"I'm impressed." Despite that, he caught her back to him again, kissed her hard.

The sweet pain of it almost made her cry out. Her mouth open, alight with passion.

He moved her even closer to him, making her shudderingly aware of his magnificent body.

The beautiful copper moon sailed down the sky; the breeze felt like scented feathers touching her skin.

"Chase…" She had to lean against him. Totally spellbound.

"Don't talk. Don't talk at all." He braided his fingers through the thick shot-silk of her hair, kissing her more deeply, letting the tip of his tongue slide over her beautiful white teeth.

Finally he had to stop to get himself under control. He was flooded with desire, trying to swim for shore.

What had happened? Anyone would think it was the first time he'd kissed a woman. He knew, had to, that he could pick anyone he liked. Then why was he so ravenous for Miss Rosie Summers, a woman he scarcely knew?

"It's all right." She was half laughing. "Blame it on the moon. The lovely big copper moon of the tropics."

"The moon exactly." Control took hold. "Anyway, it was great while it lasted," he said, counseling himself not to pull her back to him. "You have a mouth that tastes of chocolate and the most delicious wild fruit."

Rosie needed a moment to answer, such was the warm flush in her blood. "Nobody's ever topped that description."

"Hard to believe." He dipped his bronze head so he could stare into her moonstruck face. "I seek to know everything about you, Rosie."

"And I have to admit I'm intrigued by you." She, too, tried to put a stop to so much sizzling emotion. "For instance, why don't you trust your uncle?"

His smile was a little grim. "I don't think you'd have enough time to hear that whole story."

"Try me." Rosie frowned. "I know what families are like."

"Didn't you just tell me you had a childhood that couldn't have been more blissful?"

It was out before she could help herself, sprung from a deep well of hurt and confusion. "I did with my dad. Dad and I understand each other. I suppose when I really think about it, my mother and I were in some sort of competition for his affection. Or my mother thought it was so. Maybe she was right. Who can tell? I know I tried very, very hard to please her, and I did in many ways. Good grades, good at sports, that kind of thing. But basically I wasn't the daughter she wanted or could enjoy. Siblings might have taken the heat off me, but there was only me. A lot of me."

"Why are you so sensitive about your height?" he asked promptly.

"What, after years of quirky little jokes?" Rosie let out an exasperated breath. "How's the weather up there? How's it going, beanpole? Most of it was meant as fun, not cruel. I was popular at school, at university. Did well at basketball and squash... But I guess I got hurt along the way. To compound it, there's my hair," she added wryly.

"Yes, there is." Briefly he touched it. "Magnificent hair. I've never seen such a crowning glory. The color's quite extraordinary."

"You like the freckles too?" Rosie joked.

"In all honesty, I love them."

She peered up at him, looking mildly astonished. "You do?"

The moon was pouring its golden light on her upturned

face, illuminating the wonderful corona of hair. He found himself running the tips of his fingers along the line of her jaw, down the swan's throat to where the necklace lay in a shimmering garland. "I can't be the first man to tell you you're staggeringly attractive."

"Not the first, but it took me ages to believe it." Her voice wobbled.

"I take it your mother is petite?"

Rosie groaned. Whatever had happened to her customary composure? "I *love* my mother. I adore her. I've adored her all my life. She just wanted me to grow up sexy, ultra-feminine, a clotheshorse. Beside her I'm rather outrageous—a brash journalist who mostly wears pants and weird gear. I figure I'd better hide the length of my legs," she said with self-deprecating humor.

"Why don't you let me decide whether they're worth seeing?" he told her. "So, mama's about five-three. Possibly blond, blue eyes, with a gentle manner but always manages to make her point."

"What the heck is going on here, Banfield?" He kindled a fire in her. "*I'm* supposed to ask the questions. You haven't met my mother, have you?"

He smiled. "I'm what's called psychic."

"Then how come you haven't felt an ancient presence on your land? And why haven't you taken more notice of this necklace?"

"Somehow you make the necklace come off second-best."

Rosie shook her head in wonderment. "I can't understand why you're not married. You could charm the birds out of the trees."

"I don't do it all the time," he said modestly. "You've just given me an excuse."

"And you've neatly sidestepped my question about your uncle."

"You've met him." His tone was level. "You're a shrewd observer. What's your opinion? Don't worry about offending family loyalty. That was forfeited long ago."

"That's sad."

"Of course it is, but it happens. Family pictures aren't always smiling and happy. There are a lot of subjects that can't be broached. Too painful. Too dangerous."

"Yet your uncle saved your life?" Rosie spotted a park bench and headed toward it.

He followed, speaking wryly. "You don't want to hear this, Rosie. And you're not going to turn it into one of your little pieces."

"Trust me." She grasped his arm, pulled him down beside her. "I would never hurt you. I've never hurt anyone, to my knowledge. Certainly I've tried never to write in a way that causes people pain. A bit of embarrassment, maybe. Some people need the mickey taken out of them."

"Like Senator Dunne?" he asked.

"You read that?"

"Newspapers reach us even in the wilds. I enjoyed the article immensely, as it happens. He was beautifully done—you'll forgive the pun—but he didn't seem to know it."

"Can't deny that," Rosie said with a grin. "What I really want to do, though, is write an award-winning novel."

"Set it here," he suggested. "There's enough background to suit your talent. Just don't make it suspiciously like an historical account of my family."

"You were telling me why you don't trust your uncle," she prompted.

"Ah, what a musical, lulling voice you have. You forgot to mention that as an asset."

"How did he hurt you?" Rosie kept on track, though it was hard. "You were a child suffering an enormous trauma. It must have been terrible for you. I know about the fire."

"You couldn't understand." His words were harsh and abrupt.

"I know about fire," Rosie said very quietly. "I've covered a few."

"Have you had nightmares from them?" His tone was hollow.

"I have." She gave a spontaneous shudder.

"One of my most intense memories is of fire. The flames. The roar and the crackling. The black density of smoke. The *screams,*" he said, gazing at nothing. "I remember that, even if I have amnesia about all the rest. The cause of the fire was never properly investigated. This isn't any big city. Or even town. No police department—just a lone constable in a rain-forest village. The west wing, my parents' private quarters, burned to the ground. I was in the central suite, while Porter lived in the east wing. Porter risked his life to save me, or so the legend goes. It was widely believed. No reason *not* to believe it. A man and his young nephew... I've tried all my life to remember. I can't. It's a void. A black hole."

"One day it will come back," she said, sympathy softening her expression.

"What, in recurrent nightmares?" His voice conveyed his tension.

"It will come back," Rosie said soothingly. "Something will nudge your subconscious."

It struck him that he'd confided in her far more than he had expected to. Far more, in fact, than he'd ever confided in any other person. "What the hell are you? A psychiatrist?" he asked wryly.

She waved that away. "I want to help you, Chase. I can see there's so much pain in you and you can't bear to face it yet. I understand that. My heart aches for you."

He was astonished at her flash of insight. "Why would you think that?"

"Trust me. I just do," she said gently, smiling into his face. "Besides, I've met your uncle. I'm prepared to believe he lives a subterranean life."

It was uncanny. His own perception was based on years of intimate knowledge, but Rosie had met Porter exactly once. "Suppose you tell me how you arrived at that conclusion?" he invited.

"There are things buried in him," she said. "Secrets. Obsessions. It's all hidden fairly well beneath that veneer of cold, polished good manners and enormous reserve, but it's there. Why do you feel he wasn't the person who saved you?"

At her words, his whole body braced itself. Now she was applying her formidable intuition to him, drawing him out on what had hitherto been a taboo subject. To his surprise, he answered. "If he didn't save me, who did?"

Her eyes probed his. "You have absolutely no idea? Who else was there?"

He groaned and shook his head, feeling his nerves stretch taut. "Leave it alone, Rosie. I know you want to help me, but I don't want to deal with this. I only retain slivers of memory, and even they vanish. What I *can* say is that Porter might be planning a search, but not necessarily for ancient Egyptian relics."

"What?" She stared at him with acute attention. "You mean, given your knowledge of your uncle, that it's more likely we'd be looking for something other than old ruins? Like what—gold?"

"It wouldn't surprise me." He shrugged. "The necklace could be part of an elaborate front. Porter could have acquired it anywhere. He travels a good deal. He goes to the Dutch city of Maastrict every March."

"The world's leading fine-art antique fair." Rosie knit her brows. "Yes, I know. One can acquire rare and beautiful objects, paintings, museum-quality stuff."

"Classical antiquities, Egyptian works of art. Jewelry ke that." Lightly he touched the gold necklace.

"So why is he claiming he found it on Three Moons? hat and other things, as well. A magnificent stone scarab, hich you haven't seen."

"I don't need to," he said dismissively. "Look, I don't ve time for any of this."

"It sounds as though you work too hard. You should art to delegate."

"Ah, yes! If only I could. This is a hands-on business, osie. Besides, who else knows the place like I do?"

"Well—" Rosie drew in a breath "—I know your uncle as hopeless as a cattleman, but he knows Three Moons, aybe better than you do. He had years and years to ex-ore."

"So you think he's got the map of a hidden gold mine?"

"With a big cross for 'dig here'? Anything's possible. ou said so yourself. You won't allow him on the station."

"He comes occasionally. Supervised visits."

"He needs a partner, an ally," Rosie said, as though it as a revelation. "Someone with a plausible reason to gain ccess to the station. *Marley.*"

"Who, I presume, brilliant archaeologist that he is, is tally sucked in by Porter's mesmerizing story."

"I don't know. I'm only guessing."

"A scenario for your novel?" he inquired suavely. "I ppose it has possibilities—a mystery plot, maybe. Or a riller. Ah, well, much as I'm enjoying your company, osie, I think we'd better walk back. I have a feeling Mar-y's waiting up for you. Perhaps I can escort you safely your room?"

"That would be nice, but I assure you I can take care of yself."

"After today I don't doubt it." He laughed and helped r up. "Whatever I decide about the proposed safari,

would you care to look over Three Moons while you'
here?''

Rosie's knees bumped together. "I'd love to. I can mal
it anytime.''

"You said you love horses." He gave a slight smil
"Does this mean you can ride?''

"Of course I can ride," she said breezily. "I've had
couple of sorry experiences of course, but as they say, y
don't really know about horses until they've thrown you.

"Well, that's settled then." He took her arm. "I'll l
expecting you.''

No SIGN OF MARLEY as they headed along the rich orienta
carpet runners to Rosie's room. Immense quiet. Sc
lustrous wall lights.

"I suppose he could be lurking inside," Chase muttere
taking a long stride. "Want me to check?''

Rosie shied away from that one. "Good gracious, no!

"They leave the doors unlocked around here," l
warned her, still unconvinced.

"Well, I, for one, never leave my door unlocked," Ros
said. "Which reminds me, the key's at reception dow
stairs.''

He clicked his tongue, an exasperated sound, then sai
"I'll get it.''

A moment later he was back, dangling the key on a lor
tanned finger. "No point in asking me in.''

She raised her eyebrows. "I wasn't going to.''

"After such an evening?" He kept looking at her in h
intensely personal way.

"Not even then. You've got a big sign on you, Banfiel
Approach with caution.''

"Well, good night then, Summers." He caught her chi
Took her breath. Kissed her again. Making her hungi

amished, longing for splendid sex, never doubting he could
eliver.

"'Night!'' she gasped.

No MARLEY HIDING behind the shutters, though she
wouldn't have put it past him. He had a certain theatrical
ent. She wasn't in the least tired after her hair-raising ex-
eriences of the day. Body and mind were too stimulated.
Rosie took off the gold necklace and put it down on the
ressing table, where it attracted all the light. She undressed
n the soft glow of the bedside lamp, slipping into her night-
own and robe. She briefly considered not washing her
ace, just to keep the scent of him on her, but well-trained
irl that she was, decided she'd better adhere to long habit.

It wasn't until she was under the bright light of the ad-
oining bathroom that she saw the faint marks around her
eck. They followed the line and shape of the Egyptian
ecklace. How odd! She smoothed her skin carefully. It
vasn't that sensitive, surely. No soreness. No actual red-
ess. Just marks.

Wait a second! Rosie leaned across the basin, now star-
ng hard. What *were* those spidery markings? They looked
or all the world like... Way too much was happening.
Rosie took off without further thought, rushing down the
till-deserted corridor to Chase Banfield's room and rapping
n his door rather loudly, considering the hour.

For all his talk about turning in, he was still fully dressed,
ninus his jacket. "Why, Rosie!" He leaned against the
oorjamb, one long arm extended, his beautiful topaz eyes
parkling with malice, mischief, whatever. "Changed your
nind?" His eyes moved appreciatively over her sleepwear.
A long floaty purple cotton-voile nightgown with thin tur-
uoise straps, plus matching robe with turquoise binding
nd sash. The sash was fastened, allowing tantalizing
limpses of the slim white body beneath.

"I want you to tell me what you think these marks are," she demanded without preamble, pulling the robe awa[y] from her throat.

"That's an original approach."

"Can I come in?"

"Maybe." He smiled down at her. A smile that woul[d] have melted most women at the knees. "But only if I'[m] allowed to keep the door open."

She hit him in the chest. Not as hard as she could have[.] "Don't fool. I'm serious."

"So am I." Nevertheless he held the door, let her swee[p] past him.

"Here, look under the light," Rosie said urgently, he[r] green eyes filled with agitation.

"I can't wait." He had a sudden vastly exciting visio[n] of the two of them in bed, swapping confidences, minglin[g] limbs. Indulging in a little—"

"Tell me if you think this is odd."

"What do you mean? Is there a flaw in your creation?" His eyes flew over her nightwear.

"Chase." She smoothed her robe and tied the sas[h.] "Look carefully." She turned this way and that, holdin[g] her mass of hair away from her neck.

"Nothing's happened in my life for years except work,["] he marveled. "Now I get Miss Rosie Summers dashing int[o] my room, and in the middle of the night, too."

"Can't you see it?" she burst out. "The marks aroun[d] my throat."

He stared at her. "There *are* marks," he said, his brai[n] shifting into another gear to appraise the area. "No mi[s]taking it, Rosie, a tattoo. But I have to tell you, you oug[ht] to get your money back. It's fading."

"Don't they *look* like something to you?" Rosie flashe[d] him a sizzling glance.

Without further comment, he told her to lift her hea[d]

then stated, "If I can bring myself to say it, the marks are like little hieroglyphics."

"There, what did I tell you?" Rosie crowed in mingled dismay and triumph. "I'd laugh if it weren't so serious."

"But they're beautiful, Rosie. They add to your allure."

She reached out and grabbed his hand, hard. "Please, Chase. I'm worried."

"No more than I am." His voice suddenly had a sober edge to it. "What the hell are they?"

For a moment Rosie felt ice-cold. "Is it possible the necklace could be cursed?"

"No way!" he answered roughly, shaking his head. "What's happened is that you're allergic to the nickel used in making it. Unless jewelry is twenty-four-karat gold, there's always a percentage of nickel in it. Some women, obviously you, are allergic to nickel."

"I am not!" she wailed. "I've got God knows how many gold chains."

"Oh, well, it was a theory." He shrugged. "Why don't you let me put something on it? I've got a tube of hydro-cortisone in my kit."

"Well, then, find it," Rosie ordered him, "before I faint. I've never had this reaction." She walked to a wall mirror to look at herself again.

She had never seen her eyes so big and glistening. So green. Her hair a mass of flames. Her skin looked incredibly fresh, her mouth the color of wine. Did she even know herself? That siren in the mirror. Maybe the original owner had put a spell on the necklace. She touched the mirror carefully, feeling slightly crazy as she did.

"Surely you've seen yourself before?" Chase asked, coming back into the room, tube in hand.

"I could swear I haven't," she murmured. "Must be something about the mirror." *Or the necklace.*

"Well, your looks are quite remarkable," he said, taking

off the top of the tube and setting it on the bedside table
"They change all the time."

He began to walk toward her. Their eyes met. Locked
Rosie couldn't glance away.

"You planned this, didn't you?" he asked with a low
laugh.

"You don't believe that! You can't. Actually, I'm worried."

He didn't respond. "Hold your hair up, there's a good
girl."

"Woman," Rosie corrected.

"Definitely a woman," he murmured. "Just a figure of
speech, Rosie. I'll have to work on my political correctness
Now, I'm going to put this directly onto your skin. I jus
hope it works. My reason tells me these marks are just an
irritation."

As soon as his hand touched her bare skin, she felt a
flare of excitement shoot through her whole body. Even her
breasts began to rise and fall. "If it doesn't go, we'd better
get Marley," she suggested a little hoarsely.

That warranted a heavy frown. "I'm damned if we'll do
that."

"He won't laugh. He's sold on this Egyptian thing
Maybe he can read something into it. It could be an in
scription."

"Get real, Rosie," he scoffed, staring a little uneasily a
the tiny marks. The nickel was responsible, whatever she
said.

"Is the cream having any effect?" Rosie asked, almos
swooning under the pressure of his hands.

"I don't think it's supposed to happen right away. I
takes time." He rested his hands on her shoulders. "Thi
is just an interesting illusion, Rosie. Not magic. No
spells."

"The necklace has been hidden for thousands of years, waiting for someone to claim it," she whispered.

"No games, Rosie," he said sternly, stroking the curve of her neck.

She couldn't help herself. She turned her head along his hand, her heart thudding almost painfully. She didn't know what would have happened had a voice not penetrated the closed door. A rich distinctive voice, sounding somewhat ragged.

"Banfield, are you there? Banfield!" And just so there was no chance he couldn't be heard, a massive follow-up banging on the door.

"For crying out loud!" Chase groaned. "This guy has to be stopped. I'll bet he went down to your room, found it empty and headed right over here."

Rosie took a deep calming breath, realizing her robe had come open and she was showing a good bit of cleavage. She inched the robe tight. "You'd better let him in before he wakes the whole pub."

He held up a palm, speaking darkly. "I might tell him to—"

"Please, Chase," she begged.

Shaking his head, he strode to the door just as Marley knocked again.

"What the hell's going on, Marley?" Chase demanded, flinging open the door so forcefully Marley fell in. "Got a problem?"

Marley straightened, swaying. "I think I should tell you Roslyn isn't in her—" He stopped abruptly as Rosie came into view.

"Good God, Roslyn!" Marley said thickly, his blue eyes full of moral outrage.

"You have it on very good authority—mine—that she's here to demonstrate a kind of phenomenon," Chase drawled.

"What he means is," Rosie picked up hastily, feeling the anger coming off Chase in waves, "when I took the gold necklace off, I noticed marks on my throat." She turned her head to Chase, seeking his support. "Are they still there?"

"I can hardly believe this," Marley started to fume, but was rudely interrupted by Chase's moving Rosie right under his nose.

"The marks. Take a look at them," Chase said curtly.

Marley squinted at her, still outraged. "All right. What am I supposed to be seeing?"

"I hope to hell this isn't a ruse you and Rosie dreamed up!" Chase warned with some wrath.

"Mmm," Marley droned while Rosie lifted her chin, addressing Chase. "Are you accusing me of some sort of ploy?" she asked loudly.

"I'm debating it," he said.

"This is amazing!" Marley's blue eyes turned electric. "It looks for all the world like hieroglyphic writing. A magic charm for the owner to use in the next world."

"So how did you imprint it on Miss Summers's skin?"

"Imprint?" Rosie repeated. "There's no way I'd be party to any such thing!"

Marley was studying them both with a very odd expression. "Are you going to listen now, Banfield?" he asked.

"Dammit!" Chase clapped a hand to his head in disgust. "All I'm saying is, it was very cleverly done."

"Now wait a minute." The fiery disposition of the redhead was coming to the fore.

"No, *you* wait a minute." Banfield turned on her, his striking features registering repulsion. "If you think I'm going to be easy to fool, you've got another think coming."

"Please," Marley interrupted, looking around wildly. "I'm trying to understand this."

"I thought you were a trained linguist," Chase retorted.

"You should be able to read it easily. Or do you have to understand the magic to understand the writing? Tell me, are you reading right to left? Left to right? Or from the top to the bottom? Should we place Miss Summers on the bed to make the job easier?"

"The symbols are so tiny," Marley moaned. "I really need my glasses."

"And they're fading fast," Chase muttered. "Why don't I have a go? Pity to waste all that effort. Here we are—*To Hatty from Thut. Bon voyage.*"

"Say, that's good," Rosie said with a kind of relief that he hadn't said, "Watch out!" or some other warning. "Was Queen Hatshepsut King Thutmose's sister? His half sister?"

"Hatshepsut was Thutmose III's stepmother," Marley corrected Rosie testily. "The Egyptian empire reached its height during Thutmose's reign. I am certain the necklace is not of that period. There!" He threw up his hands in what appeared to be genuine dismay. "It's gone."

"Invisible ink?" Chase suggested, scathing to the end.

"This is utterly, utterly unforeseen." Marley's eyes had that fanatical gleam again.

"Darn right!" Rosie agreed. "It's a good thing I'm not a woman who scares easily."

"Pardon me, but you ran in here like a missile." Chase gave a dry laugh.

"Well, you have to admit this was odd." Her green eyes flashed him.

"I managed to keep *my* nerve."

"I assure you, Banfield, I knew nothing about this." Marley's eyes were sweeping back and forth over the white-skinned Rosie with her long cascades of apricot-colored hair. "I mean it. As far as I'm concerned it was some kind of...of manifestation."

"Scared now, Rosie?" Chase asked, annoyed that he'd been taken in for even a moment or two.

"I'm like you," she said, frowning fiercely at him and managing to look very seductive at the same time. "My reason tells me it was some kind of skin reaction, not a rash, as we all saw it wasn't red, more inky like on a papyrus and—"

"Ah, stop it," he said, dropping into a chair. "In your profession, you're a very enterprising woman. I'll bet you'd go to considerable lengths to get a great story."

"Yes," she agreed, "but nothing *dishonest*. This was pretty much what Graeme said—a manifestation."

"Marvelous, and I saw it, too. Isn't Porter going to be pleased? Perhaps next time it happens I should summon him over. Or has he witnessed this mind-boggling phenomenon firsthand?"

Marley stared at him, the picture of a proud man unfairly maligned. "I resent what you're saying, Banfield. I'm a scientist. A top man in my field."

"Which isn't Egyptology, as you very well know," Chase said in a silky voice.

"I know as much about it as many so-called experts," Marley huffed. "I have no idea how those marks came to be on Roslyn's neck. It might have been a romantic little touch of her own."

"I beg your pardon?" Rosie was stunned. The traitor!

"Really? A falling-out?" Chase's topaz eyes sparkled with black humor.

"I value my reputation," Rosie said. "I'm not in the fraud business."

"We don't exactly know that," Chase retorted. "Would you care to prove it? Give a repeat performance?"

"You mean put the necklace back on?" Rosie shuddered, turned her back on him. "No, thanks. I'll pass."

"Don't think it'll work twice in one night?" he inquired.

"I'm not going to take that chance."

He watched her, trying to decipher her thoughts. "If you're on the level, I'd say the necklace had a high nickel content. Although I haven't got the energy to come up with a plausible explanation for the series of little squiggles. I have a long drive back to the station in the morning."

"So the visit's off?" Rosie turned to him again, flooded with disappointment.

"No, the visit's on. I'll let you know. Now, if you two don't mind clearing out—" Chase rose to his full lean height "—I'm going to hit the sack."

"Can I depend on you, Banfield, to get back to us?" Marley's voice was so beseeching it didn't sound like his own.

"How many times do you give your word, Dr. Marley? I give mine only once."

"Right, right." Marley backed toward the door, tight-lipped. "I just wondered if you wanted to see the stone scarab before you go."

Chase let out an exasperated sigh. "Doctor, do you think you could accept a simple no? I'm not interested. It could be a fake. It could be a museum-quality antique. What it *isn't* is a treasure dug up on Three Moons."

Marley smiled coldly. "It appears to me, Banfield, that underneath it all, you're unsettled."

"Blame it on my instincts." Chase turned his head to address Rosie, who stood against the wall. "You, too, Miss Summers. Unless you're staying?"

"No, thank you," she said sharply, moving so quickly her robe floated around her.

"If you don't ask, you'll never know," he said breezily, touching her shoulder as she sailed out. "I'll give you a call."

CHAPTER FIVE

ON THE MORNING Chase Banfield was driving back to Three Moons with Mick Dempsey as his passenger, Porter Banfield was standing on the upper balcony of the large clifftop residence he had built for himself several miles out of town, staring out over the turquoise sea. It was an incredible view, incorporating the offshore islands, emerald diadems set in pure white sand, but he saw none of it. His mind was seething with thoughts about the project he had so carefully set up. *Operation Goddess.* That was his private little joke, but the last piece in his plan had been put into place.

All he needed now was to call Howard Siegel in Sydney—if he could reach him. Siegel was protected by an army of secretaries, as befitting a multimillionaire, but usually the name "Banfield" got him. Over the past twelve years, Porter had supplied Siegel with some of his finest antiquities, artifacts from the great archaeological sites. Most of them had been obtained through his carefully built-up sources—curators, archaeologists, explorers, businessmen of various interests. And most of them were illegally obtained in the eyes of the world, but he himself didn't, *couldn't,* see it that way. To Porter, it was a question of who observed them. His clients, like him, truly revered the antiquities from ancient civilizations—Greece, Rome, Pompeii, Babylon, Assyria, Egypt. Egypt above all. It was the stupid public, the careless hordes of tourists who caused destruction. In his own hands and the hands of his wealthy clients, these precious objects received the greatest care. Even the British Museum had damaged some of the Elgin marbles, irreparably, as it happened, when they were cleaned with copper chisels and wire brushes in the late 1930s. He shuddered every time he thought about it. Apart from some of his clients, Siegel for one, few people realized the extent of his collection—the many rare and wonderful objects from the ancient world that he had amassed over the years. It was when he'd run through his own fortune and a sizable portion of Banfield money that dire necessity had forced him into the black-market trade. It had proved extremely profitable, but not without risks. The risks both frightened and titillated him at the same time. In another life he might have been a cat burglar. Someone like Cary Grant in *To Catch a Thief.* Suave, sophisticated, handsome. Illegal dealing—as the authorities viewed it—gave him the same sense of power.

At eleven precisely, he walked back into his study, stroking the bronze bust of a satyr. Hellenistic, probably third century B.C., it sat on the massive leather-topped antique desk. Both items had been acquired legally, so he was free to display them. It was in his own interest to be seen in the great auction houses of the world. Not only to be seen, but to buy. He had long let it be known that he ran a consultancy for the very rich. And it was true. His real treasures were properly stored in his air-conditioned sanctuary. A private room that had taken a lot of ingenuity to conceal. Certainly from his nephew, Chase—ridiculous name! The boy had been christened John Chase Banfield. Chase was his mother's maiden name, more impressive in a way than Banfield. His late sister-in-law had been the only daughter of the blue blood Sir Walter Chase. Old money, while the Banfields had made their own. Anyway, Chase knew nothing of the inner sanctum. He had been in the house a scant few times, but he'd never been taken there. Chase, the usurper, like his father before him. At the thought, a great torrent of anger and bitter resentment washed over him. All his life he'd had to grapple with being second-best.

Hunched behind his desk, Porter Banfield punched in the numbers, asking for Siegel as soon as he was connected to one of those dreadful secretaries Siegel employed, not allowing the woman a minute to tell him Siegel was in conference but giving the password, the secret pact between them. "Please take this message to Mr. Siegel immediately. The books for his library have arrived." It was a blind of course, but Siegel loved books, as well. He had one of the finest collections of seventeenth- eighteenth- and nineteenth-century books in the country. Not to mention illuminated manuscripts, exquisitely decorated medieval tracts, rare manuscripts—possibly a few gone missing from private libraries. Siegel wasn't overscrupulous about how he acquired his treasures, such was his consuming passion.

A moment more, and Siegel came on the line, steely, arrogant, wasting no time in getting down to business. They spoke briefly in a kind of code. They never discussed anything real over the telephone. Private conversations could be recorded, as many a famous person knew to his cost. The outcome of the conversation was that Porter would travel to Sydney the following morning for a meeting in Siegel's office. He would be picked up at the airport in Siegel's chauffeur-driven Rolls; then he'd be offered lunch, which Banfield knew would be superb. No sandwich on the run for Siegel. No eccentric millionaire with lunch in a brown paper bag. Siegel, a huge man, was a connoisseur of great food and wine. Banfield, who still retained his lean elegant figure, privately thought that particular passion would kill him.

He arrived in Sydney the next day to blustery weather, although it had been perfect when he left home. As usual, Siegel's chauffeur was waiting for him, directing him to where the Rolls was parked. They stopped only once on the way, to pick up Siegel's dry cleaning, of all things. Which Banfield thought was very odd. He never picked up his own dry cleaning; he had it delivered. Of course, Siegel was a self-made man, with the idiosyncrasies that implied. In all honesty, he was a rogue. All his clients were rogues, for that matter. A rogues' gallery, including a seventy-year-old national icon, heiress to a shipping line, so open and forthright, so noble, a philanthropist, who'd never lost her passion for acquiring extraordinary objects by any means, short of murder. But they were faithful, his clients. They trusted him as "one of them." The powerful Banfield name. The great pioneering family of the Far North. The family that dealt in beef cattle with the odd bit of income derived from their own gold mine. The gold was long gone, though—or so everyone thought. But gold survived....

Siegel greeted him in his office high above the city, ignoring the niceties. "So what have you got for me?" he asked abruptly. He looked past his guest's tall elegant figure and frigid handsome face to the leather sofa where Banfield had been sitting, as though expecting to see a large box containing something extraordinary.

"I think you're going to like it," Banfield drawled in his upper-crust voice, withdrawing a small velvet-wrapped object from his inner breast pocket.

Siegel reached for it eagerly, his laser-blue eyes beginning to gleam. "Here, show me."

A stunningly attractive young woman in a powder-blue suit chose that very moment to sweep into the room without so much as a cursory knock. Siegel bellowed at her like an angry elephant. "Get out!" She complied without even a moue of embarrassment, while Porter's ears rang from the pounding. Evidently she had special privileges, he thought, wondering if that could be used to his advantage.

Siegel returned to his desk and sat down heavily in the

massive swivel chair. Balding, florid blotchy complexion, bulbous nose, dreadful tie. Not worth knowing, really. "Well, well, well." Siegel bent over the object, then picked it up in his chunky hands mottled with liver spots. Finally he stood and took it to the huge plate-glass window that afforded sweeping views of Sydney Harbour. "It's quite magnificent. Early New Kingdom. Around 1500 B.C.?"

Porter gave him a thin smile. "You're becoming quite the expert."

"Don't patronize me, Banfield," Siegel scowled. "Damned right I am. But I have to hand it to you. You've taught me a lot."

Don't you just hate these people? Banfield thought. "There's no record of it anywhere," he said, deciding Siegel was completely devoid of manners.

Siegel stared at him and shrugged. "You've given your whole life to this, haven't you, Banfield?"

"It's my passion. Like yours." Porter adjusted the knife-edge of his dark-gray trousers, the picture of sartorial elegance, although he might as well have been sitting in a shabby old dressing gown for all the notice Siegel took.

"A jeweled scarab," the fat man mused, gazing down at the splendid gold object in his hand. "A beetle held sacred by the ancient Egyptians. The symbol of resurrection and immortality."

"During the embalming process, the heart of the dead person was removed and a large carved scarab put in its place," Porter added, wondering what Siegel would look like embalmed.

"Curious!" Siegel grimaced. "*Scarab.* Sounds good for a dung beetle. Anyway, it's a fine piece. The workmanship is excellent. Are you going to tell me where you got it?"

Banfield never told. "Not from one of my usual suppliers. Perhaps we can talk about it over lunch."

They adjourned to a boardroom the size of a small shop-

ing mall, hung with a lot of stuffy portraits Siegel must
ave picked up at auction and passed off as relatives. A
aiter appeared to serve lunch: seared scallops with white
ruffle butter, followed by quail with buttery braised celery,
nd for Siegel, at least, poached peach in vanilla syrup with
auternes custard. Banfield decided that continuing to eat
ould be the final surrender. However, the wine was a dif-
erent matter—a luscious chardonnay. Only when coffee
as served by the same white-jacketed waiter did Siegel
esume their talk about the scarab. "And how did you get
e little trinket through customs, unless it was already in
e country?"

Banfield pondered the question, staring at Siegel intently.
"I'm going to tell you something quite remarkable. Some-
ing that might alter our whole lives."

Siegel's eyes turned opaque. "Fire away," he said in a
oice like gravel.

"What would you say if I told you that over a period of
ears I've been digging up relics of an ancient civilization
n Three Moons?"

"I'd laugh in your face. That's just bullshit, Banfield.
reposterous!" Siegel snorted.

"Well, then, you can kiss goodbye to the scarab," Baneld returned.

Siegel blinked, irritated but suddenly conciliatory. "Are
ou trying to tell me you dug up the scarab?"

Porter's glance slid off sideways as he made sure the
aiter wasn't about to come back into the room with a
owlful of chocolates for Siegel. He relaxed. "The scarab,
mong other things! A gold necklace depicting lotus lilies
et with semiprecious stones. Gold and silver coins, stone
eals, pottery fragments, other jewelry, a bronze sword."

Siegel paused, the small coffee cup, looking utterly ri-
iculous in his meaty hand, halfway to his mouth.

"I can't see you digging anywhere, Porter." He laughed

heartily, outrageously amused. "Getting down on you hands and knees, getting dirty."

Porter found himself hoping the man would choke. "A old Aborigine on the station found a handful of gold coin and brought them to me," he told Siegel, dripping disdair

"Why didn't he keep them?" Siegel was still laughing but Porter tried to put his intense irritation out of his mind

"The man was one of a vanishing breed of tribal peo ple," he explained. "The coins were no use to him. I exchange I gave him food for his family." He hadn't, bu he figured it made him sound more human, whatever tha meant. "He went off quite happy after telling me precisel where he'd dug up the coins."

Siegel slumped back in his chair, satiated while Porte waited in horror in case the man burped. No Old Worl manners there. "You're just too intelligent a man to wast my valuable time," Siegel said with just enough glimme of a threat.

"I've exercised great caution with this." Porter spoke a if it was a feat of bravery. "I can't afford to make an mistakes."

"I should think not," Siegel muttered, producing one o his dreadful cigars. "I understand that your nephew, th current *owner* of Three Moons, and you are estranged? Siegel gave "owner" great emphasis. "In fact, not to p too fine a point on it, he's outright hostile to you?"

Banfield's ice-blue eyes revealed nothing. "You've bee making inquiries?"

Siegel fiddled with his cigar while Porter serious wished he could have been spared at least this stenc Didn't anyone heed health warnings these days?

"I always make inquiries." Siegel coughed, in no tim resembling a huge chimney stack. "You should know tha Besides, it's no big secret that the place got terribly ru down during your tenure."

"A lot of wild talk!" Porter dismissed the charge, though his eyes slid off like a bar of soap. "I had to ride out some tough times. The turndown in the beef industry, for one. My nephew chose to blame me for circumstances that were quite outside my control. He always was very difficult to handle. Very hard to control. In recognition for all I'd done for him, including saving his life, he turfed me out of what had always been my home the day he turned twenty-one."

"Probably deserved it, Porter," Siegel suggested wolfishly.

"I'm aware you like your little jokes, Howard." Porter refused to bite. "If only you could come with me. Visit Three Moons. I'd be able to convince you."

"And how are we going to do that? Sneak up on your nephew? I doubt it. My sources tell me he's a pretty sharp guy. A real take-charge type." *Different from you* was never said but somehow implied. "I don't think he'd have any hesitation throwing us both off."

"I haven't told you everything," Porter said. "When I spoke to you yesterday, I mentioned I had a plan. It's as good as in place. I've managed to gain the services of Dr. Graeme Marley. You may have heard of him?"

"Archaeologist fella?" Siegel puffed, interest going up several notches. Marley had a good reputation.

"Exactly. Now I'd like you to listen." Porter detailed what had happened to date, including Rosie's part in gaining his nephew's ear.

"You don't say!" For some reason Siegel, who usually had all the warmth of an Easter Island statue, was laughing and joking. "I know Rosie Summers. Wish I was her boyfriend!" He swung his large foot back and forth. Utterly grotesque! "You're a cold-blooded devil, aren't you, Porter," he said, meeting Banfield's frozen expression.

"I like to reflect on the serious things in life." If Siegel hadn't been his one shining hope, Porter would have got up and left. "I've had a brief conversation with Marley, who's already in North Queensland, along with Miss Summers. My nephew hasn't given the okay yet, but Marley's very hopeful."

"And Marley's going for it?" Siegel's flinty gaze never wavered.

"He certainly doesn't think it's an unreasonable theory. There's sufficient evidence for him to come on board as my partner."

"So what are you looking for from *me?*" Siegel still hadn't blinked. What was he—a goanna?

"These things take money, Howard," Banfield explained, his voice oozing professionalism. "Our exploration needs a sponsor. A dedicated man. A true collector. A leader behind the scenes, if you like."

"Why are you hurting for money?" Siegel gave another hearty laugh that finished in a breathless choke.

"Aren't we all?" Porter smiled in satisfaction. "You excepted, Howard. We need to first find the site of the village, then carefully excavate it. I promise you the choicest objects will be yours."

Ah, a promising flash of greed. "And what if it's a wild goose chase?"

"Then you can decline." Porter was brisk, sounding as though they could wind up the conversation right then and there. "I have two other clients I can approach. Not as suitable as you, of course." *Nor quite as greedy.* "I'm very serious about this. So is Marley, who's entitled to a share as well as all the adulation he'll get when he finally proves an ancient Egyptian presence in the Far North. As soon as we get the okay from my nephew, I'll let you know. Perhaps you could spare the time to fly up?"

Siegel shook his head and waved his hands, as much to clear the smoke as in negation. "No, no, no. I'll keep out of it altogether. And we'll deal in cash. No checks. Nothing to trace back to me. The fewer people who know, the better. We don't want the Queensland government to get wind of it.'' He narrowed his eyes. ''I do have someone in mind to go along on your expedition, though—to protect my interests. He's not in the country at the moment, but I can have him here in the next few days.''

''Who is he?'' Porter asked, just knowing the man had to be a criminal.

''He's a lot of people,'' Siegel told him. ''Ex-army. Highly trained to do a lot of things. Mostly my bidding. He knows the jungle. How to survive. He'll be a real asset on the trip.''

''I don't know, Howard.'' Banfield was dismayed. The man sounded dreadful. A threat.

''Unless my man's in place, the deal's off,'' Siegel returned, eyes as flat as stones. ''And the deal only lasts so long. I need results. Not overnight, I don't expect that, but fairly quickly, since you're supposed to have dug up that cache. Or did you simply plant it?'' Siegel looked at Banfield with powerful suspicion, his cigar stabbing the air like a dagger.

Porter in turn looked as disdainful as only he could, staring Siegel unflinchingly in the eye. ''I would never cross you.''

''You'd be a fool if you did.'' Siegel spoke so vehemently that he started choking again. ''You seem a little pale.'' He struck his chest several times. ''Hope my cigar isn't bothering you.'' As if he'd care! ''How much do you want for the scarab? Don't waste your time going over the limit.''

Banfield named a figure that was close to astronomical, inwardly gloating when the man of steel, the Godzilla of the City, accepted it like a dupe.

THE REST OF THE WEEK was going to pass very slowly indeed if she sat around waiting for Chase Banfield's call.

Just thinking about him brought on a tremendous melt-down, a sizzling depth of feeling she'd never experienced before. No question at all: She was lovestruck. A glorious melodramatic *scary* feeling, containing, as it did, all the elements of heartbreak. Of course, he didn't feel anything even similar. She could well make an utter fool of herself. Running a huge station consumed all his energies. She had to remember, too, that a man like Chase Banfield could have anyone he liked. And yet... And yet... Those kisses!

A positive optimistic person, Rosie charged through her days chatting with the locals and working out articles that might interest her boss. Lovely man that he was, he valued her. He who blasted her off like a rocket to war zones.

North Queensland was renowned for its glorious tropical scenery, the beauty and mystery of the great rain forest one of the last natural havens left on earth. Then there was the wonder of the adjacent Great Barrier Reef, the largest single collection of coral reefs in the world. A sensory bombardment allied with idyllic weather, except for the odd cyclone, and thus the perfect sanctuary for a whole artistic colony—painters, potters, sculptors, arts-and-crafts people. Jewelry designers working with gemstones, silver, gold, opals. And a fair smattering of "characters" who had somehow existed for years without gainful employment including a few furtive-looking individuals she suspected could have been on the run, not to mention the middle-aged yuppies-turned-hippies who'd escaped to paradise. All in all, grist for the mill. She even got around to recording interviews with a few. The best was with the very attractive much-sought-after jewelry designer Silvia Gardin, prompting a phone call to her boss who, without sounding enthusiastic, thought it would make a good piece for the paper. The most touching interview was with a reclusive fiftyish painter hiding his identity—surely from his mother—with a black beard so long and voluminous it could have housed a family of possums. He even kept his paintings turned back to front until Rosie convinced him to let her take a look.

Stand back! Explosions of color! Wonderful images, soft flowers, birds, fish, sunlit beaches, green shadowy forests, haunting faces that showed a mixture of races. Rosie returned in great excitement, taking her camera. She was an excellent photographer. These paintings needed showing. She knew just the right gallery owner. Whoever heard of a painter who didn't want his paintings, his *visions,* to be seen? She was going to put this guy on the map. She was about to buy a painting, overwhelmed when he picked one up off the floor and presented it to her. The most exuberant, sensual, still-life arrangement of brilliant tropical flowers, scarlet, orange, yellow, creamy white, the great golden cups of solanders, spears of green grasses, in a cracked cobalt-blue pot sitting on a table covered with a bunched-up purple cloth. In the background a shimmering tall flute of champagne with a ruby stem.

"Radiance," he said earnestly. *"You."*

She nearly burst into tears, genuinely thrilled. And humbled. She would bequeath this painting to her first child who, extraordinarily enough, she perceived as having topaz eyes. This man's paintings would outlast her, him, give other generations great pleasure. She was sure of it, and she wasn't a bad judge. Such a body of work with its tremendous vitality was all the more extraordinary, considering that the painter himself had the joie de vivre of an undertaker.

ROSIE WAS SITTING one late afternoon over coffee and deep discussion with the pub owner, Lyn, who turned out to have a real story to tell—years of being terrorized by her ex-husband, who always begged forgiveness after each violent episode and was always forgiven until she'd finally rejected the role of victim. Or, as Lyn put it, until she'd run away. Even telling her story had Lyn trembling, leaving her in tears. Suddenly she looked past Rosie's shoulder at someone who'd just come through the front door.

Her mouth curved up with real pleasure as she dashed a few tears from her cheeks. "Chase!" Lyn patted Rosie's hand in recognition of her sympathy and understanding, shot up and went toward him, accepting his affectionate peck on the temple.

"Sorry I couldn't ring you, Lyn," said the now-familiar deep voice. "You have no idea what a day it's been. Chris Flannery nearly ripped himself to pieces with barbed wire. A fence fell on him. I've left him with the doctor."

"How dreadful!"

"Very painful for Chris." He tactfully ignored the marks of recent tears on his friend's cheeks. "Moses and I had quite a job getting the fence off him without doing more damage. Anyway, he's had his tetanus shot."

"So you're staying the night?"

"If you'll have me. Hi there, Miss Summers." Chase turned, sketched a fascinating salute by shaking his *akubra* in the air like a tambourine.

The excitement started. "Hi there, yourself, Mr. Banfield." Rosie forced herself to stop admiring the classic profile that had been presented to her and gave him a big smile. What she really wanted to do was throw herself at him. God, he looked gorgeous! That gold skin! So much for the drying effects of the harsh tropical sun. The tiger's topaz eyes. The expression in them. The stray bronze locks that fell onto his forehead. The energy that flowed out of him, charisma layers deep. Her fabled detachment was gone. This was the man she'd been waiting for all her life. Could she get a man like that? She thought instantly of her mother, of a recent conversation they'd had. "Dearest, you may be a good journalist—you were always very curious as a child, and I expect curiosity is a big factor in a journalist's success—''

"No, Ma." Her mother hated being called Ma. "My mission in life is to make people *feel* better."

"Then you're not very obvious about it, darling. As I was saying, it's all very well being a good journalist, although, mind you, most people are highly suspicious of journalists. But you have no domestic skills to offer, Roslyn."

Wounding words! Apparently without domestic skills, a woman was nothing. Many a woman, according to her mother, had been dropped because she hadn't mastered the perfect omelette. Her mother had a whole library of cookbooks written by the great chefs of the world. It was a marvel, given her legendary gourmet dinners, thirty or forty people, to see her so tiny and trim. Perhaps it was all the golf or—

"Well, I'll see to your room, Chase." Lyn's voice broke her reverie. "A husband and wife, very nice people, moved out of the end room this morning. The husband wants to catch blue marlin off Cairns." She hurried away with an indulgent smile, leaving them alone.

"I expected a phone call every day," Rosie exclaimed in a bantering voice. "I didn't get one."

"I thought of you often, as a matter of fact." He let his eyes soak her in. A tall young woman, but light as air. Her outfit for the day turned her skin incandescent. She wore a long gauzy skirt the color of the rain-forest Ulysses butterfly—a brilliant flame-blue—with a sleeveless lime-colored gauzy top, the silver belt he'd seen before clinched around her waist, flat lime-green sandals on her feet. Her unmanageable marigold hair fanned out all around her face like a fire wheel, and silver pendant earrings swung from her ears. They looked to be Indian. She was as colorful as a woman from a far more exotic background. But he wasn't about to let her penetrate his aura. "Romance and trying to run a big station don't mix, as any sensible person would know."

"Surely you're not planning to *keep* it that way?" She stared at him in mock amazement. "Why, pure self-interest alone should drive you to the altar. You need heirs to keep the Banfield dynasty alive. To till the land. To drive the cattle. Catch the rustlers. Tame the brumbies. The daughters of the family taking no part in such vigorous manly pursuits, of course."

"I can promise you that," he said, pulling a chair around and dropping into it, his body elegantly slumped. "No matter how well-intentioned, women just make the job more difficult," he said.

"You mean women are just for fun and games?" Rosie asked, feminist hackles rising.

"All right, Rosie, we can skip the sexist stuff," he said, leaning forward to set one of her earrings swinging with the tip of his finger. "Our station women have big jobs to do, as well. The home, the family, supervising staff, looking after their needs, service to the community. Helping out efficiently with mountains of paperwork. They're kept busy, believe me."

"You need someone to do this?" Rosie challenged.

The topaz eyes warmed. "Are you offering?"

"No. I love being my own boss."

"So marriage and children must wait?"

"At least until I meet my true love," she said flippantly.

"Same here, which is not to say I find any lack of magic in you. Anyway, I've come to fetch you." He presented her with the sweetest smile.

"What about Marley?" Halfway through melting, she abruptly thought of Graeme.

"What about him?" Chase's expression toughened.

"Old-fashioned, perhaps, but would it hurt to have a chaperon?"

"Chaperon? Why?" he scoffed. "I may be violently attracted to you, Rosie, but you need never fear my lustfulness."

"Who said I was talking about *you?*" The two of them alone together!

"You *want* Marley?" he asked.

She very nearly threw her big story to the winds. Then she sighed. "We *are* sort of partners in this Egypt-in-Oz thing."

"You're still hooked on it?" His incredulous grin was infectious.

"I live for it!" she exaggerated. "So does Graeme. He'll be devastated if you don't give us the go-ahead."

"Is that so?" He tilted his chair on its back legs. "When was the last time you saw him? I know for a fact he's spent a fair bit of time at Porter's."

"There's not much you don't know, is there. Your spies again?"

He didn't smile. "I want to know everything Porter and Marley are up to. And that goes for you, too, Rosie Summers."

"You haven't checked up on me, Detective Inspector Banfield?" She looked at him, defiance spilling out of her green eyes.

"They love you around here." He gave his devastating grin. "You're so *interested* in people."

"That makes me my living. Everyone has a story."

"I can't wait to hear yours."

"You will. I guarantee it." *Maybe in bed.*

"Including all your romantic entanglements?"

"There are actually very few," Rosie spoke truthfully. "That's what comes of having a pure heart."

He laughed outright. "I don't believe that. You're the

sort of woman a man would follow across continents. There's been no one? I mean no one special?''

''Not really. Finding the right person to love is a rare gift. But I haven't been lonely. If you're finished prying into my love life, what about yours?''

''I'm not as chaste as you are, Rosie,'' he replied. ''I have affairs from time to time. But every one of my ex-girlfriends still speaks to me.''

''You're shy of marriage, though?''

''Not at all. I'll get married eventually.''

''You'll have to, to ensure the continuity of the Banfield dynasty,'' she said again. ''So you can't wait *too* long.''

''Neither can you,'' he retaliated, eyes gleaming. ''After all, you're nearly thirty.''

Words Rosie set herself to considering. ''I'm in no hurry. Just like you. I've seen a lot of unhappy people frantic to tie the knot.''

He leaned forward, briefly stroked her cheek. ''Don't let that discourage you. Or maybe you want two lives. Career, plus being a wife and mother?''

''I wouldn't be willing to put my career aside.''

''I'm sure you wouldn't.'' He nodded. ''You've worked hard, and your experiences have made you the interesting person you are. Any more episodes with the hieroglyphics?'' He changed the subject rather suddenly, dropping his eyes to her throat.

''You mean the necklace?''

''What else?'' he asked cynically. ''Or has there been some *other*...manifestation?''

''I haven't been brave enough to put it on again,'' she confessed. And indeed she hadn't. One didn't go fooling around with these ancient Egyptians.

He stared at her hard to see if she meant it. ''You're going to give it back to Porter?''

"Definitely! I don't know why exactly your uncle agreed to my having it in the first place."

"Presumably as you thought—to keep you onside. It's a shame to return it, though. It looked marvelous on you. By the way, how did you actually manage those little discolorations?"

Rosie sighed loudly. "I had the feeling you were back to that. Anyone would think you were an accountant, not a cattle baron. Where's your imagination? Your sense of the paranormal?"

"I told you. I have a very suspicious mind," he said cordially.

"So do I. I'm a trained journalist. I don't believe everything I see and hear. But as far as the necklace is concerned...I don't have a clue. And I'd tread very carefully if I were you. Remember what happened to Lord Carnarvon," she said darkly.

"You mean he and Carter no sooner violated Tutankhamon's tomb than Carnarvon died."

Rosie agreed that it was a violation of a burial place. "But from all accounts there was something very odd about the circumstances of his death," she said.

"According to legend. Are you warning me against being flippant?"

"I'm only saying take care. Normally I don't think much about it, but I've come to accept that I have a sixth sense. It's developed gradually over the years. Especially when I've been in danger. My great-aunt Hester has it, too."

"Didn't I know you weren't to be taken lightly?" He was only half-mocking. "Great-aunt Hester, too? The clairvoyant and licensed tarot-card reader?"

"No, Hester Summers, Renaissance Woman and renowned painter of lovely lush nudes."

"Renoir, eat your heart out!" He shook his head. "I'd

love to see them, although I expect you're too skinny to be part of the collection."

"Indeed not! Even if I were Jennifer Lopez, I'm too modest."

"But showy! Showy as a daylily with the sun on its surface. Even to the arching satiny throat."

He said the most gorgeous things! Things that made her heart leap for joy. "So tell me," she asked sweetly, responding to such comfort. "I'm thrilled and honored to be invited to Three Moons, but can I hear your decision about our up-country safari? An American hunter, by the way, just offered the Queensland government half a million dollars to be allowed to hunt crocodiles."

"Crocodiles are a protected species," he said with a glint of fierceness.

"I *know* that, but the big-game hunter thought it was worth a try. And in case *you* didn't know, we're all descended from crocodiles."

He burst out laughing. "I thought you told me you don't believe everything you read."

"It's official." Rosie nodded her head sagely. "We came out of the sludge. Instead of being descended from the apes, our ancestors came from fearsome crocodilelike creatures."

He groaned. "Did you see this in a science-fiction movie?"

"Sorry. The Natural History Museum in London has discovered a fossil to prove it. A jawbone some 370 million years old. Surely you've met the odd human being with fishy characteristics? Especially around the jaw and the eyes?"

"The 'missing link'?" He snorted. "Believe what you like, Rosie. I'll stick with the basic theories."

"I don't blame you. I'm terrified of crocodiles." She said it so wryly they both laughed. "You can't tell me a crocodile has a soul."

"The Aborigines believe so. The crocodile is sacred to them, just as they were to the ancient Egyptians. I've seen Aboriginal children swimming safely in waters with crocodiles cruising downstream. I've seen those kids cross rivers and lagoons where no white man in his right mind would dare to go. And the ones who've tried it ended up in a death roll."

Rosie slowly released her breath. "Extraordinary, isn't it? There are more things in Heaven and Earth—"

"Okay, okay. I know my Shakespeare," he told her hastily.

"Then you can finish it?"

"I thought you were trying to get a decision out of me, instead of putting me on the spot. And I swear I know it."

"So the decision is?" She stared at him, her heart very nearly in her mouth.

"I know this comes under the heading of temporary insanity, but you've got one month to find something that will convince me to allow you to continue." He looked more skeptical than ever, but she covered his hand, squeezed it hard.

"You won't regret this. But a month's not much time."

"Stop at the various places Porter is supposed to have unearthed his treasure," he suggested caustically. "In any case, I'd like you to keep an eagle eye on him."

"I spend my life keeping an eagle eye on people." Rosie frowned. "What do you think he's capable of?"

"Now, that would be letting the skeletons out of the closet. Don't forget he's a close relative." He sobered, shook his head. "God knows, Rosie. It grieves me to say this, but I've had a profound distrust of my uncle all my life. Even before I lost my parents. I always had the feeling he hated my guts—and still does. Yet apparently he saved my life."

"My God, he'd have to have *some* goodness in him!"

Rosie burst out. "This has been a terrible burden for you to carry."

He reached out and clasped her slender fingers loosely, but didn't respond.

"Anyone short of the devil himself would be compelled to save a child," she reasoned.

"Generally speaking, yes. Don't worry about it, Rosie. It's just one of those things we'll never know. All the evidence is gone. Never examined. Although my father was very much respected and admired, people always had their doubts about Porter. He was always sore about something. He lived his life in my father's shadow, which couldn't have been easy for someone like Porter. He doesn't make friends easily. A lot of people were ready to believe the worst of him when it happened."

"Like Mick?" Rosie asked gently, listening to his heartfelt groan.

"Mick was my father's friend. He grieved for the loss of my father almost as much as he grieves for his wife."

"So Mick is part of the reason you're allowing us to go?"

He sat for a while before he answered. "Mick needs a major distraction. All his energies have been used up on drinking. Mick's emotions go deep. Besides, he's on my side. A man I can trust. That's important. And there's always the possibility that he can straighten himself out."

"You're very generous," Rosie said in admiration. "Very compassionate. If I knew you better, I'd give you a hug."

"Particularly when I want one." He hoisted his lean powerful body from the chair. "A hug it is."

Whatever he planned, it came to a disappointing halt as Graeme Marley walked from the brilliant sunshine of the outdoors into the welcoming cool of the reception area. He was flanked by a fastidiously elegant man in white linen

ousers, a white linen shirt, great shoes—had to be Ital-
an—and carrying a white panama plantation hat.

Porter Banfield in the flesh.

If he had any real life in him, Rosie thought, he'd be an
xtraordinarily handsome man, like his nephew. Instead, he
oked like a tailor's dummy in a leading men's-wear shop.

"Yikes!" she murmured, seeing Chase's face harden to
 gilded mask. He was cursing unabashedly beneath his
reath, so clearly disturbed he didn't trouble to apologize
 Rosie. Porter Banfield, too, appeared seriously taken
ack, to the extent that he backtracked into a beam of
nlight. Not Marley. He rushed forward, dripping bonho-
ie.

"Chase, how good to see you!" He held out his hand,
is distinguished face wreathed in such smiles *he* might
ell have been the uncle. "I was just saying to Porter that
is could very well be the day."

Chase felt obliged by good manners to shake the man's
and, not liking him, never liking him, while Porter Baneld approached, eyes like blue ice cubes. The man who
ad made chaos of Chase's young life, his inheritance,
hree Moons station.

"Chase, how are you?" Porter said through clenched
eth. "Miss Summers!" He acknowledged her with a bow,
 which Rosie responded with a faint smile.

"Why are you here, Porter?" Chase asked bluntly.

"Just visiting." Porter sent his nephew a long cool stare.

"You never come near the place."

"Please, gentlemen, might we not sit down?" Marley
ked nervously.

"I might not be a gentleman, but surely you're not ex-
cting me to scurry away." Rosie's tone condemned him.

Marley turned, beamed at her, his smile false. "Of course
ot, Roslyn. You're very definitely included in every-
ing."

''What's everything?'' Chase's body language was sti
aggressive.

Marley gestured widely. ''Please, let's all sit dow
Maybe a drink?'' He looked around as if expecting Lyn
magically materialize.

''If you want to talk, we'd better go into the lounge,
Chase suggested rather curtly. ''There's no one there th
time of day.''

They were all seated in the empty lounge by the tim
Lyn appeared. She did a double take when she saw Port
Banfield not only under her roof but sitting at the san
table as his estranged nephew. Chase and Marley ordere
a cold beer, Porter Banfield a vodka on the rocks. Ros
another iced tea with a splash of lemon. Better, far bette
to keep a clear head.

''How many more little treasures have you got packe
away, Porter?'' Chase asked after the drinks arrived ar
Lyn had moved off.

''The necklace is a museum piece,'' Porter said in th
manner of a particularly obnoxious curator. ''I dug that i
the summer you went away to boarding school.''

''You mean as soon as my parents died,'' Chase cou
tered.

''I always thought it a mistake that your mother electe
to educate you at home. I realize she was well qualified
do so, but—''

''The intention was always to send me to boardir
school when my parents thought I was ready,'' Chase c
in. ''Anyway, I'm not interested in all that crap. Why didn
you have the necklace melted down if you were so sho
of ready money?''

''The necklace is *far* more valuable as it is,'' Porter Ba
field returned with an icy glare. ''A genuine ancient Egy
tian relic.''

''So you're still sticking to your fantasy,'' Chase mu

red. "You've told Marley you unearthed a cache of relics
n the station." he went on relentlessly. "One by one or
t the same time?"

Porter ignored the sarcasm. "I've always had the sense
f an Egyptian presence," he said, picking up his vodka.
nstead of sipping it, he downed it in rather a hurry. His
e-blue eyes looked beyond them all, as though he saw
ings they didn't. Ancient vistas? Or modern scams. "I
now things."

"No doubt you do," Chase said, dry as a bone. "I un-
erstand you have a great desire to go exploring on Three
Moons, but I don't think the hunt for ancient Egyptian trea-
ure is legitimate, however much you've convinced Dr.
Marley here."

"And Roslyn," Marley hastened to add, seeing their
hances being diminished by the second. "Roslyn is con-
inced, aren't you, my dear?"

"Not at all." Rosie shook her head. "But I'm just as
nxious as you are to give it a go. It may be self-interest,
ut I can turn all of this to good account. I'm a writer, after
ll. I could even aspire to a novel. But the episode with the
ecklace was a bit unsettling." A shudder rippled through
er body.

"Ah, the appearance of the hieroglyphics. Marley told
e about that." Porter gazed at her assessingly. "There's
ore to you, Miss Summers, then meets the eye."

"How could you possibly know?" Chase asked rudely.
Authentic misogynist and all. What about a repeat per-
ormance, just for your benefit? The opening night went so
ell."

"Not again, thank you." Rosie spoke emphatically. "I
ave no intention of touching that necklace again."

"I wasn't going to suggest *you*, Rosie," Chase assured
er. "I wouldn't consider putting you in danger for a mo-

ment. What about you, Porter? Care to put on the necklace
Try it for fun.''

"Fun isn't what it's about," Porter hissed. "The neck
lace calls out for a woman's throat. Obviously Miss Sum
mers was some kind of medium.''

"Obviously a very good one," Chase said, his handsom
mouth wry. "And you want to lead this trip...*uncle?*''

"I'm leading the trip," Marley broke in wrathfull
"Let's get *that* straight.''

"But you don't know where to go, do you?" Chase nee
dled him.

"I'll figure it out when we get there," Marley sai
"Stop tormenting us, Chase. Do we get to go or not?''

But Chase went on taking his time. "Where do you thir
this expedition should head, Porter?" he asked, evident
unimpressed with Marley's claim to leadership.

"Up-country, where I found my other artifacts. I wa
to make it perfectly clear that I believe unequivocally
the Egyptian presence.''

Chase gave an exasperated sigh. "I've half a mind
follow behind you.''

Rosie looked at him. "You're the ideal person to lea
us.''

He smiled. "I appreciate your faith in me, but I'm muc
too busy.''

"Is this a yes?" Marley begged, realizing he wasn't th
boss here at all. A chastening experience.

"It's yes for a month," Chase said in a clipped voic
"A month only. Mick Dempsey will be going along on th
trip.''

Porter, who had been uncrossing one white-trousered le
to arrange it over the other, broke off to sneer. "That o
drunk! He'll be breaking open a bottle of whiskey the m
ment he wakes up.''

"He'd better not," Chase said. "I'll make that a co

dition. Mick was a good man. A man to depend on. He will be again."

"Hear, hear!" Rosie seconded. "Anyway, I'll be there with my eagle eye."

"And who'll keep an eagle eye on you?" Chase asked with mild reproach. "Run into trouble and there's no ambulance on the way."

"You can count on me to watch out for her," Marley said piously.

"Gee, that's a load off my mind, Graeme," Rosie said. "I can look after myself, gentlemen, thank you very much."

"Just to be sure of it, I'm sending Moses," Chase added.

"Moses?" Marley gaped at him in pure amazement.

"Not the biblical Moses," Chase said. "My boyhood mentor. In many respects, my right hand."

"And old Aboriginal stockman," Porter explained to Marley, looking as though he'd been kicked in the teeth. "Born on Three Moons. A tribal elder. He and his entire clan have lived off us forever."

"The other way round, Porter," Chase contradicted in a hard commanding voice. "It's we who've had the benefit of their loyalty, their wisdom and their expertise. I don't know what you've got against Moses. For that matter, I'm amazed you didn't try to get rid of him when you had the chance."

"Because he was too damned useful," Porter answered through clenched teeth, real hatred in his eyes. "If you must send Moses, he'll have to keep up."

"You're joking! Moses keep up?" Chase lifted his dark brows.

"He's an old man," Porter answered scathingly.

"Maybe, but he'll make light work of keeping up with you. And just who have you got up your sleeve this time, Porter?"

"Why would you say that?" Porter's eyes flickered nervously.

"Ah, come off it!" Chase felt weary of all the pretense. "You've always got someone lurking in the wings. Some accomplice. Or *assistant,* as you're wont to call them. Whatever happened to that guy who used to work for you when I was a kid? Looked like a gorilla. What was his name—Skegs? Don't know his full name. All you ever called him was Skegs. I remember my mother loathed him. She was frightened he'd do someone harm."

"That's nonsense." Porter's voice was thin and careful. "I'm surprised no one got around to telling you. Skegs was shot dead on a hunting trip in the Territory years ago. An accident, apparently. Experienced as he was, he got in the way."

"Poor old Skegs! Sounds more like he took a hit."

"I wouldn't know."

Chase laughed, a single ironic bark. "Good scapegoat material. What line of business was he in, exactly?"

"Ancient history, Chase," Porter clearly didn't want to discuss it.

"And he disappeared. You made sure of that."

"He didn't disappear." Porter's eyes were like flint. "We...lost contact."

Chase nodded. "He was no longer useful."

"I'm sure Marley and Miss Summers aren't interested in this," Porter said bitterly.

"That's because they don't know the full picture," he said equably. "I don't know it, either. Nobody does. Except maybe Moses, and he's not telling."

Porter gave a splintery laugh. "Moses is an old Aborigine. He knows nothing."

"He knows about you, Porter. Knows you're dangerous."

"I do what I have to do. You have my word that our

search is for the site of the ancient Egyptian village I believe is on the property. Our family has always locked the door on this for some reason. But they *knew*. Old Moses, too. My grandfather, your great-grandfather, gathered a good deal of information on the subject.''

''Where is it?'' Chase's eyes gleamed pure amber.

''Your father wasn't interested. I inherited it.''

''Or simply took it? Never mind that now,'' he said as Porter opened his mouth to protest. ''When do you propose to get under way?''

''Why, as soon as possible,'' Marley jumped in, frustrated at being closed out of the conversation that held Rosie enthralled.

''You don't really need Miss Summers,'' Chase said.

''You bet they do.'' Rosie frowned at him. ''You're not going to leave me out of this, Chase. I'm raring to go.''

''You're too impulsive for your own good.''

''Give me a few days to organize it,'' Marley said, eyes now afire. ''We'll need provisions. Roslyn, may I leave the foodstuffs to you?''

''Hey, organizing the foodstuffs isn't what I'm best at.''

Marley curled his hand over hers. ''Women are so much better at that kind of thing. I'll have to get my scientific equipment together. Suitable clothing. A few days, a week at the outside.''

''Then let's make it a week,'' Chase said. ''I've invited Miss Summers to be my guest at Three Moons. I'll take her back with me in the morning.''

Marley's eyes bulged like golf balls. ''You mean she'll be there on her *own?*''

''You're invited too, Graeme,'' Rosie said, renouncing the magic as if it were madness. ''Graeme's invited, isn't he, Chase?''

Mockery spilled into his eyes. ''Certainly, if he wishes to come.''

But Porter Banfield wouldn't have it. "Three Moons is a long way from town, Marley. We can't organize this trip with you out at the station. Let Miss Summers go, by all means. In fact, she'll be one of the few people accorded visitor status. You're needed here. We have things to plan."

"But I can't simply allow Roslyn to go off on her own," Marley persisted.

"Why not?" *You bloody old hypocrite,* Chase thought. *You're livid with jealousy, that's all.*

"Well...I know times have changed, but still..." Marley made a wild jerky movement with his hand.

"What do you think is going to happen to her?" Chase asked with some sarcasm. *As though it's any of your business.* "Miss Summers will be as safe with me as if she were living back home."

"I don't know," Marley was far from happy, and he didn't hide it.

"I'll be fine, Graeme," Rosie assured him, her voice not absolutely steady. "Think of it as a little vacation I'm taking."

Except there was no way it was going to be that.

Six o'clock the next morning. Another brilliant cloudless day in paradise. The cooling breeze coming through the open French doors was fragrant with the frangipani that dotted the garden. There was a brisk knock on Rosie's door.

"Are you up, Miss Summers?" a familiar voice called. "Hope you're ready."

Ready! Rosie laughed aloud, looking at the two pieces of luggage standing by the bed, one medium, one small. She always traveled light. If truth be known, she'd been ready and waiting for half an hour or more, so full of excitement and anticipatory pleasure she'd had to take periodic deep calming breaths. Despite Graeme's sizable misgivings, she knew Chase Banfield was a civilized man who could be trusted not to jump her bones. But maybe if he was invited to… Rosie gulped.

She crossed the small bedroom in a couple of strides, threw open the door, smiled up at him cheerfully. "Hi!"

His remarkable topaz eyes lit with equal parts pleasure and amusement. "Why, Rosie, such pizzazz!" His gaze ran appreciatively from her V-neck sleeveless olive-green T-shirt and the scarf of tiger-print silk around her neck to her khaki cargo pants and the stout boots on her feet. Not ordinary boots. The color and shine of an eggplant. The mane of orange, amber, gold hair was scraped back from her face to hang in a single braided rope down her back. She wore no makeup as far as he could see—she didn't need any—except for some mulberry gloss on her beautiful wide mouth. "You look great! Like we're off on a trip to the Amazonian jungle."

"Well, I figure I can handle just about anything dressed like this. It's my working uniform."

The bracket that edged his mouth deepened. "I never met anyone who could make a uniform so totally individual. I hope you've got a hat," he said matter-of-factly. "You need plenty of sunblock, too."

"Got it."

"Where's your hat? I hope it's got a good wide brim."

Rosie half turned away from him. "If you're willing to wait a moment, I'll put it on."

"All right. But we do have to get going."

She hurried to the wardrobe, pulled out an olive-green straw hat, a kind of sombrero, almost as big as an umbrella. She crammed it on her head, turned around.

He laughed. "Too fancy. Where did you get it—from a Mexican *bandito?*"

"I thought it looked rather fetching." She took it off, smoothed her hair.

"It does, but I've got something more suitable for you in the vehicle."

"You're kidding! You bought a hat for me?"

"It's a cream *akubra*. A little present."

"Aren't you nice." Unaccountably, his thoughtfulness nearly brought her to tears.

"Well, come along, Rosie," he said briskly. "Is that your luggage?" He looked past her to cases by the dark teak bed, hung with mosquito netting.

Rosie nodded, making a final check of the room. "I can carry them."

"I'm sure you can, but I figure I'm a bit stronger." He moved past her into the small bedroom, filling it with his vigor and vitality, picking up her luggage, the smaller piece stowed beneath his arm. "I should warn you, Marley is downstairs waiting to see you off."

"Gracious!" Rosie was startled and looked it. But then, Marley was the expedition leader, after all. It would be nothing personal. She hoped.

"Tell him not to worry," Chase joked. "Tell him you're wearing your chastity belt."

"I've got a couple of good ones, too, but I left them at home. But I know you're a gentleman, Rhett Banfield. I'd stake my life on it."

"So you don't think I'm capable of ravishing you?"

"No—not without an invitation."

His laugh was rich and deep. "Then maybe I should start praying you extend one."

She gave him a sidelong glance, provocative yet vulnerable. A welcome glint of mischief.

"Prayers *can* be answered when the circumstances are right," she said gently.

CHAPTER SIX

THREE MOONS HOMESTEAD was reached by a long private road that ran through as exotic a landscape as anyone could wish for. The country was awash with incredibly diverse vegetation—towering palms, lush ferns from giants to delicate little fronds that formed a thick ground cover, tropical orchids that quivered in the breeze. Many, many dendrobiums, including the rich purple Cooktown orchid, the state flower. Hardy bromeliads, agaves and aloes of extraordinary shape, some like swan's necks. Brilliantly colored foliage that rivaled the green dramatic staghorns and elkhorns fixed to tall tree trunks. Shrubs covered with masses of blossom, flowering vines cascading everywhere, the bright violet-blue of morning glories, the pink, white, scarlet, purple, sunshine yellow of trumpet flowers, rain-forest trees of gigantic proportion. A jungle, yet not a jungle. Inspired chaos. Too open to be called rain forest. In some places, the ground was bright with hot sunshine and the dazzle of huge butterflies and iridescent winged insects; in others, the canopy of trees was so dense that everything was as quiet, as calm, as shadowy, as an unlit cathedral. Birdsong floated from the green vaulted ceiling, while flights of colorful little lorikeets skimmed across their path, sunlight catching their jeweled wings.

"This is really beautiful," Rosie breathed, her expressive face transmitting her pleasure.

"It was paradise for a while," he conceded, fighting down the helpless rage that was always in him. Maybe if he'd been any other kid, if he hadn't had Porter for a guardian, he'd have received counseling to help him through that terrible trauma. As it was, he'd had to fight all his nightmares alone. At boarding school he'd taken quite a while to make friends, never letting anyone get close to him. But he was big and strong. A natural athlete. And he was smart. Not even the worst bully had entertained the idea of making him a mark. Then the genuine friendship, the mateship of the other boys, had started the thaw.

Sensitive Rosie, her ears finely attuned to him, became aware of his thoughts. "I'm sorry, Chase. I realize *sorry* is a totally inadequate word."

"It helps," he said briefly, changing his tone. "I was allowed to run wild here. My mother was always worried about snakes. But snakes aren't a problem unless you tread on them or threaten them."

"Wouldn't that be easily enough done?" She tried to imagine herself confronted by a taipan, her legs not fully operative.

"My father never let the home grounds become too overgrown. There was always a certain amount of clearing. After that, after his death, Porter left me to my chances. Having saved me, he'd apparently exhausted all his benevolent impulses. But getting back to snakes, they're usually more frightened of us than we are of them. They know instinctively to get out of the way."

"Which suits me fine," Rosie said. "Because I intend to go walking all around here. It's fascinating—it's wild and yet it's not."

Chase nodded. "I know. It looks very natural, but it's evolved over many long years. As you can imagine, in the beginning all this was dense jungle. Virtually impenetrable in some places, and it's still very wild where your expedition's going. All the women in our family took their turns in adding to and maintaining the woodland near the homestead. It's not a garden in the normal sense of the word. It's too big for that. It's actually an edge of the rain-forest habitat, which is why the lantana has always been a problem. You would have noticed it as we were coming in, great towering banks. We keep it there, under control, because it brings the butterflies. Nearer the house, there's a bit more formality. Even Porter wouldn't allow the home grounds to slip back to jungle. If he loves nothing else, he loves beauty.''

''I realize that,'' she murmured, looking around, entranced. ''This is like finding myself in a dream.''

''It is.'' Just being on Three Moons filled him with the pride of belonging. ''But life isn't a dream. It can be shattered by fate.'' His voice moved on again to a more conversational tone. ''The station's name comes from three wonderful lagoons on the property. The first, but not the main one, is coming up. It's actually the smallest of the three, but it was chosen for its extraordinary tranquillity when the homestead was sited.''

''I can see it now.'' Through the all-encompassing trees, Rosie had a view of glassy-smooth dark-green water and a wooden rowboat. As they drove slowly around the bend, the whole beautiful moon-shaped pool spread out before them, glittering in the sunlight.

Rosie caught her breath. Flowering bushes and great clumps of white arum lilies ringed it, and toward the center the sequined surface was partially covered with the most beautiful blue-lotus water lilies, native to Australia and north Africa, where it was the sacred flower of ancient Egypt. In the shallows someone had placed stepping stones to bring people closer to the water, and surely the huge sculptured boulders with tall water grasses growing beside them had not occurred naturally, but been put in place to enormous esthetic effect. It looked Japanese to Rosie's eyes, and as if to confirm that observation, she spied a tall-tiered stone pagoda rising amid the miraculous vegetation at the far end of the pool.

Chase explained, "My grandfather had a friend, a military man, who was stationed in Japan for a time, and in fact married a Japanese girl. Her father was a master gardener and a master businessman, I might add. It was he who developed the vision for the home lagoon. He never saw it. It was all done from photographs. A kind of peace offering after the war. When you have the opportunity to walk around, you'll notice a few ornamental stone objects amid the scenery. On the north side of the lagoon—you can't quite see it for the tree ferns—there's a *torii* gate framing a little Shinto shrine. I often go there to think. It's very peaceful. My mother loved it, and I often imagine her there. I think if I sit very still, I might catch her standing in the shade just looking at me."

Rosie swallowed the hard lump in her throat. "Maybe she does. Maybe God leaves little doors and windows ajar, so our loved ones can slip through from time to time."

"It's a nice thought, Rosie," he said quietly, sounding as though he didn't believe it at all.

"Life!" She sighed. "I've learned to be afraid even in the midst of the beauty and wonder. Death is always waiting around the corner. I saw terrible things in East Timor and Afghanistan. Starvation, shocking injuries, death, hopeless, helpless grief. Defeat. And the children—the children—the most vulnerable of victims." She rocked a little in her seat, momentarily closing her eyes. "I've seen our people sob with the pain—doctors, nurses, soldiers, reporters. None of us can forget. I grew up in a privileged environment, as you did, but we both know about horror. It's touched us both."

"I guess so." His deep sigh matched her own. "Tragedy can tap on anyone's door; blast its way into the safest life, not just the disaster areas where life seems to mean nothing.

just hope we don't have our nightmares on the same night.''

''If so, remind me to flip over.'' She tried a little laugh, but it didn't work.

''What does that mean, Rosie?'' He cast a swift glance at her that had her heart thumping.

''Oh, nothing. That's what I usually do. Moan to myself, then flip over.''

''Anyone on the other side?''

''I frightened them all away.''

''Same here.''

''Someone's going to be there for you, Chase. The right woman.''

''The one who's worth the wait?''

''Your own private miracle.'' She broke off as the homestead, which had been all but hidden in its grove of trees, palms and great tumbling waterfalls of bougainvillea, suddenly revealed itself.

A tropical mansion, a *huge* house, yet it had minimal impact on its glorious site, so marvelously did the landscape flow toward it. For one thing, the house was expressed in dark timber, clearly Southeast Asian in concept, with a dark-brown hipped roof, the hips extending far beyond the balconies. Timber had been used for the construction and dark-stained timber formed the balustrades. It was like some wonderful Javanese pavilion, except instead of a thatched roof, Rosie was sure the homestead's roof was cyclone-proof. She could detect absolutely no trace of the fire on the house or its lush surroundings, but then, it had happened twenty years ago, and this was the tropics.

''I don't know what I was expecting...'' Rosie was fascinated, trying to take it all in.

''What?'' He sounded amused.

''A mansion, certainly, but more like the other historic homesteads I've seen. Memories of Home. The British

Isles. Georgian, Victorian, even a French château. This is a tropical house.''

''As it should be.''

''I agree. I think it's marvelous. A fantasy tree house. You're on it before you even know it's there.''

He smiled at her, well satisfied. ''I'm glad you like it.'' He circled slowly, then parked the four-wheel drive at the base of a short flight of stairs crowned with singularly beautiful tiles. ''We'll leave your luggage. Roi will get it.''

''Roy?'' she questioned as they stood in the brilliant wash of sunlight.

He smiled down at her. ''Roi is part Malay, part Indian. He's been with us since he was abandoned and left to die in the jungle as a small child. His family obviously didn't want him. My grandfather found him and brought him home. He's been here ever since. That was nearly fifty years ago. Even then, he had great dignity, hence the name—Roi as in *king*—but we pronounced it *Roy*. My grandfather saw to it he had a good education, a real chance at life, but he always wanted to serve the family. I think he saw it as his sworn duty. About twelve years ago he found himself 'a suitable wife' those were *his* words. She's part Chinese, part Aboriginal. Together they run the house. They're also my friends, and I wouldn't part with them for the world. Welcome to Three Moons, Roslyn Summers.''

Rosie smiled up at him. ''And thank you so much for inviting me. I'm just so full of…joy.'' It was true. That was exactly the word.

The sound of their arrival alerted someone in the house. A tall, slim, dark-skinned man appeared, long dark hair tied back in a ponytail, a smile illuminating his rather austere face. His physical appearance favored his Indian blood— the finely cut features, the large black lustrous eyes. Chase introduced him as a friend, not a servant, which Roi, from his demeanor, was obviously trying to be, and Rosie found herself wondering where he had been at the time of the fire. It was apparent that he worshiped Chase, his manner displaying the deep loyalty and love that was totally missing in the family relationship.

All three walked up the stairs together, Rosie tripping a little ahead in her excitement. At the top of the stairs, she glanced along the broad veranda, recoiling in sheer terror when her eyes fell on a great crocodile, jaws gaping, splayed out on the glossy dark timber planks.

"My God!" She fell back frantically against Chase; thoroughly disconcerted, he threw his arms around her.

"What is it?" he demanded, looking as if he was going to go forward and grapple with all comers.

"The crocodile, Chase." Roi was the first to divine what it was all about. "It's not real, Miss Summers. Not real," he repeated for emphasis, smiling at her reassuringly. "It's a carving designed to look like the real thing. A spirit to protect the house."

"A live one couldn't have done the job better!" she said when she was able.

"I'm sorry, Rosie." Chase looked his dismay. "It's been here so long I hardly see it. I should have warned you."

The fear she'd suffered was almost worth it to have his arms protectively around her. "It's an absolutely smashing reproduction."

"I agree," he said wryly. "Done in the Philippines. It's as Roi explained. A guardian to ward off evil spirits."

"*Now* you tell me."

"I said I'm sorry."

"We wouldn't have had you frightened for the world," Roi seconded with great sincerity, watching her closely for any further reaction. "Tea!" he exclaimed. "Tea will make you feel better. We have our own very fine tea. Chase is partner in a plantation. I'll go ahead and arrange for refreshments. You are most welcome here."

"Thank you, Roi." Rosie smiled at him, grateful for his sensitivity and trying to hide how very shaken she was. If this was how she reacted when she laid eyes on a wooden crocodile, what was she going to do when she saw a live one waddling toward her?

"Damn and blast!" Chase was still blaming himself "Why don't we sit down for a while?"

"Later," she said, navigating her way down the veranda without bumping into anything, "when Roi arrives with the tea. I want to see the house. This wonderful house. I might even pat old Methuselah here while I'm at it. I wouldn' like to fall out with a guardian spirit."

Even patting the crocodile was an unsettling experience "Stay, boy," she said while Chase laughed.

"I forgot how terribly lifelike it is."

"Especially peeking out from the golden canes." The magnificent ferns sprouted from huge glazed pots the length of the veranda.

"Poor Rosie!" His topaz eyes gleamed. "Do you want me to move it?"

"Not even temporarily. Just make sure it doesn't stir."

"Don't worry—I'd protect you."

"I'll bet that's the real reason you keep it around."

"So women can jump into my arms?"

"Sure." She glanced around. "You've probably had some marvelous parties here."

He shook his head. "My grandparents and my parents were the ones who used to have parties. Porter didn't have a friendly disposition. And I've been too damned busy for much of a social life."

"You mean you've never brought a girlfriend here?" she asked. Of course he had. Lucky girl.

"I didn't say I haven't had one or two parties," he murmured. "But everyone knows about the crocodile. It's been there forever."

So where was the guardian spirit at the time of the fire? Facing the wrong way obviously, or the arsonist, if there'd been one, had worked from *inside*. It didn't bear thinking about, yet doubts did exist. She didn't like Porter Banfield, but he couldn't be that bad. Could he? Nothing was impossible. One had only to read the papers.

The interior of the house was stunning. A majestic central section, a soaring double space like a magnificent lobby with a gallery supported by massive timber columns encircling the upper mezzanine level on three sides. The columns had to be twenty feet high, each elaborately carved and decorated. The floor was covered in large tiles with a golden-orange cast and scattered with rugs, Southeast Asian furnishings and artwork everywhere. At first glance, it seemed to be the country home of a Thai prince.

"A girl would marry you for the house alone," she said, staring upward, wondering about that west wing.

He laughed. "You think that's all I have to offer?"

"Hey, it would probably be enough," she joked.

"Not everyone likes it, but that's neither here nor there. It reflects the taste and wanderings of *my* family. Including me. I know Southeast Asia well. Australia's in Southeast Asia, after all. This place is very appropriate for our climate."

"I feel like swooning, it's so beautiful. And so big!" Rosie lifted her arms as though about to take flight. "And the bedrooms are around the gallery?"

He nodded. "I'll take you there. You might want to freshen up after the trip. Roi always times things just right."

They climbed the staircase together, then walked along the delightful wide gallery hung with beautiful oriental panels framed in black lacquer, with tall ebony cabinets in between, decorated with jade and semiprecious stones, painted and gilded with trees, birds and flowers. Although it was a very hot day threatening a thunderstorm, it was beautifully cool in here, the breeze wafting through the opened doors leading onto the verandas. Their footsteps were noiseless on the long Chinese runner that must have been custom-made because of its extreme length.

Chase paused outside a double carved door. "I hope you're happy here, but you can change if you want." He stood back, waiting for her to precede him into what was by any standard a very large room. "You have an excellent view of the lagoon," he said. "At my end of the house, the palms have grown so much I mostly see fronds."

Rosie looked around her with fascination. Such wonders in the middle of a jungle! "I'm struck dumb."

"That'll be the day," he said with a grin.

"I feel like an Indonesian princess." She mimicked a dance she'd seen in Bali.

"I recognize the red hair."

A beautiful embroidered red-silk robe lay on the teak bed with its beautiful carved headboard, the pillows and coverings pristine white, as was the long mosquito netting draped from a teak canopy. A daybed with scarlet and gold cushions was positioned near the open doors. An altar chest sat at the end of the bed, two matching cabinets with brass hinges on either side, complete with golden lamps. There was also a small oriental table with two matching chairs, a vase of brightly colored flowers and leaves, and dominating the opposite wall, a superb large European painting. A classical landscape of a beautiful young woman with three attendants, one combing her long flowing titian hair, another holding a yellow damask-silk robe around her partially naked figure. A young boy in a white toga, a wreath around his head, held up a mirror. A marble bath was in the background, the canvas shot through with golden-green light from the tracery of trees.

"Such a magnificent painting." She went to stand before

it, trying to read the signature of the artist, stunned when she made it out. "And our classical maiden has red hair?"

"Why do you think I put it there?" He looked down at her, tugged the end of her braid. "Up until yesterday, an equally large painting of a splendid Bengal tiger filled that spot."

"How absolutely charming you are," she said, feeling he was bringing an intoxicating fulfillment to her life. "Tell me, does that tiger have your eyes?"

He made a little dismissive sound in his throat, a soft growl. "I can't say. He's in profile. Why this 'tiger eyes' nonsense? Mick's wife used to say the same thing."

"Topaz eyes are very unusual." She nodded. "Very rare."

"Do they signify a wild beast inside?"

"Not you. You have a wonderfully sweet disposition."

"You don't know me, Rosie," he said with a certain grimness.

"I know enough to come with you willingly. Eagerly. Wouldn't you call that a sign of trust and confidence?"

"It could be naiveté on your part. Come into my parlor, said the tiger to the—"

"Silly goat," she supplied with a wry smile. "I don't think so." Everything about him drew her to him.

"Thanks for that, Rosie. Your opinion is important to me. But I must tell you I get my bad days when I have to battle the demons. I love this house. It's part of me, part of my family, but sometimes *I* feel like burning it down."

Of course! Why wouldn't he? Still, she hastened to say, "Chase, *don't!*"

"You can understand it, can't you?" He met her eyes unwaveringly.

"Indeed I can. There's so much grief here. But there's love, too. And guardian spirits."

"The spirits talk." He moved about the room, almost prowled.

"Do they? They'd never harm you," she offered.

"No, I know that."

"You want a wife, Chase Banfield. Spiritual unity with the right woman. Lots of kids. You want to fill up this marvelous house. Let every corner resound with laughter."

"It's been starved of it for a long time." A magnificent wasteland, he thought but didn't say.

"Which is why you have to change your life. I'm serious about this."

"Easier said than done." He smiled at her earnestness, giving a slight shrug. "Some people, especially women, think the house is haunted, which it is. A tragedy happened here. An unsolved tragedy."

"Then we've got to solve it," Rosie said, upset by the expression on his face. "I'll help you. I'm a very good investigative journalist and, I hope, your friend."

He jammed both his hands into his pockets, his face a mask. "All the evidence has gone, Rosie. I told you."

"And *nothing* was ever discovered? An accelerant?"

"Just two bodies," he responded grimly. "But let's not talk about that. I want you to enjoy yourself, not immerse yourself in an old mystery. And don't talk to Mick about it," he warned—an order, not a request. "Mick was Dad's friend, as Bridget was my mother's." He paused for a moment, shrugged. "Neither of them took to Porter. He never attempted to make himself likable. He's just one of those people who don't care for other people."

"So to compensate, he cares for objects? How sad not to care for a living creature!"

"And money," Chase shot back. "Don't forget money. One can't come by fine works of art without money. It's absolutely essential if you're going to play the game."

"So he's an art dealer?" She bit her lip thoughtfully.

"Yes, he is. He carries on a legitimate business, at which he's very good. I haven't the slightest doubt he's involved in black-market trade, too. It's alive and well. One day he'll get caught and there'll be no one to help him. But Porter's no fool. He's a clever man, in his own way. My father always used to say he had a wonderful 'eye.' Porter could have gone places with a different identity. I think he found being a Banfield too hard to handle. You didn't know my father. You talk about tigers! He was a lion of a man. There are portraits of my parents in my study. I'll show you later on." He crossed the room at an elegant lope. "So you're happy to be here?"

"Ecstatic." Rosie joined her hands beneath her chin, her thick plait falling over her shoulder.

He smiled, thinking he wanted not only her body but her soul. "Come down when you're ready. Roi will have tea set out, and you can meet Leila. She's very shy with strangers but wonderfully sweet and competent."

Leila was an exotic little creature, hardly more than five feet, many years younger than her husband, with a mop of curly black hair, smooth round features, dark almond eyes, café-au-lait skin. Her voice was as melodious as her husband's, slightly singsong. It was apparent to Rosie from the way they looked and spoke to each other that they had a good marriage, though she learned later from Leila in a very private conversation that they wouldn't be blessed with children because of the sexual abuse Leila had suffered at the hands of a relative from whom Roi had rescued her—thus accounting for the white slash of a scar through his right eyebrow. She was a damaged little soul who had mended with very tender loving care.

Between them, Roi and Leila had prepared such delicious and plentiful "refreshments" there could be no room for lunch. Delicate little sandwiches with tasty-looking fillings, all the crusts cut off, and a whole range of beautiful little cakes, even the traditional scones with apricot and mango jam and whipped cream. Everything was arranged on a small circular table Roi had drawn up, covered with a spotless embroidered lacy linen cloth and a beautiful tea service that might or might not have been Aynsley. She could tip up her cup later to check.

"This looks even better than afternoon tea at the Peninsula," Rosie said, remembering those occasions at the great hotel in Hong Kong. "Thank you so much, Roi and Leila. It's lovely."

Husband and wife beamed at her and floated away with identical smiles.

"They really look after you, don't they?" Rosie, who had a great capacity for enjoying herself, was reveling in this glorious indolence.

"I need for nothing," Chase answered simply.

"Except maybe someone of your own." She sat back, regarding him.

"That's the plan, but plans don't always work out."

"True. But we have to keep making them."

"You think you could settle to this life?"

She hid her shock carefully. "Do I have to make a decision right now?"

"No. First we each have to learn more about the other."

A statement she agreed with. "I understand that perfectly," she said, laughing softly, "but you must admit we've made one heck of a start."

"I think you're very good at it," he said. "Very good at connecting with people." He nodded. "Roi and Leila are greatly taken with you, too. It isn't always the case."

"You mean Leila doesn't always cut the crusts off sandwiches?" she joked.

"I mean, she tends to stay well out of sight. She's like a butterfly fluttering in the air. Try to catch it and it will fly away. Stand perfectly still and it'll land right on your shoulder.''

Rosie felt a little stab in the heart. ''That's rather lovely. As Leila is herself. She need never be nervous of me. And how does Roi show his feelings—for or against?''

''Roi's quite different. He's another of the guardian spirits. He sticks around. His manner is always extremely courteous but not quite so solicitous.''

''Well, they've got my vote, both of them. Shall I do the honors?'' Rosie's hand was already reaching out for the white bone-china pot with its cobalt blue and gold decorations.

''Certainly. I want to see what you think of our tea.'' Chase leaned forward. ''As Roi said, I'm a partner in a plantation. It's on the Atherton Tableland and really starting to take off. One of these days we might take a trip over there.''

Rosie looked at him with interest. ''I'd enjoy that. I could even do an article, if you want the publicity.''

''Maybe that's why I'm asking you,'' he murmured with a carefree smile. ''You haven't figured me out yet, Rosie.''

She felt the sizzle of that smile to the roots of her hair. ''I will. I've got to keep you talking. Give you the opportunity to unload all that pain behind your eyes.''

Twenty relaxed minutes went by, during which Chase told her all about the workings of his tea plantation, thinking she had a powerful flair for asking intelligent questions.

''No way I could stay here and keep my figure!'' Rosie declared at one point.

''I'm sure you could.'' The atmosphere between them was comfortable, but with a tantalizing undercurrent of excitement. Chase let his eyes roam over her, feeling a jolt of sheer pleasure. The sunlight made her white skin almost translucent and electrified the marigold curls that had broken out around her head, despite the heavy braid. It was enormously good to see her sitting there, so strangely familiar in his home. Just meeting her had somehow enriched his life. "You're on the skinny side, if anything," he considered. "Except for those beautiful womanly breasts."

"I can live with it." She smiled complacently. "Because I'm healthy. But I've done the research and the interviews. I've seen the frightening results of taking things too far. The eating disorders, like anorexia. It's the models and the magazines that point kids in the wrong direction. They have obligations. They have to become more responsible."

"So why don't you get after them?"

"I do my bit," she said seriously. "It's hard to make young girls listen when some mothers are so heavily influenced. I've interviewed intelligent women who've put daughters as young as eight on strict diets because they were supposedly getting too chubby. My own mother used to agonize because I didn't have the right body. Too tall, too gawky, all legs! She had a terrible time buying clothes for me that would actually fit."

Chase wondered if Rosie's mother had realized the hurt she'd caused while her daughter was growing up.

"It still bothers you that you're tall and very slender?" He frowned.

"Not really. I think I've found my own style."

"You've turned stimulating and individual into an art form," he agreed. "Now, are you up to a look around the station?" he asked, moving around the table to hold her chair. "Leave that. Leila will take care of it. You can't steal her thunder."

"Just trying to be helpful." Rosie stood up, feeling a thrill of heat as their bodies almost came into contact.

"There are a few things I need to do," Chase said, moving back as though he, too, felt the current between them. "But I don't think you'll be bored."

"I'm never bored," she told him. "Will we ride?"

"Horseback?" He glanced down at her, his expression softening at the spray of freckles.

"You bet. I'm really looking forward to it, unless you need to use your vehicle."

"Whatever makes you happy." His mouth curved in an indulgent smile.

"Horses, then. I've brought boots and you've provided me with my *akubra*."

"In which you look splendid. Now, I hope you haven't been lying to me about your prowess on a horse."

"I don't believe you've *got* a horse I can't ride," Rosie returned smartly, her hands thrust into her pockets.

He laughed outright. "Rosie, it's a mistake to talk big like that."

"I'm not talking brumbies," she qualified. "Not one of your station bone-breakers."

"As if I'd ever put you on an animal like that," he muttered. "Go get your boots on. You can spend the afternoon seeing how I live."

"Wonderful!" She took off sleekly, as fluid in motion as a gazelle, running up the staircase, along the gallery until she was lost to sight.

How I live! he thought. For a moment Chase was transfixed by his thoughts. He could never draw Rosie into the dark places of his soul. He was a man whose mind had been branded, just as he branded his own cattle. Though he'd fought the good fight, survived, restored the station to its former high standing, that brain of his just couldn't clock out. The damage had been done. It was there forever. His parents' horrific death had changed his life. The terrible flames, the charred bodies, the screams that periodically brought him shaking and covered in sweat out of the deep sleep of physical exhaustion. Nothing so far had set him free of it. He loved his home with a passion, but he knew it was a place of secrets.

Bright creature that she was, Rosie couldn't be part of that, even if she wanted to. Roslyn Summers, award-winning journalist, was destined for better things, her slender feet set on a different path.

But there was great excitement here, and the promise of real friendship.

CHAPTER SEVEN

IT WAS A MARVELOUS TIME for Rosie, a time spent alone and uninterrupted with Chase. First they made a circuit of the main compound in an open Jeep, viewing the substantial outbuildings grouped at a distance from the homestead and masked by the same beautiful trees that surrounded the house. Chase pointed out all areas of interest—the administration building that housed the clerical offices, the comfortable bungalows for the office manager and his wife and another for the Three Moons overseer and his family. The general stockmen's accommodation looked to Rosie a bit like army barracks. She admired recreation rooms equipped for pool or table tennis, including even a small gym, the stables complex, the saddles shed, machinery rooms and sheds for vehicles. There was yet another large shed storing enough food rations to feed an army, as well as the station butcher shop, with a huge refrigeration room beside it. Three Moons was clearly an operation of considerable magnitude.

Afterward, refreshed by a beautiful drink made by Leila out of native limes, which tasted to Rosie far better than any she'd ever bought in city shops, they drove to the stables where an Aboriginal groom had already saddled up the horses. A magnificent bay stallion for Chase, which he sat like a centaur, and a bright chestnut mare, sweet-tempered but not too gentle, for Rosie, who displayed from the very first moment that she knew what she was about.

"You look great!" Chase's smile flashed. He was well satisfied that he had an accomplished rider on his hands.

Rosie leaned forward to stroke the mare's satiny neck. "I had my own plump little piebald by the time I was six. My father bought her for me. Owning a pony was my little-girl dream. Dad taught me to ride. My mother was so worried I was going to break a limb, which I did—an arm— but riding out with Dad was a great ritual in our lives."

"Your mother didn't ride with you?" He kept his ears tuned for the fine nuances.

"Strangely enough, my mother doesn't like horses. She thinks they're stupid animals. But then, she doesn't understand them and they know it. I suspect she used to get sick and tired of Dad's and my adventures. He was so busy for much of the time. What free time he had she wanted for herself. We used to disappear for hours, and I realize now that she probably resented that."

"You love your father." He eyed her thoughtfully from the new cream *akubra* to the old, well-polished riding boots.

"As you love yours. All through my childhood and adolescence, he was the light and joy of my life. I haven't been quite as close to my mother, but she's there for me when I need her." She didn't say her father had always made her feel beautiful, whereas occasionally her mother made her feel she was a disgrace to the family.

"Well, that's all right, then." Chase's voice held understanding; despite that, Rosie was glad to change the subject.

Thirty minutes later they were out of the small settlement and into the Vastness!

For a moment Rosie thought her heart would burst with pleasure and excitement. The mighty Outback.

Rosie slowed her horse, contemplating the vision. Spread out in front of her dazzled eyes were unimaginable distances. Great open savannahs waving an ocean of wheat-

colored grasses under a glorious cobalt sky. She saw herds
of drought-tolerant Brahmin cattle all across the landscape,
easily recognizable from their prominent dewlap and hump,
dots of dark gray on a vast multicolored canvas. Beyond
the shimmering savannahs rose timberlands to the horizon,
where it was easy to imagine humans, not only cattle, getting lost. To the east, faraway, were the larkspur hills; to
the north and west, wild country visited even in the new
millennium by only a few people, teeming with wildlife
and lots of surprises.

Gongora. The name sprang readily to her mind. The wild
river with its spirit-guardian crocodiles. The site, or so Porter Banfield would have everyone believe, of an ancient
Egyptian village.

She felt happy, her mind lucid, yet she somehow knew
they would be confronting danger. Enemies within and
without. Porter was too avid for her to doubt it. Most probably he was using them as cynically and calculatingly as
he used his rich clients.

"This is glorious!" she said, overcome by the immen-
sity, the beauty and grandeur, as she always was whenever
she visited the great desert landscapes of the Interior.

"It is." Chase narrowed his eyes against the mirage-
quivering air. Through her eyes he was seeing his home all
over again. "But it's no place for the weak or fainthearted.
It can be a cruel land. Only the strong survive."

She turned sideways in the saddle to look at him, expecting the now-familiar electric tingling. There was a kind
of fierceness beneath his pride, the indomitable will not to
give in. The years of his youth must have been very hard,
struggling to bring a once-renowned cattle station back
from the brink. No wonder there was hostility between
nephew and uncle. Perhaps hatred on the uncle's side. She
thought she'd seen more than a tinge of it. Porter Banfield
was such a joyless man.

They rode on in perfect accord, Rosie listening with interest as Chase identified plants and shrubs that yielded lifesaving bush tucker. He pointed out the ribbons of sand that in the Wet turned into dangerous rushing streams; large patches of colorful blooms rich with nectar grew close by— native grevilleas, wild hibiscus, unnamed blossoms of many kinds. Birds accompanied them on their ride, lending the scene tremendous animation. The brilliant green budgerigars, twittering and swooping, almost too swiftly to be properly appreciated, the slower flight of the gorgeous parrots, the explosions of white corellas like giant blossoms on silver-gray shrubs. The ever-curious kangaroos appeared from time to time, pausing to hold up their gentle, rather comical heads before bounding away.

Midafternoon they rode into a camp along one of the freshwater creeks. Half a dozen stockmen rose to welcome them, inviting them to enjoy fresh damper from the camp oven and billy tea. Chase introduced each man in turn, and Rosie went down the line smiling and nodding, feeling a little bit like a royal. New faces, black and white, all dressed alike, all obviously good friends, bonded like brothers. And she got to meet Chase's boyhood mentor, Moses, who charmed her in a minute. Moses had real charisma and the dignified presence of a tribal elder, repository of tribal wisdom and religious beliefs that were embedded in the landscape. Moses's ebony skin was crisscrossed with deep crevasses and a few bad scars, but nothing could detract from his gentle smile and liquid black farseeing eyes. As he removed his battered old *akubra,* Rosie saw with pleasure his high crown of pure white hair; it added a striking note to his appearance. This was Moses, part retainer, part family friend, the most loyal of them all. He was also the consummate bushman, Chase's ''eyes'' on their trip upcountry. Rosie felt they'd be far safer with the spry Moses along than they'd ever be without him. The first Australians, the Aborigines, were bound to the land. They had possessed the Australian landscape since time immemorial, surviving and flourishing for millennia before the white man arrived on their shores to change tribal life forever. One could weep for that alone, Rosie thought.

It was late afternoon by the time they decided to ride back. Chase was concerned about her comfort, saying that because she hadn't been on a horse in a few years, she might become stiff.

In reality she was a little tired, but what greeted them as they came down on the second of the station's namesake lagoons sent her spirits soaring.

"This is your lucky day," Chase told her, urging their horses into the shade of the trees. "You're about to witness a ballet by our bush's finest dancers. At least of the bird world. Native corroborees are something else again."

They dismounted very quietly and squatted down to wait, Rosie with a sense of anticipation and wonder.

In the brolgas came, the blue cranes with their rufous heads, legs outstretched and slanted slightly forward, for all the world like aircraft dropping their undercarriages. The glide to the water completed, they began to flap their wings over and over, gaining sufficient acceleration to lift off like Nureyev in his glory days—leaping, touching down, making little jetés and pirouettes, as they took up positions, bowing, bending, one to the other, following nature's choreography.

"Aren't they something?" Chase said softly. "Three Moons is putting on a show for you."

"And we're seeing it together. I don't want it to end."

But all too soon the performance was over. The big birds began to settle. Chase helped her to her feet, the desire to make love to her deep inside him, this woman who was glowing with health and a sensuality all the more appealing because she didn't realize she had it in abundance.

She smiled up at him, her breath quickening, wavelets of excitement rippling down her spine. He aroused so much in her she'd never even suspected.

But Chase hid his desire well. She was his guest. It was his duty to see that no harm came to her. Especially from him. Back on the open plain, Rosie pointed at the cloud castles that were starting to build on the horizon.

"A thunderstorm?" She looked up, shielding her eyes. "I expect you can read all the cloud formations."

"Better than the weatherman." The flames of sunset were reflected off his golden skin. "We're used to this in tropical skies." He dismissed the escalating buildup. "Probably a few fireworks tonight. Not much rain. We're coming into the Wet, which lasts, as you know, through October to April, but we've had season after season when the Wet has been a virtual nonevent. It's either flood or drought, but there's no question that the pattern of weather has been changing. I'd say we're in for one of the old-style Wets, with maybe a few cyclones thrown in for good measure. That's why you've only got one month to prove something on this expedition. If the rains come, you won't get out of there. Another thing you have to remember is that the peak of the saltwater crocodiles' nesting season is the onset of the Wet. There are wild places on the station, Rosie, where man isn't always in control. I suppose that's as it should be. This is the Wilderness Coast, after all. Three Moons isn't a managed farm—it's a vast station. Some areas are full of raw power."

"Then change your mind and come with us," Rosie begged.

IN THE EARLY HOURS she awoke to terror. She bounded up in bed, her throat aching as though she'd been screaming for hours, staring into the darkness, her eyes straining for vision, defeated by the mosquito netting that enclosed her like a shroud.

"Who's there?" Her heart pounded so painfully she held a hand to its frantic beating.

Someone seemed to be watching her. The room was full of shapes.

She threw herself sideways, wildly thrusting out an arm to the bedside lamp. Thank God she found the switch. She turned it on, watching her surroundings light up like a stage set.

Nothing. A beautiful exotic room, a veritable Aladdin's cave, full of wonderful furnishings. The light showed golden on the walls, causing the elaborate frame of the large painting to glow like gold. The scarlet-silk curtains whipped back and forth in a strong wind that was driving across the veranda. She would have to fix them.

It had been her imagination, of course. Her dream. Her nightmare. She had wanted to fight her way out of it. Couldn't. Until it became too unbearable, a scene from Dante's *Inferno*....

She'd been so immersed in her dream. She'd stood in the firelit garden of the homestead, the moonless night rent by great towering orange flames. She watched in horror, helpless as they roared through the great roof of the house. It was the west wing that was ablaze, fire and smoke billowing like molten magma. Even asleep, dreaming, she could feel the heat on her cheeks, her exposed arms, through her nightdress. She could feel her gorge rise. She wanted desperately to be sick, but it was important that she watch. She was needed to bear witness to the frightening cacophony of sound and sight and smell. The ultimate horror, the stench of burning flesh. She expected to see cruel images, figures silhouetted against the flames. She searched for them. A man and a woman. The man frantically trying to make an escape, the woman pleading for help. But there was nothing. No sign of life behind those tall glass doors. She'd heard voices close by, but numb with shock and terror, she couldn't seem to turn her head. Yet she heard words, was able to make sense of them. Maiming words. Killing words. *Destroy.*

She wanted to be brave. She wanted to risk her life to find out what was happening, but she wasn't a part of it. Just a dreamer. A watcher. There was movement through the trees. Now she could see a figure, a man staring up at the hungry fire as though mesmerized by its fiery spell. She couldn't see his face properly, only the suggestion of his profile. She could see someone else running from near the house, a squat figure crouched over, carrying something wrapped in a blanket. The figure was smoldering.

She screamed at this second figure to get clear. Finally was able to turn her head to that tall lurking figure, utterly terrified by its indifference to the terrible conflagration. But the figure had disappeared. She had a dreadful crawling feeling that he was behind her, ready to grab her, throw her into black oily waters that suddenly began to swirl around her feet. A monstrous crocodile was lurking in those dark waters, eyes just visible above the surface…. She screamed and recoiled.

Then the heavens had opened up. The whole world was in motion, awhirl in driving torrents of rain like a cyclone in full force. She could see these flooding waters pouring down on the house, sparks swirling like a million fireflies as the flames were doused. Her heartbeat kicked up another notch. *Where was the man who had started that fire?* She turned to look at him, overcoming her great fear, but was blinded by the billowing smoke, black, wet and toxic. She felt sick, choking, her throat seared.

That was the moment she'd awoken.

Trembling violently, Rosie tried to escape the dream's lingering hold. She threw the coverlet aside, kicking out with legs that had turned to sponge. Beyond the tall French doors, open to the night air, their shutters locked back, were Chase's promised tropical fireworks. They lit up the sky with a primal display, making a shimmering white rectangle of the open doorway. Now she heard the bombardment of thunder, the loud hiss and crackle of lightning, the myriad sounds of the night. Frantic rustlings from beneath the trees and the great profusion of vines, the wild clacking sounds from the blown-about palms punctuated by a night bird's inhuman shriek.

My God, my God! She felt as if she was suffocating, so deeply had she been entrenched in that dream. It was the storm, of course. Now she could rationalize it. The storm had provided all the fuel necessary for her incendiary dream, yet as she looked about the silent room, it seemed to still hold the faint echo of those voices. She couldn't shut them out. They seemed to be coming from everywhere.

Get a grip, girl! Rosie's native courage rushed back. *Breathe in. Breathe out.* This was what happened when the conscious mind had too much stimulation. The subconscious started to act up, as well. She'd always had a very vivid imagination.

Imagination! You wish! She'd never experienced anything like this in all her years. This verged on the paranormal.

Her whole body trembled as she moved toward the silk curtains that glowed so richly. They seemed to have a life of their own, flapping and flowing, leaping out to entrap her. She got hold of one, drew it back into its gold silk tassel. She went to the other, grasped the swirling fabric in her hand just as one of the timber shutters blew loose from its mooring and crashed with stunning force against the doorway.

She couldn't help it. She let out a scream, clutching her head with both hands. What the hell was the matter with her? What was she screaming about? This wasn't the first bad nightmare of her life, although it was definitely the worst. The sort of dream that seared itself into the memory. Her scream seemed to echo around and around the room, bouncing off the walls. It had probably filled the house. Woken up everyone, unless, she prayed, it had been masked by the wilder sounds of the night. She felt too thoroughly unnerved to be embarrassed, her long fingers on the curtain again, twitching. *You're really losing it, Rosie,* she told herself, concentrating on trying to calm herself.

There were footfalls on the veranda. Another minute, and she heard Chase's voice calling out to her, his tone harsh with anxiety.

"Rosie, can you hear me? What's the matter?"

It was all so melodramatic, yet it was happening. Her heart was hammering in her chest and she was snatching shallow breaths, but at the sound of his voice she experienced a great surge of relief. She reached quickly for the robe she had draped across the daybed, shouldered into it, her skin damp with sweat.

"I'm sorry, Chase." She forced her way onto the veranda, apologizing as she went. "I had such a dream. It terrified me. I should be used to them by now, but this was...different."

She could see him plainly now, his dark-golden torso stripped of clothes, a pair of dark boxer shorts his only covering. The sight of him transfixed her; she couldn't escape the almost intolerable magnetism of the man.

"It's the storm," he said, excusing her, making an impatient grab for the shutter and fixing it securely. "What were you dreaming about, for the love of God?"

"Did I bring you out of a deep sleep?" Her voice was dulled by the tension in her throat.

"I wasn't asleep at all." He reached out a hand to her, ran it from elbow to shoulder, dismayed by the visible trembling that shook her body. "Hell, Rosie, if it was that bad, it might be an idea to talk about it. You're not afraid of the storm, are you? I know it looks pretty spectacular, but it's really a lot of fuss about nothing."

"Storms don't bother me." They probably would from now on.

He dropped his hand. "Do you want me to leave you alone?"

"No." The shake of her head was very definite.

"How much do you remember? Or is it very hazy? Come and sit down while I pull some clothes on." Clearly her nightmare had been so frightening it had induced some kind of trauma. Again he reached for her, certain there was no rejection in her eyes. "There's a sitting room along here. I can even manage a stiff brandy or a scotch if you feel the need of it."

"I'll be all right. Just give me a minute." Her voice was low, almost smothered, though he could tell she was making a valiant effort to pull herself together.

Farther down the veranda Chase stepped into a room, switched on the light. It was only when he turned to her, saw her agitated breathing, the little mauve smudges beneath her green eyes, that he pulled her toward him, groaning softly. He wrapped her in his arms, his mouth dropping to her hair.

"Shh, Rosie. Everything's all right." She seemed to sag against him as though she desperately needed his support. It was an enormous erotic charge. He had believed himself to be in control, but he was instantly consumed by a desire so intense it seemed to devour him. Blood flushed his skin as he came to full arousal. Hell, why wouldn't he be? He'd been lying awake thinking about her, and now he wanted her so much he could scarcely breathe. "Rosie, Rosie." He repeated her name over and over like a mantra that might protect her. A man on the brink, trying to rein himself in.

"God, I can't believe this is happening." How could he bear to be near her and not touch her? He wanted to undress her. He wanted her naked. Now. He wanted to tell her how beautiful she was, how funny, how sweet, how clever.

She was half laughing, seeking and finding solace, but the sound held an underlying sob. She knew she was feeding on his abundant strength and vitality, her own vulnerability totally exposed. From nightmare to fantasy. She lifted her head and he leaned above her, kissing her open mouth. At the same moment she leaned into him, safe within his arms, letting herself go completely. The kiss went on and on while he ran his hands up and down her arching back. Sexual excitement pierced like a knife. It was Rosie herself who tugged at her sash, pulling it undone while his hand slid masterfully inside the low neckline of her nightdress. It sought the creamy mounds of her breasts, palming one, then the other, caressing them, his ministrations causing her to give a stifled gasp. As thumb and forefinger found a nipple, swollen as a ripe berry, she was powerless before the tidal wave of sensation. It drove out the mindless panic, the crawling sense of danger her nightmare had instilled. If only this could last forever. Her body, the body she'd always thought so very much her own, no longer seemed to belong to her. It belonged to him. A miraculous thing, shaking her to her core.

The excitement of kissing her, holding her, wasn't enough. He exhaled a breath that was clearly fraught with tension. "Look at me," he commanded, raising her chin. "I want to make love to you. I want to kiss you all over, but you've put your trust in me. The thing is, I don't know if I can let you go. Do you want it, too?"

His voice, so low and compelling, thrilled her. "I'm not pulling away." In fact, her body was clamoring for him. She was hardly able to brook having his mouth away from hers.

The rest was up to him.

He lifted her very suddenly, swept her off the ground as easily as he might have swung up a child. But she was no child. She was all woman. A woman who sent the hot blood thrumming through his veins. In his bedroom he laid her down on the bed, the cool cotton sheets so crisp, so beautifully laundered they crackled. For long moments he bent over her, studying her face and her body as though committing each separate feature, every line, every contour to memory. Her body was so slender that her breasts in comparison were almost voluptuous. He could see her long legs, beautiful legs, emerging from the gauzy yellow nightdress that was rucked up beneath her body. He began to kiss her, the side of her throat and the side of her face, her ears and her temples, her marvelous hair, which tickled his mouth. He allowed his nostrils to inhale her perfume, her essence, the freshness that reminded him of citrus fruits. Her beautiful white skin was damp, as were the glowing little curls that sprang like licks of flame from along her hairline. He captured the beads of moisture, licked them away with his tongue.

It was too much...too much... Rosie had never known such passionate abandon. She found herself moaning, her body moving jerkily, as wave upon wave of feeling broke over her, consuming her. Flesh and bone. Finally her limbs were thrashing. She had to turn to him, throw out her arms like a supplicant, aware, as she had never been before, of the power of sex as the driving life force.

Then he was beside her, the two of them in a bed that must have been specially made for him. It was big—bigger than king-size—so wonderful. So accommodating to their turning, twisting bodies. They were kissing. Such kisses. Breathing as one. Deep, deep breaths that turned into a kind of anguish. Nothing else would do—she was ready to receive him. She knew she cried out, moaned something into his shoulder, and then he was inside her. Filling her gloriously in one overpowering motion. It was so breathtaking she wept. Like a woman finding her true mate.

"Are you real. Are you real?" She guided his mouth to her breast, pressing his head down hard as he plunged deeper and deeper into her warm receptive body, oceans deep, so her heart soared to a place it had never found before. It wasn't her body he was taking; he was trying to find her soul. She felt such gratitude, such rapture, the tears gathered momentum, pooling behind her tightly closed lids. Despite all her best intentions, nothing in the world would have stopped her from having this. Not with this beautiful man who still carried the scars of his grief. She began to rock him, while he held her arms, controlling her until they reached the same rhythm. Now they were moving faultlessly together, their combined action as coordinated as that of the finest athletes', gaining speed and intensity until they couldn't stop.

Outside in the tropical night, the storm continued to rage, but neither of them would have noticed had a meteor fallen from heaven to earth.

IT WAS QUITE a long time before they could lie quietly, Rosie with her head on his chest, listening to his heartbeat, his bronze head on the pillow above her, a lazy hand making ringlets of her hair.

"That was magic." Rosie gave another voluptuous sigh, entwining one long leg around his, unselfconsciously naked as she had never been before in her life, flaunting her woman's body, the body he found so beautiful.

He looked down at her with a self-mocking smile. "Here you are in my bed with all my best intentions gone to hell."

"Heaven," she corrected. "Mine, too."

"Rosie, your middle name is temptress."

"I didn't tempt you. Did I?" She lifted her head, triumph mixed with a little remorse.

"Woman, you've plucked my heart out," he said in a deep calm voice. "If I weren't so damned exhausted, I'd get up and do a few handstands."

"I'd much rather you stayed here." She laughed. "This is such a wonderful bed."

"Don't remind me. I'm not *that* exhausted."

"I suppose we should get some sleep."

"We could try," he said, his eyes gleaming and amused.

"I've never been this way with anyone but you," she told him. "So...uncontrolled."

"You were perfect. Anyway, I think I can handle it. Now, are you going to tell me what your dream was about? It must have been pretty bad to bring the intrepid Rosie Summers to such a state."

"Pretty close. I don't know if this is the moment to tell you. I don't want anything to upset us."

He looked at her, puzzled. "Well, if that doesn't arouse my curiosity, I don't know what would."

"Are you sure you want to hear this?" Rosie felt the panic of the dream reach out for her.

"Anything that distresses you distresses me," he answered. Their bodies were so closely entwined he registered that involuntary shudder as if it had been his own.

"Do you believe in the paranormal?" She turned on her stomach so she could gaze into his eyes.

He studied her thoughtfully. "As in things that go bump in the night?"

"Want me to continue?" She gave him a look that clearly said, *Don't scoff!*

"Yes, sure." He smiled. "I don't doubt certain people have had experiences beyond the norm. People with very sensitive natures. Like you, Rosie, and Great-aunt Hester. Maybe I'll get to meet the lady."

"She'd love you," Rosie said, running her hand back and forth across his naked, hard muscled chest. "She'd love to paint you. Especially as you are now."

"She'll have to find someone else for her life classes," he protested.

"She's a serious artist." Rosie was enjoying herself, lost in sensation.

"She must have had a memorable life."

"She's an absolute darling. You *will* meet her."

"Great. So tell me about your dream. It must have been pretty nasty. You should have heard that scream!"

Residual shock showed in Rosie's eyes. "I did. Mezzo one minute, coloratura the next," she quipped, then abruptly sobered. "I'm telling you, the nightmare totally took me over. The storm was the trigger. It didn't break until long after I fell asleep, but at some level I was absorbing all the background drama. It started in the garden…" She began to describe her dream slowly, her head tilted to one side, as though listening to an inner voice.

He interrupted her. "You can't mean the dream took place *here?*" It wasn't the first time he looked highly skeptical.

She held his chin, demanding his attention. "Listen, it was the *fire,* Chase. Oh, maybe this isn't the time for it." She couldn't help reading the toughening expressions on his face.

"I don't believe in dreams, Rosie." It was a flat statement with plenty of emphasis.

"Many important messages have been expressed through dreams," she retorted. "But if you don't want to listen…" It wasn't as though she didn't know that their beliefs on this issue were in conflict. She rolled onto her back again, looking a little cross.

"Hey, don't be angry." He felt remorse and desire at the same time.

"I'm not angry. I just think you could make more of an effort to listen."

"Do you?"

After a thoroughly enjoyable struggle, he managed to subdue her, drawing her bright head onto his shoulder, trying in vain to settle the flyaway curls.

"You've taken a real shine to me, haven't you, Mr. Banfield?" She laughed softly.

"So much so, Miss Summers, that I think we'll spend the rest of the week in bed."

"An interesting suggestion, but let's use some of the time to hear me out." She turned to press her hands against his chest. "You can do that for me?"

"Sure I can." He managed a rueful smile and dropped a kiss on her nose. "You like getting your own way, don't you, Rosie."

"Look who's talking!" she mocked. "I appreciate that cattle barons don't have much time for the paranormal—they can't be cattle barons otherwise. But there is a spiritual side to life. This was the most powerful nightmare I've ever had: and I've had a few to haunt me. The extraordinary thing is that I knew my role was to bear witness...."

Chase listened in complete silence as Rosie finished recounting her dream. Sometimes he closed his eyes as though, despite himself, he might be seized by it, too, breathing in the choking smoke. Her voice genuinely trembled, the way it would if she'd been in real danger. It didn't seem possible that she could know what she did. Then again, she was a journalist. She wouldn't find it too difficult to access information. But the *storm.* How could she know the heavens had opened that night, a brief deluge that had in the end extinguished the blaze? Locked away in the safe in his study was every newspaper article about the tragedy. Gruesome details of the fire had been reported, but strangely, never the flash storm. Most accounts had been given over to the achievements of the Banfield family, the popularity of his father and mother, the immense shock and sadness within the community. It was reported widely that the fire was thought to have been started by a fallen lamp. There had been trouble with the generators; oil lamps were in use. At the time no one had considered for even a moment that it had been anything other than a horrendous accident. Speculation came later. Much later, when the numbness of shock had worn off. Lew Banfield and his beautiful wife didn't have an enemy in the world.

Not one newspaper report mentioned the storm.

Rosie's voice had petered out. Now they were both quiet.

"What I want to know is how you knew about the storm," he said finally. "You're a journalist. There must have been mention of it somewhere. You must have read it or heard of it."

"No." She moved her head so she could look at him, her gaze very direct. "I haven't heard or read a word about the fire, Chase. I couldn't bring myself to look it up like…like it was just another news item. I've seen enough fires, enough death and human suffering not to want to intrude on your private grief."

"I still don't understand how you *knew*."

Incensed, Rosie sat up. "How did I dream *any* of it? How did I hear voices? Why did I see one figure in the garden, another running away from the house? I believe in my dream he was carrying *you*."

He gave a grim laugh. "Porter would have had a hard job carrying me. I was tall and strong for my age."

"But one can do amazing things under terrible stress."

"Certainly, but I've never seen my uncle terribly stressed in my entire life."

"He must have human feelings, Chase." Rosie frowned.

"I'm not sure I agree." He sighed deeply. "I don't remember much about the storm, though I was wandering around in it soaked to the skin. It was utter hell and confusion. If there'd been any shortage of water, or if the men had been off on a muster, the whole house would have burned to the ground. Those scars you see on Moses, on his face, his hands and arms, even his legs, they came from the fire. He was in the thick of it.''

''Are you sure it wasn't Moses who rescued you? The dream figure wasn't tall. Not like your uncle.''

''Rosie, it was a nightmare.'' His voice lacked patience. ''Not a video clip.''

''It was demonic!'' Rosie found it fairly easy to ignore the fact that he didn't take her seriously. She knew better. ''A dream I'd just as soon not carry around with me. The figure in the garden. You want to take a guess?'' Her green eyes challenged.

''He wasn't *real,* Rosie.'' He kissed her forehead, then her eyelids, clearly wanting to change the subject. ''Maybe the house is haunted, after all. I sure as hell am. No matter how much I fight, I know I'm damaged for life. And you know what they say, Rosie. Damaged people are dangerous.''

A MOTHER-OF-PEARL SKY. A soft shimmering luminescence. Vanishing stars. Rosie, her yellow satin robe sashed tightly around her, leaned against the balustrade of the upper veranda in a near trance of pleasure. Her fingers reached out to the white trumpet flowers of a luxuriant vine that laced the timber columns, their delicate scent sweet to her nostrils. She felt marvelous. An initiate into the blissful realm of passionate love. It had raised her senses to a higher level. She was glorying in being alive, in being able to soak in the whole radiant morning, the deep-bush remoteness of this mystical terrain that was Three Moons.

Birdsong had woken her. The rising crescendo of sound that split the predawn silence every morning. To her utterly beguiled ear, it was like different sections of an orchestra warming up, the high sweet strings, then the deeper bell-toned voices, the punctuating clangs with the brashness of brass, until it all came together in a symphony that carried for miles and miles.

"Wait until the kookaburras start up." Chase padded as silently as a tiger behind her, his hands coming down on her shoulders. "They couldn't make it into the orchestra with their crazy crackle." He lowered his head to nuzzle her cheek and her neck, wanting her very badly again, wanting to watch her dreamy face turn desperate with long-ing, the pupils of her beautiful eyes dilate. They had ex-changed many confidences during the night, memories of childhood and adolescence, the complexities of their pres-ent lives, the relationships. He had told her more than he'd ever told a living soul. She was a good listener, Rosie. A good talker. An exquisite lover. It was the lover he wanted right now—the shuddering ecstasy, the storm of release. "Do you realize we've talked for most of the night?" His hand slipped inside her robe, moving ardently across her responsive breasts, cradling their soft weight. "Well, time out for making love."

"Do you know, I could get used to it." She leaned back into his embrace, the rush of desire stirring her blood. Risk, when emotional risk had never been something she sought. Hurt could be unavoidable in this affair, but she felt she could risk anything for him. With a few pleasurable, but not major love affairs behind her, she had just about given up hope of meeting someone who could tap into all her needs. Someone she felt she couldn't live without. It hadn't taken this man more than a day to draw her in. She was mad for him. Mad to know what distressed him and caused him pain. Mad for his company. She had given him her body without reservation, now she was about to open to him again, like a bird opens its wings. Anything to scale those heights. The moon, the stars, the galaxies. His love-making was like magic. An integral part of the man himself. Mastery, spontaneity, skills that made everything he did to her seem as sublime as nature.

"I'd love it if you'd come back to bed, Rosie," he coaxed, his deep voice little more than a seductive whisper.

Her blood bubbled like champagne. "Well, I didn't get much sleep."

"That happens." He carried her back into the bedroom, his strong arms showing not the slightest strain at her weight, allowing her to sink back against the pillows while he brought his mouth to hers, and then his warm lean muscular body. Male to female.

She clung to him, calling nis name, in a tumult of feeling from her head to her extremities, pressing her lips to his golden throat. "I don't know how you expect me to ever go home," she moaned. Wherever his fingers touched there was an expanding circle of flame.

"What about your career, Rosie?" he whispered, allowing his hands to trace a shivery line down over her long arched back to her small rounded bottom, as firmly and beautifully fleshed as two perfect pears. She was one of those women who looked even better without the adornment of clothing—the wondrous breasts, made for a man's hands, the streamlined length of her, her tummy as flat as a boy's. In the same instant he wondered how she would look pregnant, that smooth belly filled with a child. *His* child. The thought touched him deeply, even as he found it shockingly erotic.

"Rosie," he groaned, catching up a handful of her deliciously clean hair, amazed it was so soft when it looked so electric. "I don't even know how I'm going to let you go off on this fool expedition."

Her spine like a wave, she rose upward to kiss him, outlining the beautiful shape of his mouth with the tip of her tongue. Such rapture.

"So come with us," she urged.

CHAPTER EIGHT

MARLEY KNEW IMMEDIATELY when he saw them together that they were lovers. A very cozy arrangement! They didn't even have to speak to each other for the unwelcome news to come through loud and clear. Roslyn looked gorgeous, glowing with health and vitality, her eyes a blaze of emerald. A fitting mate for what he was forced to concede was a magnificent-looking man. Banfield was every bit that. Worse, he was highly intelligent, shrewd, tough, full of determination and grit. If he wanted Rosie, he would get her, make no mistake about that. Marley detested these men who were so obviously leaders. It was some element in their makeup. A quality he worked hard to acquire but knew in his heart of hearts he never would.

But Roslyn! Did she have to fall under the man's spell like some blasted teenager? After all, she was a trained journalist with a slew of awards, not some impressionable kid. Though it would be difficult indeed for any woman to overlook all the signs of wealth. He'd thought better of Roslyn. He hadn't expected her to get herself involved in this sort of thing. She'd fitted rather neatly into his plans— and now this! He felt quite victimized by her defection. Already Marley had allocated his wife, Helen, to the dim and distant past. As soon as he could, he'd get his solicitor to draw up divorce papers: it did not occur to him that Helen might already have done so.

They were seated out on the veranda, being waited on by that Indian servant, Roy. Trust Banfield to be so exotic.

Damned nearly the Raj! There was a wife, too, a little someone called Leila, but so far she hadn't appeared. As far as Marley was concerned, this Roy was on far too familiar terms with both his employer and Roslyn. It didn't do, that kind of behavior. There had to be clear distinctions.

The homestead, though... Marley, who had been invited into the homes of many rich people, was awestruck. It was like a tropical palace, definitely Southeast Asian in concept. And the furnishings! Paintings, screens, rugs, sculptures. Some had to be priceless, and they were all on show. No wonder poor old Porter was livid about his loss. It didn't seem fair, Chase Banfield inheriting the lot. The two men, close relatives, could have lived comfortably together in such a house without ever having to see each other. Yet Chase Banfield had all but thrown his uncle out. No gratitude there. None at all. He was a hard man, Banfield. As hard, in fact, as his uncle.

But Roslyn! Marley came back to his main concern. He scowled morosely, watching Roslyn, still dressed in figure-hugging jodhpurs and a crisp cotton shirt from horseback riding, laugh merrily at something Banfield said. Could it have been *that* funny? She was in a very ebullient mood. He didn't quite know how to break the news that there would be an addition to the party. Porter's man, but Porter had convinced him during a heated discussion that it would be far better to let his nephew believe the newcomer was *his* man. An associate from the museum, Porter suggested. Marley didn't like it at all. Apart from worrying about the risk to his reputation, Banfield could easily smell a rat. He could veto their plans, but Porter had been adamant this new chap, Disher—what sort of name was that?—had to come along. In fact, his inclusion was crucial to finance the trip and provide protection. Disher was ex-army, jungle-trained. According to Porter, who didn't quite seem to believe his own story, a good man to have onside.

MARGARET WAY   167

What would Banfield think? Marley sat straight with a
start as he realized Banfield was staring right at him with
those tiger eyes. Hell, did the man ever blink?

"You look like you've got something weighty on your
mind, Doctor," Chase said. He felt that from the moment
Marley had arrived, he'd seemed extremely put out about
something, and edgy into the bargain. It wasn't hard to
figure out that a lot of it had to do with Rosie and him.
Sometimes it was impossible to disguise a combustible sexual attraction. Rosie looked wonderful, more radiant every
time he glanced at her. Being in love did put a bloom on
a woman. As for him, he might just as well have had a
heart tattooed on his forehead.

Marley hurriedly realigned his handsome features. "Actually I'm impressed by what you've got here, Chase. I
hope you don't mind if I take a closer look at all your
wonderful antiques?"

"Just as long as you don't abscond with one of them,"
Banfield joked. "I should tell you the credit goes to my
family from my great-grandfather's time down. All of them
were collectors. Occasionally, when I was very hard-
pressed, I considered selling something to raise money, but
it all worked out and I didn't have to part with a single
thing."

"I take it your uncle made his own splendid contribu-
tion." Marley smiled, expecting Porter with his love of
beautiful things to have bought some of these pieces.

Chase shook his head. "If anything, the reverse. There
were huge Chinese porcelain vases that used to stand at
either side of the staircase. They somehow disappeared.
Famille noir. Quite valuable. I was at boarding school most
of the time, so I couldn't exactly tell you what else went
missing. There were a lot of things and I was just a boy."

Marley almost did a back flip in his chair. "You mean
you're saying your uncle was a *thief?*"

"Not if it's going to upset your peace of mind," Chase drawled. "So, how *is* Porter?"

Marley almost choked on his last bite of cake. "He's on top of everything. A great organizer." He looked toward Rosie, who was letting Banfield do all the talking. "He's put at our disposal no less than three Land Cruisers. There's plenty of equipment, food, drink. It must have set him back quite a bit, but he's as obsessed with this project as I am."

"Really?" Chase arched a dark brow. "I just hope you're not in for any surprises."

Now was the time to make his pitch. "Actually, I do have something to propose to you, Chase. I have a colleague at the museum, a fellow archaeologist, who would be a great help to me when we start the dig. As Porter is as good as financing this trip and we have enough vehicles, I hope you agree to his coming along." He smiled winningly into Chase's face and hoped to God his luck was holding.

"How many more people have you got lined up?" Chase asked tersely, glancing at Rosie.

"Why, no one." Marley was aware his palms were sweating. "Just Glenville. Dr. Roland Glenville." Marley whipped out the name of a colleague who was enjoying a long vacation. If Banfield happened to check, Glenville was on the museum's register. He hated telling the lie and felt extremely nervous at being put in this position, but he had a gut feeling that he was on to something huge! Why else was Porter Banfield so desperately keen on this trip?

"I take it Porter's agreeable to having this Glenville along?"

Marley all but winced, watching Banfield fold his arms across his wide chest, every inch the tough cattle baron. "To be honest, Porter was against it." How could he ever face himself in the mirror again? One lie spawned another. "The fewer people in on this the better, as far as Porter's concerned. But he fails to realize how much work there is at a dig site. Trained work, that is. Roly's help will be invaluable."

"I think I should have a little talk with this Roly before I decide."

Marley's skin reddened. "Presumptuous of me, I know, Chase, but he's already en route. You've been so good about everything so far, I thought you'd appreciate the fact that I need help."

"It's very possible you will," Chase returned bluntly, "and I don't mean on the dig. I don't understand you, Doctor. On the basis of a few artifacts that could have been acquired anywhere, plus a few old legends, you've somehow convinced yourself you're in on the find of the century."

"You forget what your uncle has told me," Marley retorted.

"Odds on my uncle telling you the exact truth are about a hundred to one. I agree. There's *something* out there. Whatever it is, Porter wants it. Maybe he's turned up the map of an old gold mine. Alluvial gold was panned in the river. Quite a lot in the early days and by my family."

"Well, I'm not interested in any hidden gold mine," Marley snapped. "The only gold I'm interested in will be in the form of artifacts proving an ancient Egyptian presence in Australia. I have a strange feeling about this. You're right—I do believe we're on to something big. All I'm asking, begging if you like, is you allow us our chance."

Rosie looked at him and nodded. "Chase has already given his permission. You should've spoken to him, Graeme, before you enlisted your colleague's help. Wait! Glenville—wasn't he the man who discovered the giant marine fossils in the Red Centre?"

Damn, he'd almost forgotten she was a journalist. Even though Glenville had never received anything like the cov-

erage *he* had, he should have guessed Roslyn would be
aware of a fact like that. She seemed to be studying him
very closely so Marley turned around in his chair and gave
her a false smile. "That's right. But it was a good few years
back. Good man, Roly. He knows the jungle almost as well
as he knows the desert. He spent some time in Java."

"I'd like to meet him, all the same," Chase said. "I have
my own little surprise for you, Graeme. I know you and
Porter are going to be pleased. I'm coming, too."

Instead of the negative reaction Chase and Rosie had
obviously been expecting, Marley slapped the table in front
of him with genuine pleasure that had its basis in relief.
"Why, that's marvelous! Couldn't be better!" He could
scarcely say it, but he was starting to get cold feet about
Porter Banfield let alone his associate cum accomplice,
Disher, who sounded as if he could rip a man apart.

"Chase would know his own land better than anybody,"
Rosie said, pleased and surprised by Marley's response.

Chase shook his head. "Except for Moses. Moses knows
and understands this country better than any white man.
And that includes me. In fact, Moses and his people know
a lot more than they're saying. They give up their secrets
very slowly. Mutual trust is the thing. Porter destroyed a
lot of the trust my family built up over many long years."

Certainly Porter didn't have his nephew's commanding
presence, nor his skill with people, but Marley thought Porter could hardly be an outright villain. Hadn't the biblically
named Moses stayed in Porter's employ? Didn't that say
something? "So he won't be coming, then? Moses, I
mean?" Marley asked, looking properly respectful of a
trusted retainer. "Initially you had him as our guide."

"This expedition is cutting into my time," Chase began,
"but I don't want Rosie put in the slightest danger. I can
ill afford to spare Moses, either, but I think it best if he
comes along. I told you that you're working to a restricted

time frame. If the monsoon comes early and you get delayed, you could be cut off in very dangerous territory. Crocodiles like to go walkabout. Plus, the onset of the Wet is their nesting season. You and your vehicles, which Porter has so generously provided, would be at the mercy of the elements." He frowned. "It's not like Porter to be this generous. Probably has a sponsor. Someone else he's reeled in."

Marley spread his hand regretfully. "I can see you two have a problem, but we can't let it interfere with our project. And there's Dempsey. Is he still one of the party? Given that you're coming now, I don't think we have any need of him."

"Maybe not, but Mick's in. He's had little enough diversion of late. Strangely enough, his sympathies are with you. But then, he's a romantic at heart. So you have a credulous audience. We've all heard the old legends. We all know there are some things that can't be explained, although mainstream archaeologists reject the possibility of an ancient Egyptian presence. I'm surprised you got your colleague interested. Scientists aren't usually interested in bizarre tales."

Marley altered the direction of his glance in case he appeared shifty-eyed. "Roly believes it deserves some serious thought." He tried to speak with authority. "He's all for our exploration. Indeed, he's painfully anxious to come."

"Another one with a febrile imagination," said Chase dryly. "When do you think you'll be ready to leave? I have to contact Mick, and if he's still keen to go, get him over here. Rosie and Mick will come with me in a station vehicle. I'd like Moses to travel with you—he can be your guide. I'll leave you and Porter to sort out the rest."

"Then you're agreeable to having Roly along?"

Chase looked over at Rosie, who nodded faintly. "If you vouch for him, Dr. Marley. You're a respected and influential archaeologist. If your colleague can help you in your work, so much the better.''

Marley knew a moment of relief mixed with nagging anxiety. He'd have to start praying Banfield wouldn't spot his ''colleague'' for a fake. There'd be hell to pay!

A DAY LATER Kurt Disher was speeding north along the highway that rimmed the Pacific Ocean in one of Siegel's brand-new Land Cruisers. He'd crossed the Tropic of Capricorn some five hundred miles back, well on his way to a rendezvous with Porter Banfield in his North Queensland hideaway.

Siegel had filled him in about Banfield. Not a lot. Just what he needed to know; Siegel liked to play it very close to the chest. Banfield was one of the landed elite, a member of a well-known pioneering family, historic cattle station, all that stuff. When he turned twenty-one, the present owner, Chase Banfield, had tossed him out. Why not? Disher would have done the same thing if he'd ever enjoyed a foray into that kind of world. Banfield was a buyer and seller of antiquities. He was well-known to Siegel, since they'd run a successful business for years. A search was being mounted for ancient Egyptian relics. What crap! He could hardly believe Siegel, the ultimate predator, ruthless in business, had fallen for that. But the old bastard was a collector. Funny thing with collectors—sometimes they lost their grip.

Disher had worked for Siegel twice before. Delivered the merchandise. His job was to stick to Banfield like glue. Figure out what was really behind this safari. If a find was made, he was there to represent Siegel, stake out his claim. Siegel had to be the winner in all this. The archaeologist guy, Marley, and the dealer were well down the line. It would be in their interests to play along. He didn't mind getting tough, but only when he had to.

There was a woman on the trip, as well, a journalist. Women meant nothing to him. Except for sex. It was a man's world. That was the way he liked it. That was the way it was meant to be.

He was well into the tropics now. Eternal green. Those bloody cane fields! Endless miles of them. He was driving through glorious country, but it made little impression on him. The colorings of earth and sky, the cobalt-blue and red ochre, every conceivable shade of green accentuated by splashes of brilliant color—he noticed it all, yet remained unmoved. The great mango plantations edged almost to the road. They also grew tea up here, and coffee. The birds had finished off any idea of growing rice. Even the air force couldn't stop them from raiding the fields. Birds. Millions of them! For a while he'd been involved in the illegal trafficking of rain-forest birds up in the Peninsula. Cape York. As wild and remote a place as you were ever likely to find. And wide open except for the blacks. There was one bird he really liked. The golden shoulder. Brilliant blue with a suffusion of turquoise around his beak, orange underside, the feathers tipped with the brilliant golden yellow of the shoulders, which gave the bird its name. Beauties, those golden shoulders. Highly sought after by the Asians. So sought after they'd all but disappeared. Yes, it was lucrative for a while, but the government men had moved in. That was when he'd moved out.

He'd done a lot of things since he'd been discharged from the army. Sexual harassment of a female officer. Rape. Bitch had come on to him. Anyway, the pay was better as a mercenary. He'd been to a lot of places all over the world. He'd assumed a lot of names. Done a lot of things. He'd heard there was still gold up here. Tin. Mount Bartle Frere was said to be solid tin. Gold, copper, silver. He recalled that some cattleman on the Palmer River where he was heading had sat on an enormously rich field without touching it. Preferred cattle, apparently. The Banfields, however, had profited mightily from their gold mine. That was going way back, before the turn of the twentieth century. While he was keeping his eye on Banfield and the crank archaeologist, he'd have a look around himself. He'd come well equipped.

KURT DISHER WAS, to all appearances, another Arnold Schwarzenegger, but without the charm. Porter looked at the breadth of muscled chest, the hard ropes of muscles in the arms, the broad neck, the deeply tanned face with its pale eyes, the fuzz of blond hair. He was terrified, certain this man was trouble.

Despite that, perhaps because of it, he went forward extending his arm. "Pleasure to meet you, Mr. Disher."

His unwelcome visitor gave him a cold smile, looking around and sizing up the place like a prospective burglar, while Porter flapped his released hand back and forth, not sure if the moron had broken any bones. "Nice house you got here." He made it sound as though Porter had come by it through a colossal con. And maybe he was right. "Is there a john I can use?"

Porter, as fastidious as they came, was disgusted. "Of course. Of course. I'll show you to the guest room. It has an en suite."

"What about a beer?" Disher threw at him. "Maybe you can rustle up a few sandwiches. I'm hungry."

"No problem," Porter said almost scornfully, then immediately regretted it as Disher turned back to stare at him.

"I'd go easy on the humor, Banfield," he growled.

"If I've offended you, I'm sorry. I apologize," Porter said, not sorry at all. He paused outside the room he'd set aside for Disher, as far away from his own quarters as possible. "Come to the sun porch when you're ready. You can't miss it. It overlooks the sea. I'll get my help to rustle up some food. What sort of sandwiches would you like?''

"The whole bit. Beef, ham, but no chicken. With cheese, tomato, plenty of onions, some jalapeños on the side. A lot of cold beer. That was a long thirsty trip.''

Porter turned away, shaken to the core. How could this…this yobbo, this muscle man, possibly pass for an academic? What an utter balls-up! Porter found his way to the kitchen, feeling utterly defeated. Did Siegel have any idea at all what he was really looking for? Porter wondered, sighing deeply. He couldn't. Porter was the only one who'd ever seen the diary, though his father and dead brother had heard about it. That was just eleven years ago, when he'd begun his search to locate the relics. All he'd had to work with was a few clues. He'd needed financing, to support both his search and his addiction to a certain lifestyle; it hadn't taken him long to start dangling a few choice pieces in front of Siegel, who threw money at him like a drunken sailor. But it all stopped the day Chase showed him the door. Cut him off from his source, as it were. He'd been back on Three Moons a number of times since, but always treated like a felon on parole. God knows how he'd retained his dignity all these years. Once he'd tried to get onto the station by stealth, coming in through a rain-forest entry. But Chase had his scouts, tribal people who crisscrossed the station with his full knowledge and consent. They got the message to Chase with their bloody drums.

In the kitchen Porter gave instructions to the help. A husband-and-wife team. Not live-in. He couldn't tolerate having them underfoot. And they might…notice things. Then he returned to do battle.

"You *WHAT?*"

Porter registered Disher's strident bark at the back of his skull.

They were sitting in the long beautifully appointed room Porter called the sun porch, Porter squirming terribly while he outlined his plan for Disher to pose as Dr. Roland Glenville of the Sydney Museum. Porter waited until Disher had properly settled back into his chair before attempting to proceed. For a moment there he'd thought Disher was about to hit him.

"You must understand that my nephew and I are not on good terms," he said, hoping this psycho could be reasoned with. "If he knew you were my man—"

"Siegel's man, don't you mean?" Disher grunted, wolfing down two sandwiches. "Mmm, great!"

Porter averted his eyes. "In this instance it's the same thing. We won't be allowed onto the station without my nephew's approval. He's agreed to our project, but he's been led to believe that the new member of the party, you, is none other than Dr. Marley's colleague from the museum."

Disher half bit off another sandwich, then put it down. "Not possible," he snorted. "I'm a hired gun, not some damned wimp. Lemme ask you something, Banfield. How do you think I'd pass muster? Do I *look* like an archaeologist? Do I *sound* like one? What the hell do I know? And *Roly?*" His swearing made Porter blush. "Try calling me Roly and I'll deck ya."

Doing a great deal of harm in the process, Porter feared. "What about Roland?" he suggested after a long moment, realizing he was well and truly caught on the horns of a dilemma.

Silence while Disher took a long gulp of beer, then a blunt "No!"

Fat chance you'd have passing as a Roland, Porter thought with contempt. "Glenville?"

For the first time, Disher looked a bit uncertain. "Glenville…" he mused, starting on the rare roast beef with lashings of red onion. "I don't mind that so much. But I have to tell ya I don't like it."

"It won't be difficult to pull off." Porter tried to keep a reassuring look on his handsome face. "Marley and I are in on it. We don't have to worry about the others. You just have to pass muster with my nephew the morning we leave."

Disher gave him a sly look from those pale, pale eyes. "I hear he's one helluva guy. People seem to think he's something special."

"Not to me," Porter said nastily. "I have little love for him."

Disher actually chortled, then sobered, abruptly sending Porter another sharp-eyed glance. "I don't like this crazy plan at all. I think I'll run it by Siegel."

"By all means. I'll get the phone." Porter stood up as Disher continued to tuck in. "I could use a pot of coffee," he called to Porter's retreating back. "Black and strong. No sugar." Obviously he was a man who took his food seriously.

Siegel, as grouchy as a brown bear because he'd been called from a meeting, gave the plan a thumbs-up. He didn't give a damn how they worked it as long as they got results. It sounded to Porter as though he didn't care if they had to kill people while they were at it.

"So that's settled," Disher said, running a hand over the blond fuzz he called hair. "I work for Siegel. What he says goes. It might be the right time to tell you, Banfield—don't ever try to cut me out of anything. You'd have cause to regret it. No hard feelings. Just business."

"We all want the same thing," Porter said, his tone icy from long habit. "The thing is, how are you going to go down with my nephew?" Porter sought for the most diplomatic way to put it. "At the moment you look like one of those…those action-men movie stars."

Another snort from Disher, who waved a huge hand. "Don't worry about me. I can alter my appearance if I have to. I've had plenty of practice. You got a photo of this guy, this Glenville? Sounds like a real prick."

"He's a very distinguished scientist," Porter said. "I don't have one, but I'll get Marley here to meet you and fill you in. He was having a photograph sent up. We don't have much time for you to make your transformation. Or to pick up a bit of the jargon."

Disher put his hand on Porter's shoulder, pressing down slightly so Porter listed sideways. "Arrogant bastard, aren't ya, Banfield? Just the type I don't like. Don't underestimate me. I know you wrote me off as a bouncer, some simple-minded tough guy, but you're dealing with a man who's got brains. If this Marley can help me, I can learn."

MARLEY WAS AS HORRIFIED by Disher as Porter had been. He was slumped in an armchair in Porter's grandiose study, trying to recover. It was more than an hour since he'd arrived in response to Porter's call, another hour while he and Porter sat in a shell-shocked near-silence. Nothing had prepared Marley for his first sight of Banfield's guest. A trained assassin! Marley felt ill. Why had he ever agreed to this deception? If he went ahead with it, it could destroy his career.

The more he thought about it, the more he was convinced such an ill-conceived plan could never even begin to work. Disher as Dr. Roland Glenville? It was ludicrous! Glenville was a brilliant man, a trusted colleague. And what if Glenville ever found out? Not that Disher would get past Chase Banfield or Roslyn, who was as sharp as a tack, or indeed anyone used to dealing with people. He looked across at Porter, who was sitting silent and morose behind the massive partner's desk. Disher, who appeared equally unimpressed with Marley, had gone off to study the photograph of Glenville that Marley had been able to bring with him. It was a good clear shot of the two of them smiling at the camera the day the museum had displayed Glenville's marine fossils. Disher and Glenville were of a height, but Disher was infinitely fitter, more muscular, while Glenville with his heavy build was slightly overweight with a tendency to shamble. Disher's hair, which went way beyond a crewcut, was blond, possibly not natural, Glenville's dark and receding fast. Their expressions were polar opposites. Glenville was a very pleasant man, liked by everyone; Disher looked as if he was ready to take on the ninjas.

It was all a horrendous mistake and Porter Banfield was responsible.

"I can't begin to understand this," Marley said, his whole body still huddled in denial. "I tell you, the man's a disaster. Seriously bad news."

"I hope you're not rash enough to tell him that." Porter aimed a cold smile in Marley's direction. "I'm as disturbed as you are. It was all Siegel's idea. If you want to place the blame, lay it at his door. He doesn't give a damn what we do, by the way. He's left me holding the bag, the old goat."

"But didn't you tell him Disher would never get away with it?"

"He seems to think he will."

"Then he's insane."

"Maybe he knows his man better than we do. Disher's worked for him before. He wouldn't still be in place if he couldn't deliver to Siegel's satisfaction."

"This could ruin me if it got out. Not that I think for a moment your nephew won't smell a rat."

Their conversation was interrupted by such a hard knock on the door if it hadn't been solid cedar it might have splintered.

Porter scurried to unlock it, falling back, frowning ferociously at the large intruder the soon-to-be-dismissed help had somehow let in.

"Gotcha!" It was Disher's voice that emerged from the intruder's mouth, the top lip covered by a peppery dark mustache. He shoved the astonished Porter aside as he shambled into the room, broad shoulders stooped, causing his impressive torso to cave in. The stubble on his head was now dark brown, giving more definition to the pale eyes gleaming behind a pair of gold-rimmed spectacles. From somewhere he had produced a loose dark-green sweatshirt with long sleeves, masking the hard-muscled condition of his body.

"That's one hell of a disguise," Porter breathed, hardly able to believe it.

"I can always find some way to change my appearance," Disher said. No boast. He'd done it a hundred times with his box of tricks.

Marley continued to stare at him. As long as Disher didn't open his mouth, he looked like some big nice guy. Even the body language had changed.

"Now I'll give you the rest." The loud gruff voice miraculously gentled, took on an upper-crust accent, although he was talking obscenities. "Well, whaddaya say?" He broke off, reverting to his own harsh tones, his gaze sweeping from Marley to Porter. "Shocked you, didn't I boys?"

"You're very good," Porter said, stepping closer. "What about that mustache? Mightn't it come off?"

"Only if someone decided to rip it off."

"I don't think that's about to happen." Porter backed away nervously. "What do you think, Marley?"

"He'd have to hold on to his nerve. He'd have to keep the pretense up. The educated accent, the lot."

"I'm gifted that way." Disher reached out a long arm and slapped the back of Marley's head. "Better work on your manners, Doc."

Somewhere Marley found the courage. He stood up, confronting Disher face-to-face. "Now see here—"

"No point in playing the hero, Doc," Disher said, adopting his previous amiable expression. And what a difference it made. "I could take you apart, but I've got better things to do with my time. As Banfield says, I have to acquaint myself with a fair bit of the jargon you people use. Think you can help me with that?"

"If you're prepared to listen," Marley said, still rocking in place.

"You a good teacher?"

Marley nodded, speechless.

"You'd better be. I've got talents you missed. You're like your pal there." He pointed a finger at Porter. "You've made up your mind I'm none too smart. Well, you couldn't be more wrong. So, how many days have we got before we leave?"

"Two full days," Marley managed hoarsely. "I'm prepared to give you all my time."

"Gee, thanks, Doc." Disher slung a heavy companionable arm around Marley's shoulders. "Just remember, if you eff up, so do I."

CHAPTER NINE

THREE MOONS HELD endless fascination for Rosie. The very vastness of it stunned her. By day Chase took her everywhere with him so she could get a good idea of what station life, with all its inherent dangers, was like. By night, they slept together, joy and passion thrilling through their blood, the sense of oneness too new, too deep, too precious to be spoken of. Roi and Leila must have been aware of this arrangement, but they appeared to live for Chase's happiness. If Rosie possessed the power to make Chase happy, it was an excellent situation as far as Roi and Leila were concerned. Rosie fitted very easily into their lives, gentle and soft in her manner with Leila, who was indeed as beautiful and fragile as a butterfly.

Each night Rosie wondered if her nightmare would return to devour her, but it never did, driven away, she supposed, by the great outpourings of emotion. They rose at first light, had a quick breakfast in the kitchen, then they were on their way, sometimes on horseback, other times in the Jeep and on those occasions Rosie took along her camera. She was an excellent photographer, and she was having the time of her life capturing the beauty and grandeur of her surroundings, as well as many action shots of the mustering, herding and cutting of cattle, and horse breakers turning the best of the brumbies, the wild horses, into acceptable station hacks. The action shots she loved best were of Chase in the saddle. Most of them he was unaware of.

All the better, she thought. He was in for a surprise when he saw them developed.

Once they stayed out long after dark, to make love under a huge copper moon, the wonderful sandalwood smell of their campfire mingling with the fresh scents of the bush. On another occasion she'd tried to get Moses to talk, sitting down beside him, a mug of billy tea in hand, trying her level best to draw him out. She was convinced the crouched running figure she'd seen in her dream was Moses, struggling to carry the ten-year-old Chase. But Moses was more than a match for her interviewing skills. He fended her off gently and with courteous determination. Indeed, he seemed to know intuitively what she was driving at. It was equally clear that he wanted her to abandon the idea. Why? Rosie wasn't about to give up.

At dawn she and Chase sat together, as they did during the tropical sunsets, when the sun went down in a glory of reds, pinks and hammered gold. At these times, nature's daily celebrations, they always turned to each other. It was a period of discovery. Whatever the future, Rosie knew she would never forget these days. Such happiness even made her half-afraid. What if the gods became jealous? She had to grasp this while she could.

When they rode in that last afternoon, it was to find Mick Dempsey waiting for them on the veranda, a cup of tea supplied by the attentive Roi in hand.

"Hi, there, you two!" He leaped up to meet them, hurrying down the steps. "Isn't that a wonderful sunset, now?"

"Glorious!" Rosie said exultantly as she leaned forward to kiss Mick's cheek. "You're looking well, Mick. What's happened to the mustache?"

Mick gave his nose a rub. "I reckon it made me look an old bloke."

Chase laughed. "You've knocked ten years off your age."

"I wanted to get fit. And how goes it, boyo?" Mick thumped Chase's arm. "It's the good life you're livin'."

Chase grinned, realizing Mick was reading all the signs. "I've been rediscovering my own land through Rosie's eyes."

"It's been a tremendous experience, Mick," Rosie said, linking her arm through his as they headed back upstairs. "I've adored every minute."

"You're staying the night, aren't you, Mick?" Chase asked.

"I don't want to be a nuisance."

"Of course you're staying," Chase said. "I hope you've brought all your gear."

"Popped it in, just in case." Mick grinned sheepishly. "Have you sighted this Glenville fella?"

"I wasn't expecting to until tomorrow," Chase said. "But Rosie's heard of him at least. He's well regarded. Marley can vouch for him. Porter is supplying his own vehicles, as I told you over the phone. You can leave yours here and come with Rosie and me."

Mick grinned. "I'd say we have Rosie here to thank for your change of mind?" He shifted his twinkling eyes from one to the other.

"I'm getting very protective these days," Chase declared, lowering his own eyes to Rosie.

"And isn't that as it should be." Mick was obviously affected by their closeness. "I just wish old Porter wasn't coming with us."

Chase nodded. "And I hope to God the whole thing isn't just another one of his scams." He indicated they should each take a chair, holding one out for Rosie. "You know, Mick," Chase said when they were all seated, "my mind's been going back to all the tales Dad used to tell me from the old days. He had endless stories.''

"More than any man I know," Mick said, nodding. "And couldn't he spin 'em."

"I used to love listening to him. I worshiped my father. I thought there was never a man like him. He used to tell me about the timber getting and the tin mining. The place-names fascinated me. Graveyard Gully, the Lord's Prayer, Starvation Gully, Mount Misery. The characters who lived in inaccessible places, scratching out a living, roughing it and loving it, waiting it out until it started to pay off, hence Mount Perseverance.''

"The German fellow who killed a crocodile with his bare hands because it was taking his dog," Mick contributed.

"Our own drovers used to swim cattle across crocodile-infested waters, running the risk of having the horse taken right from under them," Chase said. "Dad had many tales of the Palmer gold rush in the late 1870s. The names of the mines. Palmer Kate, Gentle Annie, Roaring Meg. The twenty thousand Chinese who landed on the banks of the Endeavour and trekked inland to make their fortunes. For decades after, men dreamed of finding another field as rich as the fabulous Palmer.''

"Well, the Banfields didn't do too badly," Mick reminded him with a grin. "It was your great-great-grandfather's Aboriginal boy, Kulka, who first spotted the 'yellow sand' in Gongora.''

"Alluvial gold. He scooped it up in the billy to make tea. My ancestor knew exactly what it was. He began searching to find the mother lode and the rest is history. Kulka Creek. Kulka never left Byamee's side from that day on. The family prospered from the mine, but it's long worked out. Byamee and Kulka used to do a lot of prospecting after my great-grandfather took over the running of Three Moons. They were up-country near Gongora when

Byamee became ill and died. It was Kulka's people who brought him in.''

"And poor old Kulka didn't last long after that," Mick told a fascinated Rosie. "He was way too young to die. Only in his thirties. A broken heart, you know. Byamee was dead. No point in going on living. I can understand that.''

"It was a very intense attachment," Chase said. "Something special. Moses and I have a strong bond, for that matter. Kulka, by the way, told my family that Byamee had left 'lotta writing.' There wasn't a single member of the family who didn't believe him. According to Dad, the family searched, never stopped searching, but never found any trace of these writings. Finally, by my grandfather's day, they'd put all thought of it firmly away. There was no alluvial gold left along the river. If it lay on the riverbed, no one was going to risk the crocodiles. You don't suppose Porter found something no one else did, do you?'' Chase asked, shooting a sharp look at Mick. "It's a mighty big house. Full of hiding places. He had all those years when I was gone to search it from top to bottom.''

"God knows!'' Mick answered vehemently, scratching his head. "And there's something else to be considered. One of the reasons I'm along on this trip. Your dad, when he was very young, when we were both boys, used to do his own little excavations. He used to reckon that the ancient Egyptian presence on Three Moons was more than talk. He reckoned he could *feel* it.''

Chase frowned slightly. "Oh, Mick, that can't be true.''

"No fear." Mick shook his head. "He was like you. He loved all the old stories. The two of us were riveted by them, especially after that guy dug up all the gold coins on the Tablelands. Egyptian. Well over two thousand years old. Your dad always used to say one day he'd be successful.''

"At finding Egyptian relics?" Chase stared at him.

"It's a wonder he didn't talk to you about it," Mick said, sounding surprised. "I think that, like Porter, he genuinely believed a ancient Egyptian village was a reality, not a dream. Of course when he was older, he had to turn his full attention to running a big cattle station."

"He never spoke about it, Chase?" Rosie asked, upset when she saw him flinch. She thought her heart might break for him.

"I'm not sure," Chase admitted. "After I lost my parents, I found the only way to survive was to suppress all memory of them. I carried them in my heart, but my heart was locked up. Of course, there were times when it all escaped. Then the sense of loss used to nearly stop my heart. I was at boarding school. I couldn't cry. I couldn't run away. I had no one to turn to. Now, for the first time in a very long time, I've allowed some of my good memories in. It has a lot to do with Rosie and her healing presence." He reached for her hand, lifted it to his mouth, saw the answering sparkle in her eyes. "Porter has stirred things up again," he lamented. "I've always been uneasy about my uncle. There was no rivalry as such between him and my father. My father was unquestionably master of Three Moons. It belonged to him. But I suppose I was aware at some level that Porter couldn't slough off the feeling of being second-best, even though he was left financially secure. There was no way he could have run the station. He wouldn't have taken on the job if it was offered, but I believe now he was consumed by envy of my father and, by extension, me. He'd love Three Moons as his own private kingdom. Not as a working station. His head is pumped full of the wildest notions. I know that as surely as I know the sun will rise tomorrow."

"Which is when we leave," Rosie reminded him softly, watching his eyes. Had it been wise to persuade him to come? For her sake, certainly, and for the safety of the party. Still, she recognized that things wouldn't be easy for him, not only because he'd be coming into daily contact with the uncle who had never won his trust, but because of their very destination. Gongora. She had a poignant vision of that early Banfield who'd died in the wild bush with only an Aboriginal boy to offer comfort. She would have to make every effort to ease Chase's way.

With Mick in the house, Rosie decided to return to the magnificent bedroom that had first been allotted to her.

"Why so virginal?" Chase whispered against her mouth as they parted for the night. "I want you here with me."

"I have to consider my reputation," she murmured, moving quickly out of his arms before she weakened. "No..." She tried to explain. "I want to shield what we have from the rest of the world. Roi and Leila are different. They share your life."

His eyes confirmed his understanding. "I'll miss you. You know you haven't had a nightmare since you've been beside me. Neither have I. Something healing flows from you, Rosie. I don't want to lose that."

"What are you going to do?" Her voice trembled lightly. Even she didn't know the answer. They were living in a bubble filled with excitement, but there was a greater world out there. "See you in the morning." She blew him another kiss from the tall glass doors.

"Don't be surprised if I join you in the middle of the night."

"You want an early start, don't you?" she teased.

"Hell, Rosie, I can hardly let you go." His eyes were very bright.

"You have to," she said simply.

IN HER BEDROOM Rosie slid off her robe and placed it over the back of the daybed. There was another glorious moon bathing the veranda. She wasn't a nervous woman; nevertheless, she was glad of the light. The memory of her nightmare still filled her with a certain anguish. But she'd faced many disturbing situations during the past five years. She had to tuck it away in a safe corner of her mind.

Rosie returned to the bed, loosening the ties that held back the billows of mosquito netting during the day. Free of restraint, they foamed around the bed, but needed settling into place at the back of the altar chest that stood at the foot of the bed.

It was a remarkable piece of furniture. She wasn't certain of its origin. Antique. Elaborately carved. Some six and a half feet long and quite deep. Until this moment she'd never considered doing such a thing, but drawn to it, she removed the bronze sculpture that sat atop it, then opened the lid. A wonderful exotic fragrance flowed out, physically enveloped her. She discovered the contents to be bolts of material that came up a little over halfway. A closer examination revealed upholstery fabrics. Richly patterned silks and silk taffetas, florals, sculptured damasks, stripes, in a lush array of colors. Lilac, a lovely olive-green. Exquisite! She slid her hand sensuously over the top bolt, then lifted them out, the better to admire them, remembering she'd seen at least some of these fabrics used for the large cushions that adorned the settees and sofas downstairs. Underneath these fabrics were fine-quality linens, and beneath them a brilliant yellow-silk shawl, deeply fringed and embroidered with butterflies and flowers. She adored that. She could see it slung around her shoulders or knotted over a skirt. The chest was deep enough to hold a treasure trove. The floor of the chest was covered by layers of tissue paper and aged a dark yellow. She wondered if it housed a secret compartment. That would add to its fascination. Secret compartments in chests as old and exotic as this were almost obligatory to her way of thinking. She began to examine its floor. One of the wooden fasteners that held it in place rose a little higher than the others. She tried to twirl it, but it was fixed tight. She was already on her knees, intending to get up, when the wooden bolt suddenly gave.

"Eureka!" She muttered a little cry of satisfaction. She wanted to see more. *Was* there more? She knew she was being overcurious, but couldn't seem to help it. Equally well, she knew Chase wouldn't mind. Indeed, she felt like running back down the veranda and inviting him to join her. But she knew what would happen then. Chase would want to make love to her, and she'd need little persuasion....

It took her a short time to work all four knobs loose, then she lifted them out carefully, suddenly regretting that she hadn't asked first. What if she'd damaged something? The chest was obviously valuable. And...

It had a secret compartment. Just as she'd hoped.

There it was, under her gaze, a depth of perhaps five inches with that exotic aroma like rose petals and some precious oil seeped into the wood. It was empty, of course. But something had been in there. Old love letters? Family documents? She could *smell* them. There were a few little yellow remnants of paper stuck to the sides. For a while she floated off in her imagination, coming to herself with a start.

What on earth was she doing? She'd have to replace all this right now. In the morning she would tell Chase all about it.

But when morning came, the series of events drove all thoughts of the chest from her mind.

STANDING SIDE BY SIDE on the veranda, Rosie and Mick watched the Land Cruisers move in, rolling smoothly in single file up the long driveway.

"Here comes the big bad wolf," said Mick, but his tone

wasn't joking. "It's a bloody mystery to me where Porter gets his money. He was as good as broke and deserved to be, and now he's right up there again, financing this trip. Do you know how much those vehicles cost? You can't tell me these dealer blokes make *that* much money."

"I've met art dealers who are extremely well off," Rosie remarked. "I don't know much about dealers in antiquities. I don't know where the huge profits come from, either. I believe there's a thriving black market."

"Anything dodgy and Porter would be in it," Mick said in disgust. "You never in your life met two brothers as different as Lew and Porter. Apart from the family resemblance, they might have come from different planets. I'm going to be keeping my eye on old Porter. Chase won't give me much of a hearing. Can't say I blame 'im—you wouldn't want to accuse your own uncle of murder—but Porter is such a cold fish. Reckon it twisted him somehow, walkin' in Lew's shadow."

"You don't think Chase is in any danger from him, do you?" Rosie turned to Mick in alarm.

"Now, now." Mick patted her hand, reassurance in his voice. "Chase is a man who can handle himself in any situation. All I'm sayin' is it will pay us to keep our eyes open."

Rosie straightened her shoulders. "I'll be keeping my eyes open, too, Mick. So that makes three of us. You, me and Moses. He may not be going but he's always on the move around the station. You know," she said thoughtfully, "I tried to get Moses to talk to me about the past, but he clammed up."

Mick made a clicking sound with his tongue. "Moses gives nothin' away. Reckon Porter has somethin' to do with that. I don't think Moses is concerned for himself, though. It's Chase he's protecting. I tell ya, Rosie, where there's money, there's trouble. You'd never know it from the way he acts, but Chase is sitting on a fortune. And I don't mean just Three Moons. They were into everything, the Banfields. Had the education. Knew what they were about. I'm just an old bushie.''

"A true-blue bushie." Rosie smiled at him. "Chase really cares about you, Mick."

"God, he's a prince, like his old man." Mick rubbed his chin. "Wish he was here." That for perhaps the umpteenth time.

"So do I." Rosie's response was always the same. Both of them were looking subdued.

"Never do know what's gonna happen on a station," Mick said.

"I'm coming to see that."

The excitement of the morning had been marred by a bad accident to one of the stockmen. It happened as the stockman was riding back from an overnight camp. His horse suddenly dropped dead beneath him, then rolled on his rider while his mates tried desperately to free him. On his own in the bush, he would have died. It was because other stockmen rode with him that his life had been saved. As it was, he had multiple injuries—broken ribs, a broken collarbone, a badly fractured leg and God knows what else. Chase had called in the air-rescue helicopter and flown with the man to the nearest base hospital. It looked as though Chase wouldn't be back for several hours. Neither Rosie nor Mick wanted to start the trip without him, which was just as well because they would've been going against his wishes.

"Let them drive on ahead," Chase said before he left. "Don't worry, we'll catch up with them. I know shortcuts even Porter doesn't. Until I come back, Mick, you're in charge."

"What about me?" Rosie challenged more in fun than anything. "Think I can't handle it?"

A snort from Mick.

"Mick looks the part more," Chase smiled into her eyes, his glance moving over Rosie's slender figure, all dressed up for safari with a couple of stylish touches. "You can be his deputy."

"Right." She saluted.

Another snort from Mick.

"Don't like that Marley, either," Mick now said thoughtfully. "Funny bugger."

Rosie nodded. "I think it has something to do with his not having a sense of humor. Here they come, Mick." She straightened up. "We'd better go down and greet them."

"Don't rush," said Mick, watching the three men alight from their vehicles.

Porter, Marley and, dwarfing the two of them, Dr. Roland Glenville.

"Gawd, who's the gorilla?" Mick very nearly bellowed in surprise.

"Shh, Mick," Rosie whispered, embarrassed. "He might hear you."

Mick didn't appear concerned. "My, my, ya couldn't miss *him,* could ya?"

He was proving so hard to shut up Rosie slung her arm around his shoulders. "Remember, you're the boss."

Amusement twinkled in Mick's blue eyes. "Do I really have to be nice to Porter?"

"Civil," Rosie suggested.

Mick sniffed, then gave a great explosive laugh. "I love you, Rosie."

It was Marley who made the first move toward them, grasping Rosie's hand in order to kiss her cheek. "Well met, Roslyn. Not late, I hope? Good Lord, it's a devil of a drive."

Mick, who hadn't been acknowledged as yet by Marley

for all his boss status, scratched his chin. "Thought you'd be used to long treks, Doc."

"Well, of course I am." Marley still didn't extend a hand to Mick, looking past him for signs of Chase.

Porter and Dr. Glenville ambled up. Porter nodded and tipped his white panama, not bothering with a word or a smile, while Marley introduced his colleague as though he were a Nobel prizewinner.

Rosie studied the face above her, not at all sure what she was seeing. A big benign bear of a man—or something else? His appearance reminded her of a grainy photograph, one in which the features were blurred. The sixth sense she'd inherited and developed started to kick in. She didn't like the touch of his hand either, although that could have been because he'd squeezed her fingers almost painfully in his huge grasp. Yet something was out of kilter here. Mick, too, wore a puzzled expression.

But Glenville looked around happily. "Magnificent!" he said in a gentrified, enthusiastic voice. "I'm delighted we're all doing this together. I've been out on digs with Graeme before, but searching for the site of an ancient Egyptian village is a first." He beamed into Rosie's upturned face, the sun glinting off his spectacles. "Is Banfield here? I can't wait to meet him."

"I've a bit of news for ya," Mick said. "One of the men was involved in a bad accident early this morning. Chase called in the air-rescue helicopter. He went along with poor old Davey. Expect him back in a few hours." Glenville looked deeply disappointed. Porter, on the other hand, seemed pleased. Marley couldn't hide what Rosie interpreted as positive relief.

Why?

Rosie and Mick glanced at each other.

"We were hoping to get away now if you're ready," Porter said, in his unremitting icy tone.

"Who's stopping you, old son?" Mick inquired, looking as though he wanted to say something a lot more colorful. "Enjoy the drive. We'll wait for Chase and rendezvous with you later."

"You get worse as you get older, Dempsey." Porter aimed a thin smile in Mick's direction.

"I don't see a problem," Glenville said seasonably, still staring at Rosie. "We'll get going and meet up at some designated spot."

"Is that okay with you, Graeme?" Rosie asked.

"We would like to leave as soon as possible." Marley lifted his tan *akubra* and flapped it back and forth in the heat. "You could easily come with me, Roslyn. I'd be glad of your company. I might remind you that we did start out on this venture together."

"Sorry, old sport," Mick cut in before Rosie could speak. "Chase has given his orders."

"Maybe he expects a bit too much," Marley snapped.

"It's what *I* want, Graeme," Rosie said, placing a calming hand on Mick's shoulder. "Is there anything we could offer you before you go? Tea, coffee, a cold drink?" She fully intended to sit them on the veranda, not invite them into the house. She hoped they'd decline. The funny feeling she had about Dr. Glenville persisted, like an alarm going off. And he was definitely eyeing her, despite the benign expression. Not that she wasn't used to it from men, but his particular look was too...assessing. Uncomfortable. She could feel his height and bulk cast a shadow over her, so she moved abruptly, not really caring what he thought.

For a moment it looked as though Glenville was about to say, "That would be lovely!" when Porter Banfield's frozen expression turned resolute.

"I'm absolutely certain we couldn't eat another bite after breakfast," he declined for all of them. "Thank you all the same." He sketched a brief salute. "Tell my nephew we'll camp at the Zigzag. He'll know what I mean."

"Hell, I know meself." Mick gave Porter a pained look. "Lew and I camped there many a time."

"Still worship my brother's memory, Dempsey?" Porter asked cruelly, resting back against the bonnet of the Land Cruiser, the picture of elegance.

Mick's expression took on a new cast. One Rosie had never seen. He stepped toward Porter, suddenly looking the strong tough man he'd once been before grief and alcohol had brought him down. "He'll never be forgotten, Porter. Bank on it," he rasped.

"You pathetic drunk," Porter retaliated, sneering at Mick. "Who cares what you say?"

"Okay, okay, that's enough!" Rosie threw up a palm, her voice cracking with authority. "*You* might watch what you're saying, Mr. Banfield. Mick is here at Chase's invitation. Chase won't be happy about any fighting."

"Hear, hear," Glenville said, looking at Rosie with growing approval before turning to catch Porter's eyes. He waved a thick admonishing finger. "Hop in, Porter, and we'll be on our merry way."

It was said blandly enough, but everyone, including Porter, recognized it for what it was. An order. He moved quickly to the driver's side.

"I hope we can't expect a lot more of this," Marley said, addressing Rosie and ignoring Mick. "I, for one—" He froze as Mick suddenly leaned forward and closed his hand tightly around Marley's bush shirt, bunching it up and half pulling it out of his khaki trousers.

"Since time is the essence, I won't tell you what I think of you, Doc, but get this. The man who tries treatin' me like dirt will regret it. Keep it up, and you won't finish this trip in one piece."

"Truce, gentlemen, truce." Now Glenville took charge.

He came up behind Marley, laying an enormous hand on his shoulder. "I think you might apologize to Mr. Dempsey, Graeme. You can be very arrogant at times."

The blood rushed to Marley's face. Rosie, staring in dismay, thought she saw a flicker of fear. Fear? Of Glenville, his colleague? It certainly didn't look like respect. Graeme's handsome face went from scarlet to slightly blanched.

"Sorry if we got off on the wrong foot." Marley apologized in a voice so tight one might have thought Mick had grabbed him hard by the trousers.

"And...?" Glenville prompted.

"It won't happen again."

Glenville lowered his hand, stopped to pick a flower, handed it to Rosie with some panache. "It's a great pleasure to have you along, Miss Summers. You, too, Mick. I may call you Mick?"

Mick nodded, tremors of a hot Irish temper still running down his arms. "And you, your Christian name?" Rosie had told him, but he'd forgotten.

Glenville smiled. "I don't use it. I hate it. Glenville will do nicely."

Mick shrugged. "Right." He didn't quite know what he was dealing with here. Glenville's manner was very pleasant and conciliatory, but Mick could imagine him whacking his colleague senseless. A touch of the Jekyll and Hyde. He and Rosie stood in the driveway until the third Land Cruiser, driven by Glenville, had disappeared.

"Holy Mother of God!" Mick exclaimed, crossing himself piously. "Did you see that bull neck?"

"I've not actually seen a photograph of Dr. Glenville," Rosie admitted, starting to nibble her lip.

"'Struth, you'd be more likely to find it in a police file. I don't believe that bloke."

Rosie's forehead creased. "I thought I was watching some kind of live performance."

Mick turned to stare at her. Uncertainty was in the air. "If he isn't Dr. Glenville, then who the hell is he?"

Rosie shook her head. "It has to be Glenville. I know Graeme is a pain in the neck, but he has a reputation to protect. I mean, there's no other possibility. It *must* be Glenville."

"He was pretty busy starin' at you," Mick said with evident disapproval. Mick, who had deeply loved his wife, was sensitive to and protective of women. "Can we trace this guy?"

"We can try." Rosie sighed assent. "We've picked a bad day, Saturday. What exactly is it about him, Mick, that we don't like? Apart from looking me up and down, he was perfectly agreeable, and he did exercise control over Porter and Graeme."

"Both of them needed it," he said after some seconds. "Let me think for a moment," Mick said. "The look of him, I'd say."

"His hair was alarmingly short, although I only saw it for a few seconds when he tipped his hat. What did I expect? Completely bald or soft hair falling over his forehead like some scholarly fop? Can we condemn the man because he could stand in for the Incredible Hulk?"

"A professional heavyweight, at least." Mick entered into the spirit of it. "I wish to God Chase had been around. You don't think we've got a rascal on our hands, do you?"

Rosie shook her head. "It would have to be *three* rascals if that were the case, Mick. I find it hard to believe Graeme would involve himself in any deception. Nothing would be worth it. His career could be ruined."

"Listen, you think we're overreacting?" Mick tried to cheer her.

"Maybe." Rosie still sounded uncertain. "I suppose if

he'd been a tall pale skinny guy more in line with our preconceptions, we might have accepted him more easily."

"Yeah, I guess so." Mick half laughed. "You can't judge a book by its cover. Whatever I think of Marley— and it ain't much—like you, I can't see him risking his precious reputation. Not when he's number one in his field."

Rosie was in full agreement. "That makes sense to me. I'll have a go at checking up on Glenville all the same. Even if we can't get information faxed through in time, Roi can probably get a message to us. Of course, if it *is* Dr. Glenville, and it's bound to be, and he ever found out, it could make him very angry," she added quietly.

"What are we gonna tell Chase?" Mick's voice had a hint of urgency about it.

"I don't know." Rosie threw the flower Glenville had given her away. "What's to tell? He wears his hair cropped to the skull. He looks like a big brown bear."

"Aren't brown bears dangerous?" Mick asked.

"As far as I know, *all* bears are dangerous." Rosie pushed her sunglasses higher on her nose. "Even when they're supposed to be tame. They're wild animals, after all. I think they get upset easily, even our own cuddly little koalas. I was standing right beside a colleague a few years back when he was handling one of the sleepy little darlings and got badly scratched."

"Koala mustn't have liked his touch," Mick suggested. "They're not teddy bears even if they do look soft and cuddly. They're not even bears."

"No. They're related to possums. Well, one thing's certain, Dr. Glenville isn't in the cuddly category."

"He's not Porter's friend, either," Mick said. "I think he dislikes Porter as much as I do, but Porter listens to him. Did you see how smartly old Porter moved off to the Land

Cruiser when Glenville said they'd be on their merry way?''

"Did I ever!" Rosie couldn't help laughing. "It was as though someone had called out the troops. It's a shame we're losing Moses, though. I wanted to get to know him better. I'd love to hear him talk about the old days and how his people are coping in a vastly changing world. I'd love to hear the Dreamtime legends associated with this place. There must be many."

"Well, the saltwater crocs, the big fellas, the twenty-footers, are the guardian spirits," Mick informed her. "They've existed since time began. They're sacred to the Aboriginals of the Top End. Over the years they've claimed plenty of white fellas. The killers were hunted down of course. A lot were destroyed, but the smartest ones got away to their remote domains. It might sound strange, but they never seem to touch the Aborigines. I've seen it all m'life. The crocs are a protected species now, as you know. I expect they take the view that the white man threatened *their* existence."

"Maybe we should love them," Rosie suggested wryly. "Crocodiles kill people, but their blood has the potential to save lives. Haven't researchers recently made a break-through? They've discovered that crocodiles have a gene that fights infection. It's interesting—crocs are tremendously long-lived and they rarely develop an infection, despite terrible injuries or swimming in bacteria-filled waters. Resistance to antibiotics is becoming a global concern, so the croc just might come in handy, after all."

"At least that would ensure their future," Mick reasoned. "As for Moses, I'm sorry he's not coming m'self. He's a great old bloke. Fact is, he's needed here, what with Chase comin' along and Davey out of action. Chase left it to 'im to come after us if he judges it necessary. Busy time before the Wet. I should be home meself, helping out. The good Lord knows I haven't run things for years.''

Rosie squeezed his shoulder, knowing what discipline it must take for Mick to resist having a drink. "You'll get back to it, Mick," she consoled him. "I truly believe that. So does Chase. It all had to do with sorting our your grief. I can see you're a man who feels things deeply.''

"And you're an angel, Rosie." Mick took her hand and kissed the knuckles.

Rosie smiled at him, touched by the gesture. "I don't consider myself too angelic, but once in a while, I'd like their wings. I'd fly off to Sydney right now to get a fix on Dr. Glenville.''

CHAPTER TEN

THEY WERE DRIVING deeper and deeper into the wild tropical paradise that was Three Moons. An hour on, Chase stopped for a moment to pick a handful of the scarlet berries of a wild fruit, passing them to Rosie, who popped them in her mouth, finding the taste an intriguing mixture of sweet and tart. "There's a tremendous amount of interest in bush tucker," he said, "both here and abroad. Supply can't keep up with demand. Many bush foods are being farmed now. It could turn into a big industry, as big as the more exotic tropical fruits."

"This is delicious," Rosie said. "Not like anything else I can compare it to. It has a flavor all its own. The wild limes are wonderful, too."

"A man can survive out here if he knows how," Chase said, adjusting the angle of the sunshield against the shimmering mirage.

Chase had been flown back to the station around one o'clock. The helicopter pilot had landed on the broad stretch of lawn in front of the house, the whirling rotors causing spent blossoms from the encircling trees to rise up in a great cloud. He appeared anxious to be off, pausing to give them as much news as he could of the injured stockman, changing into a fresh shirt, making a final check of the four-wheel drive and its supplies before climbing in. Rosie sat beside him, Mick in the back.

"So what's the verdict on Dr. Glenville?" he asked as

the vehicle bumped and weaved through the long grass of the savannah.

"Unusual," Rosie said, keeping her voice neutral. She hadn't been able to contact her newspaper colleague, Garry, until well into the afternoon. Hence no information yet.

"What does that mean?" Chase laughed. "He's got bat ears? Or a possum's snout?"

"He's big as a buffalo," Mick said from the back seat. "Pleasant enough, although Porter doesn't seem to be one of his favorite human beings."

"Look!" Chase didn't respond for a moment, pointing to a herd of kangaroos who rose as one from the tall shimmering yellow waves of the undulating savannah, then bounded off across the grasslands. A stirring sight when seen in large numbers. "I actually haven't met anyone who liked Porter." Chase returned to the conversation. "Except maybe for your friend, Dr. Marley." He gave Rosie a gleaming sidelong glance. "So he wanted you to ride with him, did he?"

"Of course. But I turned him down, attractive and charming though he is." She grinned, smoothing her hair that refused to lie down.

"The old goat." Chase broke off as the vehicle went into a depression, which became a water channel during the Wet, and bumped out the other side. "Sorry about that." He removed the arm he'd flung out to protect Rosie, though she was wearing her seat belt. "Some parts of the savannah can be treacherous. You can't see the depressions for the long grass. And how old is this Glenville guy?"

"Gawd!" Mick wore a lost expression. "He could be any age. What do you reckon, Roses?" He leaned forward in his seat.

Rosie grimaced. "Who cares?"

"What is that supposed to mean?" Chase threw her a searching glance. "Didn't you hit it off?"

"Well, he tried his brand of charm on *her*," Mick said, figuring Chase ought to know.

"Well, well, well," Chase murmured. "You didn't tell me everything, Rosie."

"I reserve the right to edit out the unimportant."

"If he bothers you in the slightest way, I want to know about it," Chase said firmly.

"I suppose it's no use pointing out I can look after myself. Anyway, he didn't bother me, Chase, I promise you. He's just an extremely difficult man to read. He must be Graeme's age, at least."

"Well, Graeme isn't exactly in his dotage," Chase said dryly. He shook his head. "I can't believe I'm actually doing this."

"We could always turn back." All manner of anxieties were beginning to crowd in on her. If only she'd bothered to contact Garry much earlier.

For answer Chase stopped the vehicle, bringing it to a halt in the middle of the wild bush, the dark-green outline of rain forest rising up ahead. "Look, Rosie, there's no use trying to cover up. What's the matter?"

For a moment she considered telling him the truth. But what *was* the truth? A sixth sense? A woman's intuition? "I feel badly about taking you away from your work," she finally managed.

"*Now* you tell me," he crowed, relieved it was nothing more. "Rosie, you were all for my taking a break. Is it this Glenville guy? Mick, what's the score?" He turned his head, looking directly into Mick's eyes.

"I didn't say anything," Mick muttered. He didn't want to be drawn into this. He desperately wanted to continue, Glenville or not. He'd been looking forward to focusing his mind on something other than his grief. "I suppose when you think about it, the guy's not what we expected. He's nothin' like Marley, for instance. Huge. Big black mustache. Wears those silly gold-rimmed glasses.''

''Is that all?'' Chase sounded incredulous. ''It's crazy to hold the man's unfortunate appearance against him. You said his manner was pleasant.''

Mick nodded several times, hoping Rosie would take over.

''I doubt there's a red-blooded male who wouldn't look at you, Rosie,'' Chase concluded. ''Was it the *way* he was looking at you that you didn't like?''

''Oh, hell, he was friendly,'' Rosie was forced to concede. ''We can't take to everyone. Let's get going, Chase,'' she urged.

''Yeah, come on, boyo,'' Mick seconded. If anyone could handle Glenville, if indeed he needed handling, it was Chase. He stood six-three, as superbly fit as a man could get, a good fifteen years younger than Glenville. Mick was thoroughly convinced that Glenville, for all those barely concealed bulging muscles, would suffer by comparison.

THEY MADE CAMP late in the afternoon. The other three all-terrain vehicles had already arrived as expected, parked in a semicircle beneath the branches of a massive fig. There was, however, no sign of the man.

''Probably found a load of gold relics,'' Mick said, beginning to help Chase unload their gear while Rosie wandered off, glad to stretch her legs, enchanted with her surroundings. It was already an adventure, this Outback safari. A brand-new experience. Sharing it with a man she was madly in love with made it all the more joyful.

It was easy to see how the Zigzag got its name. Even from ground level she could pick out the twisting climbing series of jumbled weathered rocks that were probably the remains of an ancient escarpment. Their multicolored contours, pink, orange, black, white, were draped by a dazzling

large-petaled yellow flower; it must have burst into bloom
after one of the brief tropical showers that heralded the
approach of the monsoon. Trees in the region of the Zigzag
also displayed bright flowers. Tall flowering grasses, vivid
green reeds and a profusion of white lilies surrounded a
small freshwater spring that bubbled over rocks some little
distance off. It looked wondrously inviting, especially after
the long drive. Rosie hoped Chase wasn't about to tell her
it was the private residence of a freshwater croc.

While the men unloaded things to their satisfaction, she
stood beneath the giant fig looking up at it in awe. She felt
utterly dwarfed by the tree's flying buttresses, some four-
teen feet or more, the front section forming a deep cave.
She didn't step inside in case it housed a snake or a goanna.
She'd let Chase check on that. A great preponderance of
thick woody vines lay all over the ground. She would have
to watch she didn't trip over them. The vines, in turn, were
covered by masses of luxuriant intertwining creepers in a
soft lime-green. Various climbing plants reached a great
height in a stand of tall slender trees without low branches
but with spreading crowns. Tiny epiphytic orchids and delicate little basket ferns clung to the slender trunks, with
long trails of some scarlet bean-shaped pods that were beginning to split open, exposing the black seeds.

It was a beautiful spot, an isolated little pocket of rain
forest, the constant damp provided by the subterranean
spring creating the atmosphere required. To one side of the
giant fig, fleshy white objects like extraterrestrial flowers
emerged from the dense layer of mosses and fallen leaves.
She thought they had to be a species of fungi, wondered if
they were poisonous.

There was so much to look at she couldn't take it all in.
She felt barely any breeze beneath the canopy of trees, but
it was delightfully cool and quiet—an astonishingly diverse
world. As she circled the rain-forest giant, the red-gold rays

of the sinking sun turned the Zigzag to magic. For a few minutes it lit up the entire area with intense brightness and a burst of hot sunshine. Just enough, Rosie supposed, for the rain-forest plants to flourish.

Mick, who was busy helping Chase set up her tent, waved to her. "We'll settle you over here, Roses," he called. "A lady likes her privacy." Mick had taken to calling her Roses during the course of the afternoon, and Rosie rather liked it. "You'd think the others would've put their tents up," Mick grumbled to Chase.

"They could have elected to sleep in their vehicles," Chase answered, not much caring. "They can look after themselves. It's Rosie's comfort I'm concerned with."

"My hero. My heroes!" She leaned over one, then the other, kissing each on the cheek. "This is such an adventure! I might even try fossicking for gold."

"You won't find any," Chase said with a laugh. How sweet her scent, her own perfume, how silky soft her lips.

"What about diamonds?" She sang a few lines from a song forever associated with Marilyn Monroe. "Alluvial diamonds." She moved easily back to speech. "They get washed down rivers. Diamonds are said to go hand in hand with gold. We're such a young country, we're only beginning to realize what we're sitting on. Queensland has the largest sapphire fields in the world, and there's opal all over the country. Look at Argyle." She named the West Australian diamond mine.

"With immense regret I have to tell you we won't be finding any diamonds this trip," Chase said, sounding amused by her enthusiasm.

"Spoilsport!" She made a face at him. "We're going to find something, aren't we, Mick?"

"'Course we are, love." Mick pushed the opening of the tent aside so he could move in, arranging a ground sheet over the soft bed of fallen leaves. "What about a small gold statue of the goddess Isis, wife of Osiris and mother of all things? That'd be nice."

Rosie shuddered. "I don't know," she said doubtfully. "That was a very strange experience I had with Porter's necklace. It shames him now to admit it, but Chase thought I was having him on about the marks around my neck."

"I don't know why you didn't wake me. I'd love to have seen them." Mick broke off abruptly as three figures came through the cover of trees and began the descent to the camp.

"Quickly, before they come." Rosie grasped Chase's arm. "Is the spring safe for bathing or is it the home of some crocodile?"

"You're in luck." He smiled down at her. "For one thing, it's too small. Freshwater crocs grow to an average of eight feet and they live almost entirely on fish. No fish, no croc. Maybe a few frogs. That's why Porter elected to camp here. It's the logical spot."

"How marvelous!" She sighed. "Is it deep or will I only get my ankles wet?"

"Roses, we couldn't let you go in if you didn't swim," Mick said. "It's deep and you'll find it pretty cold even in the heat."

"You've brought your swimsuit?" Chase asked. He found he couldn't support the notion of anyone else looking at her scantily clad body, outside of Mick, who was one of nature's gentlemen. Not Porter or Marley. Certainly not the fast-approaching newcomer who made both of them look like striplings. Interesting the way he moved. Chase would stake money on it: Glenville wasn't moving naturally. Possibly he had some old injury.

"Do you think I can take a dip while it's still light?" Rosie was asking at his shoulder.

"Wait for me." Chase didn't turn his head. He gazed unblinking, at the big man. "I can rig up some cover later on, get a fire going so we'll have enough light. It's this guy Glenville I'm more interested in right now. Look at the way he's walking."

Rosie swung around, staring.

"When I started to watch, his stride suddenly changed. Turned into a shamble."

"Wait until you see him close up," Mick chimed in.

"Now what does that mean, Mick?" He frowned at Mick. "You sound like you've got real concerns about Glenville."

Mick squinted into the rays of the sun. "Well...no. Not really." He spoke awkwardly. Because it wasn't the truth?

"I don't want Rosie involved in any of Porter's damned schemes," Chase muttered, remembering the misery his uncle had caused.

Rosie pressed her face against his shoulder. "Look, Chase, I can handle myself. Anyway, I'm certain Porter didn't want Glenville along, so he couldn't be part of any scheme."

"That's right, Chase. Rule it out." Mick seemed glad to be able to second Rosie's opinion.

"Fine. We take it as it comes." Chase shrugged. "Who can tell with these crackpots? We'd better get the campfire going, Mick. They're acting like they can switch on electric lights as soon as it gets dark. I'm damned if I know how Marley found the Winjarra paintings. It must have been a fluke."

The brilliance of the sunset was rapidly turning to a smoky-mauve dusk as the three moved on down to the camp. Glenville, apparently eager to join the main party, stumbled over a prop root and staggered sideways with a cry before eventually righting himself.

"All right there, Glenville?" Marley groaned, as though his colleague was the sort of person who tripped over obstacles on a regular basis.

"Fine, fine, Graeme," Glenville answered cheerfully, waving an arm.

"Made it here okay, then?" Marley turned to Chase with a syrupy smile, irritating both Chase and Mick no end.

Chase lifted his shoulders. "What would you expect of a man traveling over his own land? You're showing a lot of dedication, going out already—before you've even set up camp. Or has Porter been showing you where he unearthed the gold necklace?"

Marley was spared the answer as Glenville descended the Zigzag in slow motion, holding out his arms like he'd been waiting for just this moment all his life. "At long last, Mr. Banfield. Roland Glenville at your service."

"Gawd, I thought he was gonna embrace him," Mick muttered in an aside to Rosie.

Chase responded evenly, accepting a fleshy handshake that didn't seem to fit. In the falling light and deep shadows, it was difficult to make out Glenville's face. It was an odd face, shovel-shaped. The head sported an extreme army cut. On the other hand, he favored a full mustache and wore small gold-rimmed glasses, which he was constantly pushing back. The voice wasn't bad. Deep, pleasant in tone, educated. Not much to argue with there. If he stood up straight, instead of hunching his shoulders, Chase thought they would be of a height. Glenville was larger, though, heavier. His clothes were too baggy, but Chase didn't think for one moment that they were meant to disguise overweight. All in all, as Rosie and Mick had found, Roland Glenville appeared to be a jumble of characteristics, a benign bogeyman if there was such a thing. Perhaps he wouldn't look quite so odd if he hadn't shorn his hair to within a quarter inch of its life. It stood up in stiff pikes, a disconcerting contrast to the flamboyant mustache, which shrouded the mouth with its thin bottom lip. Glenville turned to smile at Rosie, barely concealing his delight at their meeting again. "How can you look so cool, Miss Summers, after a long trip like that? You're quite the fashion plate!"

"Aren't I just!" Rosie made an effort to be pleasant, aware that all her senses were on alert.

"Maybe it would be a good idea if you got your tents up," Chase said, "or are you just going to use a sleeping bag?"

"No, no, no!" Glenville shook his head. "I can deal with the tents."

"Maybe over there." Chase pointed to an area on the opposite side of the gigantic fig.

"Righto!" Glenville agreed happily. "What a backyard you have, Mr. Banfield. A tropical kingdom." He broke into an admiring chuckle.

"Chase will do fine," Chase didn't want to appear unfriendly, regardless of his mixed feelings about Dr. Roland Glenville. In the morning he'd have a clear view of the man. As it was, he'd swear Glenville was wearing a disguise.

Marley looked past the orange glare of the campfire to the beckoning pool. "Okay to take a dip, do you think?" He addressed Chase.

"Sure." Chase nodded. "You'll find it pretty bracing despite the heat. I think we'll give Rosie the chance to jump in first. I might join her. Mick can take his turn, then the rest of you can suit yourselves. While you're cooling off, we'll start laying out the food. What did you bring? We've got frozen food packed in ice in the eskies. It should have thawed out nicely, so it's fresh steaks for tonight. After that, fish. There are magnificent barramundi in the river."

"What about the crocs?" Marley asked with a shudder.

"What about them?" Chase said dismissively.

Marley dropped the subject.

IN HER WELL-ERECTED TENT, sited for maximum privacy,
Rosie stripped off her boots, then her shirt and jeans, con-
gratulating herself for having had the presence of mind to
bring a one-piece swimsuit in case there was a chance of
a dip. Not that she didn't own her share of bikinis like most
other young Australian women, with the Pacific Ocean and
the Indian Ocean at their doorsteps. But the sleek navy one-
piece was more appropriate for the trip; after all, she was
a lone female in the company of five men. Not that it bothered her. Her stints in the war zones had brought her into
very close proximity with men, even if the spartan quarters
she'd shared had always been with women. She was used
to pretty primitive accommodation. Not that this camp in
such a beautiful place resembled any of those other places.

Rosie adjusted her suit. It was cut a bit high, perhaps—
she didn't really fancy Glenville's strange bespectacled
eyes on her—but then, good swimsuits were all cut high
these days. She folded her clothes, neatly shouldered into
her beach robe, pinned her flaming masses of hair on top
of her head, then stepped outside into a star-filled night.
They crowded the sky, the atmosphere so pure, so unpol-
luted, their clarity and brilliance was extraordinary. She
could see at a glance that Glenville had erected the other
tents on the far side of the giant fig. As far as she could
see, he'd done a professional job of it. No sign of him.
Porter and Marley, however, were seated on camp chairs,
drinks in hand, while they carried on a low-pitched but
intense discussion. Graeme had his back to her. Porter saw
her, but didn't acknowledge her. Not even a wave. An incredibly disagreeable man.

Rosie made her way over to the reed-fringed pool. The
white lilies, rather like daylilies, had closed their petals, but
their musky scent hung in the air. The pool was as black
as night, yet the surface glittered with the reflection of
golden sparks sent up from the campfire Chase had lit

nearby. She took off her robe, hooking it onto a convenient branch, feeling a pleasurable shiver of anticipation at submerging herself in the bracing water. She didn't see, nor was she meant to, the bulky figure in the shadows, his body camouflaged by dark clothing, the collar turned up like a cowl around his neck....

SHE LAUGHED A LOT, beautiful white teeth glinting. He liked her voice, the pitch, the expression. A bright vivacious challenging woman, used to dealing with men. Easy in their company. Banfield was in love with her. Highly protective. She had the other one, old Dempsey the pushover, eating out of her hand. That stuffed shirt Marley had an interest in her, as well; he was plainly jealous of Banfield, who was as superbly fit as he was himself. Young, strong, the quintessential cattle baron. And he had to be sitting on millions. Millions his fop of an uncle would surely inherit if anything happened to Banfield. Chase Banfield himself would be impossible to manipulate or control. Long experience of men told him that. On the other hand, Porter Banfield would make an excellent puppet.

But the woman! She did what very few women had ever been able to do. Get under his skin. He didn't know if he liked that. It was a complication. But he couldn't take his eyes off her. He could see her white skin glow opalescent in the firelight, which was as bright as her wealth of orange-gold hair. She had a great body. Great! A *woman's* body. Just looking at it stirred him up. Beautiful straight shoulders, long lean flanks, nipped-in waist, racehorse legs and those breasts! He could imagine their soft creamy bulk filling his palms. He could imagine himself pinching her nipples hard. He could see her fighting him. Even thinking about it gave him a rush. A woman like that would always fight. The idea excited him. She was strong, too, with an athletic vitality that was indescribably sensuous. She kept herself in good shape. His eyes lowered to the secret place of her body at the apex of her thighs. He imagined himself there. He wanted this woman. He knew he'd have her before the trip was over.

Meanwhile he'd continue playing the buffoon, the jovial giant. The act had gone over very well with Marley and Porter Banfield. They lived in a dreamworld. He'd have to do better with the others. He'd recorded the way the woman had moved away from him not long after they'd been introduced. She didn't care if he noticed, either. Women were different. A lot of them had a kind of early-warning system to protect them from predators like him, no matter how much he tried to gain their confidence. Others swam easily into his trap, but Rosie Summers wasn't going to be one of those. He would have to subdue her. He was looking forward to the struggle.

Then there was Banfield, lean, powerful, nobody's fool, eyeing him warily. Even the old fellow's eyes held a shadow of suspicion. With the woman around, he didn't want to assume this crude disguise. He wanted her to see him as he really was. Of a height with Banfield. Striking, too, in his own way. Scores of women had told him so. He wanted her to see and admire the hard musculature of his body. He wanted her to see him stripped. He was as fit as he'd ever been, even back in his army days when his physical fitness had made him something of a legend, a man to be feared. He wanted *her* to fear him. Make her heart race whenever he was near.

Disher made it a rule never to get involved with a woman, but this woman was special. She had more than the others, lots more. When he took her, it was going be perfect....

She wasn't going in the water, though it was obvious she wanted to. She was looking around for Banfield. As he watched, he ran one hand across his close-cropped head and thought scornfully of Banfield's hair. Thick, deep waves, *long*, curling up at his nape. If he wasn't so damned tough, so obviously the virile man, people would be telling him to get it cut. A real man didn't want to look like a sissy. His dad had taught him that with many a belt in the lug.

Tough as he was, Banfield wouldn't be a match for *him*. Banfield might live and work in the outdoors, his job keeping his body at the peak of fitness, but he hadn't been trained for combat. He hadn't been trained to kill. He wouldn't know any of the dirty tricks. His concern for the woman and his old pal showed the weakness in Banfield's armor. Sentiment. Disher had no time for it. At some point Disher knew he'd have to engage Banfield man-to-man. He knew who would win. That thought filled him with confidence. In a way he was hoping Banfield would come out to join the woman in the bubbling spring. He'd watch for just a few moments. Not too long. He might even see Banfield pull her underwater to kiss her, to grope at her white flesh.

"WHAT THE HELL are you doing?"

The voice at his back shocked him, went beyond shock, chilled him to the bone. He was dumbfounded that his honed skills, his most bankable commodity, had failed him. He couldn't remember a time he hadn't had the edge. Now he realized many beats too late that he'd been stalked. And found. He had to do something. Fast.

The man known as Glenville reached for the front of his pants, unzipped the fly. "Lord, Chase! You scared the hell out of me. Can't a man have a pee in private?" He could sense the eyes boring into him in the inky darkness mitigated only by the flare of the campfires. His palms were wet with sweat and his stomach gave an involuntary heave.

Chase didn't say a word. Disher could sense the anger running through him.

He pretended to shake himself off, pulling the zipper back up as he turned. "Whoever taught you to move like a shadow?" And to stand immobile. "I didn't even hear a leaf crackle, and I've got pretty good ears." He kept to that goofy voice, jovial, embarrassed, but his muscles, like Chase's, were bunched, ready to uncoil.

"Don't insult my intelligence." Chase, stone-faced, put a hand on Disher's shoulder, long steely fingers reading the strength Disher had tried to hide. "You were spying on Miss Summers." His voice showed his contempt. "Is that how you get off? Playing the Peeping Tom? You took one helluva gamble doing that."

It was too humiliatingly true. How long had Banfield been there? Disher wondered. He'd heard nothing. Felt nothing. It was all the woman's fault. With a tremendous effort of will, Disher quelled his own rage and incredulity at missing Banfield's approach. What the hell was Banfield wearing on his feet? *Kurdaitcha* slippers made from emu feathers? He must have stolen the secret from the blacks. Disher managed to shrug helplessly, deliberately relaxing his body, seeking to maintain the bumbling image.

"My dear chap, you couldn't be more wrong." He used the plummy aggrieved voice of one of his army superiors who was forever hauling him over the coals. "I think you owe me an apology."

Chase broke into a grating laugh. "Think again! I took time to observe you."

Blatantly caught out, Disher had no option but to change tack. "So I've been admiring a beautiful woman." He took the opportunity to push down the collar of his olive-green shirt. "Is that a crime? It wasn't intentional, believe me. I went for a little walk to relieve myself. I was standing right here when Miss Summers appeared. I appeal to you, Baneld, what red-blooded male could turn away from a sight ke that?''

''So you're red-blooded now, are you?'' Banfield spoke uietly, but it was abundantly clear he wasn't a man to ess with.

Disher went for a touch of aggression, a hint of offended nsibilities. ''I see no reason to be rude. Surely there's no al difference between admiring a beautiful woman and a eautiful painting.''

''You're a connoisseur?''

''Precisely,'' said Disher. ''I don't know why I've made ou so angry. That's the last thing I want. I want us to be iends. By the same token, I don't want to be made feel I n't even glance in Miss Summers's direction. She's a ghly intelligent woman. I know her background. I've read ae or two of her articles. I'd enjoy her company.''

''All very plausible,'' Chase said. ''Except for the body nguage. I'm not a fool, Glenville. Make no mistake. Don't mpel me to throw you off my land. If you want to stay, is is your one and only warning. Watch yourself in Miss immers's company. Don't ever attempt to spy on her ;ain. I'll be around. Is that clear?''

''Absolutely!'' Disher threw up his hands like a prisoner out to surrender. Then, still mortified at being bested at s own game, he muttered, ''I must say in my own defense at perhaps your own feelings for Miss Summers have ade you overreact.''

Banfield's face looked fierce in the flickering shadows. don't think that's any of your business,'' he bit off.

Disher wanted to roar out his own sense of injury, but knew it was time to back off.

''And I respect that,'' he managed with a return to his :ultured'' voice. ''If you want me to keep my distance, I ll. Message received loud and clear. I'm not anxious to oil our expedition.''

"You took a big step toward it tonight," Chase told him bluntly.

"And I assure you I'm duly repentant." Before this tri was over, he'd have Banfield begging for his life.

"Then you'd better remember," Chase said. "When yo take your little strolls, make sure they're in the opposit direction."

CHASE PAUSED BRIEFLY beside Mick on his way to joi Rosie in the rock pool. He bent over Mick's reclining fig ure, one hand closing on his shoulder. "Watch Glenvill for me," he said very quietly. "Don't look in his directio just yet. But watch him from now on."

"What is it? What's wrong?" Mick had been puzzle by Chase's disappearance until it dawned on him that Gler ville was missing, too.

"You're right about one thing. He's got his eye on R(sie. Literally."

"The bastard!" Mick growled deep in his throat like dog about to tear the seat out of Glenville's pants.

"I've had a word with him. It'll do no good to make a issue of it now," Chase warned. "We're on our guard. don't think he'll offend again."

"He'd better not!" Mick snapped, obviously energize by anger.

"We won't say anything to Rosie. Not yet. Hopeful never."

"Right!" Mick said. "Who would've thought a bloo(academic would be a common peeper?" He shook his he: in disgust.

FIRELIGHT ON THE WATER.

Rosie called to him as he walked to the pool, lifting h slender arms to her hair. "I wanted to wait for you, b you took too long. Come on in." She tread water, her lun receiving the fresh moisture-laden air. "I have to warn you. It's cold at first."

"Rosie, you're talking to a bushie." He thought there could be no better place than here, beside her, breathing in her scent. Chase made short work of diving in. When he came up, bronze hair streamed away from his face, dark and sleek, accentuating his strong bone structure. "That was good!" He sighed aloud with pleasure. "What do *you* think?"

She regarded him with a sense of exhilaration that was almost dizzying. An exalted feeling that transcended anything she'd ever experienced before. "My idea of heaven. To swim in the middle of the wild bush. A bubbling fresh-water pool. Fragrant lilies all around us. A sky full of stars. The smell of the campfire. The prospect of good food. Being with you..." Beneath the leaping light that spasmodically sheened the water, she twined her legs around his, while he in turn got a one-armed grip on her wet yielding body, the other caressing her breasts below the surface.

After a moment he murmured, "Just as well the water's so cold." Her warmth was transferring itself to him. "Mind you, it's heating up." Heating up? Exquisite sensations were invading his groin. His eyes glowed in the low light. "I want to open my mouth over yours. I want to feel your mouth open to me."

Rosie groaned, yearning for the same thing. "Not with everyone watching." She continued to hold his hand fast to the rise and fall of her breasts. "I had the feeling you were checking on Glenville. Were you?"

"I thought he was missing a mite too long."

"But you found him." Rosie had to confront her anxieties.

"I crept up on him. Discovered him skulking around. I'd say I took ten years off his life, and he's not a man who cares easily." Chase gave a brief laugh that held little humor. "At least, that's my instinct despite the bumbling academic pitch. Underneath the baggy clothes he's extremely fit."

Rosie nibbled hard on her bottom lip. "I'm having him checked out," she confessed.

Chase shook the water from his ears, as though he wasn't hearing correctly. "What did you say?"

Rosie considered carefully before answering. "Just routine." She shrugged her glistening shoulders.

Chase's expression tightened. "I thought we'd agreed to accept Marley's recommendation," he said pointedly.

"We did. It's just a routine check. Nothing to worry about."

"So *you* say." No sarcasm, but hard reappraisal. "Still," he acknowledged, "none of us seem to trust him."

"The problem is his appearance, I think."

Chase looked into the middle distance, his whole demeanor changed. "I think I'd better have a word with Marley. If this is some kind of joke, I see no humor in the situation. We don't leave here unless Marley vouches absolutely for this man. If he's lying, for whatever reason, I'll make sure he pays for it. Who's doing the checking for you, anyway?"

Rosie swallowed. "A colleague. A fellow journalist. I know I can rely on him."

"How are we supposed to get the answers?"

She took his hand beneath the water. "I thought that if there's anything we need to know, Roi or Moses could get word to us."

"Rosie, this isn't the city," he told her. "You know that by now. Just getting here was quite a trip."

Rosie shook her head as though there wasn't really a problem, but privately she blamed herself. "Do you want me to speak to Graeme?"

"No, I do not!"

"No need to chew my ear off," she protested.

"Rosie, why didn't you tell me about your anxieties concerning Glenville before?"

She moved into him, put her arms around his waist. "Because he hadn't demonstrated anything in his manner to take objection to. It's purely his appearance."

"Rubbish!" Chase rejected that. "The man's a creep. Look, we'd better get out. I'll collar your blasted Graeme before he has a chance to run away. As for my uncle— you've got to understand that he's simply not trustworthy. There's only one person in this world Porter cares about and that's himself. He'd put us all in jeopardy just so long as he could benefit. The more I think of his heroics in saving my life, the more I see it doesn't fit a lifetime pattern."

"You think it's time to investigate?" Rosie followed him to the edge of the pool.

"Yeah," he said quietly, turning to give her a hand. "You know something?"

"What?"

"You're one heck of a pushy woman."

"Really?" She smiled into his eyes. "Thanks."

CHAPTER ELEVEN

WHILE ROSIE AND CHASE were cooling off in the spring, Marley and Disher went into a private huddle with Porter, keeping a close eye on Mick, who was moving back and forth, making preparations for the meal.

"You'd better watch your step with my nephew," Porter warned, holding Disher's strange flat eyes with his own. "One false move and he'll be on to you." This was said, incredibly, with a certain amount of family pride.

Marley, on the other hand, not wanting to antagonize the man he thought of as the Hulk, leapt to Disher's defense. "I think you're doing very well," he said in his rich insincere voice. "Chase seems to have accepted you."

"Accepted me enough to track me," Disher grunted, letting the accent slip.

"Well, you were gone a fair while," Marley pointed out.

"And he had to play detective?" Disher sounded amazed. "He *checked* on me. Can you beat that! I'm supposed to be a respected academic."

"You don't really believe you look like one, do you?" Porter asked in acid tones. "And on reflection, I'd get rid of the mustache," he added disdainfully. "It looks like you could sweep roads."

Disher reached out a huge hand, thumb and fourth finger digging painfully into a pressure point above Porter's knee. "Spare me your shit, Porter," he rasped. "Your dad should have belted you silly when you were a kid. That's how my dad straightened me out. Fine, the mustache goes. No prob lem. I'll shave it off.'' Despite all his training, his self-imposed restraints, Disher found himself caught in a scenario as old as time. He wanted to show off to a woman. He wanted Rosie to see him as he really was. A soldier of fortune ready to do the tough jobs anywhere in the world. Now that he was reasonably sure he was accepted—although Banfield was right, he'd have to watch his back— he could loosen up on the disguise. He was proud of his body. He needed to show it off. There had to be some recompense for all the backbreaking workouts.

"Roslyn and Chase are coming,'' Marley observed beneath his breath, watching jealously as Chase slung a towel as big as a bath sheet around Roslyn's shoulders. She had a wonderful body, wonderful! Marley felt himself becoming aroused, something that wasn't wasted on Disher.

"Fancy her, do you?'' It came out like a warning snarl.

That sobered Marley immediately. "She's a very striking woman,'' he said as though comparing her with a statue of the young Queen Victoria. "I think I'll have my dip now, if you don't mind.'' Marley began to get up from the camp chair, but Disher jerked him back.

"I do mind, old sausage,'' he said with a terrible cheerfulness. "Wait your turn.''

Disher laughed, turning as Porter said almost casually, "I wouldn't go showing off that barrel chest or the bulging muscles.'' Porter's leg was still aching, but he was quite unable to resist. "It might open up a real can of worms.''

"Worms are good stuff,'' Disher said, referring to an Aboriginal food staple. He gave Porter a revolting limp wave. "You know, Banfield, you're the kind of guy who ends up drowned.''

"My God, I think he means it,'' Marley said as Disher shambled off. He stared at Porter in a ferment of worry. "You do realize th-th-this…'' Marley was stuttering, something he'd never before done in his life. "Disher—'' he shook his head violently to clear it "—has been trained to kill. Frankly, I don't think he needed any training. What was your man thinking, sending him on this expedition?"

"Probably trying to catch me out." Porter's laugh was brittle. "Don't worry, Disher's got himself under control." Porter's own lack of interest in women blinded him to any potential danger. "I already told you he knows his job. If he doesn't carry it out successfully, he won't get paid. And you can bet your life he's earning big money."

"Well, as far as I'm concerned, it's like living with a Rottweiler." Marley couldn't conceal his deep misgivings, the overriding sense of guilt. "Something might set him off. Something to break his chain."

"Look at him now," Porter jeered, as though Marley's fears were ill-founded.

Marley turned his head. Disher was wearing a loose T-shirt over what looked like long-legged board shorts, a dark towel slung over his shoulder. Barefoot, he was picking his way very gingerly over the jumble of exposed roots splaying out from the massive fig.

"He looks ridiculous," Marley said wearily, feeling it might be time to pack it all in. His ambitions. His continuing thirst for recognition. He wanted to go to Chase Banfield, tell him what had happened, tell him of the pressures he was under.

Porter laughed again. "Who cares? Settle down, Marley. I recognize you for a wimp, but I'm not going to allow anyone to mess this up. Not you. Not my nephew. Not Disher." He stood up, looking coldly, darkly, menacingly handsome. "I'm going to my tent until the food is ready."

"Not planning to help out?" Marley wagged a finger at him. He'd come to dislike Banfield intensely, so he didn't bother to hide the sarcasm.

Porter, however, looked almost startled. "I leave that to the servants," he said, Marley's sarcasm bouncing off him.

DISHER WAS ALREADY in the pool, lost in the shadows, when Marley chanced a look. He rose slowly from his seat, thoroughly depressed. Maybe he'd do better to speak to Roslyn. She'd tear strips off him, but he knew in his heart that she was a warm compassionate woman. Easier than Banfield, at least. He was almost at his tent, intending to change into his own swimming gear, when a long arm reached out, grabbed him and drew him lurching behind the giant fig.

"Good God, Chase!" he sputtered, when his eyes became accustomed to the gloom. "That gave me a bloody fright." More than ever, he was aware that he shouldn't get on Banfield's bad side.

Chase made no apology. "I have a few things to ask you about your friend."

A great chasm opened up. "Glenville?" Marley couldn't say another word until he'd swallowed. Now was the time to put the whole matter straight, but even as he dithered he considered that Disher mightn't hesitate to eliminate him. He was a frightening, violent man who wouldn't react kindly to being betrayed. Marley felt suddenly terrified to reveal the truth.

"Who else? Don't play the fool, Marley." Chase exerted a little more force. "It doesn't suit you. I have reservations about your colleague."

Marley tasted calamity in his mouth, yet he threw up his arms as though he understood the situation perfectly. Had, in fact, experienced it a number of times. "I know. I know. Roly's a wonderful chap, a brilliant scholar, but he's somewhat lacking in social skills. He looks like a bundle of messy laundry. Always has been like that, from our student days. No woman to look after him, buy his clothes, that sort of thing. Surely you can't condemn him for that."

"Unfortunately there's more to it than that." Chase

spoke grimly. "He's not married?" Chase wanted to confirm it.

Mercifully, the real Glenville was not. "No." By now Marley was tasting bile, but he persisted with the fiction, feeling quite unable to confront Porter, let alone the barbarian, Disher. "I notice he's taken a shine to Roslyn." Was that what was troubling Banfield? "I can assure you he's absolutely harmless."

"You mean he has a reputation for being a pervert?"

Marley stiffened. "What do you mean?" He was so shocked his voice took on an odd high note.

"I caught him spying on Rosie when she went into the pool."

Disher had failed to tell them that. Well, well. Marley clasped the satisfaction of the moment.

"I've given him a warning," Chase continued. "One only, or this trip is off."

"Surely you wouldn't turf him out for a bit of voyeurism," Marley said. "I suppose he couldn't help himself. Bachelor and all that. One has no wish to pry into his private life, but I know the female staff at the museum think he's a bit of a joke. None of them takes him seriously. He's never actually *done* anything."

"Are you on the level?" Chase demanded, listening closely, searching for the lie.

"I swear." Marley made it sound like he was holding a stack of Bibles.

"When was the last time you swore to something?" Chase didn't pull any punches. "Dammit, I should have had this man investigated."

"You don't believe me?" Lying, Marley was nevertheless affronted.

"I should. You have a reputation to protect, after all. I can't see why you'd lie. On the other hand, I've learned to trust my instincts."

"Let me have a word with him." Marley studied Banfield earnestly. "He can't help the way he looks, poor chap. It didn't help when he went overboard with his hair. Had it cut short for a field trip. Let someone overzealous run a mower over it. But he knows his stuff. He'll be invaluable when the time comes."

"You still expect the earth to offer up treasures?" Chase asked with something like pity.

"I rely on instinct, too," Marley said. "I'm convinced that your uncle, in these matters at least, is telling the truth. He did find relics on Three Moons. There are more to be unearthed. With his help we *will* find ruins, some evidence of an ancient Egyptian settlement. No matter how suspicious you are of your uncle, he's not lying about this."

Chase's voice was flinty. "And you'd better be right about Glenville. A price will be paid if you're not."

"Good Lord above, Chase," Marley said beseechingly. "Can't you trust me? Mark my words, we're onto something big."

By MIDMORNING they'd left the relatively open woodland with its bright patches of color, progressing slowly into the monsoon jungle and on to the river the Aborigines regarded as sacred. Gongora. One of the most beautiful rivers of the tropical North, Gongora emptied its waters into the dense coastal mangrove swamps, a key element in the ecosystem, and then into an aquamarine bay. But just as the Garden of Eden had its serpent, Gongora had its crocodiles.

Rosie reacted with rippling thrills of horror when she sighted her first saltwater crocodile. The massive reptile with its armored ridges was sunning itself on the opposite bank of the great river along which they were now traveling.

"My God, aren't they terrifying creatures!" She gave a gasping breath, rubbing her goosefleshed arms.

"They do have a natural fear of men, like all wild animals," Chase, long used to the sight of crocodiles, said almost casually. "Tourists have been warned over and over that it's an offense to feed them, but someone always does, most often with disastrous consequences. Feeding crocodiles links food and humans in the croc's mind, as you can imagine."

"Did you know, love, you can tame a croc?" Mick offered helpfully from the back seat.

"No thanks, Mick," Rosie threw him a look full of revulsion.

Mick shrugged, a bushman all his life. "Reckon they're like lions. Some you can tame. Others can never be tamed."

"Either way, if something upsets them, they're likely to eat you," Rosie said laconically.

"True." Mick chuckled. "Look at that old boy over there. He's not as big as others I've seen. My dad shot a thirty-footer in the old days. He had to, after a woman in the town was taken in shallow water at night."

"Good grief!" Rosie said, dread in her voice.

"That's not going to happen to you, Rosie," Chase consoled her. "Just act with caution at all times. If you were in South Africa in a lion park, you'd proceed the same way. Africa has its lions, India its tigers and we have our crocodiles. I don't want to see them die out." Chase flicked a glance at her. "You wanted to come, Rosie. Anyway, Mick and I are here to protect you. That fellow over there is probably a Dreaming Crocodile, as Moses would say. The crocodile is Moses's totemic ancestral being."

"Really?" Rosie was fascinated. "So what exactly is the Dreaming?" Rosie asked. "Forty thousand years of Aboriginal history?"

Chase nodded. "You could say that. The Dreamtime was when the Great Spirit ancestors created the universe. There are hundreds and hundreds of traditional myths and legends, all about creation. They're reenacted in all sorts of ceremonies and song-poetry. The Dreamtime continues as the Dreaming in the spiritual life of the Aboriginal people today. Spirituality has a great bearing on their lives.''

"This beautiful country that is mine," Mick said. "How often have I heard an Aboriginal say that? You'd think, the way most whites talk, Australia didn't have a history before Captain Cook landed.''

"Well, Aboriginal history isn't entirely lost," Chase said. "Thankfully it's been retained in the memories of successive generations and passed on through the song-poetry and legends. I'll speak to Moses about staging a *corroboree* for you, Rosie. You'll enjoy it. Aboriginals are among the finest natural dancers in the world." He broke off to point to the forests of paperbarks that rose on the opposite shore. "The bush around here is full of fruits and berries to keep you alive. It's possible to get water from those paperbarks in the Dry. A bit salty, but it'll do if you're thirsty. Of course, there's plenty of water around in the Wet.''

"We'll be catching some wonderful barra from the river," Mick promised her. "First thing in the morning and late afternoons are the best. They lie in the shadows. Best eating fish in the world, the barramundi.''

"I've tasted it many times," Rosie said, "but I suppose it's been frozen.''

"Wait until you taste it fresh from the river," Mick crowed. "A totally different experience. I see our croc friend is moving off.''

Rosie, who'd been keeping a wary eye on it, shivered as she watched the prehistoric creature drive its claws into the sand, the great head now pointed toward them. "Won't he be waiting for you when you go to fish?''

"We stay on the bank, Rosie." Chase grinned as the

crocodile slid into the river amid a spray of water. "We won't be wading in. Pretty soon we're going to have to make camp, leave the vehicles and proceed on foot. Ready for it?"

"I'm game if you are," she said, feeling anything but game.

"I thought old Porter was betraying a bit of genuine excitement." Mick rubbed his twitching nose.

"Glenville was falling all over himself to be helpful," Chase added dryly.

"I see he got rid of the ludicrous mustache overnight," Rosie commented.

"So that's what you thought about mine?" Mick grinned and shrugged. "Ludicrous! Mine ran rings around his, too."

"It suited you much better," Rosie said. "On the other hand, I didn't think Dr. Glenville looks that much better without it."

"Mean mouth," Mick grunted. "That's why."

Rosie agreed. "When I first saw him this morning, he started swaggering around like a gunslinger. It was really quite funny."

"Maybe he's a bit of a comedian," Chase remarked briefly, his expression tight.

"I don't think he'd know a joke if it bit him on the backside," Mick replied. "Anyway, he was helpful enough. Thought I should mention it. Old Porter doesn't lift a finger. Acts like he's royalty. The kind they sent off to the guillotine."

"Well, we've reached the sacred river." Chase spoke in a terse significant voice. "The three of them had better get out there digging their holes, finding their ruins, communicating with ancient Egyptian spirits. The Wet could come early and the Wet dictates all human movement."

CAMP NUMBER TWO was a small granite plateau cushioned by patches of vegetation, mosses and lichens and a grove of flowering bottle brushes. At its feet, seeping through the bracken-covered ground, was a tiny spring that spurted up cold freshwater, much like the bubblers in city parks. This little bubbler would swell tremendously in volume once the rains started falling, but for now, Rosie found it a wonderful convenience. This had to be one of the most unspoiled places on earth, she thought as she went about making her own campsite comfortable. She was looking forward to taking more photos, even of the crocodiles, as long as they stayed on the other bank.

As they'd roared and rattled their way into camp, the ride had started to get rough, scrabbling down gullies, up the other side, flattening the long sun-bleached grasses. Once they passed a shrieking gurgling colony of giant fruit bats, thousands of them, hanging upside down from the branches of trees, waiting until just after sunset, when they would fly off to their feeding grounds. Rosie had never seen such a sight nor heard such a squabble. Chase had stopped long enough for her to add the sight to her photo collection. They were a study in ebony, compared to her study of pure-white corellas literally covering the branches of a eucalyptus. A whole canvas of landscapes just waiting for her camera. And the spectacular birdlife! Brilliantly colored birds wheeling above their heads, all along their route, while kangaroos and wallabies sprang up from the shade of the eucalypti to bound away as the Land Cruiser approached.

A little farther on, they passed a glittering sheet of water, where there were so many brolgas gathered they were standing shoulder to shoulder. This beautiful blossoming wilderness was a photographer's dream. Rosie, in a permanent state of excitement, had almost forgotten the real purpose of the trip. The others had not—Marley, Porter and Glenville, who hated to be called Roland, much less Roly.

If it weren't so embarrassing and downright unwelcome, Rosie would have thought Glenville had been parading for her benefit that morning. It seemed so idiotic she rejected the notion. Not that men hadn't made idiots of themselves in front of her before. But Rosie pushed all thought of Roland Glenville from her mind, confident that if there was some news that might expose Glenville in any way, Moses or Roi would follow them.

This afternoon, led by the enigmatic Porter, they would begin their search for more relics to prove once and for all that Three Moons had witnessed an ancient Egyptian village thousands of years before.

ON FOOT THEY FOLLOWED the course of the river as it continued to flow seaward. Porter and Marley in the lead, Glenville apparently struggling to keep up, Chase, Rosie and Mick in the vanguard. The vegetation was becoming denser, huge palms with fronds four feet across, soaring tree ferns and cycads, strangler figs with bark that reminded Rosie of crocodile hide.

They walked close to the river, but on higher ground. In fact, it was getting steeper and steeper, but Rosie, strong and energetic, was able to keep up with the men. There was an intense honey smell in the air that Chase traced to a plant with cream flowers and a brilliant yellow throat. Rosie was glad of her boots. The forest floor was alive with small creatures that the thick carpet of fallen leaves of deciduous trees camouflaged and almost hid completely. Tiny lizards in the hundreds whipped across the surface of the trail before them, and large shiny skinks slithered from their hiding places in fallen logs, taking off like rockets. There were nectar-lapping beetles of all kinds with gorgeous iridescent backs, little rain-forest wallabies standing about two feet high peering curiously through the ferns, goannas brightly patterned in yellow and charcoal feeling with their pink-

orked tongues for insects, rain-forest dragons resting on
ogs, their vivid yellow throat pouches inflated at the dis-
urbance, mouths wide open showing rows of sharp trian-
gular teeth.

As the day progressed, the magnificent birdsong and display had lessened as the birds took time out for feeding.
They had to crouch a lot and stop while Chase hacked off
a few troublesome branches, but Rosie found that every
inch of the route was filled with interest—and the odd moment of fright.

Rosie was lost in the contemplation of a gorgeous blue
butterfly winging its way between white waxy flowers
when Chase grabbed her in one rough movement, leaving
her rocking on her feet.

"Wh-wha…?" She turned her head to look urgently up
at him.

"Quiet. Stand here." He spoke in a low voice, his fingers
digging into her shoulders.

She wasn't about to argue. This was his part of the world.
No sense in asking for trouble, Chase thought. His
searching eyes always on the lookout for any possible danger, he'd spotted an amethyst python moving very, very
slowly along an upper branch, its whole attitude suggesting
an ambush. It didn't take long for Chase to spot the victim,
a placid little cuscus, a rolled-up ball of fur fast asleep in
its sheltered cocoon of vegetation.

Rosie still hadn't seen anything—until the python suddenly slid its amethyst-colored body, some twenty-five feet
long, down the gnarled trunk, coming into plain view.

"Lord!" She sucked in a breath, her limbs going weak.
Fancy having that drop on her. She cringed back against
Chase, and he slid his arms around her with relish. "Are
you sure it's not coming over here?" she whispered.

"Not this time." He shook his head. "I told you I'd
make sure nothing hurt you."

A moment more and the snake struck, its coils around its victim so quickly, so tightly, the cuscus could neither bite nor use its claws.

"Oh, that's horrible!" It would have upset anyone. Rosie averted her eyes. "Poor little thing."

"That's life in the jungle, love," Mick told her.

"It's kill or be killed," Chase murmured. "The python mostly attacks flying foxes, possums or small wallabies. All of them have the teeth and claws to slash back and inflict serious wounds of their own, but the python is super cunning. It's been known to coil itself around quite a few unsuspecting humans, just like the big six-footer goannas tangle with men and horses. Now that's a scary experience being mistaken for a tree. We can move on while our friend enjoys his meal. He'll swallow the cuscus whole."

Rosie's joy in her surroundings was temporarily blighted by the killing, but inevitably she rallied. It was so beautiful, so wild, so lush—and this was the Dry! The other three were lost to them as they forged through a corridor of ferns soaring thirty feet high, tall as trees with beautiful wide crowns. Here and there great patches of the most delicate maidenhair flourished, with coral ferns unfurling their fronds protectively over them. The rain forest had a very special atmosphere, created by the vines, the cycads, the fig trees, the ferns, the epiphytic orchids, the little ground orchids, they were careful not to tread on, the great stag horns that adorned the trunks of trees.

"It was worth coming just to see this." Rosie's expressive face reflected her pleasure. Mick had pushed on ahead to examine the spectacular rain-forest phenomenon called cauliflory, where tight bunches of flowers grew right up the tree trunk.

"Pity we're not the only two in it." Chase drew her unprotesting into the marvelous green seclusion of a tree fern with its umbrella of dense fronds. "I'm not going another step unless you kiss me."

Her skin had a wonderful incandescence, her moss-green eyes iridescent in shadow, lustrous by sunlight. Flying wisps of curls had escaped her single thick plait.

"No problem," she said huskily. "Kisses are important." At that moment no one else in the world existed for her but Chase.

He could see her beautiful teeth beneath her soft parted lips, then felt her little moaning breath come into his mouth. *This is precious. Priceless. How can I hold on to it?*

Her body clung to his, her slender arms twining like vines around his neck.

"I'm burning for you," he muttered, acutely aware of his reacting body, the blood that ran molten through his veins. Above and beyond his great desire for this woman, he needed her as a source of radiance, a guiding star, this bright spirit who could bring light into the dark places of his soul. He knew he couldn't bear the thought of saying goodbye to her. Yet did he really have enough to offer to make her stay? He had to remind himself over and over that she was very good at her job. Still, his mouth claimed hers powerfully, aggressively, responding to her present needs. His hand shaped her breast. She seemed to be melting into him, his heart, her heart, his pulse beating in unison with hers. They were enveloped in a world of verdant green and stillness, each utterly concentrating on the other.

SOME DISTANCE AWAY in the darker recesses of the jungle, a man moved stealthily through the shadows, the way a predator moves on its prey. He saw that Banfield had his hand plunged inside her shirt, feasting on her white flesh. They were totally unaware of him, their passions running high. He could see how Banfield was bent over her, the bunched muscles of his arms, his back and shoulders as he crushed the woman to him. He could tell how much the woman was loving it. Though he felt a fury akin to defeat, even betrayal, his own body was responding; he used every ounce of willpower to hold himself back. Why he craved this woman was unfathomable to him, alien. It could prove a dangerous and costly error.

Banfield and the woman finally broke apart. He could see the sheen of heat and sexual excitement on the woman's skin. He detested the way she lolled her fiery head against Banfield's chest. He imagined the two of them mating, absolutely certain Banfield had possessed her. Mating like two wild animals in the wilderness, beside themselves with passion.

Because he could no longer bear to look at them, Disher stole away, making little grotesque grunting noises deep in his throat. No one must know he'd seen them. He'd get what he wanted from the women in his own time. She'd know then what it was like to be taken by a real man.

WHEN LEILA COLLECTED the pages faxed to Rosie by her colleague, she took them straight to her husband, waiting while he glanced first at the faxed photograph of Dr. Roland Glenville, so dark and blurry his own mother couldn't have identified him, before turning his attention to the two-page article. Roi read the information through carefully, taking his time and reading aloud to his anxious wife, who hadn't liked Glenville's "aura." She'd decided this while peeking at him through a sheer curtain, Roi reminded himself, though he had good reason to respect his wife's extrasensory perception. The article was a potted biography of Dr. Roland Glenville, listing all the usual things, date and place of birth, parents both distinguished anthropologists, universities attended, Glenville's academic standing and achievements to date. Rosie's colleague had scribbled a few lines at the bottom of page two, supplementing the biography.

Glenville was a big man, around six foot three. Not really overweight but substantial. He wore glasses, was balding, had a prominent nose. Unremarkable in appearance except for this and his height. A confirmed bachelor but got on well with women, was in fact "a bit of an old woman," as Rosie's colleague had divined from his informant, a fellow academic. At present, Dr. Glenville was on a sabbatical, exact location unknown. Friendly with Marley but lacked his charisma. Roi had to read right to the end before he saw that Rosie's colleague had added an afterthought. Roland Glenville had one other distinguishing physical characteristic: he had different-colored eyes, one blue, one hazel. Neither Roi nor Leila had seen Dr. Glenville close up, but Leila remembered Rosie's mentioning that he had "eyes like stones." Leila considered Rosie as observant as she was herself; surely she would have added that his eyes were of different colors.

"Even behind the glasses Rosie would have seen that." Leila shivered as though a cold wind had blown through the house.

"You think so?" Roi asked slowly, warily, his expression deeply serious. Deciding whether to get word to Rosie was his decision to make.

"Yes, yes!" Leila suddenly buried her face in her hands. "I knew the truth about that man and I said nothing." Her slight body began to quiver with emotion.

Roi stood up at once, drawing his wife into his arms. "Hush now, my precious one. There is no need for this anguish. You forget Chase is with them. If there is any trouble, Chase is equal to it." Roi spoke calmly, reassuringly, to his timid but brave little wife. "And he has Rosie, who won't be taken in, and Mr. Dempsey. Dr. Marley did not impress me as a man, but I don't believe he would do anything to put the others in danger. I know you are very intuitive, but sometimes you get caught up with anxieties.

I recognize the symptoms. Probably Dr. Glenville is exactly who he claims to be and probably he does have different-colored eyes. Are you in any doubt about this man? Think very carefully before you answer. They will be a long way off by now.''

Leila looked up, her eyes moist with a kind of shame, her unblinking liquid gaze fixed on her husband. ''I know this in my heart, Roi. Send someone after them, and do it now.''

Immediately Roi abandoned his own duties and went on horseback to find Moses. Moses was part of it all. A tribal elder, welded to the land, to Chase Banfield, to all of them. Moses had watched over the boy, Chase, all the days of his childhood so no harm would come to him. Moses knew up-country better than anyone—what route to take, the quickest way to do it. Moses was the one to go. Roi knew he had no concrete reasons to offer Moses beyond Leila's intuition. But Moses would never sneer at Leila's ''powers.'' He had ''powers'' himself.

ROSIE DIDN'T KNOW what she expected. The Great Sphinx? The pyramids of Giza? Neither, but her sense of being on a wild-goose chase was increasing. This was the ancient land, the Great South Land, inhabited by Aboriginal tribes for untold thousands of years. Even their forty-thousand-year tenure had been pushed back greatly of recent times, experts arguing it was more like one hundred thousand. This was a land baked dry by the tropic sun for many months of the year. Grass fires scorched it, the monsoon deluged it, cyclones battered it, floods ravaged it. Not many ruins could survive all those extremes.

Chase, walking with her, offered a satirical comment now and then, eyes on his uncle's tall figure in the distance. Porter was leading them like a latter-day Messiah. But what was under the vine-covered slopes? Stone walls? Streets paved with gold?

"I know my uncle looks perfectly sane, but I think you'd better consider that he could be off his rocker." Chase paused to help Rosie up a rocky slope. "And Marley, for all his scientific background, is ego-driven. Success can't stand still. He located the Winjarra cave paintings to a considerable fanfare, and now he has to discover a pyramid or two. So we can't guarantee he's in his right mind, either."

Rosie nodded, her eyes dark with exertion.

"I suppose projects like this don't get moving all at once, but it doesn't look promising."

"Welcome to the real world, my love." He flashed her his heart-wrenching smile.

In an excess of emotion Rosie reached out to him, held his strong arm, rejoicing in his physical strength. "What was that word you used?" Love. She whispered it, though Mick was thirty meters ahead. What power this man had over her! She had never felt so happy, so *alive*.

"Only the truth," he teased.

Rosie paused to look up at him. He stood a step above her, lean and powerful, the jungle greenery and a cloudless cobalt sky for a background. His khaki hat was tilted at a dashing angle on his bronze head, but Rosie could read the naked desire in his topaz eyes.

"We use banter to escape feeling, but I'm knocked out by what I feel for you, Roslyn Summers," he said with an intensity that was new to him. "In fact, I'm starting to believe in miracles."

"God, isn't that wonderful!" His admission thrilled her, the admission that she had transformed his life. That she was his *love*. She rushed up the last few feet of incline to reward him with a kiss. She knew he would feel the love, the tenderness and— She suddenly lurched forward as though she'd been pushed, stubbed her toes against a mossy rock, felt her legs buckle. Before Chase could catch her, she went tumbling down the thickly vegetated slope, still with the presence of mind to draw in her body and limbs. Near the bottom she came to a stop so abrupt it was as though she'd slammed into a brick wall. She lay winded, scarcely able to breathe.

What the hell was going on? What had caused her to fall? She was startled and frightened by what was happening to her. Gradually, as she was able to suck air into her lungs, came the most disturbing thing. Instead of a green world, she found she was enveloped in a dark-gray cloud with shapes whirling through it. Human shapes. She was afraid for a moment that she was back in her nightmare, only this time it was different. These shapes were gods or demons. She couldn't tell which. Visions of terror from a long-ago civilization. She tried desperately to take stock of her surroundings. She didn't *want* to know about this. She hated the images that were flashing through her head, yet she was receiving them as if this was planned.

Please God, take them away. Like many another in crisis, she began to pray. With that, the whirring stopped. The cloud disappeared, along with the images, as though someone had turned off a machine.

Rosie lay very, very quietly, wondering if she needed a short spell in a good psychiatric ward. Ten days or so. She didn't really want to be like Great-aunt Hester who took such things in her stride. This revelation of her own "powers," terrified her. And…she didn't want it.

"Rosie!" Chase's ragged shout, a violent explosion of sound, sent hundreds of birds wheeling into the sky. He moved instantly, lowering himself down the slope in a fury of anxiety, his booted feet finding purchase in the ropes of vines.

A second later Mick, alerted by Chase's cry, ran back along the track, watching Chase disappear over the side.

"Wait a sec, love, we're coming," he called. He knew it was Roses. She was so impulsive. It could be her undoing.

Relief and a kind of anger rose simultaneously in Chase. He wanted, *needed* her to be more careful. She couldn't do this to him. Hell, she was too precious. He had the distinct feeling that if he lost her, it would destroy him.

But Rosie was strong, athletic, and she'd been taught how to take a fall. Furthermore, she was strong-minded. She lifted her head, still feeling pinned to whatever she was lying on, as good as staked out. She was accurately reading Chase's body language, the concern and tension that tore at him, but still felt too breathless to talk.

"Rosie, I find your antics most distressing." He bent over her, brushing corkscrew tendrils of hair off her forehead and out of her eyes before turning his attention to her limbs. He was vaguely disturbed by the way she was lying almost like a sacrifice, her arms extended on either side of her, her legs splayed. He noted without caring she had lost the cream *akubra* he'd bought her. He hadn't caught sight of it on the way down, either.

"Antics! I like that! I swear it was no antic," Rosie burst out. She stared up at him. "I was pushed."

"Rosie, darling!" He raised his eyebrows.

"I know you don't believe me. Write it off as another of the world's mysteries."

"How can I?" He laid his palms flat alongside her. "There was no one behind you. They're all up in front."

"I know. It frightens me." She began to move her arms rapidly, fanning them out over the vine-covered shelf on which she was lying.

"Is there something else?" He watched her closely.

"As a matter of fact, there is. If I didn't know better, I'd say I was lying on an altar. There's stone, concrete, something underneath me. I'm sure of it."

"Well, I'm not going to worry about it. Are you?" He bestowed a worried look on her.

"I think we should investigate."

Chase glanced about him. "Not my thought at all, Rosie. I don't thrive much on mystery."

"All right. All right. I don't blame you. I'm fairly muddled myself. But I sensed the...the weirdest things. Look, I'm shaking."

"Same here, babe." A half smile touched his mouth. "Let me get you off that bloody 'altar.'" He moved decisively, reaching out to pick her up, but Rosie waved him off, her forehead knitted with concentration.

"Give me a minute."

"Oh, hell, we can stay here as long as you want. That was quite a tumble, but even in the stress of the moment I couldn't help noticing that a porcupine couldn't have done it better."

"I was good at gymnastics when I was about eight," Rosie told him absently. "I'm getting real vibes about this place, Chase. None of them good."

"And you still want to investigate?" He gave her a look of mild disgust. "Didn't you ever see any horror movies? I know this would make a good story. Maybe you ought to write it some time. You've got a writer's imagination, but you frightened the living daylights out of me. Actually it's getting to be quite a trick of yours."

"Shh! No trick!" Her head was still tilted in a listening position. "I was only wanting to kiss you, anyway."

"Well, that's fine." He caught her chin to get her attention, bent his head until their mouths met, very satisfactorily. "I love this part, but you can't go rushing along jungle tracks. You could have fallen into a deep hole. God knows what's beneath these vines."

Rosie's green eyes fired. She sat up, clutching Chase's hand. "I told you. A flat slab of some kind. A sacrificial altar to a goddess. Not a nice one like Isis, Earth Mother. I can tell you that much. There's a priest in it somewhere, people in the background, jungle. I didn't ask for any of this, Chase.'' She shook her head. ''It's a gift—or a curse. It's like what happened with the necklace. That was no trick, either.''

Mick, who had made short work of getting down the slope, moved over to them, his face full of concern. ''You okay, love?''

''Great, Mick.'' She managed a reassuring little wave.

''She's okay?'' Manlike, Mick turned to Chase for absolute confirmation.

Chase heaved a deep sigh. ''I have absolutely no idea. I've never met such an exhilarating and provocative woman. Now she tells me she's lying on an altar.''

''I am, too,'' Rosie was so convinced she began to pound the vegetation. Her tumble had roughed her up, but everything seemed to be in working order. Except maybe her brain. ''Chase is being very sarcastic, but I think I finally have to accept that I'm psychic.''

''Or crackers.'' Chase's response was razor-sharp, but Mick focused on Rosie.

''Sure, and aren't women mysterious creatures,'' he muttered.

''Hell, Mick, we don't need this.'' Chase turned on his friend. ''If you think I want Rosie spirited away on the wings of madness, you can think again.''

''Not much we can do about it,'' Rosie said with brisk determination. ''I think we should start looking around here.''

Chase shrugged philosophically, as though he was there to indulge and cajole. ''Why not? We've got nothing better to do.''

''I love a mystery!'' Mick exclaimed. ''That's great!'' He set to with satisfaction, beginning to hack at the vines.

"Get up, love," he urged Rosie. "It's possible there's something under you. It stopped your fall. A shelf maybe." Mick's blue eyes were bright and alive, the dark smudges and little pouches caused by excessive drinking almost gone.

Chase and Rosie exchanged glances, both of them delighted at the way Mick's spirits had picked up.

"Don't you just love the way the others have come back to see if we need help?" Chase asked in an ironic voice.

"Maybe they don't realize anything happened," Rosie suggested, not much caring.

Mick didn't need to consider that. "Roses, they would've heard Chase's shout back in town. Look, we need something better than this." Mick began to shake the mashed-up vines from his small machete.

"Maybe if the two of us had a go," Chase said in the manner of a man who's decided that if you can't lick 'em, join 'em. "If Rosie's sitting on an ancient Egyptian altar stone and it's inlaid with gold, I want you to know it all belongs to *me*."

CHAPTER TWELVE

DISHER KNEW he was in deep trouble the moment he saw the old Aborigine walk out of the bush. He wasn't staying around to face it. Alerted, Chase Banfield would make a formidable adversary, and like him he had a gun.

Disher had been making his way back to the excavation site, where he'd been working like a slave to make them all happy, but now he returned on the double to where his gear was stashed. Swiftly he grabbed as much food as he could lay his hands on, although he knew as well as anyone how to survive in the bush, then collected his backpack and his rifle. It was time to make himself scarce. Not that he wouldn't be keeping an eye on them the whole while. Especially now, when things were getting interesting. The woman had come up with the site, claiming she felt "vibrations." Probably in cahoots with old Porter, who was secretly searching out the whole area, Porter who never pulled his weight. Whatever the bloke was looking for, it wasn't the old stone ruins that had that fool Marley so excited. Even if they *were* ancient Egyptian in origin, what the hell would he care? They hadn't unearthed any gold coins, gold statues, gold of any kind. Just a stone seal that put poor old Marley in a lather of excitement. Even the woman seemed interested.

These archaeologists who spent their lives poking into lost civilizations! He could understand treasure, all right. Gold. Silver. Precious stones. He couldn't get excited about little bits of rock that might or might not have been ancient

Egyptian. Chase Banfield seemed to share his private skepticism, though Disher thought he'd done a first-class job of remaining in character as Glenville. And it had had results. The woman had been a lot friendlier, her green eyes filled with approval for all the hard physical work he'd done on the site. Everything had been going along fine.

Until now.

The old black tracker, Banfield's man, had come after them for only one reason. To challenge his identity. Probably Banfield or the woman had run a check on him. This was the result. Once he reached camp two, he'd take more food and the Land Cruiser that had been allotted to him. He'd abandon it somewhere in the dense bush. Any number of good hiding places. That way they'd think he'd skipped out when he had no intention of going anywhere. The job wasn't over. There were still a few things left to do.

WHEN MOSES REACHED the excavation site, he stood stock-still, holding his side as if he were in pain. As he did he heard the soul of a long-ago victim scream in agony. This area of Three Moons spoke to him. Had always spoken to him. Visions had come to him in dreams. Always he felt ill. This wasn't a good place. There was a curse on it.

He could see everyone working below. Chase, Mr. Dempsey, Dr. Marley. Even Miss Summers was pitching in. They had uncovered a large rectangular stone slab, some six feet by four with a depth roughly the same; leading up to it was a short flight of steps and farther off, twenty or more feet of a low stone wall. This was where they were all working. So far no one was aware of his presence, but Moses realized instantly that the man who called himself Glenville was not in the working party.

Moses walked on, skirting the stone slab he knew to be a sacrificial altar, a place of violence and death. Now the spirit power in the earth had been released. Once he had held Chase's life in his hands. He knew he would do so again. That would be the night Porter Banfield would die. Still holding his hands to his side as if to contain a deep bleeding wound, Moses moved on, strange images dancing in front of his blurred eyes.

Suddenly aware, Chase turned his head, saw Moses making his way down the slope, steering clear of the flight of steps that might have eased his descent. So Moses didn't like those steps, Chase thought, staring with narrowed eyes. Obviously he saw them as unholy. Moses was an acknowledged native doctor, as well as a sorcerer, with the dislocated small toe that marked the wearer of the true *kurdait-cha* shoe. Aboriginals in general were very vulnerable to all forms of magic. Chase knew from long observation that Moses didn't like this wild area of the station. Chase put down the tool he'd been using, stood up and waved. Moses's appearance meant trouble, he told himself grimly, looking along the line to where Marley was working, with Mick as willing assistant. "Where's Glenville?" he asked, his face tightening.

Though Marley's skin blanched, suggesting he knew something, it was Rosie who answered. She was seated in the shade of a small eucalyptus, gently dusting off a few broken shards of what looked like pottery. "I think he went off to get a drink. He's been working pretty hard."

"Well, he's not here now," Chase said. "But if you look behind you, Moses is."

Rosie swung her head, fighting down panic, watching Moses walk a little unsteadily toward them, clutching his side as if he had a stitch. She knew immediately that his coming meant bad news.

"I'll go check on Glenville," Chase said over his shoulder, moving very fast up the excavated terrace. "Find out what Moses has to say."

"Oh, God!" Rosie gasped. She put the broken shard

down carefully and stood, dusting off the back of her jeans. It took less than a minute to reach Moses. She saw him give some private signal to Chase.

"Are you all right?" she asked, sounding breathless. "You're holding your side."

"Not real." Moses shook his snowy head. "It will go. Hurts like a spear."

Rosie took him by the arm, leading him to the shade of the tree. "Moses, that's your right side. It should be seen to." She stared at him anxiously, seeing the disquiet that resided in him. "Have you been hurrying?" She was worried that he mightn't have paused to rest, but pushed on in the heat.

"Don't worry, Miss Rosie. I'll be right in a minute or two." Moses pulled the wide-brimmed hat from his head. "Don't like this place. Never have. Too much sadness here." He withdrew the folded fax pages from his breast pocked and handed them to her. "These are for you to read. It's about Dr. Glenville. The real Dr. Glenville," he added softly.

"Can it be?" For all her earlier misgivings Rosie was shocked. She looked at the old man searchingly before turning her attention to the faxed pages. The photograph was useless. The rest could well have fitted the man they called Glenville. Except for the eyes. One blue, one brownish-green. The man they called Glenville had small deep-set eyes, the flat gray of stones. Was that enough to go on? Rosie felt her heart beating fast. Chase would be furious, and Graeme had sworn this man was his colleague. He had taken a terrible chance.

"Leila urged Roi to come to me," Moses was saying. "Leila told him she had bad thoughts about this man."

"What do you mean? Leila never laid eyes on him."

Moses sighed. "She saw his aura when she peered through the curtains. You haven't known Leila very long, but I tell you she is special. Roi knows this, as do I. No one chooses this. You have not. The gift chooses you. This is a bad place, Miss Rosie. Bad things were performed here. Many people died. My people. And the ones who arrived.''

"Moses, what are you talking about?'' Rosie held his arm. "Sit down. You must rest. It's quite a distance from here to where you must have left your vehicle.''

"It was nothing until the pain hit me. Where's Porter?'' Moses asked urgently, his black eyes boring into Rosie.

"He's around.'' Rosie waved vaguely, preoccupied with Moses's state of mind and the contents of the fax.

"Porter's death is certain,'' Moses said, slumping to the ground.

Rosie felt stunned. She gazed into the old man's vision-filled eyes. "Death? What are you saying, Moses?'' She didn't like it at all. Hurriedly she poured water from her canteen and passed it to him, watching him struggle to drink.

Moses could see that he had frightened her. The full extent of her powers was unknown, even to herself. She wasn't ready for this now. Impulsively he reached out, put his hand over hers. "This day I make you part of my family.''

To Rosie who had little doubt of his specialness, that was beautiful. Her skin flushed with color. "I'm honored, Moses.'' Her tone matched his. "I know you are a wise man, a tribal elder. I know you were responsible for saving Chase's life, though you have said nothing of it for all these years. Why?''

At last he wanted her to hear, though his reply was halting. "Maybe I glimpsed the devil.'' He gave a sad weary smile. "A terrible, terrible thing. I kept this secret because I was afraid. I did it out of my love for Chase and my promise to his father. It had to be so. Porter Banfield has held great animosity toward me and mine for many years, but he has had to keep it in check.''

Rosie knelt beside him, willing him to keep talking. ''You think he would hurt you? Hurt Chase? You should have appealed to the authorities that night. You should have told them what happened.''

''I don't know what happened.'' Moses's voice broke. ''To this day I don't *know*. By the time all us men rushed up to the homestead, the west wing was ablaze. We couldn't get near it—the heat was too fierce. It burned our faces where we stood. But we tried, even though it was hopeless. My own people began a sacred ritual calling on the rain. And then I heard a child's cry.''

Rosie grabbed his hand. ''So it *was* you who carried Chase away from the house. You wrapped him in a blanket. Porter Banfield was watching you from the depths of the garden.''

''What words you speak, Missy. *These* are secrets.'' Moses shook his snowy head.

''Secrets no longer,'' Rosie said quietly.

''Secrets come to you,'' Moses told her. ''One must be born to it.''

A great stillness seemed to fall around them. Rosie's skin prickled. ''I don't know that I can deal with it, Moses. I don't want strange gifts. Yet the night of the fire came to me in a nightmare. It frightened me badly. You tell me you don't know how the fire started, but you obviously believe it was arson.''

''I had no proof.'' Moses spoke as though he'd been over and over it countless times. ''Porter had injuries of his own. He was bleeding badly from the head. His hair and brows were singed, his arms burned. He was like a crazy man. Out of his mind. Bawling out his brother's name. It was terrible to hear.''

Rosie's face was a study in suspicion. ''But he pulled

himself together enough to threaten you. He wasn't *that* hysterical or mad with grief. He forced you to tell the police he was the one who saved Chase.''

Moses nodded. ''He swore vengeance on me and mine if I didn't. That night we struck an unholy bargain. I didn't know what else to do. But I told him if any harm ever came to the boy, I would kill him. By physical or magical retaliation. He knew I would do it. Then there were other issues. He was Chase's kin, the guardian appointed by Chase's mother and father. There was nothing to link Porter Banfield to the fire, and I was fearful of speaking out. No one would have believed me even if I had proof. They were his own people, his *family*. The Banfields were the richest and most influential family in the North. The authorities treated him very, very carefully. He was distraught, like a man in torment.''

''Maybe he had good reason,'' Rosie said grimly, glancing back at the site. Mick was almost at the top of the slope where Chase now appeared, Marley hanging well back. ''There was another man, Moses. Who was he?''

Startled, Moses raised his leonine head. ''There was no one, Missy. Just the stockmen. I could vouch for every one.''

''Another man in the garden,'' Rosie murmured almost to herself. ''God, I know I'm right. I felt his presence at my back. There were swirling waters lapping my ankles. Inky black. A great crocodile. I saw the gleam of its eyes above the water. That was when I woke up.''

Moses's liquid black eyes settled on Rosie's face. ''Porter had a man who worked for him,'' he began, then broke off as if dismissing the idea.

''Go on,'' Rosie urged. ''Anything you can think of, tell me.''

''His name was Skegs,'' Moses said in a low voice. ''He

did Porter's bidding. But Skegs was at Rangga River Mine at the time. He was seen there.''

"By whom?'' Rosie asked skeptically. "A couple of his cronies? We have to talk further about this. We have to uncover the truth for Chase's sake.''

Moses lifted his right hand, let it fall. Loud voices came from the top of the slope, carrying on the still air. "Porter Banfield is a man who doesn't know honor. He would be very dangerous if cornered. Dangerous like the weak often are.''

"Where is he, anyway?'' Rosie sprang to her feet, her mind racing with all kinds of frightening possibilities.

Moses wiped his weary sweating face with the bandanna around his neck. "I think you will find that Porter has disappeared. He knows this country as well as I do. As well as Chase. He has roamed it all his life trying to find the legendary gold mine.''

"Gold mine?'' Rosie put her hands to her cheeks, found them hot. She couldn't begin to grasp the full extent of what was going on.

"A legend only.'' Moses looked stern, like a man who expected to be believed without question. "Chase's ancestor wandered this country with a black boy as his constant companion. That boy was a member of my tribe. There was a chance they found something. The Banfield ancestor made many notes, but his diaries have never been found.''

"I don't believe that,'' Rosie said. "I have a feeling Porter discovered them through searching or by chance.'' She twisted her fingers.

"They're coming down,'' Moses told her, scrambling to his feet. "I don't think Chase will have to read what you've got in your hand.''

"No.''

In another moment Chase had reached the flat, striding toward them with a supple resolute pace, his height and strength emphasized. "That son of a bitch has been lying to us all along," he exploded in fury. "How could he? I don't think much of him, but I thought he was better than that. My God, the man has a reputation to uphold."

"Do you want to look at the fax?" Rosie asked quietly, ignoring the nerves in her stomach.

Chase shook his head violently, his expression thunderous. "Tell me what it says."

"In essence, Dr. Roland Glenville has a distinguishing physical feature. He has different-colored eyes. One blue, one hazel."

Chase forced himself to calm down. "I had my doubts about him from the start."

"I suppose we all did." Rosie touched his arm.

"Has Marley got no sense at all?" he appealed to her.

"Judging by what's happened here today, not a lot."

Chase turned his head to yell, "Marley, get down here!" He ripped off his *akubra* and ran a hand through his hair. "I suppose we're darn lucky to be alive. Whoever the hell the guy is, he seems to have got clear away. One of the Land Cruisers is gone. I'll bet Porter has disappeared, as well."

"No sign of him," Rosie confirmed.

"You okay, Moses?" His voice grew gentle as he spoke to the old man.

"Not in good shape like I used to be."

"We'll get you home," Chase said. "We're *all* going home. I don't know where this guy is. He could very well be playing bloody war games. We don't know where Porter is, either. The only damn reason Porter's here is because he's working on a scheme of his own. Probably thinks he's going to find El Dorado. Bank on it, he's mad as a hatter."

Mick and Marley finally joined them, Marley having a great deal of trouble meeting anyone's eyes. "I'm most terribly sorry," he said, his expression abject.

"Ah, no, you're not!" Chase contradicted him. "Don't think I'm going to take this lightly. Forgiveness isn't one of my virtues. You *lied* to us."

Marley hung his head. "And I'm sick with the knowledge. I didn't want any part of it. I was totally against having that man join us, but Porter warned me to go along with it."

"Warned you?" Chase questioned him without sympathy.

"Sorry, but I can't come up with a better word. I've really come to detest your uncle. I think he mixes with ruthless people."

"What a surprise!" Chase glanced from Rosie to Mick to Moses, his expression a mixture of anger and satire.

"Who is this man, Graeme?" Rosie asked.

Marley looked at her, grateful for her quiet tone after Banfield's fury. "His name is Disher. At least he calls himself Disher."

"I suppose he's got a choice of half-a-dozen others," Chase cut in. "And he's Porter's man? Porter's always got some vicious bastard up his sleeve."

"Porter didn't want him, either. I'm sure of that. In fact, I think Porter loathed him." Marley let out a whistling sigh.

"Then Porter's working for someone who hired Disher to keep an eye on Porter. I think that's the way things go in Porter's circle. Probably Porter's been feeding one of his big-time clients Egyptian antiquities, promising more while he scouts around trying to find the legendary pot of gold. The classic double cross."

"I wouldn't like to double-cross Disher," Marley said.

"What makes you think you're better off double-crossing me?" Chase demanded.

"I don't think you'd shoot me," Marley said.

"We could shove you in the river," Mick said coldly.

"So he's got a gun." Mick turned to Chase. "And this son of a bitch knew it the entire time."

"Why should he shoot at us?" Rosie asked. "Not that I haven't had a gun pointed at me, but that was in a war zone. I mean, what's the point here? He's probably cut and run."

"He's not that kind of guy," Chase said with certainty. "He's a mercenary. I'll bet if we got onto the army, we'd find he had a record. Probably dishonorably discharged." He shook his head. "We pack up and head back. Now."

"But we can't do that!" Marley looked shocked. "We're onto something here."

"I don't care, Marley, and I'm really pissed off. Don't make it worse," Chase flared.

"Then I'm staying."

"I'm sorry, Marley. We do it *my* way," Chase said, teeth slightly on edge. "I don't know what either my uncle or this Disher are up to, but I don't want Rosie involved." Chase caught hold of Rosie's wrist, brought her to him. "Nor will I knowingly leave you here to die."

Marley closed his eyes, then opened them beseechingly. "But if we abandon this dig, the rains will come. With my luck a cyclone. It will be all washed away."

"True," Chase conceded. "But you have no real idea who put the slab there or who built the wall."

"Aborigines didn't do it," Marley said fiercely, determined to stand his ground.

"Why the hell not?"

"I just *know*. Besides, I found the seal, remember?"

"Where is it?" Chase asked darkly.

"Oh, God!" Marley clenched his fists. "Porter was the last person to handle it."

"Porter is a true opportunist," Chase said, surprised by the tremor in Rosie's hand. "Look, Marley, I don't know why, but I'm sorry for you, even if I have absolutely no respect for you. We have to leave. All of us. I'm responsible for what happens on my land. Even if you did happen to unearth something of importance, Porter—and probably Disher, too—will be around watching. You'd disappear. Supposedly a victim of the crocs. If I were you, I wouldn't like that prospect one bit."

"The ruins will keep, Graeme," Rosie said, torn between dismay and pity.

"No." He shook his head.

"A man like Disher, living off the bush, could stay here for quite a while," Chase said. "One thing in our favor— the Wet's coming. A lot of rain. A lot of flood. We have to check out who this man is."

"But what about your uncle?" Rosie asked, disturbingly aware of Moses's prediction.

Chase shrugged. "Seems to me he's crossed the line. For years now Porter's been dealing with dangerous people."

"Suppose he has good reason to believe he can find what's he looking for?" Rosie asked a little breathlessly, gazing into Chase's face. "Maybe during one of his searches for your ancestor's diaries, he actually found them. Suppose his story about digging up all the relics on Three Moons is true? I know it's hard to believe, but there was no trickery attached to the gold necklace. It did make those odd marks on my skin. Like hieroglyphics. You saw yourself that the marks disappeared." She raised her eyebrows. "Maybe all your uncle had to do was follow some chart to unearth the relics."

"You mean my ancestor knew all about ancient Egyptian relics and left them in the ground?" asked Chase in a highly skeptical voice.

Moses, who had been very quiet, suddenly spoke. "Where they are meant to stay, as your forefather found out. No good will come to the person who has them."

Marley made a fist and whacked it into his other hand.

"Hang on! That's absolute nonsense!" He tried to look Moses in the eye. Failed. "It's my job to uncover such things. To show them to the world."

"Just as men like you have defiled Egyptian tombs and taken the bodies of the dead for your experiments," Moses said. "This is not right. It is a desecration. Evil clings to this part of the bush. My people know it. They don't come here."

Marley burst into wild laughter. "Good God, who'd listen to an old witch doctor?"

"I'd listen to Moses any damn time over you," Chase broke in harshly, his anger running high. "I would've thought, Dr. Marley, that you'd have learned respect for native doctors from your travels in the Outback. There are far, far too many examples of how magic works. Good magic and bad."

"I apologize if I've caused any offense," Marley answered dully. "I don't want the pointing bone entering me," he said, only half joking. "What I want is to continue with this project. We've already accomplished much."

Moses lifted both arms to wave the thought away. "Go from here," he said in a voice as deep as thunder. "You have no understanding of what happened here a long time ago."

"Well, what happened, then?" Marley demanded, almost hysterically.

"Can you not smell the stench of blood?" Moses asked him, calmer now. "Spirits are still here. I've seen them."

Rosie shivered. She couldn't shake her own strange experience. "I think we should listen to what Moses has to say, Graeme. Whatever was here, however distant the time, some aura remains."

Marley looked at her in mingled amazement and despair. "And you've felt it?"

"Some people have all the luck," Chase murmured laconically, stroking Rosie's hair.

"What's happened to you, Rosie?" Marley moaned. "This could be a world scoop for you."

"I'm already beginning to feel it wouldn't do me much good," Rosie said. "I don't know that I want to be a part of it anymore, Graeme. This place isn't welcoming."

"I can't say it thrills me, either," Chase drawled. "And I know this land."

"There aren't any monsters lurking around here, love." Mick had decided to enter the argument. "We *were* beginning to get somewhere."

"You want to stay, Mick?" Chase turned to his friend.

"Hell, son, this was your dad's and my territory when we were in our mad teens. Used to scare the hell out of us then. But that's ancient history."

"Ancient history is what we're talking about, Mick," Rosie pointed out. "Some things are best left alone."

"You mean you're giving in to superstition?" Marley's blue eyes bulged with disbelief.

"No, she's going home where I know she's safe," Chase said in a clipped voice.

"Great heaven!" Marley shook his head. "And here I was thinking you were so well balanced."

"I hope you're not talking to me," Chase said ominously, looming over him.

"He means me." Rosie took Chase's hand soothingly. "I have to admit that out here I'm a little more highly strung."

"It's the isolation, love," Mick said. "It gets to people."

"Oh, bugger off, Mick," Rosie said. She couldn't help laughing. "I've been in some bad places and my nerve has held."

"Maybe your nerve's been booted out of you," Marley

suggested disgustedly, causing Chase to swing on him, strong chin jutting.

He stared so fixedly at Marley that Marley began to back away. "You must be doing this on purpose," Chase said angrily. "One more remark like this and—"

"I'm sorry, I'm sorry. I'm going too far." Again Marley apologized. "But I'm convinced we're onto a great find!"

Chase shook his head. "You haven't found a damned thing, apart from that stone object you say is a seal. Beats me how you let Porter have it. Now, before any of you say another word, I suggest we all go back to camp two, which at the moment is unattended. Disher could be anywhere out there. It's his job to keep an eye on my uncle. Whoever stays alone will be caught in the middle."

THEY ARRIVED AT CAMP to find the three remaining vehicles disabled, the rotor buttons removed from the distributors.

"Disher must have doubled back as soon as I took off," Chase told Rosie grimly. "There's a quantity of food missing, too."

"Couldn't it have been your uncle? Couldn't he have done it just as easily?" she argued.

"I suppose, but why? Unless he wants everyone to continue working at the site while he follows his own agenda. He couldn't be fool enough to think Disher wouldn't be watching him."

"He must have a map, Chase." For the first time Rosie told her story of the hidden compartment in the antique chest in her bedroom at Three Moons homestead. "There were little scraps of paper still attached to the sides."

He smiled at her. "Rosie, darling, I can't turn into a believer overnight."

"How did the chest get to be in my room?" She ignored the sarcasm.

Chase shrugged. "I have no idea. I had the painting brought in. To my knowledge, that's all. I couldn't even tell you when I last opened that chest. It's been in various parts of the house since forever. Maybe Roi did it or Leila. I know nothing about a secret compartment," he added flatly, his voice trailing away as he looked around the campsite. Marley was slumped dejectedly under a tree while Moses and Mick went into a huddle.

"Well, I'm not about to abandon my theory," Rosie said doggedly. "I'm not saying I'm in Great-aunt Hester's class, but a few things that have happened to me lately have given my theory a lot of weight—in my mind, anyway. Porter found the diaries and ever since then he's been making a financial killing. The necklace, apart from its spooky elements, would be worth a good deal of money."

"But wasn't Porter going to present it to you?" Chase protested.

"Sure, so I'd shut up and get on with it. That was the whole idea, wasn't it? Keep the project going. While we were all preoccupied on the site, Porter was conducting his little forays into the bush. Poor old Graeme was really led astray. Something entirely different from ancient Egyptian ruins is going on."

"So it would seem," Chase said. "Lots more. And this expedition was the only way Porter could get on to my land. So he could search for…whatever it is."

"The legendary gold mine," Rosie suggested with a considerable degree of conviction.

"The gold is finished," Chase said. "Completely played out."

"Maybe your great-great-grandfather stumbled onto something when he and the Aboriginal boy were out prospecting. Maybe they saw something dazzling. Maybe your ancestor didn't have time to tell. He died in the bush. In this area. The Aboriginal boy died not all that long after."

"And he spoke of nothing except the existence of 'lots of papers.'"

Rosie remembered that. "Maybe he didn't want to be part of it. You know what Moses is like. They're not material people. A gold strike would have been taken out of Aboriginal hands."

"Not by my family," Chase said.

"You don't know that. Gold made your family fortune."

"Let's get this straight." Chase caught Rosie's chin, raising her vivid face to his. "I'm a cattleman. Like my father. This is an industry that earns billions of dollars in exports each year. I'm proud to be part of it. If there's more gold out there, I don't have the time to search for it. Maybe my children or my grandchildren will want to find it—if it's there. You've seen the country. They'd have to have a very exact map."

"Porter's got it," Rosie said.

Chase counted to ten, then he kissed her roughly, yet sweetly, on the mouth. "You think so?"

"I can do better than that," she said breathlessly. "I'm absolutely certain."

"I'd better find Porter, then," Chase said after a full minute's thought. "We have at least something in common, apart from our surname. We both know this country. We both know how to live off it. I think we'll find that Porter's friend, Disher, was once a professional soldier who had jungle training."

"Tracking down Porter could be dangerous." Rosie's green eyes were anxious. "He wants to keep what he knows to himself."

"Well, he can't." Chase ran a distracted hand through his thick bronze hair. "God, I can't believe I'm giving this serious consideration. You're a witch, Rosie Summers."

Rosie shook her head modestly. "Let's say I have good

intuition. Porter can't keep what he finds unless..." She couldn't get the words out. She choked up.

"Unless he gets rid of me?" Chase prompted.

"Maybe he tried to get rid of you last time." Rosie looked off into the distance, eyes glittering with unshed tears. She would withhold what Moses had told her for the moment.

"I want you to go back, Rosie." Chase grasped her shoulders, his whole body exuding determination.

"Aren't you forgetting we don't have a vehicle?" She was almost grateful.

"I'm forgetting nothing." He shook her lightly. "Moses is much too wily to fall into any trap. I think you'll find he has the Jeep stashed away somewhere. He's obviously not well. He has to go back with you. Mick can drive. Moses can ride shotgun, just in case there's any trouble. But Disher's real concern is my uncle."

"I don't like this." Rosie turned her beautiful eyes up to him, misty and soulful.

"I don't like it, either." He kissed her nose. "But I want you back at the homestead where you'll be safe. No one would get past Roi. If Mick wants to return to the site, that's up to him."

"What about Graeme?"

"As far as I'm concerned, he's a real no-hoper," Chase growled. "I don't think either Disher or my uncle have any interest in Marley or his excavations. If there *was* something there and you're right about Porter's finding the diaries, chances are Porter knows about it."

Rosie allowed herself to lean into him, gathering strength. "You know, your uncle must be involved with some pretty weird stuff."

"You could say that," he muttered.

"I want to stay, Chase. Someone has to watch out for you. I'm of no interest to anyone."

"Don't be silly." His voice grew resonant with longing. "You're of great interest to me. I want you back home, Rosie. I want you out of it."

She shook her head. "I'm a grown woman, Chase. A good reporter. I didn't write social columns, you know."

"Ever thought of astrology?"

"Enough of the sarcasm!" She adored the way his eyes crinkled at the corners with humor. "Are you going to bundle me up forcibly?" What an experience that would be!

"If I have to," he said slowly, their eyes locked together, turmoil forgotten.

Rosie raised her hand, drew it lingeringly down his cheek. "Chase, my love, let me take responsibility for myself."

His handsome face tautened. "I can't lose you, Rosie. I've lost too much already."

"You're not going to lose me." She made it sound like a declaration. Everything she had yearned for in a man was standing right there in front of her. "If you want me, I'm yours forever." Her eyes were eloquent with the depth, the wholeness, of her feeling.

Though his heart was filled with a great hope, the fear of loss had never left him. "Don't make promises you can't keep, Rosie," he warned her. "I don't want an affair. I want everything from you. Absolute love and devotion."

Flames of warmth were spreading through her body. She was so happy she, too, was half-afraid of it. "You want me to give up my career?" Her career? Her career had been good. She had grown with it, but there was more to life than a job. "I suppose I can write anywhere…"

"I want you to marry me, Rosie," Chase said gravely. "To be my life's partner. To achieve immortality through our children. Be very sure before you choose. Sex alone won't hold us together."

This, when she was already planning her once-in-a-lifetime wedding. "We might be well into our nineties before we find out," she leaned forward to whisper.

"Strangely enough, I think so, too." He drew her toward him, resting his chin on the top of her head. "It's been heaven and hell having you so near me without being able to make love to you. Not that I don't intend to make up for it when we get home."

Home! What a beautiful word, deeply woven into the fabric of life.

"I'm staying with you," Rosie said, feeling his glance like a perfect kiss on her mouth. "Now and always."

A BROWN TREE SNAKE with its prominent eyes fell on him, forked tongue darting. It had poison fangs at the rear of its mouth, but the forked tongue was only a sense organ. This one wasn't big enough to be dangerous. Porter kept absolutely still as it slithered from his shoulder down his arm, desperate in its own way to escape the alien human presence. He'd been perched in the branches of this strangler fig for close to half an hour, watching what was happening at the site through his powerful field glasses. He was certain, like Disher, that the appearance of Moses meant the moment of truth had arrived. Damn Siegel and his insane paranoia! Porter thought, characteristically overlooking the fact that paranoia was only paranoia when it was groundless. Nevertheless, Disher had been found out. Now the whole venture was about to explode in their faces. His nephew would break camp, insist that the lot of them get off his land. With the exception of the Summers woman. Porter wasn't such a fool that he hadn't noticed his nephew couldn't take his eyes off her. The feeling appeared to be mutual. The classic *coup de foudre*. Powerful and compelling. Another triumphant love story, like Lew and Carole. He felt closer to their ghosts than he had in years. Years of blocking out that dreadful night when all his jealous ravings, his mind-bending fantasies, had been put into action by the loathsome Skegs. A mere hireling, but the man had thought they were friends. That one day they would live at Three Moons together. Partners. Partners in a horrendous crime of Skegs's devising. A crime that would deliver up a fortune. Lew's son had survived, but Porter became guardian to the boy, who could in turn be removed when the time was right.

For a moment Porter Banfield bent over as if racked by nausea, his mind recoiling in horror from the events of that night. At least old Moses had kept his part of the bargain. He had never spoken out against him in return for the boy's safety. But Porter knew that once Skegs had crossed the line, he could cross it again. He should have listened to his brother, who'd told him Skegs was mad. Skegs who had killed for *him*. Skegs felt no guilt, only ugly anger when his crazy ambitions crashed around him. That was when the extortion started; it had stopped only when he paid to have Skegs's life terminated. Wasn't that grotesque? He hadn't really wanted any of it. But in the end he had to make an arrangement. It was the only way he knew to get Skegs off his back and keep the boy safe.

He could never sort out his feelings about his nephew. He hated and resented him—he was far too like his father—but he wanted no more blood on his hands. Not as long as he lived. Yet if Moses ever talked, the whole case could be reopened. The question of Skegs's exact whereabouts the night of the fire? His own false statement that he'd been the one to rescue his nephew. No one, including the boy, had doubted it. *Then.* For one terrible moment Porter Banfield thought of suicide. But not before he located the gold mine. He unbuttoned his breast pocket, slid his hand inside and found to his sick horror that the page torn from the diary wasn't there. He concluded Disher had taken it. Now two people knew of the mine's existence, a twist of fate that made him a victim again.

He'd been returning to the excavation site from the western side of the low escarpment that formed part of the upland forest. That was when he'd seen Disher halt in his tracks, then double back the way he'd come, keeping to the thick cover of the casuarina forest with its heavy undergrowth of fallen needles, shrubs and seedling trees. Moments later he himself caught sight of the old black walking out of the bush and readily understood Moses's presence.

Now the old man was slumped under a tree with the Summers woman down on her haunches talking to him ninety to the dozen. Extracting information. Wasn't that her job? Thanks to her, this might be the very day the old man decided to unburden himself of a secret he had carried for twenty years.

The Summers woman still held the pages Moses had handed her. Without a doubt, a rundown on Marley's colleague, the real Dr. Roland Glenville, who probably had some distinguishing feature like a wooden leg. On the rise above the excavation site, in the same vicinity where years ago he'd found the gold necklace, his nephew was giving that fool Marley a good dressing-down, his voice steely with rage. It rang around the upland plateau. His brother's voice. His brother's style. Lew the great man. Lew the favored son. Lew the heir. All his life he'd walked in his brother's shadow. He'd hated him. But he had never wanted him or his wife dead. Or so he'd made himself believe.

Fighting vertigo, Banfield climbed down the strangler fig, his right palm scraped raw by the rough bark. He'd have to keep moving. Disher was on the loose. Porter began walking, clutching his rifle, vaguely conscious of frightening shapes all around him. Shadows. Yet they took on human form. Memories streamed back with dreadful force. Wherever he walked, Lew seemed to walk before him. Tall, broad-shouldered, loping like a jungle cat. Faceless. The face was burned off.

Porter clutched his gun closer to his side. Maybe only death would set him free.

"WHAT ARE YOU complaining about, Marley?" Mick finally exploded, sick to death of the other man's nonstop grievances. "The game's up. We've got Porter and this guy, Disher, on the loose and you want to go back to the dig. Hell, it's hot," Mick broke off to groan. He wiped his face and cast his eyes upward. "You'll get sunstroke out there."

Marley refused to take this seriously. He frowned. "It's only a matter of time before I unearth something truly important. I'm not asking you or Roslyn to come." He was unable to keep the deep resentment out of his voice.

"Just as well." Rosie looked at him, her green eyes glittery from the heat, damp curls ringing her forehead, color staining her high cheekbones. "Chase told us to stay right here until they get back." Chase and Moses had set off to retrieve the tucked-away station Jeep.

"Do you have to do *exactly* as he says?" Marley focused on her pugnaciously, although only half an hour before, he'd been utterly chastened. "I'd like a private word with you, Roslyn."

"You can speak in front of Mick, Graeme," Rosie said. "Is there something else you want to add to this sad tale? What do you suppose the real Dr. Glenville is going to say when he finds out about this?"

"*If* he finds out," Marley sneered with no visible sign of concern. "He'd be put out, of course, but if we manage to find proof of an ancient Egyptian site! Well, that's something else again. This storm in a teacup would be swept away."

"Would it?" She shook her head. "You don't appear to

be listening, Graeme. Chase wants us to go back. He believes, and I fear he's right, that Disher is a man well used to violence. He's been sent to see exactly what's uncovered. And to keep his eye on Porter, who appears to have his own agenda. Disher won't take long to find out what it is. They'll either come to some agreement or there'll be trouble. But one way or another, the authorities are going to be brought into this.''

"So what?" Marley sputtered, a man in the grip of obsession. "It would take a very big leap to make *me* a criminal. I was acting under duress. I'm absolutely certain neither Porter Banfield nor Disher were interested in me. I need to continue my investigation. Who knows what we might uncover? But I need help.''

"Well, I'm not going anywhere, Graeme," Rosie informed him sweetly. "I'm going to do what I'm told. Wait here until Chase and Moses get back.''

"Then you're not the woman I thought you were," Marley said, turning on his heel. "You were supposed to be my partner.''

"Ah, yes." Rosie gave a wry smile. "But that was in the days when I thought you could be trusted. Think about it, Graeme. You were party to a cover-up that could put us in danger. And you still have to answer for it. I don't think Chase is about to save your reputation.''

"I'll just have to live with it." Marley sounded as though he thought she was vastly overestimating Chase Banfield's ability to influence anything. "I gather you think a lot of him." His eyes bored into her, desperate to see into her heart.

"Could be I love him," Rosie answered simply.

Marley recoiled as if she'd struck him. "I wouldn't bet on your chances of getting him to the altar," he snapped. "You're just in the grip of an affair. A few weeks on, and you'll be just a memory.''

''We'll see!'' Rosie nodded. ''It's you who's going to get shown the door, Graeme,'' she added lightly. ''Have a nice day.''

Mick swore softly. '''Course he's jealous, love,'' he said as Marley stomped away. ''Cheek of him, looking at you when he's still a married man. That's not on. Anyway, love, you couldn't meet a finer young man than Chase. And you're just right for him. Knew the moment I saw you that you were special. It would be the most marvelous heart-warming thing to see Three Moons come alive again. It's been a sad old place, but if anyone can bring back the sunshine you can. It takes a woman to make a home.'' Mick rose almost happily to his feet. ''What about a cup of tea, Roses? Amazing how it cools you down.''

''That would be lovely, Mick.'' Rosie sighed gratefully, thinking with satisfaction that Mick had come a long way in a short time. Now a good cup of billy tea was the beverage of choice. ''Want a hand?''

''No thanks, love. You sit there and cool off. Reckon the Wet's gonna come early. Today's a scorcher. Just look at that sky! We could have a storm. Notwithstanding all this business, love, I've enjoyed myself.'' He turned back to face her. ''Not exactly fun and games but much better.''

''You have a future, Mick. Not just a past. Good friends.''

Mick nodded. ''I don't doubt that for a moment. Life is worth having.''

Rosie smiled at him with understanding, a smile Mick returned.

''So, where do you reckon that stone seal got to?'' He returned to the less emotional.

Rosie threw her thick plait over her shoulder. ''Pretty straightforward answer. I'd say Porter's got it. I'll even bet he found the legendary Banfield diaries.''

''A very long shot, love.'' Mick scratched his chin.

"They've been looking for them for fifty years. But I have a feeling that even if old Porter found them, they'd not do him much good."

That had already occurred to Rosie—and to Moses.

While Mick got the fire going, Rosie closed her eyes, unfastening a button of her cotton shirt and fanning back the collar. Not only was it very hot, the humidity was high. The sky above her, electric-blue. It would be a relief if they did have a downpour. The rain would clear the air. She allowed herself to drift. Drifting...drifting, carried by a languorous tide. She hadn't been getting much sleep lately....

FROM A DISTANCE Disher looked down on the scene with his savage grin. With Banfield out of the way, it was time to take the woman. His lust for her was overriding every other consideration, though he knew that was a mistake. He knew it could end very badly, but couldn't seem to help himself. Up until now women had been necessary for one thing only. He used them and threw them away, sometimes badly beaten up. It depended on what triggered him. But this woman was fascinating. He liked to listen to her, liked the way she talked and her infectious laugh. The way she moved. He liked her physical strength. On the site she had worked like a man. He liked the way she could run, those long legs moving like pistons. What fun it would be to hunt her. How much better to *find* her. There could be only one outcome. After that, he knew he'd have to get away. No big deal. He'd disappeared many times before. The treasure Siegel had hoped for just hadn't come to pass. Though he had in his backpack the map Porter Banfield had been concealing from all eyes, it told him nothing. He couldn't work it out. From his constant surveillance of Banfield, that arrogant bastard couldn't work it out, either. Maybe landmarks that appeared on it were long gone, swept away, reduced to rubble, or maybe the map was a hoax. Either way, he'd pass it on to Siegel when he collected his fee. Siegal couldn't afford to cross him. He had too much on the old vulture.

From his vantage point he saw Dempsey turn away to collect firewood. The woman was lying back, slowly, seductively opening the collar of her shirt. For a woman so slim, she had full beautiful breasts. He stood up from his green hideout, excitement thrumming through him like a buzz saw. He was going to have this woman. Now.

FROM THE CORNER of his eye Mick saw a movement. He swung around sharply. Nothing. Could have been a wallaby. There were plenty in the woods, nice little fellows. He was taking his time making the tea. He could see Roses had dozed off. She'd had rather a rough time of it camping here in the wilds, but never a word of complaint. Mick hoped with all his heart that this love affair between Roses and Chase would work out. They were both terrific young people. Best of all, they were his friends.

Mick began to whistle very quietly. One of his favorites, "When Irish Eyes Are Smiling." He'd been a whistler all his life. Bridget used to say his whistle was as true and sweet as a bird's. These days he felt Bridget especially close to him. Willing him to survive. To live out the rest of his time as she would have wanted him to. And to be, once again, the man she married. Comforted, Mick bent again to the fire, stoking the orange-gold flames. Like Roses' hair. Extraordinary color. At least one of her kids would be a flaming redhead. Whistling happily, Mick didn't even see the rifle butt that arced through the air before it found the base of his skull.

ROSIE'S EYES snapped open in fright. Standing above her, his legs straddling her body, was the man called Disher.

He was dressed in jungle gear, a large grin, more like a grimace, on his strange granite face.

"Hope I didn't wake ya," he muttered. The Glenville persona was entirely gone. The voice was grating, the accent rough, the gaze so frankly sexual that Rosie felt as revolted as she did fearful.

Instantly she shuffled back along the ground until she was able to spring to her feet, clear of his bulk. "Well, well, Mr. Disher. What a surprise!" As she spoke she half turned, her eyes sweeping back to the campfire, looking for Mick. She drew in her breath as she registered his prone body. "What have you done?" She turned back to Disher with tremors of fury. This shouldn't be happening. But it was.

"Nothin' much." Disher shrugged. "Your pal's out cold. When he does wake up, he'll have a powerful headache."

"You brute!" Rosie was too angry to be cautious. "Why did you have to do that?" She began to go to Mick, but Disher shot out a detaining hand, pinning her arm in a painful grip.

"Don't bother about him, Rosie. You've got *me*. You and me are gonna play a little game together."

Rosie struggled until she threw off his arm. "Or what?" she asked contemptuously. "You'll kill me? I should remind you that Chase will be back very soon."

"And he's the boyfriend?" Disher tensed like a jealous rival.

Incredible! Rosie found it hard to believe Disher was actually attracted to her. But it seemed that he was, which seemed distinctly bizarre.

"This is his land," she said matter-of-factly. "You're here on false pretenses. Why?"

"Don't waste time askin' questions, Rosie." He nudged her breast with the rifle. "Get goin'."

"Where?" She refused to let him see her pant with fear.

"Ever heard of hide-and-seek?" He gave her a dreadful leer that might have been meant as a smile.

"You want me to run?" she asked incredulously, keeping her voice neutral. "You could overtake me easily. Some game!" She shrugged her shoulders critically, letting her mouth pucker in reproof. She hoped to God Chase had located the Jeep and was on his way back. Sure, she had a black belt and she was in good shape, but she'd be no match for Disher, who could knock the living daylights out of her...although he was starting to look as if he had something different in mind. She had to take advantage of that. It was probably her only chance.

"I'll give you a good start," he said, like a man determined to play fair.

She cast her long eyelashes down and fluttered them. "So what's the prize?" The longer she kept him talking drivel, the more time she gave Chase.

"You, sweetheart." The stony gray eyes actually smoldered. "Truth is, I like you."

"Ah, now I understand." Though she had her work cut out, Rosie smiled at him, a slow burning smile. It seemed to have an immediate effect on him.

"You're gonna know what it's like to have it off with a real man." He flexed his impressive pectoral muscles.

A real man like Chase. A real man who'll find you, Rosie thought grimly, but managed to will admiration into her eyes. "I appreciate your frankness. I think I might have made a mistake about you, Disher." She gazed up at him attentively. "This might be fun. But only if we stick to some rules."

There was a slightly puzzled look on his face. "Like what?"

"Well, where do I start?" Rosie stared at him boldly with the exhilaration of a rival sporting competitor.

He continued to study her face, trying to read it, frowning in concentration as though he didn't quite get what he was hearing but was immensely gratified all the same. "How about that backdrop of trees?" he suggested.

Rosie turned her head. "You're getting mighty close to the river. It might look beautiful, but it's dangerous territory."

"Crocs don't worry me," he said with a swagger. "I've got the gun."

"What about me?" She smiled at him again, all feminine sweetness and light.

"I won't let anything bad happen to ya."

It was said with something like genuine feeling. Rosie couldn't be sure.

"If you ask me, you're the one who should've been leading this expedition," she said. "You can't just go and leave us now."

"I could take you with me," he offered. "Let's see how this shapes up."

Like a death trap, Rosie thought. "How do I know you're going to keep your word?" She directed another admiring glance at him, wondering why one of his eyes was fully open and the other was scrunched up.

"'Cause I'm a man of pride. You have until you get to the woods. Right? I've seen you run. You're good."

"You're good, too," Rosie said, feeling as if she was beginning a slide into madness. "A man to be taken seriously."

"You bet!" A besotted smile spread across his face.

Adrenaline pouring through her body, Rosie took off like a rocket, running in a direct line. She knew the name of the game, all right. One of the oldest games in the book for a psychopath. Native fear mixed with hope put wings to her feet. She was flying along like a star of track-and-field, her long legs extended to their fullest as she leaped over a near-hidden boulder that rose in front of her. Now wasn't the time to break a leg.

When she reached the shelter of the trees, she could have mopped herself with a towel and found it soaked. Her heart was pounding as she stared about her trying to decide which way to go. How could Chase possibly find her in this jungle? She ran on, dodging in and out of trees, clinging to the trunks of some to catch a shuddering breath. She could see the line of the great river through the trees. Caught glimpses of the sandy banks. Where the hell could she hide? What could she do? Caught between the crocs and a monster.

Think.

He'd expect her to cover as much ground as possible. She ripped the yellow ribbon from her braid, laced it around a low branch, then doubled back, plunging into the deeper bush, with its densely matted canopy of trees and profuse vegetation. She could feel the sting of scratches on her hands and arms as she fought her way through the undergrowth, panic tearing through her at the sound of a large body rushing toward her.

Rosie acted instinctively, scrambling up a tree just as a wild boar roared into sight, the light glancing off its twin tusks. It was only a few feet away, aware of her presence, the snorts growing louder, its little eyes glaring its displeasure at the invasion of its territory. If she fell, she was certain it would kill her. Gore her to death. It had happened to others.

"Go away, you bastard," she hissed, stretching out a hand to grab a bunch of hard purplish berries and hurl them at the boar.

The pig roared in rage, but instead of standing its ground, to Rosie's immense relief it continued its forward charge, breaking through the scrub to the clearing while brilliant parrots flew from the tree branches to wheel above the forest canopy. A few minutes later Rosie heard a rifle discharge.

Poor little piggy. Bad piggy. She was shaking all over, her hands swatting at a cloud of iridescent insects going for her face. The gun—that had to be Disher. Still, he'd have quite a time finding her before the crocs did. She'd never been so frightened in her life. Not even when a warring soldier in Afghanistan had pointed his rifle at her.

Where was Chase? She made no attempt to run on. Her only plan was to try to fool Disher. If that failed? She began to think of ways she could save her own skin. Flatter the monster until she could get in a stupefying blow. She would have to seize the right moment to render him unconscious. She could do it if she was able to catch him off guard. Ugh!

Rosie kept to her hiding place in a tree, straining to peer through the leaves. No sign of Disher. Thank God. She was climbing a little higher to more shelter when she heard, like a clarion call, Chase's shout.

"Rosie, Rosie, where are you? Call to me!"

Disher would hear him, as well. That ruined her plan. She had to get to Chase first. She dropped to the ground, grateful at least that the wild boar was accounted for. Unless it had a mate. Chase kept calling while Rosie, hidden by cover, followed the sound.

Disher grabbed her without warning, one arm coming around her waist, the other clamped across her mouth. She let herself yield against him, feigning compliance so successfully his harsh grip relented. That was when Rosie swung on him, bringing up her knee with full force so it smashed into his groin. As he doubled over in agony, Rosie took off like a starburst, running as she'd never run before.

"Chase, Chase, I'm here!" she yelled. "In front of the camp." She tore on, with Disher's cries as maddened as the wild boar's behind her. A prop root was her undoing.

She tripped over it. Fell. Disher was on her in a minute, wrenching her up, smacking the side of her head with the flat of his hand. "Bitch, bitch, bitch."

Rosie felt it like a dozen punches. The force of the blow snapped her head to the right. She tasted the salty metallic tang of blood. Dazed, her ear ringing, Rosie was aware that he'd begun dragging her off into the bush when Chase suddenly burst into view, his rifle trained. "Let her go, Disher," he thundered. "You can't get out of this. Let her go."

Disher strengthened his cruel hold, and Rosie's pain went up several notches. "I'll kill her first," Disher warned, his voice full of bitter betrayal. "Break her neck. Bitch. She tricked me." An irredeemable mistake.

Rosie tucked in her head, directing her full weight to her legs, making it harder for him to manhandle her. Her mind was clearing. She had to be ready. She needed an opportunity to use her hands, but Disher was putting such pressure on her arms she thought he'd break them.

"Throw your gun here, Banfield. I mean what I say." Disher grasped a handful of Rosie's hair and jerked her to her feet so violently that she was engulfed in pain, her cry uncontrollable. If only he'd give her an opening. An opening. That was all she needed, but his strength was appalling.

Chase wasn't taking any chances. Though he was desperate to run to Rosie, he held on to discipline. He threw his gun toward Disher—knowing, as Disher didn't, that Moses was there in the shadows. Moses knew his job. He'd shoot if he had to. And he wouldn't miss. Only then did Chase begin to walk very slowly toward them with little fear for himself. At that moment, survival without Rosie seemed impossible. His whole mind was concentrated on getting the woman he loved out of Disher's murderous grip. "If you let her go, I'll guarantee you safe passage from my land."

"And after that?" Disher kicked Chase's rifle away, hefted his own in one arm, the other keeping his stranglehold on Rosie.

"After that, you're on your own." Chase's voice cut like a sword.

"Except I'm takin' the woman with me." Disher gave his crazy grin. "We have a little score to settle."

Every muscle in Chase's body was ready to explode into action. Rosie's life could be in the balance. "That sounds like a very bad idea," he warned.

"I don't think so. Back out of here, Banfield," Disher ordered, "and you won't get hurt." As he spoke Disher was unconsciously moving backward into the scrub, half dragging Rosie with him.

It was then that Chase's blood froze in horror as he spotted what no one else had. In the thick vegetation a nest of huge pale-gray eggs was suddenly revealed. "Croc!" He yelled a warning with powerful urgency, breaking into a full forward run in a heroic effort to save Rosie. Seconds later, with the speed and ferocity of a raging bull, a crocodile's monstrous head burst through the dank green vegetation to snatch at Disher's leg, the vast jaws opening and shutting with an unearthly bang. Disher scarcely had time to register what was happening. He looked back in shock, then began screaming, while Rosie sprinted off in a great burst of energy and fear. Chase's arms locked around her with stunning force as he pulled her away, half carrying her in the direction of the camp. Every muscle in his body clenched in violent protest as Disher, still screaming, was brought down, his thighs crushed and pinned in the crocodile's viselike jaws. No human had ever been able to release that ferocious grip.

Like the most dreadful nightmare, crocodile and victim disappeared into the dank greenery that led down to the river. Even before Disher's cries were extinguished, another crocodile even more massive and terrifying than the other, thrashed into sight like the prehistoric monster it was. It stood in a full threatening display, swinging its powerful ridged tail, its open jaws showing its yellow mouth and its countless hideous teeth.

"God almighty!" The oath surged into Chase's throat. This was the male. He flung Rosie away from him with all his strength, calling on Moses to shoot, expecting to be obeyed without question. But Moses came out of the bush a short distance off, waving a sheaf of burning dry grass. He faced the crocodile, putting his body between the monster and Chase, directing words in his own language to the great reptile as though the monster would understand.

Rosie, in shock now, felt every bit of strength leave her. She lay on the ground shivering, convinced Moses was about to suffer Disher's terrible fate. She had to bite down hard on her lip to stop herself from screaming and screaming.

But nothing happened the way she'd dreaded. Extraordinary things could and did occur, unfathomable to the rational mind. The massive crocodile's yawning jaws slowly closed. The enormous head came down as it swung about, its powerful tail flattening the undergrowth as it headed back to the nest.

"Move out," Moses called to them quietly, still holding his ground, burning torch aloft.

Neither of them had to be told twice.

Chase tore to Rosie, hoisted her over his shoulder. "And Disher?" he yelled back to Moses, the horror of what was happening sounding in his anguished voice.

"Him tucker now," Moses responded, not without a certain grim satisfaction, watching the male crocodile oversee the nest before disappearing into the undergrowth.

ONCE THEY REACHED the safety of the clearing, Chase lowered Rosie to the ground, keeping his arms around her.

Tears were streaming down her face, the left side red and
swollen from a blow, the eye closing at the corner. It would
undoubtedly turn black. He looked with tremendous remorse at her slender arms and elegant hands. They were
covered in scratches and welts, beads of blood drying on
the surface. Shudders racked her entire body.

"Rosie, darling." He rocked her back and forth, gripped
by a terrible sense of guilt, of responsibility for what had
happened.

She would not let him go, her arms wrapped around him
as though he was all that could protect her from her unrav-
eling world. "Can't we do something?" she implored.
"God, its horrible!"

Chase's face was a taut mask of revulsion and pity. "The
croc will have taken him under, Rosie. No one could have
saved him. It all happened too fast. Wild animals are at
their fiercest when the nest is threatened."

"It's so dreadful!" she gasped, trying to stop sobbing
but actually crying harder. "I'll never ever forget it as long
as I live."

THERE WAS NO STAYING after that. The authorities had to
be advised and a search mounted for possible remains.
Also, Mick was found wandering around dazed, looking
for them, a splitting headache testimony to Disher's blow.
Still, he had enough common humanity to be aghast at
Disher's fate. Marley's reaction, on the other hand, was
quite the reverse. The croc could just as well have taken a
wallaby or a wild boar for all the feeling he displayed when
told the shocking news. As Rosie commented later, he
didn't actually *say* Disher had it coming, but his whole
attitude clearly said goodbye and good riddance. It made
her feel positively queasy.

"I hope his wife never goes back to him," she raged to
Chase. "He has no heart at all."

"Not much of a head, either. My uncle is not to be trusted. You can be sure he threw in the stone seal for Marley's benefit. Now he's taken it back."

Though Chase was still full of skepticism, no one could convince Rosie the place wasn't cursed. Too much blood had been spilled there.

A futile hour was spent trying to flush Porter out of his hiding place, Chase calling the ghastly news about Disher, as well as his own intention to return to the homestead. But Porter had gone to ground.

AT FOUR O'CLOCK that afternoon, when Chase and his party had safely reached camp number one, the storm came in from the Coral Sea, unleashing its full tropical fury. The lurid sky, purple-black laced with silver and vivid green, was illuminated by jagged bolts of lightning that fell from the great curling cumulus clouds to the earth below. The canopy of the rain forest, lashed by high winds and lightning strikes that felled slender trees, opened in undulating waves, allowing great torrents of rain to pour down with such force the earth was unable to contain it. Every depression, every rock pool, every swamp and lagoon filled, every creek of the lowlands overrunning its banks. Torrents of rainwater seeped through embankments, becoming subterranean waterfalls. The sheer volume of water was astonishing. In the space of an hour eucalyptus woodland had turned into lakes. The fauna had all taken cover. So had Porter Banfield who, when the storm was over, discovered to his growing excitement a sinkhole in the small wooded plateau. He had searched over and over. Now this. He moved cautiously along it, and as he did so other sinkholes formed.

He knew now that he had found the mine, but how to get back? He watched with mounting panic as areas of heath and scrub collapsed into an opening crevice in the earth. The soil simply gave way. In another moment Porter, too, fell through the roof of the eroded plateau into an old mine. The same mine his ancestor had recorded. Mounds of loose earth were piled up behind him, but in the low reflection of sunlight that canted in he saw a tunnel ahead. His heart thudding madly, he found the powerful torchlight in his backpack. He began to burrow forward, taking shallow breaths, the beam of light showing him the way. Soil clung to him. To his clothes, his boots, his hair, his face. He took no notice. Now he could see thin ribbons of bright yellow in the rock walls. He shifted the direction of the beam to examine them more fully, and as he did so, terror gripped him. A grotesque human skeleton dressed in tatters of clothing was propped against the rock wall, one skeletal arm extended. The sight nearly stopped his heart. For long moments he fought the panic that overwhelmed him, the shocking sense of claustrophobia, but he forced himself on, his face ashen. So someone had been here before him. Had died here for his pains. The Banfield cousin who had vanished into thin air? Just as he decided it was far too dangerous to continue lest the whole roof collapse, Porter Banfield saw something he had dreamed about all his life.

Exultation burst like a flame in his mind. Porter stared in wonderment at the treasure before him. Piles of gold coins, artifacts, jewelry, ceramics, golden boomerangs. And beyond and above all of it, the statue of a goddess. She stood in all her sinister splendor, some four feet high, basalt most certainly, but wearing the most marvelous headdress fashioned out of gold. It ringed her head, a serpent, fanged jaws opened wide, questing forked tongue extended, a single glittering jeweled eye. A cabachon emerald.

Porter took a deep shuddering breath, so elated by his monumental find that he paid no attention to the low rumble that seemed to come from deep within the bowels of the earth. While he stretched out his body, abasing himself in adoration before the goddess, the entire plateau collapsed. Cubic tons of earth caved in on the underground mine, burying its ancient treasure and the men who had exulted in it so briefly.

EPILOGUE

PORTER BANFIELD was never found. A search party directed by the local police constable and manned by twenty local cattlemen and farmers failed to find any trace of him. Two of the searchers, in fact, became lost, drawing away some of the main party to go after them. Every member of the team, which included Chase as unofficial leader, had real concerns about the threatening monsoonal rains. If they were heavy, there was every chance the search party could get cut off as streams rose dramatically and swamp areas turned to impassable mudflats.

When it came time for the inquiry, the whole township of Isis crowded into the small courthouse. After hearing all the evidence, the visiting magistrate brought in a verdict of "death by misadventure," even in the absence of a body. Up-country was crocodile country. According to eyewitnesses, a crocodile had taken Kurt Disher who, it was soon discovered, had been dishonorably discharged from the army and subsequently figured in a lengthy police file under a string of other names. It was considered highly possible that Porter Banfield had suffered the same fate. Although Banfield was as familiar as anyone with the remote up-country, no man could consider himself entirely safe during the crocodiles' nesting season. Whatever his private reasons—and they never fully came out—Porter Banfield had put himself in danger and paid the price. Had Disher not suffered his own terrible fate, he would have finished up behind bars.

The whole story consumed people. For weeks they spoke of little else. This was another legend out of Three Moons. It would pass into the folklore of the wild North.

Rosie and Graeme Marley had been required to remain in the area as a matter of course. They were required to tell their story at the inquest, but afterward Marley, disgraced by the deceptive role he had played in the whole misadventure and the great volume of criticism that came in from his colleagues—not the least of them the real Dr. Glenville—took off for parts unknown, still maintaining that he'd been on the verge of a great discovery.

Two DAYS AFTER the inquest, Chase flew Rosie by helicopter to the nearest domestic airport for her return to Sydney, where she had long-standing commitments to attend to.

"I love you," she whispered to him when the call came for her to board the aircraft. *Love you. Love you.* Only another woman so madly in love could understand.

"You're here in my heart, Rosie," he responded gravely, bending his head to kiss her mouth.

"Don't make it sound like you'll never see me again." She didn't know whether to laugh or cry.

"We agreed, Rosie—I'm going to give you a little time. Now, you have a plane to catch, my love."

Fighting back a sudden welling of tears, Rosie gathered her things. "I'll speak to you tonight."

"I'll be there." He saluted her, a tiny smear of her lipstick at the edge of his beautifully defined mouth.

She gestured to let him know it was there, but his smile said, *I like it.*

DURING THAT LONG two-thousand-mile flight from north Queensland to Sydney, Rosie went endlessly over the night before, when she and Chase had sat up for hours discussing their future. They were desperately in love. Both were certain of that. But Chase had serious concerns. Rosie couldn't so easily give up her career. He didn't feel he had the right to ask it of her; neither did he want a wife who'd be away from him for long periods. This state of affairs had to be resolved to their mutual satisfaction.

"It's the isolation, Rosie," Chase had stressed. "You could find it intolerable after the active interesting life you've led. You'd practically have to reshape yourself."

As though she couldn't do it! At one point, frustrated and distressed, she had accused him of trying to drive her away, but his lovemaking had shown her in glorious fashion that this was far from the case.

She had to be certain; that was all he asked.

Rosie had argued her case—convincingly, she thought— but this was a man who had sustained and survived terrible losses. A lot of pain there. A lot of pain that would never leave him. But he could escape much of it in her.

She knew she could bring him comfort. She'd had plenty of time to know her own mind. She, too, had given the situation very serious thought. No woman could overlook the isolation. And she'd miss female companionship, all the things that went with big-city life, the stimulation of her career—but love was a massive force in a woman's life. She'd found out that for her, love was just about everything. And she did love Chase. She wanted *belonging*. The right man to love. That was her road to heaven. Moreover, she wanted children. Now was the time to have them. They had a great many things to build on, she and Chase. She loved Three Moons as he did. She wanted him to have faith in her. Besides, she had her writing; had he forgotten that? She'd always wanted to write fiction. She had proven literary talent. Why shouldn't she turn out a brilliant first novel? Follow it up with another? The idea filled her with enormous exhilaration. Paradise Coast was a fantastic environment, her country's pioneering past. Lots of material for a book! There were countless stories from the old days passed down through generations. She was thrilled by the chance to learn more about the Aboriginal heritage. Isis was full of characters; she'd interviewed only some of them. Life was what you made it, Rosie would tell him. To keep working was good, and her writing would be a great diversion and, more than that, immensely satisfying. She would derive purpose and direction from it and from playing a positive role in the running of the station. She had a good brain and lots of plans. They all included him.

This was one great romance that was going to have a happy ending, Rosie determined long before her flight touched down in Sydney.

ONE IDYLLIC AFTERNOON in late April, when the cyclonic weather had finally settled into the brilliant Dry, Chase Banfield and his very popular bride, the award-winning journalist, Roslyn Summers, were married in the home gardens of the bridegroom's historic cattle station, Three Moons. Three hundred guests came from all over the country and overseas to attend. They came by jet, by light plane, by helicopter, by boat, by bus, four-wheel drives, some even on horseback. Most of Isis town arrived in their best bought or borrowed finery, everyone thoroughly enjoying themselves at such a wonderful wedding, celebrating a true love match in such a glorious setting. No one spoke about Porter Banfield's bizarre death. This wasn't the day for it. It had been whispered in the weeks preceding the eagerly awaited wedding that the bride, a "very clever girl," intended to write a novel about the entire affair. No one could wait to read it. The wedding was seen as Chase Banfield's reward for years of backbreaking hard work. Not a single person could think of anyone who had a greater right to a happy successful future than this favorite son of a pioneering dynasty.

AT THE END of the following month the Australian *Woman's Day* and *Women's Weekly* had a picture of bride and groom on the cover, both looking brilliantly happy and full of optimism. Several people, including Rosie's mother who had taken the greatest fancy to her new son-in-law, and Mick Dempsey who was keeping an eye on Three Moons in Chase's absence, bought copies and sent them to the Capriani, the honeymooners' hotel in Venice. The first copy to arrive Chase and Rosie read in bed over a bottle of vintage champagne. Inside was a four-page spread covering the happy event.

"My Rosie! I'll never forget how you looked that day," Chase toasted her before gently taking the magazine from her hands. "I'm happier than I ever imagined possible. My world's in perfect balance, thanks to you."

There was such a depth of feeling in his voice Rosie felt her heart dissolve. She turned to entwine herself in his arms. "You're the center of my life."

"Mmm." He gave a small satisfied grunt, dropping kisses all over her face. "I think we both got what we prayed for."

"Amen." She gave a voluptuous sigh, already sinking into their private dreamworld. He had a real genius for lovemaking, her husband. The sweetness, the tenderness and the wild passion. "Darling, I've had the most wonderful time in this most fascinating of cities, but do you know something?" She held his deeply desirous gaze, watching him shake his bronze head.

"What?"

"You have absolutely *noooooo* idea?"

He growled deep in his throat, tenderly nipping her

creamy breast before bringing his lips to the tight-furled velvet bud. "You want to try another position?"

She laughed, knowing she would love this man forever. "Is there one? I thought we'd tried everything possible."

"Not yet." His handsome face was etched in sensuous lines.

An electric pause, torched little cries.

Then Rosie breathing hard. "What I'm trying to say is, there's a call inside me. I can hear it. Maybe you can hear it, too."

A hesitation in the caresses, the stroking, while his strong hands perceptibly trembled. "You're not trying to tell me you're pregnant, are you?"

She pounded the soft bed with her feet. "Just like that? I'm sure I will be!" She laughed delightedly. "But no. We'll settle down first. A year, no more. This is another call. It's coming from Three Moons."

He had to laugh and adore her both at the same time. "Go on, tell me. I've come to admire your psychic ability."

"That's good news." Rosie settled down into her husband's arms, green eyes glowing. "Because Three Moons is telling me it wants us home. And we're going. All right?"

"All right." He hugged her, thrilled that her feelings matched his own. "We may even get around to going back to the site. Investigate it properly. Sometime," he qualified.

She tilted her face to him. "So you're willing to accept the possibility of an Egyptian presence?"

"It's like I told you, Rosie," he said slowly, thoughtfully, "there's something there. I'm not gifted like you, so that's all I can allow."

"Good enough." Rosie nodded. "But whatever's there isn't necessarily benign." She shivered in remembrance. "I suppose we could speculate for the rest of our lives, but we'll never know for sure what happened to your uncle."

"No." Chase's voice momentarily turned grim. "Porter had it all planned—but the plan fell through. He wanted Marley to unearth more treasure for him while he went off in search of the fabled gold mine. His way of killing two birds with one stone. As for what happened to him—he could have been buried beneath a mudslide. Who knows? Areas of the landscape experienced change. I'm afraid that Porter, without wanting it, has become another of Three Moons' legends."

"Maybe his end fitted his crimes," Rosie said, wishing they'd learned Porter's exact role in the fire that had taken the lives of Chase's parents.

"It seems very much like it," Chase agreed after a minute. "Let's not talk about Porter anymore. Better yet, let's not talk at all."

The moment before he gathered her gorgeously familiar body to him, it crossed Chase's mind that he had married a witch. Natural, warm, generous, clever. A witch he knew he wanted forever.

AN INTERVIEW WITH MARGARET WAY

Margaret Way, known worldwide for her passionate
and memorable writing about Australia, answers our
questions about her beautiful homeland.
Please join our conversation!

Margaret, readers love your books for—among other things—the passion and beauty with which you write about Australia. Why do you think people all over the world are so fascinated by the land Down Under?

Fascination with Australia is probably due to a number of highly alluring factors: its geographical remoteness; its size, roughly the same as the U.S.A.; the fact that it's a bulwark of Western civilization in Southeast Asia, where it stands tall. Word has got out, too, of its natural splendor, the uniqueness of its landscape, unique flora and fauna. And life is good in Australia. A massive ninety-two percent of the population agree. This state of affairs is made possible by the national character—"a fair go for all," a remarkably stable political system, a wonderful climate and a huge continent to work and play in, the lure of the bush to one side, glorious blue oceans to the other. Australians have a unique devotion to their country, which we must have picked up from our Aboriginal people. A kind of non-Aboriginal dreaming. On the same survey mentioned, eighty-seven percent of the population (Australians are great world travelers) voted their own country "the best place to live." One can conclude Australians are happy with their lot.

Australia has so many different and unique kinds of landscape. How many places have you been to? Do you have favorite ones?

I've managed to travel through most states of Australia—and it's a big country. Air travel is the only way to get around it (up until recently very expensive). I know my own vast state of Queensland (some 667,000 miles) the best, but there are many, many places so wild and isolated few white people have seen them. My travels took in the Daintree Rain Forest of far North Queensland some thousand miles from where I live in Brisbane, the state capital. I've reveled in the astonishing beauty of the Great Barrier Reef, I've seen mango plantations, tropical fruit plantations, coffee and tea, the sugar lands, the citrus and cotton belts, the mining areas right down to the magnificent beaches of the Gold Coast, then west across the Great Dividing Range to the legendary Outback with its great sheep and cattle stations, again more than a thousand miles away.

My favorite place, the place where I think one feels the greatest spiritual link with one's country and the most sadness and sympathy for the displaced Aborigines, custodians of the land for more than sixty thousand years, would have to be the Red Centre, Australia's Wild Heart. No other region has its extraordinary drawing power. The landscape is stark, very primitive, but so spectacular with the great monuments and ever-changing play of colors. Sometimes in different lights the landscape appears not only mysterious but forbidding, as it must have been to the early explorers. The Red Centre is home to two of our most powerful monuments—Ayers Rock (Uluru), the world's mightiest monolith and the source of countless Dreamtime legends, and the domes, minarets and cupolas of the Olgas (Katajuta), some thirty kilometers west. These great monuments, rising as they do from the flat desert plains that stretch to the horizon, dominate the eye from every direction. They strike awe and reverence into the heart.

The Cattle Baron gives us a sense of how weather affects people's lives and livelihoods in North Queensland. Would you say this is true throughout the country? What's the weather like where you are—and how does it affect you?

Australia is blessed with a wonderful climate pretty well all over. This makes it a marvelous playground for times of leisure, which Australians insist on as their God-given right. As a nation, we're sports-mad; as well, we love tearing off to our easily accessible beaches for the weekend. The good life is a way of life. My own state of Queensland, "The Sunshine State," bisected by the Tropic of Capricorn, is famous for its beautiful weather. "Beautiful one day, perfect the next." The beauty and consistency of the weather affects us all, contributing to a sense of physical and mental well-being.

It's clear from your books that Australia is a melding of many different influences. How successfully are the various cultures integrated, in your view?

When I began writing thirty years ago, around eighty-seven percent of the population's forebears hailed from the British Isles. Today that's been halved. Australia is becoming an increasingly multicultural society, with big intakes from Europe, mainly Greece, Italy, Germany and most recently, migrants from Southeast Asia. This has worked extremely well, though it has not been without its early adjustments. Migrants who arrived in the 1960s and 1970s are well and truly "old" Australians. It is still quite possible for a penniless person with enough ambition and drive to become a millionaire. Australia is a very tolerant society, as societies go. Racism is pretty well socially unacceptable. The fact is, multiculturalism has added a dynamic, colorful and vibrant new dimension to this country, an exciting diversity of cultures that enhances life. No matter what the color of your skin, if you have an "Aussie" accent you're as Australian as anyone else.

Is there an Australian *character*, would you say? Or particular Australian characteristics?

There is a definite Australian character. People from around the world who have taken the time to get to know us and our country will agree with that. So far as I'm concerned, the defining characteristic is "mateship" and the mate can just as easily be female as male. Mateship goes deep. It implies obligation, "helping out," which goes back to the earliest days of colonization. Men and women had to carve an existence where everything was wilderness, a vast remote wilderness far from everything they had ever known. In Australia, men and women are good friends. Good pals. There is little segregation. At the same time, women are much respected for their special skills and qualities. "Mum" is very important in the scheme of things. Women, on the other hand, like a man to be a man. We're not terribly interested in the sensitive New Age guys, which is not to say we don't expect sensitivity from our men. The ideal Australian male exhibits a rugged individualism. He is confident, easygoing, proudly masculine, with a good sense of humor. A man can handle himself well in any situation but still retains a definite "courtliness" toward women and children.

Has life in Queensland, and in Australia generally, changed much in the last few decades? With the advent of new technologies, do Australians now feel more connected to the rest of the world?

Australia is much more forward-looking than it was, say, twenty years ago. There's a real buzz in the air. A sense of achievement. The cosmopolitan elements have added to this dynamism. People on all sides express a lot of confidence in Australia and in its future. There has been a huge development in our film industry and in the arts, technology and medical science. As I've said, Australians love their habitat and their way of life, which in the best respects hasn't changed. Americans who come to our shores inevitably say with more than a touch of nostalgia "Australia is America thirty years ago." Perhaps things were freer, more open, then? Of course, almost everyone has every possible appliance, better houses, better cars, access to all the new technologies, but these things don't necessarily make people happier. It's the quality of the lifestyle, the capacity for simple engagements and relaxations, more than an increasingly higher standard of living.

There seem to be a great many deadly dangers in Australia (and maybe especially in Queensland), some of which are mentioned in *The Cattle Baron*: poisonous snakes, poisonous spiders, jellyfish, the crocodiles, of course... How aware of these dangers are you on an everyday level? Is this something you think about in your day-to-day life?

I would think there are deadly dangers in most countries. Certainly those that lie along the tropics. The dangers are mostly confined to the bush. In the outer suburbs of sub-tropical Brisbane, where families live on acreages, there are snakes, some poisonous. But unless one is unfortunate enough to tread on them, snakes keep well out of the way. (Antivenins are readily available.) The same goes for spiders, who keep to dark, out-of-the-way places. Jellyfish don't bother us where I live. They float in now and again. Far North Queensland is a different story, and during certain months when poisonous stingers come from the Coral Sea, it's not safe to go into the water. As for crocodiles, Far North Queensland and the Northern Territory live quite successfully with them. One takes the necessary precautions and doesn't invade their territory. They don't waddle into town. But I can tell you, sighting an Australian salt-water crocodile is a truly terrifying experience.

Far North Queensland is over a thousand miles from Brisbane, and there are few, if any, dangers of this kind in city living.

Why do you think Australia has been such a popular setting for romance?

All of us, wherever we are in the world, are drawn to the great outdoors, the thought of great open spaces and freedom. The Outback has plenty of that. So has the rest of the country, for that matter. We're a vast island covering nearly eight million square kilometers, the coastline nearly the circumference of the Earth. Occupying our great land mass are some nineteen million people, which explains why Australians are bred to a great sense of freedom and a certain "innocence." I know my readers love reading and learning about my country. In a way, trying to convey my own devotion has been my life's mission.

Tell us how you started writing. Have all your books been set in Australia?

I started writing when my son was an infant. A friend visiting me in the maternity hospital brought me a pile of Mills & Boon novels to pass the time. I read them all, thought "I can do that," which I very quickly did while my little son was sleeping. I was at that time a professional musician, pianist, accompanist, teacher, but I had no wish to disturb my son's sleep with my practicing. I wrote instead—in longhand at the kitchen table. This was in beautiful New Zealand. My husband and I went there for our honeymoon, stayed for over two years. When I returned home, I bought a typewriter. That was the start. All my books have been set in Australia.

Can you recommend books or movies—apart from your own, that is—that will give readers an accurate picture of Australia?

The finest Australian writer in my opinion is Patrick White. He won the Nobel Prize for Literature in 1973. His works can be daunting but he is so Australian with a profound love of the Australian landscape. I love Morris West, though his books are set all over the world. David Malouf is another Queensland-born writer I admire. There's Thea Astley and Venero Armanno, son of Sicilian migrants looking at Australia from a new Australian's point of view. Helen Garner, Rosie Scott, Robyn Davidson. So many... As for movies, *My Brilliant Career,* the film with Judy Davis and Sam Neill, is true of the Australian experience. Another is *Oscar and Lucinda* with Cate Blanchett and

Ralph Fiennes. Though Colleen McCullough wasn't happy
with it, I enjoyed the dramatization of "The Thorn Birds."
It was stamped with a wonderful sense of place.

**If any of our readers are planning to visit Australia, what
would you recommend they do and see?**

For first-time visitors to Australia, I recommend landing in
Sydney with its truly magnificent harbor. Experience what
our biggest, most dynamic city has to offer, then come right
on up to Queensland. The Great Barrier Reef is a must. The
Daintree Rain Forest. All the scenery in the tropics is glorious.

Don't travel in the summer months, although it's always
summer up there. The heat is intense from November
through February. The so-called winter months, June
through August, are superb. Then you must go Outback,
specifically to the Red Centre and if you possibly can, visit
Kakadu National Park along the edge of the Arnhem Land
escarpment in the Northern Territory. It's one of the
world's great wilderness areas, along with Queensland's
Cape York Peninsula, wonderful frontiers we're fighting to
keep for the benefit of the world.

As for our cities, in other heavily populated parts of the
world the big cities swallow up the surrounding country-
side. Our cities, much smaller with only a fraction of the
population, somehow retain a kind of "holiday" atmosphere. As a Canadian university student recently remarked,
"Australia is one big adult playground." Not quite, but I
know exactly what she meant. The bush and the ocean
fringe all our cities.

There are birds, flowers, scented trees everywhere, like
gorgeous wattles, which I love, and Australia's acacias. The
tang of the ocean with seagulls wheeling overhead in the

cities' parks and gardens. Sydney and Melbourne are our biggest cities, Sydney the most cosmopolitan, Melborne very elegant. The rest of our cities, including my own much-loved Brisbane, are—compared to them—country towns. (Actually, for those of us who live here, we find that wonderful, but don't let on.) The Apple Isle of Tasmania, separated from the mainland, is a lovely place to visit. It's closer to an English landscape than anywhere else, with a glorious wilderness area. To my own regret, and I must change that, I have never been to Perth, which has to be one of the most remote cities on earth, even for other Australians, three thousand miles away across the Nullarbor Plain (nullabour is Aborigine for treeless) and separated by the great inland desert. Yet Perth is always described in glowing terms by people who have visited it. A handsome thriving city, it's the headquarters for the great mining industries and the increasingly important Argyle diamonds.

Do come and visit us! As a notoriously acid-tongued English journalist once remarked, ''Up close Australians are as cuddly as koala bears.''

In March 2001,

Silhouette® Desire®

presents the next book in

DIANA PALMER's

enthralling *Soldiers of Fortune* trilogy:

THE WINTER SOLDIER

Cy Parks had a reputation around Jacobsville for his taciturn and solitary ways. But spirited Lisa Monroe wasn't put off by the mesmerizing mercenary, and drove him to distraction with her sweetly tantalizing kisses. Though he'd never admit it, Cy was getting mighty possessive of the enchanting woman who needed the type of safeguarding only he could provide. But who would protect the beguiling beauty from *him…?*

Soldiers of Fortune…prisoners of love.